THE
DREAMING
TREE

THE
DREAMING
TREE

MATTHEW
MATHER

**BLACK
STONE**
PUBLISHING

Copyright © 2019 by Matthew Mather
Published in 2019 by Blackstone Publishing
Cover and book design by K. Jones

Printed in the United States of America

First edition: 2019
ISBN 978-1-5385-8941-0
Fiction / Mystery & Detective / General

1 3 5 7 9 10 8 6 4 2

CIP data for this book is available
from the Library of Congress

Blackstone Publishing
31 Mistletoe Rd.
Ashland, OR 97520

www.BlackstonePublishing.com

For my mother, Julie Mather,
who is the real heroine in all my novels.

1

Such a beautiful day to die. The man took in the view over Long Island Sound, the sun low enough on the horizon to spit pink into the clouds and a chill returning with the creeping darkness.

"Excuse me, sir?" A young woman in a fleece top and jogging sneakers approached. "Do you know which way to Kings Park Bluff? This is Nissequogue State Park, right?"

"You live around here?" the man asked.

He spun a key with an orange plastic handle around on his finger.

"In New York," the woman replied. "First time out here. So is it that way? Or back where I came from? I got turned around."

The man looked back and forth up the beach. "It's that way. Look, up there. You can see the edge of the cliff. Next to the asylum." He pointed behind her, indicating the way with the orange key.

"Asylum?" She turned and held up one hand to follow his.

"I'm sorry," the man whispered.

As she faced away, he slipped the steel wire around her neck.

The woman's hands went straight to her throat. She tried to scream, but it was too late. The wire cut into her windpipe. He swung around, grunting with the effort, and lifted her up onto his back. Her feet dangled off the ground. He watched the darkening clouds on the horizon while her body spasmed for a few seconds before becoming as peaceful as the scenery.

What a beautiful day.

2

"What do you mean?"

Blue eyes came into focus. A mane of gray hair, a huge beard. Soothingly familiar but alarmingly unknown. "Buddy, take it easy," the man said.

Hidden lights glowed in fuzzy eggshell white.

A new face appeared. Angular features. Green eyes this time. "Tell me your name," New-Face said. The accent was foreign. New-Face scowled and spewed out a tumble of words at unseen recipients before asking again: "Do you know your name?"

My name? What is my name?

The question echoed from one side of empty mind-space to the other. The answer tickled the back of the throat—a too-distant taste of the past, gulped back by the terrifying nothingness.

"Royce."

The word rolled out by itself, a stray rock fallen from unseen heights, whispered as if from someone else's lips.

"Royce Lowell."

These two words were more confident—still whispered, but attached to a bloom of recognition coloring the empty canvas of the mind. *I'm Roy,* he thought. Relief tingled his scalp, but then … *Is that right? That's not my name, is it? Am I Roy?*

"Good. Very good," New-Face said. "That's right, and I am Dr. Danesti—"

"Roy, it's me. My god, baby, this is all my f—"

"Please, Mrs. Lowell-Vandeweghe." Dr. Danesti held up one hand, his fingers spread wide.

Roy's head was propped up. He tried to turn it but couldn't. Tried to shift his body. Nothing. Panic trickled into his veins. *Where am I?*

After a few long seconds, he recognized the woman's voice. *That's Penelope. Penny. My wife.* He rolled his eyes as far right as they could go and caught a glimpse of her cropped blond hair. His wife and the gray-bearded man and the doctor hovered close.

Three more people were at the back of the room.

One of them, a large African American man sitting in a corner chair, asked, "What do you remember, Roy?"

And that's Atticus. The dark-skinned man in the rumpled suit was Atticus Cargill. Their family lawyer. His bald head reflected the overhead lighting. A wide nose, flattened off-center from some offense given or received, slouched over his thick white bristle of a mustache.

The lawyer sagged forward in his chair and wheezed as he stood, but then, he was huge. Six and a half feet and at least three hundred pounds. Mostly fat, but enough of it muscle. *A Marine, served in Vietnam*—something he never let Roy forget.

"Do you remember what happened?" Atticus asked again. More insistent this time.

Standing beside Atticus was Roy's mother, and the other guy with her looked familiar. Drops of memory spattered onto his mind. *A policeman?* Right. That other guy was Captain Harris from the East Hampton Police Department. He was always at the parties, waiting by the entrance.

Dr. Danesti shushed them. "Do you remember who *I* am?" he asked.

I know you, Roy thought, but he couldn't mouth the words. A wheezing rattle of air through a constricted windpipe. *Are those my lungs?* He tried to breathe deeply but felt nothing. Still-smoldering fear tightened its knuckles around his brain stem.

"Blink once if you can hear me," Danesti said, his voice rising in pitch.

Roy blinked once, twice, three times in rapid succession. An alarm sounded. A white-clad figure materialized to his left, then disappeared just as fast. Languid ooze settled into his mind. The room went quiet again.

He remembered what he was trying to remember. He muttered, "You're my mother's doctor."

"That's right." Danesti's voice regained its calm. "And now I am *your* doctor."

And the shaggy-beard man is Sam. Samuel Phipps. *My best friend.* The cool ooze filled more of his brain, the familiar patina of drugs sliding over his mind's eye. "Am I paralyzed?" The question came without fear now.

If yes, then turn the machines off, his inner voice urged. *Kill me. Make it painless. Or maybe painful. You deserve* some *pain.* He frowned. "What did you say before? About a transplant?"

"Relax, buddy," his friend Sam cooed.

"But what did you say?"

Roy's wife stepped away, raising her hand to her mouth. Her watch hooked the bedsheet, and she managed to pull it halfway off him, exposing his right arm, torso, and right leg and foot. He focused on his big toe. Except that it wasn't *his* big toe. His eyeballs rolled left. *The leg. That hand.* Was he hallucinating? The room seemed to swirl, sucking the air from his lungs.

Dr. Danesti gently spread the sheet back over him. "We had to perform an aggressive surgical procedure to save you."

"What did you do?" Roy strained, but he still couldn't move anything except his eyes. He darted them back and forth. Up and down. Side to side.

The beeping machines quickened in tempo, their beat faltering into a staccato arrhythmia.

"We call the procedure a body transplant."

"What body?"

"You were crushed in the accident." His wife leaned over him and kissed his cheek. A tear slipped down her face. "There was no other way."

The doctor added matter-of-factly, "We replaced your body with a donor's. You are very lucky, one of the first—"

"What do you mean, *donor* body?" Roy's eyes swiveled down as far as they could in their sockets. Black dots raced and coalesced in his vision, the machines' stuttering beeps merging into a single high-pitched whine.

"Nurse," Danesti called out. "Nurse!"

Roy's mind dropped backward into the maelstrom churning behind consciousness.

3

A flash, white-hot, bright enough to leave a floating yellow afterimage in Roy's eyes, lit up the rain drenching the backyard. Then came the air-shattering boom.

"The storm's right on us!" Roy's father yelled, one hand shielding his face from the tipping deluge, the other holding his son close. "Do you understand?"

Roy wagged his head up and down in mute fear. Trembling, his clothes wet-stuck to his stick-thin limbs, he clung to the warmth of his father's body. Another stuttering lightning flash, the tearing-splitting crack of thunder right on top of them this time. His father let go and ran doubled over, his blue oxford shirt soaking dark.

Roy hesitated before sprinting forward, arms and legs pumping in a flood of adrenaline. From the driving rain appeared a red-and-brown woman. A bright red dot hovered over her. He ran around her, following his father's yells. The streaked walls of the greenhouse materialized out of the gray blur; behind it loomed the skeletal branches of late-autumn trees, the smell of dirt and dead leaves thick in the air.

* * *

"Jesus! Are you awake?"

The image of the rain faded, the red-and-brown woman disappearing last, replaced with the dim outline of Roy's prison. The hospital room. He recognized the voice. "How long have you been here?" he said.

"Half an hour."

In the dim light, Samuel Phipps's bushy gray beard and mustache twitched around his ever-present grin. That was the Sam magic. The man was always smiling—an energy that made him fun to be around, as if something exciting was always about to happen.

But even he couldn't make any of this fun. Three months stuck in this bed, each waking minute like an hour, each day a year without escape.

"Is Penny still here?" Roy asked.

"She left when I arrived," Sam said in his faintly southern accent. His family had come from South Carolina when he was a kid.

Roy closed his eyes tight before opening them again. He couldn't wipe them himself. Squeezing them shut was the best he could do. "I was dreaming."

"About what?"

"My father, that old house on Mott's Point. Near where you lived on Long Beach."

"Sold that thirty years ago, didn't you?"

"My dad did. I loved that place."

"I remember your mother hated it. Right under the flight path of JFK."

And for Roy as a kid, that had been the best part. He remembered lying on his back in the grass by the water, imagining the cargoes of business-suited men off to negotiate exotic deals in those massive aircraft that somehow levitated into the air. How in the world could something so huge disappear into the clouds? When he got bored watching planes, he'd hunt for crabs under the rocks by the dock. A perfect world for an eight-year-old boy.

Strange, the things he could remember now—and the things he couldn't. Bright canvases of memory between black rifts of nothingness.

"So a dream about your dad—dead twenty years—makes you dance like a bean on a hot tin roof?"

Roy didn't understand the expression, but then, half of what Sam said didn't make sense. "I was asleep on the twentieth anniversary of his death." March 12 of every year, he marked the day. This was the first time he'd missed it.

"You were in a *coma*. I'm sure he'd understand."

"It's the implants that make me jump around when I'm asleep."

"The what?"

"Electronics stuck in my legs, arms, back, head. When I'm asleep, they get stimulated—gets me moving around to keep from getting bedsores."

His friend smiled as if it were funny, to hide the uncomfortableness. That was what friends were for, but then, strangers did the same thing. Maybe it was just that nobody liked the uncomfortable things—the reason so few people came to visit in hospitals. The awkward silences, the forced smiles. The empty platitudes.

Or maybe it was just the friends and family Roy had.

He looked down at the alien finger attached to the alien hand attached to the alien body stapled to his neck. He'd gotten used to the shape and color of the donor body, but the smell—how did you get used to someone else's *smell* in your nose?

This body—barely able to move, opiates pumped into its veins the only relief for the pain—perspired a lot under these sheets, but even the *sweat* wasn't his. Didn't smell the same. It had a slick tang that gave him headaches, enveloping him, drowning him in its sickly-sweetness. How the hell was he supposed to get used to that?

Roy turned his head an inch—a small, hard-won victory. "Suzi, could you bring up the lights and fade the wall?" he said to the digital assistant that routed all his requests.

"To fully transparent?" a disembodied female voice asked.

Roy signaled his response with a feeble nod.

On command, the recessed lighting glowed bright in daytime colors, and the window wall to the foot of the bed faded from black to smoky to clear. Directly in front of them, due west, the top of the Rockefeller Center loomed into view three blocks away, the pregnant clouds above it almost at eye level. Beyond that stretched the rest of the New York skyline, with gray patches of the Hudson River peeking out between the buildings down Fifty-Third and Fifty-Fourth Streets.

Eden Corporation's New York offices took up the top floors of 601 Lexington Avenue in the heart of Manhattan. The fifty-eighth floor, almost eight hundred feet above street level, was the rehab wing of Eden's transplant surgical unit.

To the right, the square-faceted pinnacle of 432 Park Avenue towered over them and into the clouds. At 1,400 feet, it was the tallest dedicated residential building in the world. He had heard that the penthouse alone, with its own lap pool and climate-controlled wine cellar, was worth most of a billion dollars. An Arab oil prince owned it. Half the remaining units were owned by foreign businessmen who left them empty most of the year. Roy and Sam had gone to a few parties in the building. Great parties—what he could remember of them.

Roy took a deep breath and concentrated, grunting with the effort. His right arm twitched and then, inch by inch, bending at the elbow, slid across the bedsheet toward his head. He did his best to aim a trembling index finger at his forehead, which he tilted downward.

Sam pointed at the arm as if at a tarantula that had crawled over the sheets. "Oh, my god. You *moved* that arm. You did that with your head? I mean, your brain? You moved your *arm!*"

"Look, there's implants in my skull," Roy said. "Can you see them?"

Sam leaned in close, his eyes narrowing.

"One in each temple, two in the forehead. The machines know when I'm asleep, even when I need to go to the bathroom."

"My smart watch knows when I'm snoozing." Sam brandished the device on his left arm. "It's the only way I know what time I got to bed after a late night."

"But it's not stuck into your head. When I fart, someone three rooms over jumps."

Sam grinned, the yellow-gray of his mustache widening. "Have you seen that body you're attached to? The muscles on it?"

Yes, Roy had seen the body. He had stared at it for hours: the stubby fingers, the strange hands that seemed as big as dinner plates.

"Hey, hey." Sam slid his chair closer to the bed. "What's going on?"

Roy had been body-numb when he woke up a few minutes ago, but the automated spinal tap dripping anesthetics had stopped when his brain waves tipped into consciousness. The buzzing, maddening pins and needles returned. He could control it, ask Suzi to administer a dose of analgesic—not an anesthetic, not to block it completely, but just an analgesic. It masked the pain, but it didn't let you forget about it.

He had become an expert in pain these past months. That was all he could get now when he was awake: an analgesic. Dr. Danesti said he had to take as much of the pain as he could bear, that it was his neural system trying to communicate with the donor body's. They had started him on this new torture regimen six weeks ago.

"That arm I moved?" Roy paused, clenched his jaw muscles and grimaced. "I can't feel it, but out there, two feet to its right?"

Sam held up a hand in the approximate location.

"I can feel my old arm, right there. Flares up like it's on fire from time to time, just to tell me it's gone."

Roy bared his teeth. He felt a jackhammer cutting deep into the side of his brain. "Phantom limb, the doc calls it. My old feet itch like mad, but I can't even feel these clubs."

"It'll get better."

"I can't feed myself. I'm spoon-fed like a baby. I piss myself. Sometimes, the only time I know I've taken a crap is when I smell the stink in my adult diapers. I'm so drugged up, I drool. Can't tell day from night, dreams from reality."

"You moved that arm. That's progress. We gotta work through this."

"*We?*" Roy laughed between barely contained sobs.

You shouldn't have bothered, should have just let us die.

He frowned. *Us?*

Me. And I can think of a few million reasons why my mother and Penny might be doing this.

Don't say that. That's not nice.

Christ, what's wrong with me?

"Three months, and I can barely budge fingers I can't feel. This body reeks. I can't ... You shouldn't have let them do this to me."

Roy's autonomic nervous system was making faster progress than the rest of his peripheral nervous system in fusing its neural machinery with the donor body. He had heard Danesti tell the staff doctors on their rounds. He was getting used to the medical jargon—no other choice, really, sitting here for weeks in the most solitary of confinements.

Sam said, "There *is* light at the end of this tunnel. There's been three before you—"

"And how did they work out?"

The first two had died.

"Shelby Sheffield, he's out of here."

The pulsating pain seemed to subside. Roy said, "What do you mean, *out* of here?"

"That's why I came in today. Penny and I were supposed to tell you together. Shelby's gone home. Walked out of Six-Oh-One Lexington this morning. All over the news today."

"Shelby *walked* out of here? By himself?"

"Kinda herky-jerky, but yeah, the man walked straight out of the lobby and across the sidewalk to the car waiting for him. Totally by himself, arms swinging—even waved to the crowd."

Shelby Sheffield was Danesti's third attempt at a full-body transplant, performed eighteen months before Roy's. A sixty-four-year-old British banker, former head of the IMF. His room was on the opposite side of the floor, but he had come in a few times on his robotic-walker legs, shuttled over by Nurse Juan to say encouraging things.

He remembered the man's black eyebrows, incongruous under the shock of white hair. Flaccid tanned skin hanging beneath tired eyes, jowls forming at the sides of his mouth, but the man had a kind voice. Said nice things. Terrible breath, but nice words.

Sam said, "Two years after his surgery, and Shelby is home. Walking around by himself. Check out the video clips on the web. I bet he felt like you a year ago. We'll have you home for the next holidays, buddy. We'll celebrate your forty-fourth birthday in style. That's your inheritance day, old buddy."

4

Officer Delta Devlin tried to control her rapid breathing. She checked and rechecked the straps on her ballistic vest. The apartment hallway smelled of mildew and urine. The concrete floor was littered with chips of paint and plaster from the walls. Bare incandescent bulbs, one above each doorway, threw stark shadows. Sixteen units on the second floor. She looked at the door again: 14B. This was the one.

She unholstered her Glock 22.

Most of her peers went for a Smith & Wesson or SIG, but she didn't find them as comfortable for the weak-hand-thumb-past-the-straight-strong-thumb grip that trainees were taught to adopt. Also, the grip and barrel were shorter and easier for her to handle. *Fifteen rounds in the magazine.*

"It's your bust," said the Nassau County police officer, pointing at the 14B doorplate as an invitation to take charge. He backed away from the door. So did his partner.

Were they being polite, or cautious? Or just tired old men? This was her big collar. Maybe. Second year on the job, but still a rookie. She was the one who got these two cops here in such a hurry. The warrant still stuck out of her pocket.

If she stepped back, asked them to initiate, she would look weak.

Control the fear. This was what she had always wanted, right? To be like Dad? Her gun hand shook. That was the adrenaline and cortisol. Natural. It was normal to be scared. The unknown was behind that door. Should she wait for more backup? But she knew he had already been tipped off.

No time to wait.

She stepped forward and rapped hard on the door with her left hand, her right holding the weapon down and away. "Open up! This is the police. We have a warrant to search the premises."

Anyway, Pegnini, the guy she was looking for, was just a small-time bookie for the Matruzzi mob family out of Queens. Wasn't as if she were hunting the cartel. Maybe she was being a little dramatic.

One second. Two.

Nothing.

No sound except the faint crying of a baby two or three doors down. She glanced at the two Nassau County officers behind her.

"Open up," she repeated, louder, hammering the door hard with the fleshy part of the fist this time. "Open up, it's the—"

The hallway went pitch black.

Del waited a beat, but the emergency lights didn't come on. She checked down the hallway to the only exterior window, but even the streetlight outside had gone out. "*Damn it!*" she muttered under her breath.

She gritted her teeth, stood up, and piston-kicked the door with her heel. It budged a half inch. She backed up and lunged. This time, her blow splintered the door frame. Jet black inside as well. She took a tentative step forward, fumbled for her flashlight, felt the other officers coming in behind her. A ghostly image in smudged red stepped into her field of view and swung something up. She knew she was the only one who could see it in this darkness.

She screamed, "Get down!"

The shotgun's muzzle blast lit up the room for a split second before the boom. Del dropped to the floor, felt the whoosh of projectile sucking the air back. The oily blackness returned, but overhead she saw the hot scattershot glow red. Whoever it was had aimed high, into the ceiling.

Hadn't tried to hit them—just scare them away. There was a noise in front of her. Someone opening a door.

A light flicked on. One of the officers managed to find his flashlight. "How the hell did you see that?" he asked. He crouched and waved the beam of light around the small apartment.

"He's going out the back," Del said, ignoring the question. "One of you go out the front; one of you stay here." She had already pushed past them and was sprinting down the hallway.

She had her flashlight out now and hit the stairwell at a run. She made the first landing in three careful leaping steps, and in three more she thudded into the emergency exit door. Outside, it was almost as impenetrably dark—just the haze of industrial lights a few hundred feet away through the trees. Somehow, the perp had switched off the streetlights, too. *Damn it.* The area behind the complex was the Bethpage Solid Waste Disposal building. No telling what bolt-holes someone connected with the Matruzzis would have back there.

In the distance, the whine of police sirens. A flicker of red.

The apartment complex was bordered by a high wrought iron fence, more to keep people away from the waste-disposal property than out of the apartments. Playing her flashlight beam along the old, twisted barrier, she found a gap and squeezed through. Her light flickered. Maybe the battery? With no time to change it, she felt her way through the mud and low brush. She circled around and stopped. Listened.

Beneath the wailing sirens, a soft gurgling.

Step by careful step, she angled her way to the rear of the building, hoping to triangulate 14B's location. Her breath came in quick pants. The flashlight beam shimmered. In the blackness, her uncommon visual acuity picked up a shape glowing faint red. The figure seemed suspended in the air, a hundred feet away. She quickened her pace and almost tripped over a branch.

"Back here!" she yelled.

The strobing lights of the arriving police cars lit up the trees to her right, but the back of the apartment complex was still black as a mine shaft.

She took four more steps and shined her light upward. It flickered on and off again, then back on. She recognized the face. It was Pegnini, on the second-floor balcony. "Hold it right there!" she yelled, raising her gun and the light. "Put your arms up and don't move."

The light flickered, but the man kept his arms by his sides, seemed to wriggle.

"Don't you goddamn move," Del repeated, "and put your arms up or I will shoot you."

This asshole had just blown off a shotgun at three officers. What game was he playing? She still couldn't see him clearly, but he was too far from the back of the apartment to be up that high. More flashlight beams scissored across the back of the building. One shone straight into Del's face, and she squinted, holding up one hand to block the glare while she looked up.

"Mother of God," someone said.

Two more flashlight beams fixed on Pegnini. He wasn't on a balcony.

The man had jumped from the second floor, but clever as he'd been to rig shutting off all the lights, he hadn't quite calculated his escape properly. Part of the fifteen-foot iron fence had pulled away, and one of the ornamental spearheaded rods was angled toward the back of the apartment.

The rod had entered through Pegnini's right groin, protruding through the top of his left shoulder blade. Both arms were caught in the fence, his feet twisted together. He looked as if he'd struggled to begin with, but his desperate flailing had just driven the post deeper and deeper through his body. His legs and arms still quivered, but the blank stare and silent-screaming slack-open mouth said he was already gone.

"Jesus Christ," said another officer.

More beams of light fixed on the hapless bookie.

Del pulled her gaze away.

A split-open briefcase was on the ground. Papers lay scattered all across the grass and into the scrub forest of the waste-disposal site. She holstered her gun and bent down to start gathering them as quickly as she could, leaving the other officers to figure out how to get Pegnini down. She could barely pick up the papers, her hands shook so badly.

5

FIFTEEN MONTHS LATER

"Welcome home!"

Roy's mother, Virginia, stood in the entryway of his house, arms spread wide.

"Did you walk the whole way? Showing off?"

She wore sheer yoga pants and a sparkling black tank top under a frayed jean jacket. Waves of platinum hair cascaded over her shoulders. Not your average seventy-seven-year-old, but not that unusual for the Hamptons.

Roy said, "Just wanted to get a look around." He walked up the driveway, past the manicured twelve-foot cedar hedge that secluded the grounds from the road. His soft exoskeleton hissed quietly with each step.

One of the last days of summer. Sweat dripped down his back after the two-block excursion. Gravel crunched underfoot, and cicadas buzz-sawed loudly from the triad of stately elms that provided some relief from the midday swelter. A salt breeze, just enough to hold back the stifling humidity, rolled in from the Atlantic, the sea air perfumed by the red roses lining the house.

Roy had had the driver drop him off a few hundred feet down the road, at East Hampton Beach, amid the crush of holidaymakers' cars lined up to drop off and pick up; mothers holding boogie boards, kids in wide-brimmed hats balancing cones of disintegrating ice cream in their sticky hands while dads yelled for everyone to hurry up.

On days like this, he would roll up with his big-wheeled cooler brimming with bottles of chardonnay, on the usual circuit from the house to erect a circle of beach chairs near the pounding surf. And by this time in the afternoon, he would be most of the way to stumbling drunk, wandering to the boardwalk to stand in line for a lobster roll, wondering whether he'd remembered to put on sunscreen.

Was it that easy? Could he just fall back into his old life? The cooler was probably still in the garage. Could he load it up with a few bottles, call Sam, put on some board shorts, and head out to the beach? Pretend the last two years were just a bad dream?

Something about the idea felt as if it were someone else's life he was remembering. The trip in from Manhattan a re-creation on the true-crime channel, a step-by-step replay of the night of the accident. The drive down the Long Island Expressway, turning off onto the Montauk Highway—he experienced it like a film he'd seen before, one he hated but couldn't stop watching, toothpicks propped under his eyelids to keep them open. This was supposed to be his happy day, his return to freedom. So why, the farther he ventured onto Long Island, did it feel like a descent ever deeper into some dark pit?

"Nothing has changed." His mother held her arms wider, her teeth perfect and white in the afternoon sun.

While nothing here had changed, she seemed younger than he remembered.

"Come here," his mother said. Virginia jogged down the front steps, leaving the glass entryway doors open. "Come on, give me a hug."

Roy quickened his pace and closed the last ten feet with his arms open to embrace her. "Thanks for coming," he said.

"So good to have you home."

Both sounded insincere, though both tried not to.

The black Escalade ground to a halt behind Roy. He had asked his wife and the driver to follow him in the car, to give him a moment, but they were home now. He heard the car doors open and shut and the crunch of footsteps behind him.

"Bring all the bags into the house," Penny told the driver.

Roy and his mother released each other from their awkward embrace to follow his wife into the house, into an oasis of air-conditioned coolness. Dark-stained wide-planked oak floors, cheery whitewashed walls—everything looked just as he had left it two years before. Through the glass wall of sliding patio doors, the pool glistened in scrubbed-clean pale blue.

He had rebuilt this house almost from scratch after buying it as a broken-down eyesore twenty years ago. His friend Sam had helped in what became a sort of bonding session between them right after Roy's father died. Before, Roy had thought of Sam as an uncle; afterward, as a friend.

"You were supposed to be here an hour ago," his mother exclaimed, clapping her hands together. She glanced over the granite kitchen countertops to the digital display on the gas stove. "It's already two."

"You didn't need to come, Mother."

"I did, but can I go?" She crinkled her nose. "Is that all right? I have tennis with Maurizio."

"Go. I'm going to take a nap anyway."

"I'll take care of him," Penny said.

"You certainly have." As always, Virginia delivered her sarcasm with a smile.

Silence, broken only by the driver asking, "Is that all, ma'am?"

"Yes, yes, here." Penny tried to hand him a fistful of twenty-dollar bills.

The driver refused. "All paid for by Eden, but thank you."

"I'll see you soon," Virginia said to Roy, stopping to peck her son's cheek on her way out. "And don't forget tomorrow night. Seven sharp. And wear a decent jacket, for God's sake."

She followed the driver out.

"I don't trust your mother," Penny said after waiting for her mother-in-law to get out of earshot.

It had taken less than a full minute of being back in the house for the circus to start up. "Tell me something new."

"I heard some things when you were in the hospital. She wants to take your money, Roy."

"Like I said." To change topics, he added, "Who's Maurizio? She's not seeing Thomas anymore?"

"That was three boy-toys ago—not that I'm judging."

"Is that jealousy?" He let the comment linger an instant. "Can we not do this?"

If he had to pick one thing that had attracted him to his wife when they first met, it was her innocence. That free-to-be-you-and-me attitude and lack of pretentiousness, but then, men always loved women for what they were—right up until they changed.

She was easily bruised, and his mother's circle of friends wasn't gentle. Penny had transformed—*transmuted*—in the six years since they'd married, and he had been in the hospital for two of those years. Roy knew she was only trying to protect herself. Even before the accident there had been a distance between them. Since then, the rift had widened into a gulf. Some relationships grew stronger through adversity; others couldn't bear the strain.

This wasn't easy for her, either.

"I'm sorry," Roy said. "I'm tired. Really tired."

"I'm sorry, too," Penny said. "You're right. And this was all my fault."

She had been the one driving when they had the accident. It was something she had apologized for a thousand times, try as he might to get her to stop. He noticed again the pink scar on her forehead. Her only injury.

"It was an accident."

"Still my fault."

Roy paused a beat and said, "Hey, I was thinking, maybe after a nap, of dropping by the animal shelter."

It had been the closest thing he'd had to a full-time job, helping with their paperwork. Technically, he *had* a job—on the board of directors of his father's company. But twenty years ago, when he showed up there after his father died, they had made it clear they preferred that he not come. He still got a salary, and after a few years, he had given them what they wanted: he'd not bothered to show up anymore.

"Everyone you know at the shelter is gone," Penny said. "I don't think anybody would know you there."

"Really?" Two years swallowed in a time warp.

His house keys in his pocket, he reached in to pull them out and drop them on the side table, just between the picture of his mother next to

Diana Ross in Studio 54 and the frame of his father arm in arm with Steve Robinson at the release of the HighSoft Corporation's first cell phone. HighSoft had become one of the world's most valuable companies, but the picture was from its uncertain early days.

Roy tossed the keys unconsciously, automatically, then noticed that he'd used his left hand. Things like that gave him fleeting bouts of vertigo. He was right-handed—at least, he always had been. Now it was a little of this and that, an ambidextrous struggle between his mind and body.

Shaking it off, he took two steps to the couch and slumped into it. "I gotta get out of this thing."

He began unstrapping the Velcro ties that held the soft exoskeleton to his legs. Wearing it outside his jeans had been mostly a publicity thing for the reporters when he left Eden this morning. He could walk on his own now, at least around the house. The exoskeleton wasn't metal struts, but hair-fine shape-memory alloy wires sewn into a fabric to allow free movement in certain directions while restricting it in others. The nickel-titanium filaments contracted to encourage his muscles to work in concert with the implants. He carried the batteries in a small backpack.

A bit more than a year after he first managed to make one of the donor body's fingers tremble, he could now pick up pens and tie a Windsor knot. The human brain had an amazing ability to rewire itself, Danesti liked to tell Roy at every opportunity. Danesti loved to tell anyone who would listen. Roy even had a little numb sensation in some toes now.

He even started to think of it as *his* body … sometimes.

As excited as he had been to finally get out of Eden, he was emotionally flat. What had he been expecting? A surprise party? Balloons? One thing he was expecting, though, was the pitter-patter of paws. "Where's Leila?"

"I have something to show you," his wife said.

"What?"

"Come on. Get up."

Roy extricated his legs and unstrapped his waist from the exoskeleton, stood up slowly, and stepped out of it. Soon, it would be gathering dust in the corner of a closet. "Do I have to close my eyes?"

"Just come on." Penny grabbed his hand.

He followed with shuffling steps, his unassisted gait still penguin-like. She led him to the doorway to the garage and put one hand over his eyes. He played along and closed them. She opened the door and flipped on the lights, then took her hand away. In front of them, his old baby-blue Porsche 356's chrome glistened under the fluorescent tubes overhead, the whitewalls pristine, the tan interior leather perfect.

"Is that …?"

It was the car that had tumbled off the cliff in Montauk with them in it. Penny had been driving, but only because he was too drunk even to get in the car without some help. He still didn't really remember the night, but seeing the car, he felt a lump in the pit of his stomach.

She handed him a note in Sam's unmistakable scrawl: "*Better than new, just like you.*"

"Sam had the car rebuilt. Dragged it off the beach and reconstructed it. Said it was a good—"

"Metaphor?"

"Something like that."

Even before the accident, Sam spent more time than Roy on that car. He was always in here putting in a new fuel line or replacing the wiring. Said it was good bonding for them to work on stuff like this. He did a lot of that ever since Roy's father passed.

"And I have something else to show you." Penny pulled him back down the hallway and turned right.

Roy didn't recognize this corridor. "Wait, was this …"

"This is new." She opened a door in front of them and stepped into a huge atrium, glass walled, with a complete gym and workout machines.

"A gift from Eden. They did some other upgrades to the house. For your rehabilitation."

"How much did it cost?"

"Free."

Nothing's free. Roy imagined the press tours he'd have to go on to repay in kind. Still, here he was, walking around his house, maybe even heading down to the beach, when by all rights he should be dead. "Please thank Dr. Danesti."

"You can thank him yourself."

A purposeful sigh. "Do we have to?" He remembered again that he had agreed to attend an Eden fund-raiser tomorrow.

"You said you would."

"I'm tired."

"Of course you are."

"Then can't we cancel?"

"But he has a lot of people coming. A lot of *important* people."

Roy pulled his hand out of hers and turned to walk back to the front of the house. "I've still got blank spots in my memory."

"It'll come back. He says that going back to the—"

"I'm not so sure." There wasn't a lot he could do about it, so he switched topics. "Where's Leila? Is she out in the yard?" The house suddenly felt empty. "Where is she?" He shuffled faster, turning past the kitchen, to the sliding doors looking into the yard.

"Leila's dead."

A silent thunderclap. Of all the things he had looked forward to when he got home, seeing his dog was right at the top of the list. Leila. A little caramel-colored pit bull he'd rescued from the pound ten years ago, before he met Penny. It had been just him and Leila. These past months, he had asked about her, wondering why nobody brought her into Manhattan.

"What happened?" His legs deadened, and he staggered to the edge of the couch to catch himself.

"She was ten, Roy. She was old."

His wife had never liked the dog. He often thought she was jealous of the bond he shared with Leila. She often said he spent more time walking the dog than talking with her. In truth, his girls had been jealous of each other. "What happened?"

"Sweetheart, are you okay? Can we stop talking about the dog? I have something important to tell you."

Roy squeezed his eyes shut and fought the dizziness. Maybe he should have stayed at Eden.

Penny took his hand, held it tight. "I want to have a child, Roy. That's what I've been thinking about, what I've been waiting to tell you. I wanted you home. We can have a real fam—"

The front door chime echoed through the house.

Husband and wife stood a foot apart. They stared at each other, then both turned to look at the shadows on the front stoop. The doorbell rang again. His mother wouldn't ring. Nobody rang a doorbell anymore. These days, any visitors would call ahead—or any *known* visitors would.

Roy said, "If it's reporters, tell them to get lost." He sat at the kitchen counter, head in his hands, and tried to make the room stop spinning.

Penny opened the inside door, then half-opened the screen door.

"Mrs. Lowell-Vandeweghe? I'm Detective Devlin with the Suffolk County Police Department."

Roy pulled his face up from his palms just in time to see the attractive face of a dark-skinned woman in uniform with short black hair holding up a badge. Beside her stood another policeman, young and pale-faced. Penny pushed herself through the door and closed it behind her.

He rubbed his eyes, still trying to get through his shock over Leila's death. Now cops were here? He struggled back to his feet and was halfway to the door when Penny reappeared, thanking the police and wishing them a good day.

The smiling policewoman glanced from Penny to Roy, but then her eyes swiveled back to Roy, her casual glance intensifying. Her partner sensed this and also took a look at Roy. Behind them, in the bushes, another figure lurked, but Roy couldn't see much before Penny backed through the door, thanking the detective again.

She closed the door.

"What was that about?" He had heard the man call the woman "Del."

"Some hiker is missing. They're looking for her."

"A *hiker*? Around here?"

"Up in Nissequogue, near the state park."

"Why are they at our front door?" Nissequogue was halfway across Long Island.

"Someone saw her around here. I said I hadn't seen anyone, that we just got back in from Manhattan."

"Why did she look at me like that?"

"Like what?"

"She stared. Like, *really* stared."

"Your face was on the TV news all week."

"And who was that out in the yard? Behind them?"

"Maybe a reporter? Dr. Danesti said they'd be sniffing around."

Roy was too tired to pursue it. "I'm going to take a nap for a few hours. I'm wiped out."

His wife put her hand to his cheek. "Are you sure? I might just go out to the Habitat for a bit, then."

"Habitat?"

"For Humanity."

"Oh, right." He had almost forgotten.

She was working half days at the Women Build program. It paid a nominal salary, but then, it wasn't a matter of their needing income. She also volunteered at the East Hampton Historical Society. Of the two of them, she was by far the less slothful. Or at least, she had been. After almost two years of grueling rehab, now he could hardly resist the urge to jump on an exercise bike. He had never been so fit, yet he was exhausted.

"Is that okay?" his wife asked. "Or do you want me to stay here?"

"You go. I'm hitting the sack. I've got my phone and medic alert button."

"I'll be a few blocks away if you need anything. And don't forget your medicine, remember—"

"I know. If I don't take it, I die."

6

Detective Delta Devlin stared at the closed door.

"Did you see that?" her partner, Officer Coleman, asked her.

Del saw something, that was for sure, but she wasn't sure what. She always preferred getting a lot of information before giving anything away, and Coleman seemed to know something she didn't, so she asked, "What did *you* see?"

"That was that guy. You know, *that* guy."

"You gotta be more specific."

"He was on the news this morning."

Del rarely watched current events—rarely watched television at all. Her partner needed to up his descriptive game if he wanted to get the detective stripes she had earned only a month ago. "What for? What did he do?"

"Got his head cut off."

"He *what?*"

They turned and jogged down the front steps onto the gravel driveway. Too hot to be in full uniform, but the deputy chief had insisted on it, especially if they poked their noses into East Hampton's backyards. Both of them. Told them to shine their shoes, too, which bordered on insult coming from a white man to a person of color. But then, he was speaking to her whiter-than-white-bread partner at the same time.

"He had a full body–replacement surgery last year. Got sent home this morning. It just clicked when you said his name, DeWay. That was him right there—Van DeWay! Not exactly common."

"No kidding? *Body* replacement? Like from the neck down?" Even she had heard of it. "And FYI, his name's not 'Van.' That's part of his surname: *Lowell-Vandeweghe*—one of those hyphenated blue-blood names."

"And they cut off his head. Creepy, huh?"

Sure, creepy, but then, she'd seen creepier things on the job. A soft gurgling and squirming and black, blood-soaked dirt crowded her mind. The image of the scarecrow, that bookie Pegnini impaled on the fencepost, was never far from her nightmares.

But Coleman's account explained it.

The guy's face she had just seen inside the house was flushed, *ishma*-red in anger, but the wife's face had that tone of pink-orange-*ishma* that often crisscrossed people's cheeks when they were lying. She figured they were having a fight, which wasn't unusual on any given house call where a man and a woman were involved.

What *was* unusual was the shade of his arms. She saw colors differently from everyone else, and had her own systems developed for describing what she saw. His arms were blue-green-pink against the steady blue-blue-pink of his face. She had never before seen someone with differently colored skin like that, not ever, and she was a careful cataloger of everything skin and color related. When she saw him standing there, it was like seeing a unicorn. She couldn't help staring. It was not often you saw a unicorn.

"You didn't recognize him?" Officer Coleman asked.

"I noticed his wife was lying."

"You think so? About the hiker?"

"Not about the hiker. Something else. They were arguing."

"Nothing to do with us, then?"

"Don't think so."

"What else did you notice?"

"The way the wife only spoke to you even after I introduced myself as the detective."

"You think because you're a woman?"

"Or not white, or both. Take your pick. This place is a WASP nest, isn't it?"

She regretted the words even as they came out of her mouth, but Officer Coleman laughed it off.

"You haven't spent much time in this part of the Hamptons, have you?"

"Not exactly my cup of tea." She affected an English accent, but it came out more Irish. "Just know it by reputation." They cleared the end of the driveway and made their way to the next house. Their cruiser was parked at the corner of Ocean Drive.

"One thing out here, Del: new money is colorblind. This place has as many Jews as whites, and blacks and all the colors in between. You want a WASP nest? Head over to the old money in Southampton."

"Thanks for the pointer." They reached the next house on the block: a sprawling gray-shingled mansion.

"I think Jon Bon Jovi has a place on this road," Coleman said.

"You bring your autograph pad?"

"I just don't think we're barking up the right tree on this, Del. That girl that's missing—she wasn't a hiker. I think she was out there, well, *working*, if you get my meaning. And she's been missing more than a year and a half."

"That mean we shouldn't try and find her?"

"Just don't think we're going to find her out here."

"Want to go back to traffic stops in Brookhaven?"

Officer Coleman gave a snort and started up the drive. "Just hope this isn't that goddamn psycho starting up again. The Fire Island Killer? The thought of that guy still being out here gives me the creeps."

1

"Death is something we must get rid of as soon as possible," Dr. Danesti said to Roy. "Do you know how long humans would live if we removed disease and age as causes of death? If the end only came from a sudden mishap?"

It was a rhetorical question.

"An average of eight thousand, nine hundred and thirty-eight years," the doctor continued. "That's how long we would live."

Roy focused on the stepped-pyramid shape of the top of the Rockefeller Center a few blocks away, the ziggurat to the new gods in sharp relief against the clear blue vault of the firmament above. He had come back into Eden's Manhattan offices for another in the unending string of checkups.

Danesti hovered by the edge of the gurney Roy lay on. He pricked his patient's right-hand fingers one by one, and Roy blinked each time he felt the pressure. An imaging device watching his face calculated the reaction time between pinprick and blink—or whether he blinked at all. Apparently satisfied, the doctor moved to the bottom of the bed and began to prick Roy's toes.

Roy blinked, then blinked again. The pinpricks felt numbed out, but almost every day his sensation seemed to improve, the pain and buzzing pins and needles settling down sometimes to a bearable level.

"I've done dozens of full-arm transplants," Danesti said, "and nerve regrowth progresses at about an inch a month. But eighteen months after your surgery, and already …" He pricked Roy's big toe, and Roy blinked. He continued up the leg.

Some places were still totally numb.

Done, the doctor picked up a glass of water from the bedside table and took a sip. "Almost *nine thousand years*. Imagine that lifespan, if we died only by accident. The number one cause of death would be suicide."

"I wouldn't classify suicide as an accident."

"You are so right, Roy. Everything starts with brain health. Keep the mind happy and active. Remove suicide, and we could live fantastically long lives. Perhaps forever. Our work here with you at Eden is to break the link of being imprisoned for life in our birth bodies."

"I wish I had mine back." He still couldn't get used to the size of his hands, but the smell was the worst. He doused himself in cologne every morning.

"I know you do. I know." The doctor adjusted his glasses with his left hand, the glass of water still in his right. "But the body can be reconstructed. It's the mind and the structure of the brain that are the key to longevity. Did you know"—Danesti's voice took on a dreamy tone—"that your brain is being washed with the blood of a man half your age? This is the *real* fountain of youth."

Roy was forty-three. He hadn't taken care of himself before the accident, and that was an understatement. Fifty pounds overweight and with the beginnings of what they said was cirrhosis of the liver. Too many late nights with Sam.

"So how old was my donor?" Roy asked.

They'd never talked about it before. The question of the identity of Roy's donor forever circled in the back of his mind, like a maddening buzzing insect he tried to ignore and hoped would go away, but never did.

The doctor focused a clinical smile on his patient, pulling his mind back from its daydream. "I can tell from the muscle and skin tone that it was a man about twenty years of age. In excellent physical condition."

Roy paused a second, and then another, before asking, "Can I find out who he was?"

"That, I'm afraid, is impossible. Unless the family requests it."

"Even for you?"

"The donor system is confidential and beyond even my access." Danesti reached over to put the glass of water down on the table but released it in midair, two feet off target.

Roy's hand shot out and caught it almost before he even registered seeing it.

A beat of silence. They both stared at the quivering surface of the water in the glass. Not a drop had spilled.

Danesti said, "Amazing," and retrieved the glass.

Roy was just as surprised. He had never been very athletic or even coordinated.

Dr. Danesti retreated to the attending chair beside the bed. He folded his thin hands into his lap—a bird perched on the arm of the chair—and smiled a toothy grin that stretched his facial skin tight. He probably practiced this in the mirror every morning to improve his bedside manner. A large mouthful of straight teeth, but not bleached white. Slightly yellowed, with one incisor chipped at its edge. Perfect imperfection.

"Did you take your antirejection drugs this morning?"

"Every morning."

"And the fentanyl?"

"I'm taking it easy." The truth was, he needed more.

The doctor stood and straightened, his face loosening up. He opened his mouth and rubbed his cheeks. The actor getting ready to go onstage. He took a step for the door. Outside was a small mob of reporters. Each time Roy came for a checkup, it was an implicit invitation for a press conference.

Roy said, "Before we go out there, I have another question that's been bugging me."

The doctor waited.

"How much is all this costing? How is it being paid for? I checked our insurance, and it maxes out at a million a year, but for almost two years I took up half the top floor of one of the most expensive buildings in Manhattan, plus a staff of a dozen doctors and nurses. And then there's the exoskeleton ..."

"Please, Roy, we don't need to—"

"It's not like I'm some combat vet that Uncle Sam is footing the bill for because I got my legs blown off being a hero. We crashed my Porsche when I was wrecked after a party—almost killed my own wife."

"It was your wife driving."

"Because I was wasted. But to my point—why do I deserve all this?"

"Your fate in this will equal my own."

It was an odd choice of words. "I need to know."

The doctor's face creased up, but some inner wall was breached. "The Chegwiddens made a significant contribution."

That made some sense. The accident had been on their property. Probably worried about liability, and Primrose Chegwidden was as rich as a Rockefeller.

"And your own trust fund is paying part of the costs."

That caught Roy off guard. "*My* fund? You mean Atticus approved this?" Their family lawyer—Roy's lawyer—was managing director of the trust fund set up after Roy's father died. Under his breath, he muttered, "There won't be a penny left in it."

His father had left a few million in the trust two decades ago, but anything left would be gobbled up by what this had to be costing.

Danesti said, "Most of your trust is intact, because I am funding the largest part myself. For you."

Roy's cheeks burned—embarrassment but also relief. "Ah, well, then, thank you."

"Because you are helping me. Do you understand? The first two surgeries I attempted were on patients who had underlying medical conditions that made their recovery difficult. They died within months, and our great enterprise was on the verge of failure. But you, and Mr. Sheffield before you, represent a new beginning for Eden. Two successes to show the world, and both within, let's say, a certain *circle* of people."

Roy was always quick to spot an angle. "Rich people."

"Money is not the purpose, you understand, but a necessary evil. A means to an end. Eden Corporation is nonprofit."

So it wasn't so much the money Roy *had* as the pond he swam in.

People like his friend Sam, the Chegwiddens, and the other billionaire diaspora that his mother clung to, with her the glittering dominatrix socialite at their center. Danesti had been his mother's doctor before the accident—not for plastic surgery, but for "rejuvenation" treatments. The transfusions of young blood and plasma. Perhaps his mother had begged Danesti to save her son, had made the case for it. If she had, there was something in it for her, too. There always was.

Danesti put a hand on the door. "And now, you help me?"

He opened the door. At the other side of the rehab room, an expensive gym-like space forty feet across, waited a gaggle of reporters surrounded by cameras loaded on their operators' shoulders. The lights blazed on, the glare dazzling his eyes.

Time to get the show on the road.

Roy strode confidently behind the doctor. He smiled for the cameras, waved to them. Maybe he would even get onto Page Six or the evening news. Or the national news. He bet his mother would be cursing his choice of the old T-shirt he had on.

Dr. Danesti walked ahead, leading a round of applause, which the reporters joined. "I present to you Mr. Royce Lowell-Vandeweghe. A terrible accident destroyed his body, and now, less than two years later, he is up and walking, through the miracle of body-transplant surgery.

"Decapitation is an extremely complex surgery," the doctor explained, his cheek hollows dark in the bright camera lights. "Even after cooling the bodies and heads of patient and donor to ten degrees Celsius, we have less than an hour to reconnect the blood supply to the brain, and then a few more hours to complete the most complex of procedures. In Mr. Lowell-Vandeweghe's and Mr. Sheffield's cases, we have shown that it can work."

Roy picked up three tennis balls and began to juggle them. He dropped one. The reporters laughed and made notes. The prize pig, but not that prized. He'd seen clips of Shelby Sheffield when he did his walks of fame, and there were dozens of reporters. He counted four cameras here. The next guy getting his head chopped off would be getting only a pat on the shoulder and a sugar biscuit.

Danesti, ever the showman, didn't miss a beat. He stepped in front of the cameras and gave the best serious-thinker pose he could do standing up. "When Louis Pasteur first said that microbes caused disease, he was ridiculed, just as I was when I first proposed the idea of a complete body transplant."

"Don't you feel like you're playing God?" asked a squat young reporter in front.

"When they carried out the first human heart transplants in 1967, there was moral outrage that it went against God. The same thing happened with the first test-tube baby in 1978: cries of blasphemy, that we were playing God. Now all these things are so common, we don't give them a second thought."

"But don't you think we're taking this a little too far, too fast?" the reporter pressed.

"This is not just *my* life's work. Soviet pioneer Vladimir Demikhov transplanted a dog's head in 1954, and in America, Dr. Robert White performed the first head transplant on a monkey in 1970. This is a progression—"

"How did you reconnect the spinal cord?" an attractive blond reporter asked.

"An excellent question. Fusogen is a neural-growth factor. A waxy chemical that we insert into the surgically cut interface between patient's and donor's spinal gray matter, it encourages them to grow together. Remember, there is none of the messy neural-tissue trauma you see from an accident. It is clean-cut surgically and reconnected within minutes. In tests with mice in 2016, we had them walking around two weeks after cutting their spinal cords."

"Isn't it a stretch to go from mice and monkeys to humans?"

Danesti affected the look of an adult explaining to a child how to tie shoelaces. "The mind is contained within the brain, and that's what makes us human, what makes us *us*. The reconnecting of blood vessels and fusing of spinal cords is more a matter of mechanics and rehabilitation." He cocked his head to one side. "And some luck. We do need a compatible donor with good genetics and a blood match. Mr. Lowell-Vandeweghe was very lucky."

Roy couldn't help snorting at that, and the reporters' heads turned his way.

"I sure don't feel lucky," he blurted. "I mean, I do, but … you know what I mean. It's been hard."

"What *do* you feel, Roy?" asked an attractive blond. She held out her microphone just inches from his face. "I'm Susan Collins, from the *New York Tribune*. The technical stuff is interesting, but I want to know how you *feel*."

The room went silent.

Roy stared at the reporter. Her hazel-flecked green eyes didn't waver.

What do I feel?

Sick at his stomach, which was sometimes a queasy phantom stomach that floated in front of him—that was how he felt. Drowning in someone else's sweat while his brain floated in opioids, his mind unable to grasp on to reality. Shooting pain from arms and legs that weren't there anymore, and drilling pins and needles from a body he was stapled to, half of which he couldn't feel—a body he felt he'd somehow *stolen* from someone. Propped up on a robotic walker for months, primped and preened for the cameras.

His cheeks burned.

"I … uh," Roy stammered. "I feel, uh …"

"This is a very challenging time for Mr. Lowell-Vandeweghe, as I'm sure you all can appreciate," Danesti said, stepping in front of Roy. "But what I want to make clear today is that death is not an absolute."

"You think you can cheat death?" the reporter Susan Collins asked.

"Death is not an *entity* to be cheated, but simply an invention made up by nature to help life adapt to changing conditions. We are now at the juncture where, through technology, using our God-given intellect, we can unmake that once-inevitable condition of our existence. The Methuselah Foundation, the Singularity Institute—they take different approaches to the idea of ultimate life extension, but who really wants to upload their mind into a machine?"

This earned chuckles from the reporters.

"That is science fiction," Danesti continued, "whereas today I present to you flesh and blood." He nodded at Roy. "With our therapies, many clients of Eden will now live more than a hundred years, as will many of you"—he pointed at the cameras and, by extension, to the millions of people watching—"but Roy and Shelby represent the first steps to something more. Something greater. This is the goal of Eden, the age-old quest for the Holy Grail. Ladies and gentlemen, the beginning of everlasting life is *now*."

8

From a black hole, a screaming face appeared. Blue eyes so pale, the sky shone straight through them. Red hair. She was screaming but silent. Lips closed. A noose around her neck.

"I'll get us out of here," Roy promised, but it wasn't his voice.

They had to hurry. The police were coming.

In the grass ten feet below the wooden platform, his whole family watched. Why were none of them helping him? His dead father stood, impassive, his eyes urging him to do the right thing. Roy heaved and strained to lift the woman but couldn't.

"I'm sorry," he said. "I'll come back. I promise."

On the grass below, a tiny red-haired girl watched.

Roy gasped for air, blinked, and looked around. Penny was asleep beside him. He was drenched in sweat. He'd been dreaming again. Not really dreams. Nightmares. The alarm said 3:05 in the morning.

* * *

"It's getting worse," Roy said.

His friend Sam took a swig from his bottle of beer, the neck almost disappearing into the gray nest of his beard and mustache. "You gotta expect some weirdness."

They stood at the back of Roy's yard, at the edge of the line of cedars between his property and the neighbor's. The lawn service had been there in the afternoon, the cutters and mowers giant ants that swarmed about for an hour before leaving a sudden stillness behind. The air was filled with the strong organic smell of the fresh-cut grass that stained Roy's tennis shoes. It was the end of the day, the shadows of the trees growing across the house.

Roy said, "I'm even afraid to go to sleep. It's like ..."

"What?"

"The dreams are getting more real."

"Than what?"

"I don't know."

"You sure you don't want a beer?" Sam had another one in his hand. The guy was always ready.

Roy shrugged—why not?—and his friend went into the garden shed and found something to open the import with. In the shadows of the back of the structure a kitten mewled, its tiger stripes just visible in the twilight.

"Come on, it's okay," Roy said.

He put down the bowl of milk beside the food he'd brought out. The little cat took a tentative step forward, a step back, and then trotted up to the milk. Its brothers and sisters followed until the bowl was surrounded by whining kittens. The mother and father had kept their distance to begin with. They waited for Roy to leave before they would come to eat, but he was slowly gaining their trust.

Sam came back out of the shed and handed Roy the bottle. Sam smiled at the kittens and retreated a few steps so he wouldn't spook them.

A month had passed since Roy came home, and it felt like house arrest. A month of working out all day with a parade of rehab specialists, making sure his body was connected into the central data collection. He was in better shape than ever before. He had run three miles on the treadmill this morning and barely broken a sweat.

Between rehab and workout, he had taken to wandering on the beach and around the garden. It was on one of those rambles that he spotted the cats, behind the shed. None of them had a collar. If it were up to him, he'd bring them inside, have the whole gang of them crawling around over his head in the mornings. Penny hated cats even more than dogs. That wasn't entirely fair—she was allergic. He should have just taken them up to the animal shelter, but right now he was enjoying them.

He thought of his dog Leila the last time he saw her. He'd taken her for a walk and gotten impatient when she'd wanted to stop and sniff a lamppost. He wished he had just let her be. It was the first and only time he'd had a dog he could really call his own, and in hindsight, the experience was like no other. A fearless, uncompromising love that he missed more than he ever thought he could.

Sam said, "What about volunteering at the Southampton Animal Shelter again? You used to love that."

"I don't know anybody there anymore." He had gone back, but the place just didn't feel the same.

"Did you think any more on what we talked about?" Sam asked.

Roy looked down at the cats. Strays, but at least they had each other. "Yeah, I did. It makes sense, but I don't think I want Penny coming. She seems to want to insert herself into everything."

"She's just trying to help."

"I guess."

"Hey, I need to get going," Sam said. "Give you a call later?"

"Yeah." Roy didn't take his eyes off the kittens.

"You take it easy." His friend walked off across the back lawn, giving him a small wave goodbye.

Roy sat cross-legged in the grass and gave the cats space. The mother and father joined the scrum around the bowls. They circled and rubbed against the others. They looked so happy together. They understood each other.

"Hey, buddy, can you stop doing that?" His neighbor stood on his balcony. The people next door had just moved in, and Roy hadn't met them yet.

Roy waved back. "They're hungry."

"I don't want them around. They're pissing in our shed. Can you not feed them?" The man waved dismissively and turned around to go back inside. "They need to be gotten rid of," he said over his shoulder.

What an asshole.

* * *

The rain hammered down.

Roy's eight-year-old body tensed.

"Richard, hurry up!" his mother screamed from the veranda. "They'll be soaked. We'll be late for the show."

Everyone else called his father Dick. She was the only one who called him Richard.

His dead father hunkered low, looked his son in the eye. "You ready?"

Roy nodded. Small white rocks appeared at their feet. Covered everything, flattened the grass. The shush of the rain replaced with a clattering racket against the glass of the greenhouse.

"That's hail, Bucky." His father always called him Bucky. "We'd better hurry. You first, I'll follow."

The heavens ripped open in another flash.

Roy shivered, his teeth chattering.

He blinked, then looked around again.

But now he was sitting in a seat.

In a car.

Rain drummed on the windshield.

Dark.

The only illumination was from a streetlight forty feet away. The leather seat felt cold against the hand he had just put out to steady himself. The dream of his father faded. After a second, he clicked on the interior light and blinked again to clear his eyes. This was his Range Rover. The last thing he remembered was feeding the cats, but that had been when it was still light out. He was still wearing his tennis sneakers and jeans, the same shirt he had on before. But he was soaking wet. The clock on the dashboard said one fifteen. The middle of the night.

Five hours missing. Maybe six?

In the center console was his phone.

He clicked it on, his mind still swimming. Penny had called him twice, but he hadn't answered. No other calls or messages, incoming or outgoing. He clicked the map app. He was on Middle Country Road, just west of Calverton on the north side of Long Island. A fifty-minute drive.

What the hell was he doing here?

9

"Careful of the ghost."

Officer Coleman stepped square in front of the East Hampton detective. "What's that supposed to mean?"

"Woo, woo-oo-oo." The jokester waved his hands in the air, miming an apparition, then chuckled as he reached out his hand.

"Relax, Coleman," Delta Devlin said, grinning. "That's my nickname from the academy. 'Ghost.'" She shook the man's hand. "Nice to see you, too, Hulk."

"Still doing the law degree?" Detective Hogan shook her hand.

"Almost done," she replied.

Twenty-seven-years old, four years on the job, and still not sure what she wanted to do with her life. Become a lawyer? Try for the FBI? She had just earned her detective badge—one of the youngest on Suffolk PD ever to manage it. Could she do it all? Her mother still wanted her to find a nice boy, settle down, and take up painting full time. Less chance of getting shot, Mom never tired of pointing out.

Hogan said, "Nice to see you again, and best of luck." He pushed his way out through the station's double front doors.

Coleman watched the guy jump down the front steps. "Ghost?"

"'Cause I see things other people can't." After a week with her new partner, she was surprised this hadn't come up sooner.

They reached the front desk, and she said to the shift officer, "Detective Devlin from Suffolk County. Deputy Chief Alonzo told me to come see XO Harris."

Where else but the East Hampton PD would they have an executive officer? Captain Harris was a pain, but one her deputy chief had made her promise not to aggravate.

The shift officer didn't bother to look up from his paperwork. "Take a load off," he said. "I'll tell him you're here."

Del thanked the officer and sat in a soft leather chair to one side of the reception desk.

"I'll bite," her partner said, joining her. "What do you mean, you can *see* stuff?"

On the side table between them was a pod-fed coffee machine, with instructions saying to ask for decaf if needed, and stacks of *Sailing* and *Hamptons Living* magazines. Not linoleum floors like every other police station she'd ever been inside, but marble with a logo engraved in the floor, as if this were the FBI headquarters. It even smelled like—what was that, *patchouli*?

"I'm a tetrachromat."

"A whatcha-chromat?"

"A tetra …," Del enunciated slowly, "chro … mat."

"Still no idea."

"It means I can see more colors than you."

"Like how many?"

"Like, you can see a million, and I can see ninety-nine million more."

"Bull."

"Are you color-blind?"

Coleman had to think for a second. "Nope."

"If you were, you'd be a dichromat. '*Di-*' means 'two' in Greek. Dichromats can see only about ten thousand colors, and that's most animals, like dogs. Their eyes have only two different types of these things called *cones* that see colors. *Trichromats*—three kinds of cones—are regular people."

"So you're a tetrachromat; you have four cones."

"Ladies and gents, we have a winner." Del gave him her you're-not-so-stupid-after-all grin.

"I still don't get it. You see more colors than me? Like what colors?"

"A color-blind person can't see the difference between red and green. To you and me, the difference is night and day, obvious as a slap in the face, but they just see the same red-green shade of gray."

"They just see *gray?*"

Del crinkled her brow. "I don't know *what* they see, to be honest. Color is subjective. We call red 'red' just because everyone else calls it that. I can never really know what you see. So I can't explain the colors I see that you can't."

Coleman still had the same blank expression.

"Look, color-blind people see red and green as the same color. So me, with my extra cone, I see a color I call *ishma*. I've called it that ever since I was a kid. A word I made up. You see it as the same color as red or green, but to me it's as clearly different as night and day. It's slightly higher up the frequency scale toward ultraviolet, and I can perceive my reds a little deeper."

"Are you bullshittin' me?"

Del's easy smile faded. She whispered, "When we go to crime scenes, I sometimes see blood spatters on walls that have been cleaned—stuff nobody else can. I can detect things in the dark. That's why they call me 'the ghost.'"

"So you're telling me you're the only person who can see like this?"

"A small percentage of females—*only* females—are tetrachromats, but they only discovered it a few years ago. I mean, we were all here before that, but it was discovered as a *thing* only about ten years ago. I knew I was different when I was a kid—could see stuff. But reading an article a few years back, I found out what I actually was—at least, the name for it. It's a mutation."

"So you're a mutant."

"In the flesh." Del let her smile return.

"Mutants have been living among us all along?" Coleman grinned back at her.

"That's what I'm saying."

"In the land of the three-coned men, the four-coned woman is king."

"That's pretty good, Coleman."

"What else can you see?"

"That guy Royce Lowell we saw the other day? You remember?"

"The head-chopped-off guy?"

"To me, the skin of his face was totally different from the color of his arms. And his wife—I could see that she'd just been lying about something. Remember?"

"You see that just by looking at them?"

"A lot of people, a lot of the time. It's not just the colors, but body language, too. More of a feeling than anything else."

It was a skill she'd worked on over time. Maybe she should have been a professional poker player. An easier way to make money, but then, girls wanted their daddies to be proud, and her father wouldn't have been happy to see her become a gambler. Then again, police work was gambling of another sort.

"Maybe the wife wasn't exactly lying," Del added, qualifying her statement, "but she wasn't happy with *something* when she opened that door. It's all in the blood vessels near the—"

"Devlin." The shift officer was on his feet, pointing to the door at the back of the station. "Detective Devlin, he'll see you now."

* * *

"So that's it? Nothing else?" Captain Harris leaned back in his reclining leather chair. Behind him, floor-to-ceiling windows framed a bucolic scene of woods and a stream. Between the mahogany bookcases and the credenza to his right, plaques and awards decorated the walls. He glanced at his computer screen.

"We don't know who called it in," Del said, admiring his office. "Probably a crank. Kids being a pain in the ass. Didn't find anything unusual."

A week ago, someone had called in to Suffolk County a report of the missing person—missing over a year now. Said they saw her, unequivocally *her,* on a road near Ocean Drive in East Hampton. The sheer detail of the call forced them to come and check it out, door-to-door, but nothing. The deputy chief of Suffolk didn't want to find out that some rich nutball was hiding a girl in the backyard, so he told them to come check it out for themselves, but quietly.

"Good. Don't like bothering my people with stuff like this."

My people—it was an odd turn of phrase to describe the citizens of East Hampton. "Gotta do it, much as I hate it, Captain."

Captain Seamus Harris. His red crew cut was as Irish as his name. Half of her found him comfortably familiar, while the other half felt on edge. Del inspected Harris's face: the color smooth, the capillaries as pink and relaxed as the forest behind the glass.

He'd already lost interest and was looking at his emails again.

"One thing that was noteworthy, though," she added.

He looked up from the computer screen. "What's that?"

"We met Royce Lowell-Vandeweghe." After Coleman told her about him, she'd looked Royce up, read the stuff in the papers. "The guy who underwent that head surgery."

She didn't need to be more detailed. The relaxed pink shade turned darker. "That is an amazing story."

"You're the one that pulled him from his car? After the accident?"

The effect was immediate. A mottled explosion of orange-*ishma* bloomed on Harris's face. Del was taken aback. She hadn't expected that. Hadn't expected anything, really. Was just curious. The captain maintained an even smile, though. A regular person wouldn't have noticed anything.

"Thank God I could help," he said after a pause.

"But you happened to be out there, way out in Montauk. That's gotta be a—"

The smile slid away. "Listen, Detective Devlin. I don't want you causing trouble where there isn't any. That family has gone through enough. I want to make it clear that you leave the Lowell-Vandeweghes alone."

She didn't reply.

"Is that clear?" he repeated.

"Sure."

He looked at his screen.

In Del's vision, his face was crisscrossed with patches of orange-pink. It wasn't just that he was upset. Harris looked as though he was *lying* about something.

"Anyway, you got other fish to fry. They just found your hiker." He swiveled his monitor around to an email he had opened, and clicked the image files. A weathered sack filled with gray-brown lumps. "Or at least, parts of her."

10

"Two more."

The trainer, a burly Asian man with a shaved head, straddled Roy's body on the bench in his new home gym. The man got his meaty hands under the barbell to spot the weight. "Grip as hard as you can and push. Come on, push!"

Roy strained. Inch by inch, the massive weights rose.

The dreams were getting even more vivid. He could still see the little girl's eyes from his dream again last night, as blue and pale as the woman who was always with her. Their hair flaming red. Or images of his mother, screaming at his father. One second, Roy was here, sitting on the couch watching TV, and in the next, he'd be off in a dream world.

Sometimes, he would dream about the accident.

He still couldn't remember it all.

His mind slid back as he lifted the barbell.

He remembered that they'd driven in from Manhattan, waited for the traffic to ease off first. He had asked the concierge to bring around his baby-blue 356 Speedster. Penny hated it, couldn't stand the way it blew her hair around when he took the top down. She had tried to insist that they get the driver to bring them in the Escalade, or take the helicopter shuttle from West Thirtieth, but he had told her it was too expensive, that they weren't that rich. And anyway, he said, it was his birthday. New Year, every year—a cursed day for a birth if ever there was one.

Images of the drive on the Long Island Expressway flashed in his mind: the smell of the leather seats, the bite of the frigid air, Penny's hair flying in the wind. Then scraggly chokeberry and bayberry bushes half-lit in the headlamps, the washed gray cedar shingles of the Chegwiddens' rambling New England–style home rising up out of the gnarled, wind-blown pines. White-framed windows cast warm yellow light over patches of sea grass atop sand dunes. A distant crash of waves, the full moon reflecting off the Atlantic. Strains of a cello, soft clink of plates and glasses, black-liveried kitchen staff serving hors d'oeuvres on silver platters, hushed conversation and peals of laughter, a flash of a diamond necklace, and then …

Screaming, but not in the accident. Someone screaming before it happened.

He was yelling at someone.

Or was someone yelling at him? Was it Penny? Or his mother?

"One more," the trainer encouraged. "Come on, you can do it."

The barbell descended to bounce off Roy's barrel chest. He gritted his teeth. The bar started to move back up again.

"That's ten. Can you do one more?"

Roy held the bar aloft, his breathing fast and shallow. He nodded. The weight training was about the only thing that kept his mind centered. Someone whistled. Roy strained again and pushed the weight all the way up, banging it onto the rack. Sam ambled toward them, limping with his cane.

"You can bench *four hundred pounds*? That's insane! Thought I'd drop by to say hello, see how my boy is doing."

"We good for today?" Roy asked the trainer.

The trainer nodded and offered a hand to haul him to his feet. "Why don't you go get hydrated?"

"My thoughts exactly," said Sam.

* * *

"Maybe you should talk to your mother?" Sam said. "I think it would be good for you. Get things out in the open."

"You're right," Roy said.

Two months had passed since he got home, and the blackouts were getting worse. Sometimes, he couldn't remember what he'd been doing for an entire evening. It wasn't alcohol—that didn't seem to make much difference. The events seemed random. Danesti said it was normal, that his body and mind were repairing themselves. He said the medical team was keeping track of him remotely. He said that nothing about Roy's recovery from such an extreme surgery was abnormal. He just needed to stay calm and things would improve.

Sam asked, "You got a beer in there?"

"Sure." Roy opened the refrigerator and pushed back a bunch of kale, frowned, and looked down another shelf. "Actually, no. Looks like Penny took it all."

His friend opened the cupboard over the dishwasher and clucked. "Cleaned out all the booze, too."

"You want a bottle of water?"

"Try not to touch the stuff."

A loud ringing interrupted them. It was the house phone, set on the counter under the microwave. No one called the house phone these days except telemarketers.

Roy picked it up anyway. "Hello?"

"Mr. Lowell-Vandeweghe?"

Roy remained silent.

"This is Susan Collins," the caller continued, "from the *New York Tribune*. We met at the press conference at Eden."

"We met?"

"I asked you how you felt. Do you remember?" After another pause and no response, she added, "The blond one. You looked right at me."

"Oh, right. Listen, I'm not doing any more interviews."

"This isn't really concerning you."

"Who is that?" Penny called out from the upstairs hallway.

"Just a telemarketer," Roy yelled back with his hand over the receiver.

Then, in a lower voice, he said to the reporter, "I can't really talk now, but—"

"I've been researching Eden Corporation's finances," she said.

Ka-click, ka-click, ka-click ... Penny's high heels announced her descent of the stairs.

"I really can't talk right now. Maybe later."

"Roy, I would really—"

He hung up just as Penny appeared.

"Why do you talk to them?" she said straightaway.

"Maybe because I'm lonely?" He let the half joke hang in the air a split second before adding, "I feel bad for them." Roy fidgeted with his water bottle for a few seconds. "I'm going out."

"You're not supposed to go out. Remember what the doctor said about infections?"

"I'm just going to my mother's."

"Why would you want to go see her?"

"I need to speak with her."

"You want a lift?" Sam offered.

"I'm just going out for an hour," Roy said.

* * *

"Would you like a drink?" Roy's mother asked.

"Ah, I don't think so."

She checked her watch. "It's six o'clock. You going to make your mother drink alone?"

"Scotch, then, a few ice cubes." He never needed much arm-twisting.

"I've still got some of your father's. Give me a second." His mother sauntered into the kitchen, her heels clicking against the Italian ceramic tiles. She had on black slacks and a matching top covered by a tailored dinner jacket with sheer lapels.

"Going out?" Roy asked.

"It's the sick-kids fund-raiser tonight," she said from the kitchen, out of sight.

Roy inspected the array of pictures in silver frames, on display on a high table in the entryway. There were black-and-white pictures of his mother with Bob Feldman, the civil rights activist arrested at Columbia. Another with blood on her face, being dragged away by the New York Police Department after the raid on Hamilton Hall. Over a hundred students injured in the occupation, one of the most famous in the civil rights struggle of the sixties—at least, as his mother liked to describe it. She always claimed she was the seventh of the "IDA Six," a group of students who were expelled for uncovering the Institute of Defense Analysis, which hooked Columbia to the Vietnam War.

Truth be told, she wasn't even really a student at Columbia at the time, but it cemented her street cred with the Hampton crowd. Virginia always denied being anything important, just before regaling them with a steamy tale of her short-lived affair with Feldman. There were pictures of her at Woodstock, with flowers in her hair. That generation always liked to think of themselves as unique, as having fought "the man," pushed for the good of humanity. But from Roy's perspective, they were just a bunch of selfish kids, doing whatever they wanted, and they'd grown into a generation of selfish adults, and now selfish retirees who controlled the country.

There were pictures of Virginia standing with Diana Ross in Studio 54 and of her posing with a range of other celebrities. Right at the edge of the table were some wedding photos of her and Roy's father, Richard. Just one shot without her—the only one with a celebrity: Richard standing with his arm around tech entrepreneur Steve Robinson.

This was their family home—a big step up from the one at Mott's Point, and at least twice the size of Roy's house. His dad had bought the place in 1994, just after he started his private equity company, right at the start of the original dot-com boom. Located in Sagaponack—although his mother would always say it was Bridgehampton—it was a fifteen-minute drive from Roy's house in East Hampton, but a totally different feel, with a riding stable across the street, and a still-operating farm behind that.

"Here you go." Virginia handed him a crystal tumbler with an inch of Scotch. "Why don't we sit? I do need to be going soon."

They went to the living room, to an ornate glass table between two overstuffed couches. Roy dropped onto one. "Just wanted to stop by and say hello."

"Well, then, hello." She took a sip from her drink, a vodka soda with a lime twist.

"I have a few things that have been bothering me."

She took another drink. "I'm sure you do. I know this is very difficult. I'm doing my best to help—"

"The night of the accident, did you see us leave?"

"I already told the police everything."

"You mean Captain Harris."

"He *is* the police, dear."

"But did you see anything … I don't know, anything else? Was I angry?"

Her bright-red lips took to the edge of the crystal glass. She took another sip before saying: "I think you were having a fight with Penny."

"A fight?" That dim recollection of someone screaming. Was that his wife screaming at him? Or him at her?

"But you were very drunk."

"And Penny decided to drive me home?"

"I don't think you should trust Penny."

"So you didn't see us get in the car."

"No."

"But you did try to get Atticus to change the terms of our family trust when I was in a coma."

The grandfather clock in the hallway ticked through the seconds of silence.

"So that's what this visit is really about." His mother lowered her drink to her lap. "Did your wife tell you that?"

"Is it true?"

Virginia looked away. She pursed her lips, the edges of them crinkling with lines. "You were dead for half an hour after the accident, before they resuscitated you—*and* almost another hour during the operation."

"Dead?"

"Legally dead. I was just trying to protect us, to protect *you.* You know the terms of the trust."

If Roy died or went to prison, the entire contents of the trust was directed to go to charity. His mother had barely been able to contain her rage when the executor read out the terms after the funeral.

Roy had just come home after being expelled from Yale for selling pot, just before his father's heart attack. That little stunt hadn't made things any better—maybe had caused the heart attack. It was one of Roy's most private fears, something no one ever said but everyone had considered.

His father had been under investigation by the SEC at the time, regarding questionable financial transactions in tech IPOs during the height of the dot-com crash, when millions of investors had lost billions of dollars. The charges were dropped, but then, the terms of the trust weren't really about that.

His father had never really trusted his mother.

"I know the trust ends with me," Roy said. "Is that why you pushed Danesti to keep me alive?"

"That's a horrible thing to say. You're my son."

"Who you barely ever paid any attention to."

"You always were a little monster, you know that?"

She was already drunk. "The apple doesn't fall far from the tree."

"You didn't fall from *my* tree."

"Meaning what?"

She closed her eyes and seemed to count to ten before reopening them. "I'm sorry. I just mean, you're very much like your father. Bullheaded. And yes, I know I wasn't a good mother. It's something I regret, Roy. And seeing you there, on that table …" Her upper lip trembled, and she brought her hand up. "I realized that I might lose you. I did everything I could, begged everyone. You don't know how hard … but you're here now; that's all that matters."

Was that a tear in the corner of her eye? She dabbed it away, her hand shaking.

Roy gulped a mouthful of whisky. Was he always this awful with her? How had they gotten to this place? This was his *mother*. He sighed and said, "I don't mean to be ungrateful."

"Just nasty."

"You can come over anytime."

"But ... *she's* there." Virginia finished her drink.

Roy had always been perplexed by the animosity between his mother and his wife. Was it simple jealousy over taking away her little boy? But his mother had never really made an effort to be close to him.

She added, "Anyway, in a few months, the trust will be done. You'll have your inheritance."

On Roy's forty-fourth birthday, the trust fund would dissolve, and all the remaining cash left in it would be transferred to him. Two months from now. His dad had started his company when he was forty-four.

"This house is worth way more than what's left in the trust," Roy pointed out.

The property had to be worth ten million, and while technically it was still part of the trust, he had promised a long time ago that his mother could keep it. You could say a lot of things about Roy, but he always kept his word once he'd given it.

He said, "I'm still leaving it to you. It's written down. Atticus has a copy."

"Thank you, Roy." Another tear welled. It was either honest or a damn good performance, or she was drunker than usual. Maybe a combination of all three. "That woman—"

"Has a name. It's Penny, and she's my wife. Now, can we just stop?"

"If something ever happened, you could come and stay here. You know that, right? I love you, no matter what."

Roy finished his drink in one gulp. "One more thing."

"Yes?"

"What happened to Leila?"

"She died, dear. Why do you keep asking about that dog?"

11

The Chegwiddens' property sat at the edge of Montauk, where the steep white-sand beaches of the Hamptons began to spread wide and flat. The house had the same washed-gray cedar shingles that Roy remembered, the white-framed windows still staring out over dunes and sea grass.

"Everyone, everyone, our guest of honor has arrived," Charles Chegwidden announced, his cheeks already florid with alcohol. "Just in time for dinner."

He had opened the front door before Roy and Penny reached it.

An attendant took their coats as the driver circled the Escalade behind them to find a parking spot down the scrub-lined road leading to the beach. His mother got out of the car and went straight into the house, but Roy and Penny had stopped briefly to inspect the new reinforced-concrete wall before the forty-foot drop to the beach. Two years ago, it had just been a low brick wall and wooden fence with stairs leading down, before Penny had plowed through it in the dark, sending them tumbling into the abyss.

Dr. Danesti had said it would be good for them to face the past head-on, that it could help with memory recovery. All Roy knew was that his stomach felt as though something inside had been trying all afternoon to stab its way out. But coming here did feel good, as if they were starting to put the past behind them.

"Sorry for being so difficult," Roy whispered to his wife, holding her hand for both comfort and balance.

"Don't worry," she replied. "I know it's been hard." Then she added, "Did you hear? About Roger? Our neighbor in the back?"

The guy who wanted to kill the stray cats. "What about him?"

"He's been missing for a month."

"This way, this way," Charles said, urging them through the entryway. The Englishman had a habit of saying everything twice—a tic accompanied by brisk hand motions. Sam was already here. Seeing Roy, he raised his glass.

When they were here the night of the accident on New Year's Eve, there had been a crush of people, hundreds of them. Tonight was more intimate, less formal. Roy wore a black turtleneck and patch-elbowed sport jacket, but most of the sixty- and seventysomething men wore open-necked shirts, the much younger women accompanying them in short black dresses or close-fitting jeans.

Ambient electronic music played from hidden speakers. In the middle of the great room straight off the entrance, a thirty-foot table was set for dinner. The white leather couches beyond it spilled out into a rough marble exterior courtyard and swimming pool.

"Charles, I didn't get to thank you and Prim yet for helping with the costs of—"

"Oh, please, please, think nothing of it," Charles said, with more fluttering of hands. "Least we could do, old boy. Such a terrible, terrible business, all this."

"Well, thank you, all the same."

"Ah, Alexi," Charles said as they approached the first pair of couples. "I would like to introduce you to—"

"No introduction needed." The short, almost cylindrical man nearest them thrust his hand forward. He spoke in a thick Russian accent. "Alexi Berezovsky, and this is Anastasia." He motioned with his eyes to the pretty brunette at his left, a full foot taller than him. "It is a pleasure to meet you, Mr. Royce."

Roy took the man's hand, which gripped tighter and tighter as they shook. Roy returned the pressure, and Alexi's eyes widened. An old game, which Roy won.

"Amazing," the Russian said after Roy let him have his hand back.

"And this is my wife, Penny."

The man to Alexi's right was someone Roy recognized. Bobby.

"My god, you look good!" Bobby said. "It's been too long." The guy didn't try to shake hands, instead reaching in for a hug. "And holy cow, the muscles on you!"

"Thanks." Roy remembered that Bobby did something in pharmaceuticals and ran some kind of bodyguard army in sub-Saharan Africa. He'd told him once, *if you go down there, call me to make sure you're safe.* A nice guy.

Roy never stopped being amazed at what people in the Hamptons did for a living.

One by one, they went through introductions. Roy had never been good with names and didn't even try to remember the twenty-odd people he didn't know. A collection of characters, to be sure, but they all had a certain sameness to them, a perfectness that was unnatural but beautiful at the same time, as if the lines of their faces were sculpted by the same expert hands.

The last person they greeted was Danesti himself.

"Thank you for coming," the doctor said. He had a house just down the beach.

"Everyone, everyone, let's sit," Charles said.

Penny and Roy took their arranged seats at the center of the table, straight across from Charles and his wife, their hosts. Roy's mother sat at the head of the table, three people to their right. Maurizio—a thirtysomething Spaniard, her "tennis partner"—sat to her left.

Sam seated himself to Roy's right. "Glass of wine?"

He hadn't taken a drink when they came in, but one or two couldn't hurt. "Sure, some red?"

Sam motioned to the waiter. Dinner conversation murmured in the background.

Although Roy took center stage tonight, Primrose Chegwidden was the real star in the room. Both she and her husband were psychologists, but she had turned her practice into a television show, syndicated internationally—"Dr. Rose," as she was known to millions of adoring fans.

Primrose sat straight across from Roy, inspecting him. Her thin fingers matched lips pressed tightly together, her short hair dyed red beyond anything close to natural. A web of fine lines at the edges of her eyes—not the fat, good-natured lines born of laughing, but more like cracks in porcelain, and unalleviated by the hard black arcs of mascara and the thin flaring nostrils.

"How are you feeling, Roy?" she asked. She picked at the amuse-bouche that a waiter had set in front of her.

"Good. Better than new."

She smiled, but not in a way that made Roy feel that he'd said something funny. He felt like an exotic insect being observed under a bell jar. Primrose's face had that expression of bored indulgence that the English once reserved for their colonial subjects—one that barely concealed the unspoken understanding that they had somewhere better to be.

"It is so nice to see you," she said. "Thank you for coming."

Her husband, Charles, was the yin to her yang, the jovial British counterpart to her cool intellectual conceit. Ruddy-cheeked and snaggletoothed, with a quick smile that invited jocularity, he was reliably the only one wearing a tie, which was always a little off-center. He was the researcher, Roy had heard—the behind-the-scenes part of this partnership. Primrose was definitely the one who wore the pants.

"Isn't it wonderful?" Roy heard a woman next to his mother exclaim. "Dr. Danesti helped me arrange a surrogate mother in India. I had my eggs frozen when I was forty-two"—the woman was probably pushing seventy—"but I just met Matty," she said, squeezing the hand of the young man beside her—"and we're going to have children."

"Congratulations!" Roy's mother replied to the woman. "You're going to need to stay healthy, Angela. Talk to my microbiomogist. Your microbiome is the most important thing. He gets samples from first-contact tribes in the Amazon ..."

"Poop. Fecal transplants. They're talking about someone else's excrement," Sam whispered under his breath, the ever-present grin barely visible under his bushy mustache.

He handed Roy a glass of wine from the waiter and explained. "They get it from some god-awful country they'd never set foot in, yet they're happy to stick some smelly native's poo up their asses. Something poetic in that somewhere, no? I just can't quite put my finger—"

"I think I'll stop you there." Roy grinned and lifted his glass. "Cheers," he said, and they both took a sip of their drinks together.

Whatever else, it was good to be back goofing around with Sam at these things.

The couple across from them was talking about bee-venom therapy, and Alexi, the Russian fireplug he'd met on the way in, was deep in discussion with Danesti about a liver transplant.

They finished the opening course, a lemon-and-pine-needle sorbet, each tiny bowl topped with a sprig of pitch pine that Primrose explained she had collected that very morning from the woods surrounding the house. More wine and drinks followed before a rustic soup arrived in clay bowls. Charles—after asking everyone whether they could believe it twice—said Primrose had thrown the bowls herself in the pottery studio by the beach. Everyone responded with coos and congratulations. As they awaited the main course, which the head waiter announced as a boeuf bourguignonne garnished with microgreens and fresh herbs from the garden, people came up in twos and fours to talk to Dr. Danesti, stopping on the way to congratulate Roy and ask him how he felt.

Dr. Danesti stood and clinked a spoon against his wineglass. "Everyone, I would like to be the first to announce the upcoming Art for Humanity exhibition and auction, organized by our own Virginia Vandeweghe."

Roy's mother smiled but held up one hand in feigned embarrassment at the attention.

"I trust that everyone will be attending. All proceeds will be donated to the Women Build program of the Habitat for Humanity."

Roy frowned in surprise. That was his wife's program. "You didn't tell me that," he whispered to her, leaning over to get close. Was this his mother's way of melting the ice?

"I was as surprised as you," Penny replied.

"You know, you two could almost be twins."

"Pardon?" Roy looked up. The alcohol was already hitting his bloodstream.

A beautiful brunette in a form-hugging black knit dress and red stilettos stood to one side of Dr. Danesti, resting a perfectly manicured hand on the doctor's shoulder. It was Anastasia, Alexi's date. She smiled at Roy, then at Danesti, then back at Roy. "You two. Roy and Dr. Danesti. Is it just me? Don't they look like brothers?"

That got Sam's attention. "Hey, she's kinda right. Minus the glasses ..."

"How old are you?" the brunette asked.

"Ah, forty-three," Roy replied, still off balance. Did he look like Danesti? Maybe. He hadn't thought of it before. His own family was solidly midwestern, but he thought his great-grandfather was from Europe. "Doctor, where are you from?"

Danesti took his seat and smiled awkwardly. "I was adopted."

"But that accent?"

"My adoptive father was Romanian. Hence the name."

That made sense. Roy's head was swimming. The brunette was still smiling at him, her lips as bright red as her fingertips. Danesti kept speaking, but the words garbled together. Roy grabbed his water and downed it, and the words began to make sense again.

"This is what we call 'newgenics,'" Dr. Danesti said loudly, picking up where he had left off. "Preimplantation genetic diagnosis. By taking a dozen fertilized embryos and making modifications, we can test to make sure the DNA is complete and unmutated, while still allowing nature to play its hand. The genome can then propagate by itself in the germ line. Just as a résumé uses past performance to judge the future, genetic enhancement is what you might call a 'présumé.'"

The assembled guests clucked at his clever wordplay.

"Can we do that?" Angela, Roy's mother's friend, asked. "I mean, could we do that with my surrogate?"

"Chinese scientists have already produced the first genetically altered children."

"So it's possible?"

"Not here, and not without strict state oversight, even in China. The only sure way forward would be to create our own sovereign nation-states floating in international waters, outside the regulatory environment of America or any other country. But that is a discussion for another day."

"Are you okay?" Penny whispered to Roy.

"I'm fine."

"I remain committed to the faith of my teenage years," Dr. Danesti proclaimed, his voice rising in volume. "To authentic human freedom as a precondition for the highest good. I stand against confiscatory taxes, totalitarian collectives, and the ideology of the inevitable death of every individual. For these reasons, I call myself a libertarian, and as proof, I present my greatest achievement, Mr. Royce Lowell-Vandeweghe."

The gathering erupted into applause, and Roy raised a hand in acknowledgment, but the images and faces melded and merged into one another. He had another drink in his hand and was laughing with someone, and a moment later, he was again sitting by his wife and Dr. Danesti.

"I can repair your body, your physical self, Roy, but do you remember what I said in the hospital?"

"I remember every-shing." Roy blinked and tried to clear his eyes.

"There's only one thing I need you to do."

"Wash that?"

"You need to stay sane, Roy, for your sake as much as mine. Remember, brain health before all else."

Roy narrowed his eyes and tried to focus on the doctor. *Brain health? Sane? Why would you say that? If anyone is insane, it's you—cutting off people's heads, chopping them into pieces ...*

* * *

The fluorescent lights of the home gym's new glass atrium glowed bright under the trees.

Roy said, "Stay sane; stay sane."

He rocked back and forth.

"Stay sane."

He was sitting cross-legged in the grass out by the shed. Out in the backyard. A bowl of what smelled like mushed cat food in his hand. He blinked and looked around. How did he get here? A second ago, he was at the Chegwiddens' house, and now he was sitting in the dark, out by his shed. He staggered to his feet.

The sound of a patio door sliding open. "Roy, are you out here?" Penny's voice.

He looked at the bowl of food in his hand. "Yeah, I'm just … I came out to find the cats. Is everything okay?"

"Everything is fine," his wife replied. "Those cats have been gone for weeks. Come back in. It's cold. You'll catch your death."

12

The meeting was in Hell's Kitchen, in the basement of the Church of the Sacred Heart of Jesus, a red-brick megalith towering over the two- and three-story apartments on West Fifty-First Street, a few blocks over from Times Square.

The location alone—in a *church*—was almost enough to send Roy back to the subway the moment he arrived, but Sam had scoured the message boards for him. It wasn't easy to find a support group for transplant patients, harder still to find one that focused on body dysmorphia issues.

That was what Sam said he had: issues concerning his perception of his own body.

Roy couldn't disagree, and he didn't have any better ideas. Something was better than nothing, and the support group was run by Dr. Kenneth Brixton, a renowned British transplant surgeon. Sam said maybe Roy could get a second opinion on what was happening to him, or something like that.

"Just sign here, and print your name here with a phone number," the woman said in a singsong Caribbean accent. A pudgy index finger pointed out the correct spots.

Roy hesitated, then went ahead and filled in his real name. What was the point of faking it?

He had talked to Penny about the dinner party, and she said he was just drunk, but he hadn't had that much. Two drinks? Maybe three? The more he told his wife, the more she wanted to keep him under lock and key. So he didn't tell her everything.

He was scared.

He had gotten up yesterday morning and decided he needed to heed Sam's advice and go to a support group, talk to some people who shared his experience or at least some part of it.

The receptionist was a big woman, and proud to be, in a flowing orange sari with floral lace fringe and great, dangling silver tiger's-tooth earrings. Dark-skinned with a broad, smiling face, and long straight black hair pulled back in a ponytail, she radiated a readiness for work and business. Her gap-toothed smile was infectious.

"We are glad to have you, Mr. Roy," the woman said. "My name is Fatmata Johnny." She held out her hand to shake. "I run the support groups for Dr. Brixton. I'll tell him you're new here to the group if he comes up.

"This way," she said, leading Roy toward the stairs down. She had scribbled "Mr. Roy" onto a sticker, and she gave it to him.

"Everyone, this is Mr. Roy," Fatmata announced. Then she whispered under her breath to Roy, "One of our group died this week. And you might speak to Mr. Mario. He had a double hand transplant. I'm just trying to be helpful."

Eight men and three women sat around a circle on metal folding chairs. They all said hello and introduced themselves. The scene was as depressing as Roy had feared. Two men wore identical blue T-shirts with the message, "Don't take your organs to heaven; heaven knows we need them here!"

Roy could already feel the sweat trickling down his back, and not because of the turtleneck shirt. *Just leave,* his inner voice told him.

I can't, he replied to himself. *It wouldn't be polite.*

Screw polite. Get out of here.

He took a chair from the stack against the wall, unfolded it, and joined the circle.

The man Fatmata had identified as Mario said, "Victor had been waiting for his second heart transplant and died within a few days of finally getting it. He rejected his new heart."

Roy could just see the edges of the scars on Mario's forearms.

"But he lived two good years after the first transplant," a woman said—Sylvia, according to her name tag. "Every day is a gift. Just because Victor died doesn't mean it will happen to us."

"For the first few months after surgery, I held my breath, waiting in fear for my body to reject my new organs," said a man named Carroll, from Brooklyn. "The medical staff at the hospital tried to help, but their main priority is to fix bodies, and they didn't have time to offer me emotional support. Talking to a psychiatrist who hadn't experienced this wasn't the same as talking to people who've been through what I have."

Sylvia said, "One of the most difficult things is living with the guilt over the donor dying to give me what I needed to live."

This was part of what Roy was struggling with. Sam had been right. Roy spotted a large stainless steel coffee urn on a table, then nodded to the group and went to get a cup.

"We carry guilt around the fact that we were waiting for someone to die so we could live," he heard the man Carroll say behind him. "We have to help each other ease the guilt by reminding ourselves that these people would have died anyway. They just would have gone to their graves with their organs. When I first heard the word 'transplant,' my hair stood up on end. Today I'm fifty-seven on the outside, but inside I'm thirty-seven."

"I gave this heart life the same way this heart gave me life," Sylvia said. "That's the way I think about it."

"But once you take them up on their handouts," said Mario, the guy with someone else's hands, "they pretty much own you. Promotional functions, distributing intimate studies about you to anyone who can get hold of a lab coat. Like I'm more of a specimen than a human."

Roy pushed the spigot on the coffee urn and filled a Styrofoam cup. He could definitely empathize with what Mario was saying. He put the cup down to stir in some creamer. Behind him, the group leader asked everyone if they wanted to take a five-minute break.

"My name's Fedora." The wiry man in a leather sport jacket seemed to come out of nowhere. He stood next to Roy. Right next to him. He held out his hand. "I didn't introduce myself before."

"Roy." He shook the man's hand.

Was the guy Mexican? Italian, maybe? Roy wasn't sure. He had a black mustache flecked with gray, a tuft of a soul patch, and sideburns as long as the mullet haircut. He smelled of equal parts cheap cologne and cigarettes.

"What are you in for?" Fedora asked, his eyes narrowing. "Heart transplant? No, let me guess. Liver, right?"

"Well …" Roy sagged.

"Take your time. We're here for healing, right?" Fedora began filling a cup.

"I'm new to this."

"It'll be good for you. Trust me."

"And you?" Roy asked. "What are you here for?"

"My arm—it's someone else's!" He theatrically held out his fist, then snickered. "Bad joke. No, man, this isn't just a transplant support group—it's a body-dysmorphic thing. My problem is, I'm in the wrong body entirely. That's a trip, right? Man, I got arrested by the cops last week for carrying fake papers. Passports and everything."

"And this is a support group for *that*?"

Fedora scratched the back of his head. "Maybe, maybe not. The judge let me off and said I had to go to therapy. It's close, right?"

"If it works for you."

"It does."

"Is Fedora your real name?"

The guy smiled an intense grin. "It's more like a hat I put on."

Roy nodded, not sure what to say to that, and turned back to the circle of people, who were chatting in twos and threes. He had decided that Fedora was probably Latino, partly from the accent. Weird guy, but Roy liked him.

Maybe he should just go introduce himself to the group, say what happened. Get it out in the open. Part of the problem was that he didn't even want to talk about it. He didn't want to admit the freak he had become—the guilt and anger and, worse, the fear.

The pain he could deal with, but the fear seemed bottomless.

"Mr. Lowell-Vandeweghe," said a loud male voice with a British accent. A man strode purposefully across the linoleum floor in the time it took the stairwell door behind him to swing shut. "What a bit of luck! It is you! I'm Dr. Kenneth Brixton. Do you suppose we might have a word?"

* * *

"So what can we do for you, Mr. Lowell—"

"Roy, just Roy."

"Ah, yes, of course. And you can just call me 'Brixton'; everyone does." The doctor gave a rosy-cheeked smile through two days of stubble. His suit looked as if he'd just woken up in it. "Now, what can we do for you?"

Was this normal? Did this famous surgeon do one-on-ones with everyone who walked in the door? The guy didn't exactly look prosperous. "I don't know. I, uh …"

The room was to one side of the large open basement, with a dividing window wall of glass crisscrossed with embedded wire. Above the row of cast-iron radiators along the street-side wall were two half windows reinforced with metal bars. The doctor had closed the disintegrating wood-laminate door, the only way in or out. The enclosed space smelled strongly of floor polish with a faint note of mildew.

"I know who you are, Roy. We can dispense with that. And I know Dr. Danesti only too well. My question is, with all the resources Eden has at its disposal, what are you doing here, in a musty church basement west of Times Square?"

"To be honest, I don't know."

"I think you do."

"How do you know Danesti?"

The doctor pressed his lips together. "A better question is, who *doesn't* know him these days? Am I right? And I knew him professionally, of course."

Roy leaned forward to rest his elbows on his knees. "I'm having trouble."

"And who wouldn't be, in your shoes," Brixton murmured. "I'm sorry," he said in a louder voice. "Look, chap, the first rule of medicine is to do no harm. You are facing some unique challenges. Honesty the best policy, and all that."

"I'm scared shitless. That's about as honest as I can be."

Brixton gave him another hobo smile. "Before surgery, people are usually dying, and they're terrified," Brixton said. "Their main concern is getting that transplant so they have a chance to live. After the transplant, recipients realize that things aren't perfect. They must deal with harsh realities. They have to be permanently on expensive medications that may have side effects and may play havoc with their moods. They may have to go in and out of hospitals. In essence, they've traded a terminal illness for a chronic illness."

"This wasn't my decision. I was in a coma."

"So then you're stuck living with the consequences of someone else's decision."

Roy's stomach churned. "This was my fault, not theirs."

"Guilt is a common reaction people have after a transplant. Patients often report thinking a lot about the donor and feeling guilty about benefiting from the donor's death. After the procedure, some get the feeling that they had been wishing for someone else to die. And to further complicate those feelings, at what point can we really say that someone is dead? Who makes the decision to harvest organs? A tricky thing, cheating death."

Maybe it was the church basement, but Roy suddenly imagined the undead—long curling nails, pallid skin, and misshapen fangs. "I was dead for more than an hour, they say. Maybe I should have been the donor."

"But luckily, you're rich." The doctor seemed to catch himself. "Excuse me, that wasn't fair."

Roy leaned forward to get to his feet. "This was a mistake."

Brixton laid a hand on his arm. "Just tell me, why did you come here?"

With a sigh, Roy eased his weight back onto the chair. "I'm getting these dreams, almost every night. The same dreams, over and over."

"You are a body dreaming it has a head, or a head dreaming it has a body?" Brixton said. "Is that it?"

"Something like that. I don't feel normal."

"But what is 'normal'? Medicine has no way of really knowing. We define it with mirror writing, by seeing our reflection. Only the limits of abnormality define normality. Deviance defines the limits of conformity. Perhaps you are the freak now, but perhaps just the first exemplar of the new normal."

"You're losing me."

"I'm not sure that Dr. Danesti has fully informed you of the challenges you face. Is he keeping you confined? Away from prying eyes?"

Yeah, he is. "I'm here, aren't I? I just need to talk to someone."

The doctor leaned back and looked at the ceiling. "You know, I like to think of the human nervous system as a tree. If you invert the human nervous system, look at the pattern of nerves spreading out from the brain. It looks like a tree—but this is a tree that dreams. And the tree does not survive without the branches and leaves. What has happened to you isn't the same as grafting a single branch onto an existing, healthy organism."

"So you're saying the dreams—they're not just me?"

"The question really is, *who* are you now? Your conscious stream, the record of one moment to the next, is in the brain. But the bulk of your nervous system and gray matter is foreign to you. Ninety-five percent of your body is not *your* brain's body. You now have two sets of DNA. You are a chimera."

Roy remained silent, though he glanced at the door.

"Just hear me out," Brixton continued. "While we might be able to reconnect the tissue and blood vessels in the surgery you underwent, the mind is a whole different thing. Change the body, and you change the mind. Do you ever get a '*gut feeling*'?"

"Sure, who doesn't?" Just words were enough to knot Roy's stomach in a churning roil, as if something were fighting to get out of him.

"You see, Roy, there isn't just one brain in the human body. Did Dr. Danesti explain this to you? There are, in more than a figurative sense, two brains."

"Danesti said that what made me *me* was in my head. He said it would …" Roy shifted in his chair, searching for words. *Two brains?* The walls of the room seemed to warp and bend in his peripheral vision.

"There is a secondary brain in the human body—in fact, some would even say that evolutionarily speaking, it is the primary brain. The mass of nerve cells around the gut is the vestige of our most primordial brain …"

Roy's stomach clenched again. Painfully this time.

"Connected to the modern brain by the vagus nerve, it controls the heart, the lungs. We all began as worms from the primordial soup, and this ancient brain was the thing that made us survive, made us into the killers we are. The modern brain is a recent offshoot, and there are dozens of mini brains throughout our bodies, which provide body control and reflexes. 'What your gut tells you' is not just an expression, but a real thing. Your body now has two connected nervous systems."

The pain intensified. Roy gritted his teeth. The doctor's face ballooned cartoonishly in his vision.

"… Connecting two parasympathetic nervous systems … two different unconscious systems connected together. You are not just *you* anymore, Roy …"

The words became disconnected.

"Do you hear an inner voice?"

A pause in beats as the room faded in and out.

"Dementia … two brains. This is what … Are you all right? Mr. Lowell-Vandeweghe …?"

* * *

"Roy, sweetheart, is that you?"

A light clicked on. After the cool blackness of a second before, the brightness of it almost blinded him. He held up a hand to shield his eyes.

Penny squealed and scrambled back against the mahogany headboard of the bed in their spare room, her lacy nightgown up around her midsection. She almost fell out of the bed. "What are you doing!"

"What's wrong?" Roy's mouth felt full of molasses. He could hardly get the words out. "I was just … I'm just …"

"Don't … don't hurt me," she stuttered, eyes wide.

"I'm not doing anything." Roy wiped his face with his hand. He looked at the hand. It was covered in mud. Not just that. Something red. Blood. Still hazy, he looked at his other hand. It held something aloft.

"Put the bat down, Roy! For God's sake, I'm calling the police." She had her cell phone in her shaking hand now.

Roy put the weapon down on the bed. How had he gotten here? A second ago, he'd been talking to Dr. Brixton. *God damn it.* Another blackout. "Don't do that. I'm just sleepwalking. I'm sorry. I'm okay. I was just sleepwalking. I thought I heard something."

13

"Drop them there," Del said to her partner, indicating a wooden table by the open door. Officer Coleman tramped up the last two stairs and nodded.

She wasn't entirely sure why, but she had asked him to pick up the Pegnini files from almost two years ago. She wanted to look through them again. It was Friday, and she had spent the day filling in paperwork online, so Coleman had volunteered to pick up the boxes and some other files they were working on from storage. She pushed the image of the impaled bookie from her mind. The Pegnini case had opened a treasure trove on the Matruzzi crime family, earning her a quick promotion, but it was also something she tried to forget.

She asked, "Did you get the Lowell file, too?" It was the same building as the medical examiner's office.

Coleman dropped the stack of files under his arm, picked up one, and waved it before putting it down.

It was the first time she had brought her new partner here. She walked over to the pile of documents and scanned through them.

"So this is your place?" he asked.

"My mother's, really. Rent control. Had it since the seventies. She used it as her painting studio—used it as everything back then. Rented it out for ten years, but she lets me have it now."

The loft, sixty feet deep and twenty wide, was the top floor of a five-story walk-up on Barrow Street, just off Bleaker in Greenwich Village. The back and side walls were red brick, with the only light coming from the large metal-framed windows at the front. The highest building in the immediate area, it just cleared the treetops, affording nice views of the uptown skyscrapers, but the view of the blue skies was what Del loved. Not much blue sky in Manhattan. The back wall was interrupted only by a steel fire escape door. In summer, Del would sometimes open it and barbecue off the back—illegal, of course, but then, she was a cop. The job did have its "cheeky perks," as her dad would say.

Coleman walked down the opposite wall and inspected the wood-framed canvases hung on wires from the exposed pipes of the sprinkler system. Dozens more paintings were haphazardly stacked on the floor, four and five and six deep against the walls. The parquet floor was speckled with a rainbow of dots and smudges. The place smelled of wood and turpentine and, more faintly, of boxing-gym leather and sweat.

"Your mother was an artist?"

"Still is, but these paintings are mine. She was well known in her day. Amede"—Del enunciated it clearly, *AH-med-DEH*—"Bechet."

"Amede? That's unusual."

"Like *Amadeus.* Means 'lover of God.'"

"So your family's religious?"

"Complicated topic in our house, but sort of. My mum's side of the family is Creole."

"You're Cajun? I kinda thought you were Mexican or Porter Rican or something. No offense."

None taken. "Not Cajun. Creole."

"Would I know her?" Coleman asked. "I mean, heard of your mother?"

"Only if you were into the Greenwich art scene in the late seventies." Which was almost thirty years before Coleman was born. The young officer shrugged.

Del picked up the medical examiner's report from the night of Roy's accident, out of curiosity more than anything else. A hunch, but hey, she was a detective, right? She had to listen to her hunches. She leafed through the file and walked over to sit down at a pocked and paint-spattered desk against the brick exterior wall halfway down the loft.

A heavy bag hung from a steel chain from one of the roof joists in the corner. She used it for *muay thai* and boxing—an easy way to de-stress and keep fit in limited space. She thought of this place as her personal office away from her office, the one where she painted. Her Murphy bed was stowed against the wall, so it wasn't as if she were bringing her partner into her bedroom. Still, she put the file down for a second to hide a pair of Manolo heels behind some boxing gloves—fancy shoes were a vice she struggled to indulge on her cop's salary.

"These pictures," Coleman said, standing in front of a canvas hanging near the front window. "They're, ah, nice, and all, but they're all kinda white. All the same."

"To you they are, but to me, they're filled with color and images. You can't see what I see. I see ninety-nine million colors where you see only one. Like I said." She reopened Roy's ME report and started reading again.

Coleman squinted at the picture. "Right."

Del said, "I mix my own pigments. Some have chemicals that phosphoresce in ultraviolet; some are heat sensitive. I'd love to show you what they look like to me, but that would be tough."

"So these are just for you? Nobody else can see them?"

"They help me think—something you might want to try sometime."

She winked at Coleman and went back to reading the file.

"Doesn't it take a long time to commute?" Coleman asked. He had moved to the next painting.

"I take the One train to Penn Station, then the Port Jefferson out to Hicksville. Takes about an hour. I leave my car there."

"Why don't you get an apartment closer to the Second?"

The Second Precinct of the Suffolk County Police Department, where their two wooden desks faced each other in the middle of the common area, was south of Huntington, about a third of the way into Long Island. Del tried to spend as little time there as possible. The thought of living in the suburbs made her feel as though she'd be giving up her soul, and the Second was as close to the city as she could get without being *in* the city.

She hadn't wanted to work for the NYPD. She needed her own space, needed to spread her wings away from her father. And the Suffolk Police Department was still one of the largest in the country, with three thousand sworn officers, and two million citizens to protect.

"I still go to night school at NYU," she said. "For my law degree. It's easier from here. And sometimes I stay in Brooklyn with my folks."

She put Roy's file down.

Coleman saw her expression and asked, "What?"

"Something's not right."

14

"I'm sorry," Roy said. He and his wife sat in silence at the breakfast counter, the distance between them growing by the second.

"Sorry isn't good enough. You could have hurt me—maybe *killed* me."

"I told you, I thought I heard something," Roy lied. But was she right?

"We need to get a full-time nurse."

"You mean prison guard."

The landline phone on the counter rang.

Penny leaned over to push the speaker button. "Could you please take us off your calling list?"

A woman's voice said, "Mrs. Lowell-Vandeweghe? This is Detective Devlin with the Suffolk County Police Department. I was hoping I could speak with your husband."

"Regarding what?" Penny answered, her voice coming down a notch.

"I'm afraid I'd like to speak to him about that, if possible."

"And I'm afraid that's *not* possible. My husband is in a home-care situation right now, and if you have any questions, please address them through our family lawyer, Mr. Atticus Cargill. Would you like me to spell that for you?"

A second of silence, and another. "That won't be necessary. Sorry for the intrusion."

The caller hung up, and Penny punched the speaker-phone button to turn it off.

"Home care?" Roy said. Then, "Did you call the police last night?"

"Of course not."

"Then what do they want now?"

"If it's anything urgent, we'll find out from Atticus."

Roy ran his hand through his hair. "I need to go out. Get some fresh air. Is that okay?"

* * *

"You did *what?*" Sam took a swig of his beer. His mane of gray hair ruffled in the wind coming off the ocean. It was almost seventy degrees, unseasonably warm for the end of November, and Sam wanted to make the most of the balmy weather.

"I was standing right there over her," Roy repeated, "holding a number thirty-three Louisville Slugger."

"And not on purpose?"

"Before that was a total blackout. I don't remember a thing."

"Sit down. Relax. Have a drink. Let's talk this out."

A cooler filled with Budweiser occupied the space between two Adirondack chairs on the seaward deck of Sam's sprawling Southampton estate. A perfect blue cathedral of sky encompassed a glittering view of the Atlantic, just beyond two hundred feet of bayberry bushes, sedge, and switchgrass and a hundred feet of empty white-sand beach.

The beach was technically public property, but Sam made it clear, using fences and signs, that nobody was to trespass on his virgin fifty acres. He even set up video surveillance. Both his parents had died ten years ago, and Sam, an eternal bachelor, lived alone in the massive ten-bedroom, nine-bath house. Off to their left was a seventy-foot swimming pool, and beyond that a double set of tennis courts, even though it was adjacent to the Meadows Club grass-court center just up the road.

"What about, uh …?"

It had taken Roy a while to find Sam after driving up the winding road in, past the stands of miniature elms, pitch pines, and crimson-ruby stands of chokeberry bushes. The front door was unlocked, the cavernous house echo-empty as he called out. Roy had given up and was about to leave when he saw two figures out on the sea deck: Sam and a young woman, whose name Roy couldn't recall even after just being introduced.

"Eva was just about to leave," Sam said loudly, turning in his chair. "Weren't you, honey?"

The girl sauntered up the boardwalk from the house—a cat on a catwalk, in tiny shorts and high heels, but with an oversize sweater on top. She had a ham sandwich in one hand, a bottle of rum in the other. And "girl" seemed the apt word for her—the beautiful Latina with flowing auburn hair couldn't be more than twenty.

"Whatever you say, *Papi*," she said as she put the sandwich and rum down on the table. She cast a quick smile Roy's way before asking Sam, "We all done today? What about—"

"It's on the counter. The usual spot. The usual amount."

She kissed Sam on the cheek, smiled again, and walked back the way she had come.

"I'm not even going to ask," Roy said, trying not to watch her leave.

"Hey, you always pay for it, one way or the other. Come on, sit. Beer?"

"Not for me." He flopped into the chair next to Sam.

He felt exhausted. He had barely slept, and the unease in his belly had only worsened as he drove up Sam's driveway. The sense of foreboding had intensified the closer he got to the beach.

A loud, almost ear-splitting whistle sounded, but it was just Sam goofing around, wearing his usual ear-to-ear grin. "So a man goes to see a magical bird—a parrot that, it's said, can remove any curse."

"Oh, God, *really*?" Roy wasn't in the mood.

"The guy spends years searching the mountains and forests, until he finally comes upon the magical parrot." Sam whistled again, two loud bursts. "'What can I do for you?' the parrot asks the man."

"'Can you remove a curse I've been afflicted with for the past thirty years?'" Sam said in a lower voice, now imitating the man in the joke.

Yet another loud whistle. "'Maybe, maybe,'" Sam said in a squawky nasal voice, this time impersonating the parrot. "'But I need the exact words that were used to put the curse on you. Do you remember them?'" Sam's eyes twinkled. Here it came. "And the guy says without hesitation, 'I now pronounce you man and wife.'"

"That's very funny," Roy said.

"You're the one waking up over your wife with a baseball bat in your hand."

"I think I will take that beer."

"How was the support group?" Sam asked.

"You mean before the blackout?"

"Yeah, before that."

"Depressing."

"That's all?"

"I mean, those people are dealing with sort of the same thing as me. The guilt. Except some poor bastard checked off 'organ donor' on a card and expected maybe they'd give a *kidney* to someone. Did they know they might end up giving their entire *body*? I've got that extra bit of guilt to deal with."

"Minus the brain," Sam pointed out. "An entire body *minus* the brain."

"Maybe not. This Dr. Brixton? He was there last night. Had a chat with him. He says the body has two brains—that there's an ancient one in the gut, connected via the vagus nerve."

"Sounds like a cheerful guy."

"He said that as my neural connections solidify, this other guy's ancient gut-brain is going to start talking to me. *Gut* thinking. Danesti never told me any of that. Never said anything about it."

"I read more about this Brixton guy," Sam said. "He's a bit of a flake. Not doing transplants anymore—something about a donor that wasn't fully dead."

"You're the one who sent me to him."

"Was it helpful?"

Was it? Roy at least felt that he had more people to talk to, an outlet. And if Brixton was a flake, he at least gave a different perspective on what was happening in Roy's head. "I guess."

"Something's better than nothing, right?" Sam raised his beer to clink with Roy's. They both took a sip.

"Except for the blackout," Roy added.

"Maybe that's just part of the process. This was never going to be easy."

"Easy?" Roy jumped out of his chair. "My wife finally wants to have a baby, she says, but what? I'm going to have sex with her using some other guy's penis?"

"Did you ever touch it?" Sam asked. His grin gave a little twitch. "I mean, like, held it, and—"

"Can you be serious for just one second?"

"Sorry."

"Even if I got her pregnant, it's not even my sperm. It's not my DNA coming out of there. It's this other dead guy's that I'm attached to. So it would be *his* kid."

"I gotta admit, that is kinda messed up."

"And I'm taking immunosuppressant drugs, just like the other people at the support group last night—but the drugs are to prevent this body from rejecting my head. If I don't take the drugs, will my head drop off? Explode? They say it'll start to rot like dead meat."

"Calm down."

"This wasn't *just* an accident." The thought had tickled the back of his mind, circled around and back, but it was the first time he'd said it out loud.

Sam got up out of his deck chair to join Roy at the railing. "What wasn't an accident?"

"Penny said she was driving that night, but she doesn't know how to drive stick shift."

"Better her grinding the gears than you—you were howling drunk that night."

"Did you see her drive?"

"I saw both of you leave together."

"Were we fighting?"

"No more than usual. So you think she crashed the car on purpose? Why would she do that? She could have killed herself."

"Maybe that's what she wanted, or maybe she wanted to kill me." For all her carefree attitude, his wife did have a dark streak. "What did she tell you about my dog, Leila?"

"What does that have to do with anything?"

"She's lying about it, or somebody is. My mother said something else, too. No straight answers."

"What are you talking about?"

"It's not just that, Sam. Things don't add up. Maybe the crash was an accident, but *this*?" Roy pointed at his body. "You know what the odds are of getting a healthy young body, undamaged, with a blood and genetic—"

"Sometimes luck happens, man. Sometimes it doesn't. When it does, take it."

The man was an inveterate gambler. He had even dragged Roy in from time to time, mostly for the World Series or Super Bowl games. It was about all that kept him busy, he liked to tell people. His family was old money—started with distributing booze after Prohibition, with connections to the Anheuser-Busch families. He had helped Roy's father get started when he first came to New York, introduced him to the Hamptons crowd.

"It's a gut feeling," Roy said. He gulped down his drink. *Gut feeling.* There it was again. He'd said it without thinking. "That's the best I can explain it."

Sam finished off his drink, too. "Let's take a walk."

They got new beers and started off on the boardwalk to the beach.

"So you think Penny faked the crash?" Sam asked. "Did you remember something new?"

It was a constant topic of conversation. Roy still didn't remember anything from the end of the party. "Something doesn't feel right."

"No kidding, but I mean—what do you mean?"

"And if it wasn't an accident, then I'm not safe and Penny isn't safe, either. Not least of all from me. I could have killed her last night!"

"But you didn't. Did you talk to Dr. Danesti about it?"

"I don't trust him, either. I'm just a building block for his billion-dollar empire."

"You think maybe Danesti arranged this? With your mother? That's dark, man, even for her."

"He was my mother's doctor before this. Don't you think that's a little too much?"

"Your mother can be a battle-ax, but she's—"

"She's trying to get at my trust fund. I asked Danesti how all this was being paid for. He was vague. Said he was paying for most of it, that the Chegwiddens paid, too, and my trust fund was paying part of it."

The family lawyer, Atticus Cargill, was executor of the trust, but Sam had been named a secondary trustee, not that he paid much attention. "Could you ask Atticus about that for me? I want to know what's going on."

"I'll see what I can find out. Sure."

"Danesti's got too much invested in me. I don't trust the guy."

"He did save your life."

"Maybe so, but even if he did, for what, exactly? What pound of flesh do I owe?"

"I think you're being paranoid. The doc said this would happen. I think you need to go home and calm down."

They had reached the beach and were walking across the sand, toward the water.

"That day I got back to the house?" Roy said. "The first day?"

"What about it?"

"The police came to my door. I've never had police come to my door, *ever*, and they come on that day. And they called again this morning, but Penny wouldn't let me talk to them. She passed them on to Atticus. Then there's this reporter calling me. An investigation into Eden."

"I'm getting nervous listening to you, buddy."

They stopped at the edge of the ocean, a wave just lapping across the sand to wet Roy's sneakers. He squinted at the horizon, the thin line that separated heaven from earth.

15

Roy jogged up eight flights of gray granite steps to the top floor. There, on a claustrophobic red-brick landing whose only light came from a cracked skylight twenty feet overhead, stood two massive wooden doors. Apartments 4A and 4B. The doors were finely engraved in trapezoidal patterns, but a dozen layers of black paint over the years had smoothed and glossed the features. He tried to focus on the design, but the edges seemed to blur into each other. At the center of each door hung a heavy brass knocker. Roy grabbed the one for 4A and was about to rap when he saw that the door was ajar.

"It's open," a voice announced.

"Mr. Rodriguez?" Roy pushed the door slowly, feeling its solid mass and noticing the four locks down the left edge. Why bother having all these locks if you were just going to leave it open?

He peered around the corner at green ceramic floors and clean white walls. An open loft some fifty feet long and thirty wide, with a ceiling that went right up to the pyramidal roof twenty-five feet up. Potted eucalyptus trees, artfully placed, defined the open space, and spider plants and creeping vines draped from the rafters. In the middle hung an intricate Native American dream catcher.

A compact olive-skinned man sat reading a magazine on an overstuffed green couch, his black-socked feet up on an ottoman. He had on jeans and a crisp white dress shirt unbuttoned at the collar. Cuban guitar music played in the background over the distant honking of car horns on Third Avenue below. Eden's corporate headquarters stood on the same Third Avenue, just three miles away but an entire world apart from the barrios of East Harlem.

"Come in," the man said, putting the magazine down. He nodded toward the matching couch opposite him and handed Roy a business card. Thick stock, very simple, with small, neat letters: "Miguel Angel Rodriguez, Private Detective."

"You can call me Angel, or Miguel, but my friends call me Angel." The way he said it, it was clearly better to be a friend.

This wasn't the dingy, cramped ashtray of a place Roy had imagined on his way over. The west-facing wall was lined with five-by-five squares of industrial-style windows looking onto the bare treetops at the north end of Central Park. Spanish Harlem. Bright sunshine streamed in, lighting up dust motes floating in the air.

"Would you like a drink, Mr. Lowell-Vandeweghe? A coffee"—he pronounced it "coif-ee"—"maybe Perrier?"

"Roy, just call me Roy. Do you have anything stronger?"

"Sorry, don't drink. Would keep booze around, but …"

A recovering alcoholic. At least this much fit Roy's idea of a private eye. "I'm fine."

Angel leaned forward and steepled his hands together, elbows on knees, his chin resting on outstretched thumbs. "Okay, Roy, so what made you call me?" A shiny red slash ran down the man's left cheek, just inside the jawline. He stroked the scar with the back of his right hand.

"I have a problem."

"Everybody's got ninety-nine of those, but how'd you get my name?"

"You'll laugh, but the Yellow Pages."

The private investigator didn't laugh. "And you took *Rodriguez*? Needed a Puerto Rican for some dirty work?"

The man sat straight upright, his palms coming apart, his eyes opening wide to expose the whites, eyebrows raised. Almost comical, but also threatening, in a way that Roy imagined only a Latino could manage without looking ridiculous. Or maybe an Italian. The man's accent sounded more Brooklyn than San Juan.

Roy said, "I looked at your website, too."

"So you did some research."

It wasn't a question, but the steady unblinking eyes made it feel like a test.

"It said you were a Navy SEAL."

"You want someone killed, is that it?"

"Wanted someone strong, I guess. Liked the sound of it."

"So you don't feel safe? Is someone threatening you?"

"I don't feel anything, to be honest." Roy scratched at his neck under the polo top. "And no, I don't want anyone killed. I just need information."

A pause stretched into uncomfortable silence.

"I did my research, too." Angel leaned back into the couch. "And I know who *you* are, too, Mr. Royce Lowell-Vandeweghe. That must itch like hell." He put a finger against his own scar. "Tingles where the nerves were cut, but man, they cut *all* your nerves. I got buddies that came back all busted up, but my god, what they did to you ..."

"His handle in Afghanistan was 'Angel of Death,'" said a new voice.

Roy turned. A pink-faced, freckled man, six feet and chubby, closed the front door and locked it.

"Is that your partner?" Roy asked, turning back to Angel.

Angel gave a lopsided grin. "Yeah, this is my partner. Charlie."

The newcomer stopped to shake Roy's hand. The fingers were thin and warm, the grip soft. He deposited himself next to Angel, then turned and kissed the former frogman tenderly on the lips. "You want me to put some coffee on?"

Roy's eyes must have widened.

"You okay?" Angel asked, looking straight at Roy.

"He's an investigator?"

"He's a veterinarian, man."

Charlie was at least a foot taller than Angel but looked as though he'd never been to a gym or seen the sun in his life—a sharp contrast to his tanned and muscled lover. The realization was a mind flip, like seeing a line-drawn 3-D cube switch orientations.

"My mistake," Roy said quickly. "I thought you meant business partner."

"Business partner, life partner, everything partner." Angel gave Charlie's leg an affectionate squeeze as Charlie got up. Roy must still have been staring, because Angel added, "What, you didn't think there were any gay SEALs?"

"None of my business."

"If we're going to work together, this is *exactly* your business."

"I don't ... I mean, it doesn't—"

"I'm one hard-core-as-fuck operator-killer, my friend, but I'm queer as a nine-dollar bill, too—that's 'queer' squared." He pointed at his midsection. "Every cracker's nightmare, in a sleek brown Puerto Rican package. You got a problem with that?" Angel's nostrils flared.

No one would suspect that this guy was a private investigator. "No problem with that."

"Don't pay any attention to him," Charlie called from the kitchen area at the end of the loft, singing the last few words. "He's just teasing."

Angel slouched back into the couch and laughed. "Sorry, man. Part of my process."

"So a thousand a day—is that the rate?"

"How many days you need?"

"As many as you got."

Angel looked at his feet, back at Charlie, and then back at his feet.

Roy thought he was about to turn him down. "I can pay more if—"

"I can start full time, tomorrow after I finish a few things, but it'll be fifteen hundred per diem, plus expenses, a month in advance. Can you get that?"

"No problem." Roy pulled a fat wad of bills from his coat pocket. "Here's for the first ten days. I can write you a check for the rest or be back in half an hour with cash."

"First, let's talk about what you need done."

"Right." He put the cash down on the table anyway.

"So explain to me the situation, my newest friend. What do you need to find out?"

Roy pointed at his own chest. "Who this body belongs to."

* * *

"Always follow the money, that's my golden rule," Angel said. "How much is in this trust fund? Your best guess?"

Through the windows, the setting sun lit stratospheric clouds fiery red over the north end of the park. Angel and Charlie sat side by side on the opposite couch from Roy, so close that their thighs touched. An empty coffeepot and half-full cups encircled a plate of biscotti rapidly turning to crumbs.

"Maybe five million, at a guess. It started off at ten, but with the annual allowances, upkeep on the houses …"

"And you and your mother get payments from it?"

"About three hundred thousand a year. Started at a hundred and thirty each, twenty years ago, indexed at four percent per annum."

"That's after-tax money?"

"The trust pays our taxes."

"Not bad for sitting on your ass. And five million is still a lot of money."

"Not really, not anymore."

"Excuse me if I don't feel sorry for you," Angel said.

"Hey, be nice," Charlie admonished.

A veterinarian who was an amateur sleuth. Or maybe both he and his boyfriend were. Roy had no way of determining whether a Navy SEAL had what it took to be a detective, but he liked Angel and his boyfriend.

"You know the things I've seen people do for money?" Angel replied, slapping Charlie's knee. "But if you die, all this cash …"

"Would go to charity. That's the deal."

"Same if you went to jail."

"Before my father died, I'd just been kicked out of Yale. I was dealing pot."

"Just pot?"

"And some other stuff," Roy admitted. "Stupid. Not as if I even needed the money. No other college would take me after that. It was the second one I'd been kicked out of. Only added to my father's stress. He was being investigated by the SEC at the time. Then he had his heart attack."

"So nobody wants to kill you to get your money. They need you to stay alive for that money to stay alive. *That's* a twist."

"Right."

"What was your dad being investigated for? Is that important?"

"Can't see how it would be. Was twenty years ago."

"And your dad set up this *trust* fund because he didn't *trust* you?"

"Or my mother. I figure she was sleeping around, but I don't know."

"Something else to find out. Why not get a divorce?"

"He was old school."

"I don't get it," Charlie said. "I thought we were supposed to be finding out who Roy's donor body belonged to."

"Honey, leave the investigating to me, okay?" Angel said. "Why don't you go make us some sandwiches?"

Charlie pouted but didn't budge.

"He's right," Roy said. "What I really need to know is whose body this is."

"Because you think something isn't right, right?"

"Right."

Angel sat up straight and smoothed his jeans. "We gotta go on your instinct. Your gut feeling. If you think *something* about all this is wrong, then we gotta assume *someone* is to blame. When you first woke up, who was in that room? Your lawyer, Atticus—he was there. Was that normal? My lawyer doesn't turn up at family functions."

"Normal enough. He's an old family friend."

"Like your friend Sam."

"He's more a part of my family than just a friend."

"And your wife? How's home life? Is she happy about you giving that ten-million-dollar house to your mother like you promised?"

"Penny's family has their own money. To be honest, she married down. They'd be just as happy if she left me and went home."

"Was there anyone there who didn't fit?"

Roy rubbed his face. They'd been talking for two hours already. "Captain Harris, from the East Hampton Police. Barely met him before."

"And your mother was there, too." Angel scribbled more notes. "So that just leaves Dr. Danesti. He was your mother's doc? For these, uh, *rejuvenation* treatments?"

Roy had explained about the young-blood transfusions. "That's right."

"That is goddamn creepy." Angel looked at his notes, then glanced at Roy and cringed. "Sorry. I didn't mean ... And what about the Chegwiddens? You said they paid for part of your medical costs. Maybe they were worried about you suing them."

"I wouldn't do that, and they know it."

"But maybe your mother and your wife would."

"They're barely on speaking terms."

"You said they're working together on that new charity, right? And who knows what deals they made when you were in a coma."

"Are you serious?"

"That's what you're paying me for."

Roy sat back in the couch. A headache began to pound in his sinuses. He rubbed his eyes again, then looked at Angel and Charlie, then Charlie and Angel. He laughed. "Oh, I get it. You're Charlie's Angel." He frowned, then laughed again. "And you're both vets."

Angel smiled but didn't look up from his notes.

"So we're looking to find out who the donor body is," Charlie said, his pale brows furrowed. "And we think there's foul play, so maybe someone killed your donor? So Roy could inherit a few million dollars?" The veterinarian took a biscotto and bit off the end. "If that's true, then someone is *protecting* you more than anything else."

"But even if they killed someone to get the donor body for Roy, you don't just drop a body off," Angel pointed out. "Transplants are controlled by—what did you call it?" He looked at his notes. "The Organ Procurement and Transplant Network. OPTN. That's who controls the body parts?"

"It's operated by the United Network for Organ Sharing—UNOS. Headquartered in Virginia but has a big office here in Manhattan.

16

"Hey, man, you got some money?"

The too-thin young man hopped and skipped backward in front of Roy along the gravel path through Tompkins Park. The greenspace was in the middle of Manhattan's Alphabet City neighborhood, just at the edge of the red-brick towers of Stuyvesant Town.

The young man cracked a hopeful grin—he hadn't been shooed away yet—and asked again. "Just a few bucks, man. My Ferrari's in the shop, you know?" The kid cast a sidelong grin at his hoodied crew of friends lounging on and around a green park bench.

"That is a shame," Roy said, but he smiled, too.

It was still warm enough for T-shirts, but Roy had on a thick high-necked sweater and scarf. He'd read in the *Times* that the crustypunks and pushers had moved west to Washington Square Park, but as the last rays of slanting sunshine gave way to almost-winter twilight, the creatures were coming out in Heroinville.

The kid in front of him backpedaled, not giving up, his brown Afro swaying in time with his oversize Ramones T-shirt and blue-checked flannel pants ripped at both knees. After another pleading request, he spotted another target and moved on. Roy still had an hour to kill, so he let his feet wander, circling back around past the dog park and stone

I already sent in a letter. Recipients can send letters to the donor families, requesting to get in touch."

"And you already sent a letter?" Angel said. "So if they can get in touch, that means they have records of who the donor is. So *some*body knows. We need to find out who. Not sure if it's legal, but not exactly illegal … probably."

"A few million dollars is a drop in the ocean to these people. It's something else. Something …" Roy couldn't articulate what he felt. "I just want to find out whose body this is. Can't we start with that?"

"But you didn't get a letter back from UNOS. You said the donor families could respond. Doesn't that mean that maybe they don't want you to know? Maybe they got your letter." Angel's voice softened. "You sure you want to open this can of worms? Some of this stuff might be better left buried. Maybe someone *is* trying to protect you. You might want to let sleeping dogs—"

"And my dog—I want you to look into that."

"Your *dog*?"

"When I was in the hospital, my wife said my dog died, but I've never gotten a straight answer."

Angel didn't look convinced that this had anything to do with anything, but he wrote it down just the same.

"What should I do about the policewoman?" Roy looked down at the arms that weren't his. The creeping sense of vertigo was never far away. "This Detective Devlin?"

"Did you talk to Atticus—your lawyer—about it yet?"

"Not yet."

"You want information? You get out there and do some digging. Go meet Detective Devlin yourself."

tables. The soft exo-suit whirred and whined under his jeans. He must look like a junkie himself, complete with the stuttering walk.

The day before, he had rented a basement walk-up on Eleventh near the corner of Avenue C, just across from a bodega. Seven hundred bucks a week, fully furnished, the landlady had explained before asking, with her hand out, for two weeks' advance payment. "Furnished" was optimistic for the haphazard stained and scratched contents of the apartment, but Roy had paid at once without even looking. Something about it fit, like easing into a worn but comfy chair to watch the big game. Two days before, he had told Penny he was leaving, that he needed some space. He said he was freaked out about the baseball-bat incident, that he needed to think.

All this was true, as far as it went.

More of the truth was that he needed to escape before he couldn't. He had to get out from under the smothering weight of the mansions and manicured hedges of the Hamptons. His wife had protested that it was dangerous, saying that she was going to call Dr. Danesti. Roy had replied that he was available by phone at any time, but he'd ditched his cell phone as soon as he got into the city, then picked up a pay-as-you-go cheapie from a Duane's drugstore in Times Square.

He had taken his passport with him and withdrawn fifty thousand in cash from Chase Manhattan, half of which he'd given to Angel the day before. The rest, he'd hidden at the apartment. He had a thousand in cash on him—enough to buy some serious drugs. And if he was really being honest …

"Hey, man, you got some …" The gaunt-faced kid with the swaying Afro skipped in front of him again, stopping in midsentence as he recognized him.

"My Ferrari's in the shop, too," Roy said, keeping his pace.

"Little hot for a scarf, ain't it?"

Roy didn't reply.

"You looking for something, bro?"

Roy hesitated but shook his head and kept walking.

"You sure?"

"I'm sure." He kept moving.

Looking for something? asked the voice in Roy's head. *Sure as hell.*

He had originally planned to rent a room at a hotel in Times Square, where he could melt into the obscurity of the crowds there, but somehow he'd ended up in the east of the East Village, getting off at the Delancey subway station and letting his feet lead him. Walked up and down the blocks until he saw the rental sign. After getting the keys, he'd gone out yesterday to meet Angel, then come back and slept. He got up in the morning just long enough to get a coffee and doughnut from the bodega and then slept like a dead person all day. He left his exo-suit plugged in to charge it all the way and put the spare battery in his backpack. A down-at-the-heels Six Million Dollar Man.

There was another reason he had circled back around the park, though. Someone was watching him. A lurking figure just out of sight.

Did his wife have someone following him? It wasn't out of the question. He had just hired a private investigator to look into *her*, after all, and he was the one going off the ranch. Or maybe it was Dr. Danesti. The man had a lot invested. Whoever it was, they were good at their job. A shadow just out of sight.

Roy took an abrupt turn onto the gravel path that led to the southeast corner of the park, and then exited onto Avenue B, past Sixth Street, where community gardeners were busy pulling up their last winter harvests of potatoes and carrots. A homeless man had his hand out in front of a CVS pharmacy, his dog curled up beside him. Roy looked over his shoulder, then ducked inside. He went up and down the aisles, looking for dog food, but really looking outside to see who was following him. He found the pet-care aisle, bought a small bag of kibble, and left the store. He looked left and right, up and down the street. Nothing. He stopped for a minute to feed the dog, left the bag with the panhandler, and took an alleyway north.

He wound up and down the side streets, stealing glances behind him where he could. He hid behind a dumpster on a Second Street construction site, then leaped out. A woman carrying a bag of groceries shrieked and spilled three oranges, which Roy picked up right away, apologizing profusely all the while, saying he thought she was someone else. Up and down the alleyways, always looking over his shoulder.

Twilight dimmed to evening. Whoever it was, he had lost them.

His breath came in and out in heaving gasps. He hadn't realized he was running. He ran a hand through his hair, which was soaked with sweat. Still warm and humid in November. He had lost track of where he was. He looked up, squinting in the semidarkness. He wasn't sure what street he was on. A neon sign buzzed and clicked over his head.

What did it say?

"Inn."

The light flickered off and back on.

The "Never Inn."

Off again. Then on, bathing him in blue neon light. It was a walk-up, the stairs to the hotel right in front of him. Another neon sign in the window. "No vacancy," it said in glowing red letters. Roy stood immobile. The Never Inn. Had he been here before? *Never.* He'd never even been to this part of Manhattan before.

He checked his watch. "Damn it."

* * *

Roy nudged and sidled his way to the bar, past a bearded hipster in a lumber jacket talking to a spindly-legged woman in a loose gray dress and laced-up Converse high-tops. A muscled bartender in a tight pleated white shirt asked him what he wanted.

"A beer," Roy yelled over the noise. What kind? Whatever, something blond. The bartender nodded.

The guy had on a bow tie and suspenders, his head shaved on one side but the long brown hair on the other side combed over—the speakeasy Viking of Death and Company bar on Second Street. Roy introduced himself to the bartender, who said his name was Alex and then plunked the foam-topped glass on the counter.

Roy had already stopped for a quick drink on the walk here and was half an hour late.

He took a long swig of his beer—*God, it was good*—before looking around. Maybe she had left already? He realized he'd only half-glimpsed her when he first saw her. Would he recognize her?

"Mr. Lowell-Vandeweghe. Thanks for agreeing to meet me."

Someone tapped Roy's shoulder, and he turned, glass still in hand. There stood a dark-skinned woman with full lips, a broad, smiling face, and a sprinkling of freckles over her nose and cheeks. Intelligent hazel eyes, though slightly tired-looking, he noticed. Her black hair was cut short, and she wore civilian clothes: a green tank top and jeans, with dangling square-hoop silver earrings. Attractive. Young. He glanced down. Nice shoes.

He switched his drink to his right hand, then back to his left so he could shake hands. It made for two confusing seconds.

"Pleasure to meet you, Detective Devlin."

17

"Thanks for agreeing to meet me," Delta Devlin said.

She gripped Roy's hand firmly and pumped twice. The guy didn't offer her a limp-fish handshake the way some men did. She despised that, as if it were a tacit deference to the "weaker sex." Then again, some people just had weak handshakes. From a young age, her father had taught her to shake hands as if you meant it. Do everything as if you meant it.

Good handshake. She liked that.

"Sorry for being late," Roy said.

"Not a problem. I just got here, too."

That wasn't quite true.

She had arrived at the Death and Company bar an hour before they were supposed to meet. She scouted it out, watched the patrons, and found a second-floor coffee shop across the street, where she could wait. She'd watched Roy walk up Second Street, not from the direction of the closest subway. He was late but walked fast, which meant he *cared* about being late. Not just being lazy. No cab. He had walked. No driver following him. Was he coming from somewhere local?

He also kept pretending to window-shop, so he could check for a possible tail.

He stood five-nine or -ten—a good three inches taller than she—with thick, well-proportioned shoulders. Looked as though he did a lot of cross-fit training, not like someone who had just been through a massive surgery. She had scanned his social media from before the accident, and he looked as though he'd lost fifty pounds of fat but gained most of that in muscle. Square jaw. Attractive. Except ...

Those glassy eyes. The green seemed unstuck somehow.

Was he drunk?

Or high?

Or might it be something else?

"Maybe we can find a quieter place to talk?" She gave the slightest tilt of her head toward a corner in the back, away from the speakers and the growing after-work crowd.

"Sure," Roy said. "Can I get you a drink?"

Technically, she wasn't on the job, and she wanted him relaxed. Besides, it wasn't polite to let someone drink alone. "Vodka soda, with a lime. But let me pay."

"Oh, no, I insist. Please. I was late." He turned and called out the bartender's name.

She had waited and watched outside for a few minutes after Roy entered the bar. He came alone. No lawyer, no wife or friend. From the way he had checked his six coming up the street, she wondered whether he was being followed, but she hadn't seen anyone.

Even after she went in, she had hung back for a minute. Watched him order a beer, introduce himself to the bartender. Friendly guy. A beer drinker. Down to earth? Or liked to think of himself that way, at least? Didn't seem pretentious. He didn't order a fancy cocktail or ask for some rare scotch, and he didn't seem to care which beer he got, either. So either easygoing or an alcoholic.

He turned back to her with a tumbler. The vodka soda.

"Thank you," she said.

His hands. They looked like a fighter's, the knuckles swollen as if with underlying scar tissue or something, and she couldn't help staring at the color. To her, his arms and hands were completely different from his face, as different as red and green. To everyone else, it would look basically the same, but to her … She blinked and looked away.

"After you," Roy said, gesturing with his arm toward the back of the bar.

That, she didn't mind. Just because she liked a firm handshake didn't mean she felt put off when a guy opened a door for her. Chivalry needn't be altogether dead. A man could still be a man, and a woman a woman, as long as the respect was there.

She led the way, squeezing past the other patrons.

Roy followed.

She felt his eyes on her.

They sat at the back on wooden benches, facing each other over a table. He had checked his phone a few times already—a bad habit nearly everyone had. He put his phone facedown on the table.

"I heard your partner call you 'Del' when you came to the house," Roy said over the noise. His eyes scanned the crowd before he looked at her. "That short for something?"

"Delta."

"Pardon?"

"Delta—that's my first name."

"Delta Devlin? Sounds more like a musician than a detective."

"I think that's actually what my mother wanted. I've never really liked the name Delta Devlin, to be honest." It couldn't hurt to share something personal, see if this opened him up. "And please, you can call me Del, too. This is informal. Not official."

When he had called her out of the blue yesterday, he said he was in the city. She had said maybe it would be better if they got a drink, kept it casual, unofficial. She said she didn't want to bother him but she did appreciate him calling her back. Said it wasn't serious, that she just had a few questions—and also something she thought might interest him.

Roy picked up his beer and downed two, three, mouthfuls before putting it down empty. "Beats having your parents name you Royce Buckminster Lowell."

She grinned. "That sounds like a bit of a rich man's problem."

"We're not rich."

Odd. That seemed like a sore spot. "I was kidding."

"I know, I know," Roy said, rubbing his thumb and forefinger together. "The world's tiniest violin, being played just for me." He flagged the waiter for another drink.

"Sorry, that wasn't fair," Del said. Something about him was off. A bit flippant. "I can't even imagine what you've been through. But it has to have been a very difficult time, Mr. Lowell-Van—"

"How about 'Buck'?"

"Buck? Ah, right, Buckminster, your middle name?"

"Named after my uncle Buck, my dad's younger brother. He died when they were kids."

"His younger brother was named Buckminster?"

"Just Buck, like I said. My father insisted on the middle name Buck when I was born, but my mother was horrified. Refused to name her son like a redneck. He suggested Buckminster instead. Sounds stuffy as hell, which my mother liked, and my dad could shorten it. My dad made his fortune himself—grew up coal-miner poor in West Virginia."

That explained a few things. "And everyone calls you Buck?"

"Only my dad, and he's been dead twenty years." The beer arrived, and Roy thanked the waiter before taking two more big gulps. "Roy, just call me Roy."

Del took a sip of her drink. "Can I be frank?"

"If I can be Roy." A half a beat later, he added, "Sorry, that was dumb. I guess I'm a bit nervous."

"Are you sure you're okay?" Del asked. She looked straight into his eyes. A little bloodshot, but not exactly drunk. "I mean, are you supposed to be away from home? Is this safe for you? After the operation, and all?" She paused. "Are you taking painkillers?"

"Am I under investigation for something?"

"Like I said, this is unofficial."

He leveled a steady gaze at her. "Did you have me followed today?"

This question blindsided her. She rocked back on the bench. "Absolutely not."

"Did my wife ask you to find me?"

"Why would she do that? Are you hiding from your wife?"

"Why did you come by the house that day?"

"We were looking for a missing woman."

"And you just showed up there on the day I came back from the hospital?"

"Someone called in a sighting. On your street. We weren't targeting you personally."

Roy leaned back on the bench and drank another third of his beer. He seemed to be sizing her up. His eyes narrowed. She took another sip of her drink, stopping to hold the glass against her face. It was hot in here.

"Why did you ask to see me, then?" Roy asked.

"I wanted to talk to you away from your wife."

"Why?"

"Because I called twice, and she sent me to your lawyer both times."

"You called *twice?*"

"Then I got a call from Captain Harris telling me to stop bothering you. I'm not here officially, you understand? You called me, asked to speak with *me*. Otherwise, I wouldn't be here."

"Did you talk to Atticus?"

"Your lawyer, Atticus Cargill? He never called me back, either."

"So I'm not under investigation for anything?"

What was he so worried about? "No, one hundred percent. Nothing."

He seemed satisfied this time. He took another sip of his drink, a smaller one this time, and looked around the room. A few seconds passed. So far, his face hadn't betrayed anything other than worry. Stress. It had cooled outside, but the heat indoors was turned high. He had on a heavy sweater, and a scarf still pulled snug around his neck. He had to be hot, sweating.

She figured the scarf was to hide the neck scar.

But not all scars were as easy to hide.

"You know, I also have some experience being half one thing and half another—in a way, two things stuck together."

"How's that?"

"My dad is Irish, full-blooded, off the boat. Lived in Ulster until he was twenty and came here with nothing but the shirt on his back."

Roy considered that. "Devlin ... right. You ever go back with him?"

"Not once, even when I begged him. And my mother is Creole, from Louisiana. Those are two very different worlds. My mother called me Delta, to always remind me where that half of me came from."

"The Mississippi Delta."

"Easy, right? And my dad liked 'Del' because it's a bit Irish, too—at least, Gypsy Irish, which his grandmother was. Means 'giver.' So I'm never quite sure what, exactly, I am. Half one thing and half another, while not really one of anything."

"So you're part Gypsy, too? Quite the mixture." Roy stared past her, at the window beneath an orange neon sign for Stroh's beer.

"Did you get a lot of support from your family?" she asked.

"My wife, of course." Still he stared past her. "My mother ... She only made things worse, I think. She was worried about money, about herself more than me. Maybe that's not fair. It was my friend Sam who was the most help."

"Sam?"

"Phipps. Family's a big booze distributor."

The name seemed to ring a bell somewhere in the back of Del's mind. Some rich guy she'd read about, maybe? "And when I came to your door— they'd just sent you home that day? Your first day out?"

"We did outings before that." Roy still seemed to be off somewhere else. "Field trips. Like in school." His gaze returned to her. "Why are you asking me this?"

"Just interested."

"So what was so important that you called me twice? You said you had something you thought would interest me."

Del sucked the last drops of her drink from the ice cubes. "You were medevacked by helicopter to Stony Brook Hospital, up in our neck of Suffolk County. Might be East Hampton PD's case, but the medical examiner was ours. I pulled the report from your accident."

"Why'd you do that?"

"I'm a detective—it's what I do."

"Valid point."

"Seeing you that day," Del continued, "it was unusual, and when I read the report—did you know the tox screen said you had blood alcohol of point two two?"

"Is that good or bad?" Roy gulped down the last of his beer.

"Most people would have trouble walking, but you had cocaine and ketamine in your system."

He put his glass down. "It was a New Year's party."

"Those details didn't appear in the East Hampton police report. None of the tox screen results were filed."

"Why would they be? I wasn't driving. Is it a crime to be high?"

Roy didn't flinch when he said it. His facial color didn't change at all.

She said, slowly and clearly, "You weren't driving?"

"No. My wife was. Said I was too drunk."

"Roy, I read that report. The steering column of that car impaled you—almost went straight through your body and into the back seat."

"I, uh ..." Roy was at a loss for words. "So what? Does it matter anymore?"

18

Why had Penny lied to him? Roy seethed. She told him she was driving. How could the steering column go through him if she was behind the wheel? And the obvious next question: *Was she even in the car?* The scar on her forehead—where did that come from? And why was she lying about Leila? Did she kill the dog, too?

What was going on?

Roy took a sip of his beer, then motioned to the bartender for another shot of Jameson. Detective Devlin—*Del*—had left hours ago, but instead of leaving with her, he had deposited himself on a stool at the bar. The after-work crowd had thinned out to a few late-night stragglers. It was a Tuesday night, and even in the East Village people had to get up for work. But not Roy. The bartender ignored him, so he waved again for the shot of whiskey.

"Hey, watch it," the lumber-sexual beside Roy complained. "What's your problem? You just knocked my drink over."

"Shorry." *Lumber-sexual.* Roy giggled to himself at his funny word, a compression of "lumberjack" and "metrosexual." The complainant had on a red-checked shirt and heavy work boots, but Roy was sure the guy had never gotten a callus or nicked a manicured fingernail in his life. "I'll get you another one. What is that?"

"Forget it. Just stop hitting me."

"Hey." Roy motioned at the bartender. "Another shot. You want one, too? On me?"

Bow-Tie-and-Suspenders put down his dishrag. "Maybe you've had enough, mate?"

In the months at Eden, they had injected opioids into Roy's bloodstream, and he wished he could dive into that sweet nothingness again. Maybe he should go back to Tompkins Park, find that kid who had offered him "something." He had experimented with drugs in college, but he'd been too scared of the heavy stuff, instead opting for a steady diet of alcohol and safer recreational drugs. *Cocaine and ketamine were in your bloodstream.* "Safer" was a relative term. Right now he needed another drink.

"Just one more," Roy said. He waved an arm, holding up a finger.

"I said to knock it off, pal," the lumber-sexual growled as Roy bumped into him again.

The bartender said, "I can't serve you."

"I'm not drunk." Roy held out a fistful of hundreds. "Just one more? And could you plug me in?" He pulled the charging cord for his exo-suit battery from his pocket.

"Jesus, did you spill your drink on me?" The lumber-sexual turned to face Roy. He had a bushy red beard, with his hair side-combed in the same style as the bartender. Maybe he hadn't worked outside in his life, but the kid sure had spent some time in the gym. He was huge.

Roy looked down. The kid's jeans had a dark stain along the outer seam, but Roy's khakis were soaked.

"What the hell! Did you piss yourself?"

"Ah, damn it." He should have put on the adult diapers before going out. Control of his bladder was still hit-and-miss. "I'm—"

"That is *disgusting*. What the hell is your problem?"

Roy stumbled off the barstool to his feet. His charging cord dangled to one side. He couldn't even feel the dampness between his legs. Couldn't feel anything. "*My* problem? What's yours, asshole?"

Is this smart? a voice inside asked. *You just had this head surgically attached to this body.* Metal pins still held some of the vertebrae together in his neck. *What if this kid hits you? He might literally knock your head off.* And then another voice answered, *I don't care. Just let him try.*

The lumber-sexual stood up. He towered a good six inches over Roy. "You've been banging into me all night. And now you're *pissing* on me?" He lunged forward to shove Roy.

Roy saw it coming before it even happened. Sidestep and deflect, then disable. The thought came automatically. In one smooth motion, his body turned sideways and ducked. The kid's hands slipped past him into thin air. In the same motion, Roy's left hand shot up and grabbed the kid's wrist, wrenched it around. *Crack.* The six-four, 220-pound bodybuilder dropped as if his legs had been cut out from under him. His friend was almost as big, and seeing Roy standing over his buddy, twisting his arm, the friend didn't hesitate. He threw a straight jab right at Roy's face.

Momentum, a knowingness in Roy's muscle memory said. *Slide past it and use your opponent's momentum.*

Letting go of the lumberjack's wrist with his left hand, as if in slow motion he spun around, lifting his right elbow up. It felt like dancing. The momentum of the friend's punch carried him forward. Slipping just outside the jab, Roy turned from the hip and brought around his elbow, crunching it into the friend's temple. The kid crumpled onto the drink-and-urine-wet floor.

"Hey, hey!" yelled the bartender, palms up in surrender. "We don't want any trouble."

"They came at me."

"Yeah, I saw. Just, no more trouble."

Roy wasn't even breathing heavily. The friend lay sprawled on the floor, with an upended bar stool across one leg. The lumber-sexual groaned, cradling his hand in the crook of his other elbow, and backed away as he got to his feet. He looked terrified.

The wave of rage crested, ebbed, then disappeared below the horizon of Roy's mind. What just happened? He'd never fought anyone in his life. His hands were shaking, his exo-suit cord still dangling from the pocket of his pee-stained pants. He had never even thrown a punch before, and he just felt as though he could have killed those kids with his bare hands. *Wanted to kill them*—that's what he'd felt.

He reeled out of the bar without another word.

19

"Have you seen the house?" the old woman asked.

She pointed a gnarled finger at a shantytown of corrugated metal and plastic sheeting. It was the red-brown woman from the backyard at Mott's Point, Roy remembered. Her skin so papery thin, it could burst into flame over the cold blue veins beneath. Roy floated down the stairs, his tiny eight-year-old body lighter than air.

Long grass waved in the sand.

"But don't worry, your secret is safe," the woman said, her lips not moving, eyes opaque. "Some gold paint will hide the bones."

"What do you want?" Roy tried to get away, but the air was like molasses. He knew they had buried a body, but it was forgotten, wasn't it? Behind the woman, a young girl with flaming red hair—just a baby, not more than four—ran squealing in terror.

"Get her!" Roy screamed. "It's not safe!"

He pushed the air aside and slid forward through the space it left.

"Get the girl!"

Roy's feet touched the ground, and he fell forward. His face lay flat against a striped floor. He rolled over and blinked, reached out again for the girl. His hand slapped into something hard that wobbled and crashed. He rolled over again and breathed deep. His eyes focused, and he inhaled the stale reek of sweat and old cigarette smoke. Spat out crumbs his half-open mouth had gathered from the sheets. He rolled onto his side. The dream faded, replaced with dingy reality.

"Oh, my god."

His mouth felt stuffed with cotton balls. His brain, too. There was throbbing pain behind his eyes. He rubbed his face but couldn't feel his hand. The already-numbed sensation he had of his body was almost gone, replaced with pulsing pins and needles. And nausea and gut-wrenching vertigo.

Roy propped himself up on one elbow on the stained mattress. He still had on the khaki trousers, now two-toned from dried piss. The exo-suit cord still hung out of his pocket, the batteries long since dead. He struggled to shift one leg and then the other and felt some sensation through the pulsing static of his nerves.

With a grunt, he threw his legs over the side of the bed. His socked feet slopped into the water from the glass he had just knocked over.

Dim light filtered in through the dirt-streaked window of his new basement apartment. The knuckles of his left hand were scraped, his hands and forearms covered in caked dried blood. From the fight? The fight was the last thing he remembered, but there hadn't been any blood. What else had he done?

He struggled to his feet, teetering sideways until he caught himself on the wall. He clicked on the incandescent bulb in the tiny bathroom and looked at himself in the mirror. The jagged scar that encircled his neck—the literal intersection of his old life and new—was red and inflamed. His eyes were bloodshot, rimmed with angry blood vessels.

"Damn it," he mumbled.

* * *

"You look like hell," Angel said cheerfully. "You want a mango-chutney smoothie? I'm telling you, they're the best." He hunched lower to get a better look at Roy, then motioned to the waitress as he held up his glass. "Excuse, please, another one of these over here?"

They sat perched on blue wooden stools at a brushed-aluminum table on an enclosed sidewalk terrace on First Street. After Roy said where he'd rented an apartment, Angel had told him that the best juice bar in town, Juicy Julie's, was right next door, and why not to meet him there? It seemed like a good idea yesterday, not so much today. Death would be an improvement on how Roy felt.

In a playground across the street, children chased each other, screaming like banshees. He glanced over from time to time, watching three little girls in parkas and scarves and mittens playing a game of tag. Angel was depressingly chipper, his square jaw, aviator sunglasses, and razor-creased slacks looking as if he'd just stepped off a movie set.

Even from five feet away, he smelled clean—or maybe it was just that Roy stank.

"Here you go." The waitress set a tall glass of orange-yellow sludge on the table.

"You okay?" Angel asked. He had already finished his smoothie.

"Gotta excuse me. This is the first hangover I've had in this body." Roy grunted, picked up the drink with one hand, and rooted in his pocket with the other for his pills—three of the antirejection medication, two ibuprofen for the headache, two blood thinners, and two others whose names he didn't recall, only that they were blue and he had to take one at night and one in the morning. He assumed he'd forgotten the one last night.

"Sure you should be drinking, brother?"

"Orange juice ain't gonna kill me."

"I mean whatever you had last night. You got that sour stench, man. Those blackouts you talked about? Might not be safe. You gotta take care."

"It's like I've been in jail for two years, and anyway, I got a brand-new liver." He gulped down the mouthful of pills. "Someone's following me."

"Pardon?"

"I said, *someone* is *following* me."

"Who?"

"That's your job, isn't it?"

"My job—"

"Is whatever I'm paying you fifteen hundred a day for."

Angel's expression changed. The eyes narrowed. "You're being followed *now*? Here?"

"Not sure. It's like someone is there but just out of sight. Can you tail me?"

"Is this turning into a bodyguard gig? 'Cause the rate goes up."

"Charge me whatever you want."

"Fine. I'll arrange it. You still want to talk? You look like you need to lie down."

"I met the cop yesterday. There's a medical examiner's report from Stony Brook about my accident. Seems to say *I* was the driver, not my wife—at least, it says the steering column tore my body in half."

"That wasn't in the East Hampton report," Angel mused. "Did you see the report? With your eyes?"

"Just what the detective told me. No reason to doubt her, but she said I had to go through official channels to get a copy."

Angel said, "I'll get it, but I might need your signature. So your wife might be lying to you. Any idea why?"

Roy shrugged. No, he didn't. His brain wasn't quite firing on all cylinders yet.

"Can you find out if my wife filed something with the police?"

"For what?"

"Domestic disturbance. Something like that."

"Did you fight with your wife?"

"Not exactly. Just what I told you."

Angel looked at him as if he weren't telling him everything.

Roy said, "Devlin told me I wasn't under investigation for anything. She has to tell me, right? If I was? Otherwise, it would be entrapment?"

"Doesn't quite work like that."

"She said it was only coincidence she came by that morning I got home."

"Because of that hiker?" Angel tapped his phone and brought up a story on the web. "They found her a week after you got home, cut up in pieces. In a bag on the beach."

None of this was news to Roy. "Did you do any real detective work yet?" He was in a foul mood. The sunshine was too bright, the people on the street too happy.

"Is that your blood?"

"Just dirt." Roy had changed his shirt—another black turtleneck—and washed his hands, but he hadn't been thorough. There was still blood caked on his forearm, visible as he leaned against the table and the sleeves edged up.

"You get into a fight last night?" Angel's expression made it clear he wasn't convinced. He pointed at Roy's chafed knuckles.

"Only with the sidewalk," Roy lied.

The detective gave up, dragged a hand across his black buzz cut. "I looked into this OPTN—the Organ Procurement and Transplant Network. Set up by Congress in 1984, and in 2012 they started allowing face, foot, hand, and arm transplants. So they started collecting those body parts. Three years ago, they opened limited trials for whole-body transplants—"

"You do all your detecting on Wikipedia?"

"I mean, how can you tell when someone is really *dead* dead?" Angel said, ignoring the sarcasm. "I read stuff where people were in a vegetative state for ten years—the doctors said they were *brain dead*—but their families kept them alive, refused to turn them into sacks of body parts, and now they're waking them up. Coming back to the land of the living. Stimulating their vagus nerve—that thing you were talking about. Man, I ain't *never* donating my organs." Angel rubbed the scar on his cheek with the back of his hand.

"Thanks for the advice."

"You died, right? Dead for an hour, you said. I'm Catholic, or at least, I was, but I mean … what was it like? What did you see?"

I was dead. Maybe I am *dead. Even now. Maybe this is hell.* What did he see? Just flashes. Light. The past. "I don't remember. What about their databases?"

The private eye looked disappointed but didn't press. "I called them, said I was your lawyer." He snickered. "They told me they had your letter, but the donor family wasn't accepting any communications. I tried, but they get this stuff every day. Locked down tight as a nun's panties. There's this Transplantation Society, an international group. Danesti's involved in that, I think. Some very shady stuff going on out there. Organs taken from living donors, from Chinese prisoners—there's big dinero in the shadows out there."

"Can we stick to my case? What about hacking them? The OPTN?"

"You watch too many movies." Angel looked away and up. "But maybe there's a way. Easier to send someone in on an intern job, but that takes time. What we need is another transplant surgeon, like that Brixton you talked about? Someone who has access to the list. Did you ask Danesti? I mean, what did he say about your body?"

"He only said it came from the OPTN. That it was a young guy, early twenties. Bodybuilder or something."

"So at least, we know you're American, or that body came from inside America, anyway." Angel wasn't quite sure how to refer to Roy's lower half. "Male, Caucasian, early twenties. That narrows the search to just half the country."

"I'm going to look into the money." Roy planned to go to his dad's old office today. Usually, he just showed up for board meetings, and he hadn't been there in over two years.

"It's always about the money," Angel said. He sighed, whistling the air out and shaking his head. "Are you sure about this? The donor family seems like they don't want to be contacted."

"Family? How do you know it's a family?" Roy looked again to his left, at the screaming little girls running in circles around the jungle gym.

"That's just the word they use." Angel tracked his client's eyes. "Might not mean kids. It might just be a brother. Cousins, maybe. Might be nobody. Maybe that's why there's no response. I have no idea."

"Exactly, so just keep digging."

"You sure?"

Roy said, "That's what my gut tells me."

20

"So you're back?" Gary asked Roy. "You look great."

The man sat just on the edge of the chipped wooden table that was Roy's desk. They were in Roy's office, which was twenty feet square but devoid of any other furniture except for a computer screen and the chair Roy sat in.

The window behind Gary was arched into a point at the top, the letters "LCT" at the apex. All the doorways and hallways were arched in this neo-Gothic skyscraper built more than a century ago. Walking into the lobby had felt like entering St. Peter's Basilica.

Gary half leaned on the desk, giving the impression he wasn't staying, and also that he didn't want to wrinkle his four-thousand-dollar bespoke Italian suit. His full head of hair was coiffed to perfection, as if he had just come straight out of a salon—his nails buffed, his blue silk tie gridded with tiny Louis Vuitton logos.

"I thought I'd get back into the swing of things." Roy gave an artificial grin. He had on old sneakers and loose jeans from the Gap and hadn't showered in two days.

"That's great. That's really great." Gary didn't look Roy in the eyes but picked with a manicured fingernail at the edge of the wooden desk.

From the ninth floor of the Woolworth Building, they had a nice view of the arcing fountains of City Hall Park just across Broadway, the last yellow leaves hanging on to the treetops as winter set in. Beyond the skyscrapers lay the flat gray of the East River.

They were turning the top two-dozen floors into ultraluxury condos now, but almost thirty years ago, when Roy's father rented the ninth floor, this place had been deserted. Mothballed. The old dame of a building had been at the sleazy end of the shooter alley that the Bowery was at that time.

Roy's father almost rented this floor for free, and the long-term renewable lease was so cheap now, it was almost a crime. Just at the edge of Wall Street, it stood at the gates of Tribeca. Trendy old money was the vibe.

"How are things going, Gary?" Roy asked, stretching out his name like a kid taunting another on the playground.

This douchebag was the new general manager of LCT Capital. A slimy pump-and-dumper who had climbed through the ranks. Roy's father would be horrified. But then, maybe Roy hadn't known his father as well as he thought, and this was his dad's partner's son. Then again, maybe Roy was just jealous.

Gary Tarlington, "Tarlington" being the "T" in "LCT."

"Things are great," Gary said. "Amazing." Still the guy didn't look up.

Maybe that was because Roy had rolled down his turtleneck to expose his garroted-throat scar. He leaned his head back to expose it even more. "Like, how good? Sounds exciting."

"Twelve-point-five on the last quarter for the main fund."

LCT Capital, the company Roy's father had founded, had morphed from helping technology companies start up to becoming a balls-to-the-wall hedge fund over the years since his death. From white knights to mercenaries.

"And my trust?"

"It's indexed to the main fund; you know that."

When Roy's father had died, his shares in the company were sold back to the other partners, with the money placed in Roy's trust. So he didn't own any part of LCT except for the financial interest in his trust.

He did, however, have a permanent seat on the board—a growing point of contention with the other directors—and an annual stipend of a hundred thousand dollars for doing basically nothing. Which was most of what he'd done the past ten years, after trying to get involved the entire decade before.

How the hell did that much time pass?

The contract stated he had to have an office, but the partners were just as happy that he was never in it. Indeed, they had made it clear they preferred it. "No-show" jobs were a staple of New York mobsters, and financiers could play the game just as well.

Roy said, "I'm thinking of getting into some deals. Do you have my password?" He cut a glance at the blank computer screen.

"You can get that from Roxanne at the front," Gary said. Still he picked at the wood. "Look, we all feel terrible for what happened to you. I can't even imagine—"

"You can't, let me tell you," Roy interrupted. "I know I've been an asshole in the past, but this whole thing … I really want to start over. Can we do that? Maybe try?"

"Yeah, of course." Gary let the words roll out slowly. "But here's the thing …"

"The 'L' in that name is Lowell," Roy said. "*My* name."

"Sure, but you know, it might be a distraction having you in here."

Roy had breezed in past reception, earning frowns from the front desk staff. Then whispers in the secretary pool.

"A birdie told me you were in here, young man," said a voice full of gravel.

It was Atticus Cargill. His mountainous frame loomed in the arched doorway, almost blocking out the fluorescent hallway lights. His blue suit looked two sizes too small for the belly it must accommodate. He shuffled forward and put out a hand the size of a supermarket chicken.

Even at seventy-five years and moving slow, he gave the impression he could crack you in half with his bare hands if you riled the bear. His white-bristle mustache elongated into a smile.

"I'll leave you to it," Gary said, getting up off the chair. He gave Roy a less-than-sincere handshake and nodded at Atticus as they passed.

Atticus's grip felt like a warm-meat vise. "I wondered when we'd see you here. Penny told me you were in the city."

"Thought I could start doing some work."

"Don't you think it's maybe a little bit soon?"

"I think it might be therapeutic. You know, help get my head straight."

Atticus's smile was the sort a grandfather might give a grandson who didn't understand what he did all day when he went to work. "It's a good thought, Roy, but we had some losses here last year. Lot of people laid off. I'm not sure this is the right time."

"Gary just told me you did twelve-point-five last quarter."

"That was just one quarter."

"How much is left in my trust fund, Atticus?"

"In a month, you're going to find out. The trust dissolves and you inherit it. Why not just wait?"

"Why can't you just tell me now?"

"Rules are rules. I can tell you the value that was registered when the trust was set up—ten-point-four million—but then it was sealed under court order. Half of it went into our main fund, and we did well with it—paid out all your allowances, you and your mother. I saw you took out fifty thousand in cash the other day."

Roy forgot that Atticus had power of attorney over his estate while he was incapacitated. "Just needed some cash."

"That's what it's there for. You accumulated quite a bit while you were convalescing. And I didn't tell Penny. We can keep that just between us." The old lawyer smiled conspiratorially.

"How much is left, Atticus?" Roy asked again. "Just between us?"

The smile melted away. "Honestly, I don't even know myself. And even if I could tell you how much we're managing for you, the other part is investments your dad made. Lock and key, court order. Nobody can look at that until your forty-fourth birthday. In one month. Four weeks. Like I said."

"Can you at least guess? Just ballpark?"

Storm clouds seemed to build behind the furrowed white hedge of eyebrows. "Why are you pushing this?"

"I just want to know." Roy leaned back in the chair. "Wouldn't you?"

The old man's expression changed. "Look at you. Hands all busted up, stinking like booze, walking in here like you own the place."

"I did, once."

"You know the pain and suffering your mother went through? Your wife? Me, too. My god, I promised Richard I would look after you. Now you're back to drinking again? And who knows what else? After all the time, the money, the connections, the pain ..."

Maybe he'd been feeling stirred up from meeting that slimeball Gary. Whatever the cause, Roy's combative tone evaporated. "Atticus, I'm sorry. It's a weird time. I just need to know."

The old lawyer took a deep breath. "I don't begrudge you blowing off some steam. That's why I didn't say anything to Penny or your mother about the fifty grand."

Roy said, "I've been going to a support group."

"Good. That's good." Atticus exhaled, eyes closed, and shook his head.

"What did the police want?" Roy asked. "Detective Devlin from Suffolk County."

"They were just looking for that hiker," Atticus said, opening his eyes.

"That doesn't make sense." Roy said, "I went and talked to her. Had a drink with her yesterday."

"You did *what*! God damn it, Roy, you shouldn't be doing that."

"Are you having me followed, Atticus?"

"Am I ... Sweet Mother of God! Dr. Danesti said you'd be paranoid. You should get home, young man. Go see your wife. Get your head on straight."

"Maybe I will."

The room went silent. Roy sat splayed out on the only chair in the room, Atticus towering over him.

"Eight million."

"Excuse me?"

"Don't tell anyone I told you—I could get disbarred. That's how much I estimate is in your trust, or will be when you inherit it next month. Eight million, and that's cash."

21

The eyeball exploded. Needlepoints shot straight from the center in perfect fivefold symmetry. A blob of black held the center, with spatters of smaller orbs spiraling away in a widening vortex held together by a haywire of metal struts. The edges of the eye shape sprouted outward as if in surprise, while, below and to the right, a sail appeared to pull the whole assembly forward. A rectangular wire mesh reminiscent of a skyscraper protruded from the top of the image.

Del took a step back to appreciate the work in full.

What did she see? More importantly, what did she *feel*? An intensity, as if some squashed giant animal were trying to leap out. Its arms seemed to reach up at the skyscraper, but the movement felt circular, as if it were a creature forever stirring in the depths.

That was the problem with art.

Someone else might just look at it and see a splash of brown paint over metal.

Which was exactly what it was.

This work, ten feet tall—"in welded steel, porcelain, and wire mesh on canvas," read the inscription—stood against the wall. Six other installations graced the cavernous room. Thirty-foot ceilings, the walls matte-white, with bright wide-spectrum bulbs casting careful light over polished oak floors. Hushed whispers came from knots of patrons who walked soft-shoed from one spot to the next. She had taken the day to come look at the new exhibit at MoMA—the Museum of Modern Art, on Fifty-Third Street, almost right in the middle of Manhattan.

People paid millions for a Pollock, but the artist might have just been having a laugh and slinging paint randomly on a canvas when he made it. Did that make any difference? Or when Warhol inked soup cans for even more millions?

To some, it might seem nonsense, but then, art was a language unto itself. An esotericism that demanded study. The rebirth of the Renaissance, to the baroque and its flourish and splendor for God; neoclassical to Romanticism and the triumph of imagination; the fleeting effects of impressionism to the rustic charm of realism; modernism versus postmodernism. Artists of each era and school building on the insights of their predecessors to see further and deeper into the human psyche.

Beauty was in not just the eye, but also in the mind, of the beholder.

For Del, the keys to understanding art and people were the same. To really understand, you had to trace back to the roots, know where they came from and how, and understand who created them.

"Amazing, isn't it?" said a quiet voice.

A woman had appeared beside Del. She had short-cut platinum hair, with asymmetrical bangs falling playfully over her left eye. She'd been a striking beauty in her youth, Del could see, and had carried that aura into her later years. Floral notes of an expensive perfume drifted with her.

Del nodded appreciatively. "It's from her later period, but evocative of her primal works from the Leo Castelli days." The piece before them was by Lee Bontecou, whose body of work she was familiar with. "We have one at home."

"How *wonderful*." The woman extended her hand. "Virginia Lowell-Vandeweghe," she said. "I'm running the auction today."

Del took the woman's hand and got a limp fish in return. "Delta Devlin."

Del's father used to love telling her how a degree in fine arts would never be useful in police work. She wished he were here to witness this.

"What a lovely name," Virginia replied. "Are you a collector?"

"I have to admit, my mother studied with Lee at Brooklyn College, back in the seventies. That's how we came to have one of her works." Del had used her mother's connection to get an invitation to the event today. It wasn't open to the public.

"Lovely." But the brightness in Virginia's eyes diminished a shade, probably as she realized that Del didn't have a million-dollar checkbook. "And would I know your mother's work?"

"Amede Bechet. She and Lee shared a common family history."

"Ah, yes, I remember. Often showed in Greenwich?"

"That's right."

Virginia gave her a tight smile and started to move away.

"I do have something else to confess," Del said.

The older woman stopped.

"I know your son as well."

"Royce?"

"That's right."

Now Virginia sized Del up and down, as if she were inspecting a show horse. "He's been through so much lately. We're very proud of him, of his strength." After a few seconds, she added, "Are you the reason he suddenly took off into the city?"

Del studied the woman's face. Faint capillaries at the edges of her eyes lit up and seemed to pulse. So Roy had taken off into the city? Why?

"I'm not sure it's just me," Del replied with an appropriately demure grin.

"A pretty thing like you? Don't sell yourself short." Virginia's smile took on a more carnivorous aspect. "But I must warn you, his wife is just over there." She pointed in the corner.

So Roy's mother and wife were here in Manhattan, but it appeared neither of them knew where Roy was. Interesting. And the first thing that came to his mother's mind was that he was having an affair?

Del saw something else interesting and decided now was the moment. "And I'm just wondering," she said, lowering her voice, "why you were trying to steal your son's money when he was in a coma."

She expected an explosion of color in Virginia's forehead after such a combative and unexpected accusation, but the woman remained almost preternaturally calm. Just a flicker of heat across her face. "Who did you say you are, again?"

"Nobody important."

"I think it's time for you to leave."

But Del was already walking away, following her next target. "I think so, too."

* * *

Del exited from MoMA onto Fifty-Third Street, wobbling just a little on her four-inch Christian Louboutin heels. She looked up and down the street, trying to spot the mass of flowing gray hair and beard she was tracking. She had run down the last set of stairs—no mean feat in the stilettos.

"Careful on those," said a man's voice behind her. "Love the red soles, but not exactly athletic wear."

She turned.

"Do you have a light?" Samuel Phipps stood leaning against the wall, a cigarette in his mouth.

"Sorry, I don't smoke." Del steadied herself and smoothed down her dress, then ran a hand through her hair.

Sam took the cigarette from his mouth. "Damn things. Me, either." He tossed it into a trash can near the entrance. "Least, I shouldn't be." He held out his hand. "My name's Sam."

"Delta." This handshake was firm. "I saw you upstairs."

"I saw you, too." Sam's eyebrows raised a fraction, just enough to show what he meant but not enough to seem boorish.

Confident—that was the impression.

She would have put him in his fifties, but she knew he had just turned sixty. Rich people were easy to research on the internet. She'd read all about his family business in the liquor trade, read about his enormous house in Southampton. Didn't dye his hair. Proud and gray, long and flowing and natural. Read enough about him to know he thought of himself as a ladies' man, and he certainly played the part. His pale-blue shirt was open two buttons under his full beard, and he wore a brown tweed sport jacket and faded blue jeans with scuffed loafers.

Sam asked, "So what's the connection? You a friend of Virginia's? I saw you talking."

"My mother worked with Lee Bontecou many years ago."

"Interesting. Hey, you must be freezing. Can I lend you my coat?"

The past two days, the temperature had dropped thirty degrees to a more seasonal range for the end of November. She had on only a thin-strapped dress. She had left her coat upstairs in her rush down. If she went back up to get it, she might lose this opportunity.

Sam added, "Maybe you want to grab a coffee?"

Del replied, "Sure, why not," to both.

* * *

"So you're an artist?" Sam asked. "Because you know what they say about artists."

They'd found a spot around the corner. He had an espresso, black; she was having a filtered coffee with milk. It was midafternoon, and the café was almost empty. They sat on stools facing the window and watched people walk by. They'd been talking for ten minutes now, with Sam edging a little closer every now and then.

"I consider myself one," Del replied. "So what do they say?"

"That artists mix with the highest and lowest of society, and therefore, that makes them the most dangerous. I think it was Queen Victoria who said it."

"So that makes me dangerous?" Del said.

"I think so. Sounds pretty dangerous to me. And I do mean pretty."

She ignored the pickup line. "Do you consider yourself an artist, Sam?"

He laughed, his blue eyes steadily on Del. "I do. Perhaps a *great* artist. Perhaps the greatest." His eyes narrowed, and then he laughed at his own joke.

"I have heard of you before," Del admitted. "Doesn't your family have that big place in Southampton? I've seen it in the magazines."

"That's right. You should come out sometime. What do you think?" He took a card from his jacket pocket. "Call me. This is my private number."

Just a phone number. No name. No address. Just numerals on expensive card stock.

Del took it. "Thank you. Maybe I will."

She studied his face. The guy was charming, she had to admit, even though he was more than twice her age. "One more thing I know."

Sam's grin widened, and he leaned closer to her. "We sharing secrets now?"

"You should be careful of the Matruzzi family."

The man's grin faltered for barely half a second. She had gone back and checked through the files. That was what triggered her memory when Roy mentioned Sam. She'd seen Samuel Phipps's name on the list of accounts from the Pegnini case, attached to a debt of a shell company of the Matruzzi clan.

Sam's smile widened and he asked, "Who are you, really?"

"I already told you. Delta Devlin."

"But you're not just an artist? A reporter?"

"A cop, actually."

Now she really studied his face. A flicker of heat across his forehead and cheeks, but his grin just intensified. The knowledge seemed to excite him.

"A woman in uniform. Well, then, you'll definitely have to come over and inspect my place. Make sure it's safe." He rubbed one temple. "You know, that was a legitimate expense. Tony Scalisi's construction company did work on my house. How was I supposed to know it was connected to some mob shell company? Their laundering companies do real work, too. I explained all this years ago."

"Two million dollars is a lot of money."

"Maybe to some people." The way he said it, he wasn't lying.

"You sure it wasn't a gambling debt?"

"Like I said." He leaned back. "Who was your mother, again?"

"Amede Bechet." No use in lying.

"Ah." Sam's face lit up. "I remember her. Our family supported her work, back in the seventies. I've got some of your mother's art on my walls. So you're her daughter? Now you *really* should come over."

Del didn't bite. "One more thing."

"Sure."

"Do you know where your friend Roy is?"

"I have no idea."

She watched him. He looked as if he was telling the truth.

"But I hope you'll find him," Sam added. "He's been having blackouts. If you do find him, give me a call. Promise? I'm worried."

"Sure."

Sam said, "You know who *you* should be careful of?"

Del waited.

"Dr. Danesti. I get the feeling you're barking up his tree. There's something not right about that guy, if you ask me."

22

Water radiators clanged in the church basement, urging some heat into the damp space. Roy had slept through the whole afternoon after collapsing on his bed the day before, when he got back from his dad's office. Today, he felt much better and had bought some clean clothes, taken a shower, and shaved.

A new man.

Literally.

It could also be the Oxy he bought from the Afro kid in the park. He felt in need of a little extra pick-me-up for his second visit to the transplant group. He'd sat through an hour of stories and confessionals, but that wasn't what he was here for, not really. Finally, there was a break, so he headed for the doughnuts and coffee urn by the wall.

"You feeling any better?" Roy asked his new friend Fedora. He filled Styrofoam cups for both of them.

"I could ask you the same thing," the Mexican replied.

The man had a habit of tucking in his chin when he spoke, so that he looked at you from the tops of his perennially bloodshot eyes. It made the skin around his neck bunch up in flaccid rolls. *A little crazy* was the overall effect. Today he wore a dark-blue faux-silk shirt, open almost to his navel, with a thick gold chain hanging over his sparse salt-and-pepper chest hair.

Still rocking the leather sport jacket, full sideburns, and mullet. He reeked of cheap cologne.

"The cops, man—they won't stop bothering me. Tell me I can't have three passports with different names." Fedora took the cup from Roy and blew on it. "I mean, I got medical papers saying my condition. I need it, man, when I'm not in the right body, you know? I need to have the right papers. Know what I mean?"

He did know what Fedora meant, even if it sounded nutty. Right now, he liked nutty. It made him feel more normal.

Roy said, "It's not easy. Take it slow, one day at a time."

He couldn't believe that he was the one dispensing advice. That was what support groups were for, he guessed. Shared experiences. Shared fear. He'd read that people did exercise classes together, like the spin classes that Penny loved, because humans could tolerate pain better in groups. People could withstand more suffering when they shared it.

"Thanks, man." The dysmorphically confused fashion victim took a sip of his coffee, then asked, "Hey, you ever heard of celebrity poop?"

"Is that a website or something?"

Fedora laughed. "No, man, It's actual poop. Celebrity shit."

"You mean, as in *excrement*?"

"Yeah, dude, that's the stuff." He leaned in to Roy as they sat down in the group circle. "These rich ladies, they pay crazy money to get the poop of famous people. Fecal transplant—supposed to help the microbiome in your gut. Makes you super healthy. They say the celebrities already have the best stuff, you know, from Indians or something. I just think they like the idea of sticking Brad Pitt's turds up their asses." He giggled hard enough to spill his coffee.

"I *have* heard of the procedure," Roy said.

"I'm going to go looking for celebrities around town. You want to come? Maybe have a few drinks?"

"I can't drink, not tonight."

"Just come. It'll be a hoot."

"Let me think about it." The group looked as though it was settling in again for another session, and Roy wasn't sure he was up for it.

"Mister Roy!" It was Fatmata Johnny, the receptionist. She waved a pillowy arm, today's yellow-gold-embroidered sari floating around it in circular waves. "Dr. Brixton is here!"

* * *

"Ah, Mr. Roy, Mr. Roy! So good to see you again, sir." Dr. Brixton beamed a buck-toothed grin. He had shaved within the past day and a half, but his comb-over was matted and the green sweater was a painful match with the wide blue tie and frayed brown jacket.

Roy shook his hand and sat down as Fatmata closed the door behind him. "How's the group going?"

"We lost another member last week, I'm afraid. Rejection. As always."

Join the club, said a voice in Roy's head. "I was hoping you could help me."

"That's what I'm here for." The smile made his ruddy cheeks puff out.

"I need to find who my donor is."

Brixton indicated two wooden chairs beside a fold-out table. Roy took the seat opposite the doctor, who sat and craned his neck back to stare at the ceiling as if he expected something to crash through it. Still looking up, he said, "You can write a letter to the donor family. Have you—"

"They won't respond."

The doctor leveled his gaze at Roy. "Then I'm afraid—"

"I know you were on the British equivalent of our organ transplant board. You know how it works. Couldn't you call someone?"

"I get a lot of these kinds of requests."

"I know you don't like Dr. Danesti."

Roy waited. He had sensed it before: something more than mere professional envy.

The doctor smiled, this time without showing any teeth. "Did you know that the Danesti family is from Romania? An old family, the Danesti—they were once cousins to the Dracul dynasty, did you know that? It's a real family, if the history has been, um, *gorified.* But then, the younger Danesti seems to be making good as the prodigal son."

"Maybe more Frankenstein than Dracula, but I get your meaning."

Dr. Brixton's eyes seemed fired with an inner glow. "Do you know the life expectancy of a woman born in Monaco today?"

"No idea."

"Ninety-four years. That's just the *average*. Do you know what it is for someone born in one of the southern United States? Seventy-two. Yet these are both rich countries, and these humans aren't genetically different. Interchangeable people, vastly different lifespans—almost twenty-five years—and the difference isn't fried chicken and okra. Do you know what *is* the difference?"

An easy guess. "Money?"

"Our northern friends in Alberta live ten years longer than someone in Alabama, yet they pay half as much on health care. How is that possible? Because the health system focuses more and more of its money on the wealthy. Dr. Danesti and his friends don't just want to live longer; they want to live *forever*."

Brixton let the word hang in the air a beat before continuing. "You, Roy, are the living embodiment of the medical divide between the rich and the poor: a rich head living out its life on a body of the poor dead."

How do you know my donor is poor? Roy wanted desperately to ask. "And you want to stop it?"

"I'm not sure we could stop it. Slow things down, perhaps. I want to help you, Roy, but Dr. Danesti—he wants to stop death itself. What he doesn't understand is that death *literally* is life."

"How so?"

"It's an evolutionary mechanism that didn't always exist—Danesti is right in that—but death is the tide of life that cleans the beach. Malthusian limits are reached in a population when bleak new conditions are imposed. Darwin's finches starved when leafy plants died out on their island, but in a population of thousands, a freak eventually emerged with a hard beak that could crack nuts. A mutant. The leaf eaters died, and the mutant freaks survived and flourished."

"I've heard of that." The doctor was rolling now, and Roy was giving him lots of runway. He couldn't help being a little bit fascinated—but that word "freak." He felt like the freak, the mutant with the hard beak.

"Do you know what happens if we stop the death of just one human cell out of *forty trillion* in our bodies? We can do it. Just disable the human gene BCL2 to stop cell death, so that a cell can literally live forever. Do you know what the result is?"

It was a rhetorical question.

"Cancer. That is the result. The uncontrolled growth of a malignancy. Death of the larger organism. Can you imagine what this would mean for the global *human* organism? What uncontrolled malignancies will grow within the soon-to-be ten billion people on this planet if some of them stop dying? Can you imagine what would happen if a Vladimir Putin ruled for a thousand years over a new Russian Empire, amassing trillions of dollars and an iron grip over the world? Or if John D. Rockefeller had lived into the present day?"

"I hadn't thought of it like that."

"And Dr. Danesti isn't just stopping there. He and his friends call it 'newgenics'—making genetic modifications in the germ line. Cloning bodies, transplanting brains—have you read what the madman wants to do?"

Brixton was up out of his seat now, pacing the room, waving his arms in the air.

"Are you aware of things British doctors have done in the past? My antecedents? It was Darwin's cousin, Francis Galton, who laid out the simple idea for improvement of the human race. His cousin Charles put forth *natural* selection, so Galton proposed to improve on this with *unnatural* selection."

"Eugenics," Roy said. "I've heard of that."

"It was a word before genetics itself was even invented. Led to the horrors of Nazis in the mid-twentieth century, but the madness has returned."

"I don't think we're talking about Nazis. Right now it's more about housewives in the Hamptons."

Brixton's eyes were wide and wild. He had a sheen of sweat on his forehead. "You don't need dictators for mass eugenics programs to exterminate millions of people. Did you know that the largest eugenics event in human history wasn't the mass extermination of the Jews by the Nazis?"

Seeing Roy's stare, he said, "Arguably, at least. You could say the dubious distinction would go to India and China in the recent past, where more than *ten million* females are missing from the adult population, thanks to infanticide and neglect leading to death. These were free citizens—your housewives and their husbands—enacting one of the largest mass exterminations in human history."

"Are you okay?" Roy asked. The doctor was flushed.

"I do tend to get a little worked up." He wiped his forehead and stopped pacing. "I'm trying to make the point that all we have is our morality. When it becomes distorted, we are capable of horrific things."

"I wouldn't argue with that."

"And I've heard rumors about Eden Corporation in the background. Illegal international trade in organs. India and Bangladesh and such."

"You think Danesti is involved?"

"He's pushing that line too far. His ethical protocols are compromised."

"So if I help you find some dirt on Danesti, you'll figure out who my donor is?"

"Down to the point right away, eh?"

23

"That Brixton is *loco*, yeah? I heard him yelling at you. We all heard him."

Fedora brought his face up so close, the fumes of his cologne almost made Roy's eyes water. He was a close talker.

After the support group meeting, they had taken a taxi down to Meatpacking. It was Thursday night, and the streets were jammed with revelers lining up outside the door-to-door clubs. Bouncers with big muscles and tight black shirts manned the red velvet ropes that held back the hopeful masses.

Fedora added, "Kind of a nutball, but at least, he's *our* nutball." He threw his arm around Roy's shoulder and cackled, chucking his head back as if he had just come up with the funniest joke in the world.

"What happened between him and Dr. Danesti?" Roy pulled back an inch. Fedora definitely had something with garlic in it for dinner.

"I don't know." The edges of Fedora's mustache tilted down as his eyebrows rose. "But I can tell you, that day when you walked through the door, Brixton's eyes just about popped right out of his head. You were like manna coming from heaven to him, I think. He's got an ax to grind, that's for sure."

"*Est-ce-que on peut jouer de poker?*" the young man next to Fedora asked.

Tall and thin with a bit of a stoop, he wore a red-and-white Canadiens baseball cap. Guillaume was his name, Fedora had explained at the support group, Guy for short—"rhymes with 'tree,'" Fedora said—but everyone called him Rat. *Guy le Rat.* He'd had a heart transplant last year at twenty, just after his family moved from Quebec to New York to have the operation performed privately. He didn't speak much English.

"Poker—he wants to play poker," Fedora explained. "Not tonight," he told Rat. "We're looking for celebrities. Anyone famous."

Rat's eyes lit up. "Ah, *oui. Célèbre*—famous." His eyes narrowed and began scanning the crowd—a task his height made easier.

"Come on, this way, I know a place." Fedora still had his arm around Roy as he muscled through the crowd.

Brixton had told Roy that he couldn't access the specific registry to find out where a single donor came from, but that in Roy's case, the problem was somewhat simplified. As a transplant surgeon himself, Brixton *could* access the list of recently deceased donors. It now stayed active for years since they could freeze skin samples for genetic matching.

The list would still number in the tens of thousands, but they could cross-reference by age and narrow the date of death to not long before Roy had his operation. It had to be someone young who died in a way that left his entire body intact and unharmed. A time-consuming process to sift through all the files manually, but Roy had Angel and Charlie to divide the labor with.

Even then, Brixton had said, there would still be some uncertainty.

"Hey, *c'est* Georges Clooney, no?" Rat said, tapping Fedora's arm and pointing.

"Nice work." Fedora got up on his tiptoes for a better look. "Come on, let's go."

He pushed them through a knot of people, toward a black-painted brick wall with a pink neon sign: "Heaven."

"Are you serious?" Roy said. Before, it had been a bit of fun—*let's go to Meatpacking and look for celebrities*—but now it was getting real. "You think we can just go up to George Clooney and ask him to take a crap in your hand?"

Fedora still had his elbow hooked around his friend's neck. "You kidding me, man? You know how messed up these people get at these places? He'll take a dump on your *face* if we ask nice."

Roy grimaced. "Don't ask nice."

"I've done this before. Leave it to me."

They shoved through the last of the crowd, stopping at the impassable wall that was Heaven's head bouncer. The guy was seven feet if he was an inch, with biceps like bowling balls. He looked at them with disdain but still asked, "You on the list?"

"Ah, maybe, but we were with George," Fedora said. "Didn't he tell you we were coming?"

The bouncer's sloping forehead didn't register the least bit of surprise. His eyes returned to scanning the crowd. Roy and Fedora had ceased to exist in this Neanderthal's mind.

"George Clooney, man, we're with Clooney," Fedora protested.

"Please step back," the bouncer instructed, sweeping them aside with a scything motion of one bulldozing arm.

Four young ladies traipsed past in impossibly high stilettos and skirts the length of Roy's boxer briefs. One of them gave the bouncer a kiss on the cheek, and the sea of people closed in behind them, swamping Fedora, Rat, and Roy in their wake.

* * *

"Come on, it's been an hour." Roy liked these guys and was even intrigued by the subversive thrill, but enough was enough.

Having given up on the bouncer, they hung at the edge of the crowd outside Heaven. Three anorexic models in bikinis would have been a shoo-in, but three guys? Even Sisyphus would have given up by now. One by one, Rat had named off the celebrities going inside, which only intensified Fedora's mania.

"You know how much a pound of pure George Clooney is worth?" he said. "Like fifty, maybe even a hundred grand, man. And Bieber! You saw him go in, right?"

"We're never getting in there," Roy groaned.

"This right here, *tonight,* is my retirement, brother."

Roy had already begun to walk away. "It's been fun, but—"

"Hey, isn't that the doctor lady?" Fedora waved at someone. "From that show?"

"Royce, is that you?"

Roy turned. Short ginger hair and alabaster skin. Blood-red lips, thick layers of dark eyeliner covering brittle lines. Gold segmented fish earrings—her signature jewelry. What on earth was his mother's famous psychologist friend doing in the Meatpacking District? He hadn't seen her since Thanksgiving dinner at their place, out in Montauk. Images of the cliff Roy had crashed over rushed through his mind.

"Primrose," he said. "What are you doing here?"

"I could ask you the same question."

The sixtysomething-year-old had on a one-piece form-hugging jumpsuit and heels, one hand on hips tilted jauntily to one side. She waited.

"Sorry, this is my friend Fedora," Roy said, "and Guy. Fellas, this is Primrose Chegwidden. You've maybe seen her on TV?"

Fedora's face beamed. They both mumbled hello.

"Are you going to Heaven?" Primrose asked.

"I don't think so. We were just walking by."

"I'm going in. Why don't you come with us?" Behind Primrose were a half-dozen elderly men and women who looked as if they shouldn't be outside their assisted-living homes unsupervised, never mind trying to get into a bar. "Come on, let's go."

She sashayed forward, the crowd magically parting before her. Roy held back, but Fedora grabbed him. "How do you know her?"

"Are they with you?" the mountainous bouncer asked Primrose. He nodded at Roy and Fedora.

"They are my special guests," she replied.

The bouncer's slab-face remained impassive, but he opened the velvet rope and swept back the rest of the crowd. "*Asshole,*" Fedora whispered as they passed.

* * *

The pounding bass was so loud it rattled Roy's teeth. Under the strobe lights on the main floor, a sweaty mass of dancers jittered in stop-action. Purple leather booths on platforms defined the edges of the dim bar. On the tables ice buckets overflowed with bottles of champagne and vodka.

One of the bouncers had followed them in, clearing the crowd so Primrose's elderly entourage could get through. A waitress slid past them holding a magnum of Dom Pérignon with a sparkler hissing flames from its top.

A fluffy white halo hovered over her head.

Fedora yelled in Primrose's ear, "Do we have a table?"

"We are the VIP, dear," she replied. "The real party is downstairs."

She led them past the neon-and-glass main bar with its glowing and bubbling multideck fountain. Men in black ballistic vests and earpieces nodded at the bouncer accompanying them, then opened a set of nondescript double doors at the back of the bar. Down black nonskid metal stairs—one flight and then another.

"Don't be scared, we're just going to Hell," Primrose said, laughing now, scarcely able to contain her sudden giddiness.

"I've heard of this place, man," Fedora whispered.

Two more men in ballistic vests opened doors at the landing. Roy followed Primrose, expecting another blasting assault on the senses, but instead they entered an eerily quiet, pristine white room.

Hospital gurneys, arranged side by side in pairs, lined all four walls. By each pair were beeping machines, and an IV pole hung with a bag of dark liquid. Young men and women, dressed up for their night out, lay on every second bed, a needle inserted in one arm. They chatted happily with each other and waved at Primrose and her arriving crowd. Nurses in scrubs hovered over some of them.

Roy had trouble computing what he saw.

"I suppose we could call this purgatory," Primrose said. "A pit stop between Heaven and Hell. If you can wait for me, we'll go to the party in a minute."

She pointed at a large set of doors, inset and almost invisible. Roy heard the dull thump of dance music just beyond.

Primrose took Roy's hand and led him to one of the beds.

"This is Sophie, my donor."

A young woman—girl, really, in her teens—with ethereal blue eyes, pink lipstick, long red hair, and a face sprinkled with freckles. She looked shyly up at Roy from her gurney, smoothed down her miniskirt, and said, "Hey."

"Is everything ready?" Primrose asked one of the nurses in green scrubs. She laid a hand on Roy's forearm and squeezed.

Roy felt queasy and pulled his arm away.

"Already did the CBC and tox screens, Mrs. Chegwidden. All the lab work is done. She's clean and matches perfectly." The nurse busied herself on one of the machines.

"Buddy, some water?" Fedora asked. "You look like you could use some." He held out a full paper cup, and Roy downed it in a gulp and asked for another.

Primrose sat on the gurney next to the girl's and swung her legs up, crossing her ankles as she lay down. "Your mother was just here before us. Don't look so surprised, Roy boy. I would ask if you'd like to try it, but then, you're already flowing with the blood of a youngster, aren't you? You've taken the whole *body* of one. You're a bit famous in our circle."

One by one, the oldsters who had followed Primrose in took their beds beside the bright young things.

"How do you think those Hollywood stars stay so young-looking?" Primrose said. "You think it's by hitting the treadmill? Quite simple, really."

The nurse inserted a needle and catheter into Primrose's left arm, then repeated the process on her right.

"They pump her blood into me while they refill my donor with bagged blood and empty some of mine into the trash. All it's good for, at my age. Like getting an oil change."

Primrose eased back on the bed and closed her eyes as the blood of the teenager snaked its way along the empty tube between them, passing en route through a tiny pump attached to the IV pole. The nurse made an adjustment. The dark liquid completed its circuit and flowed directly into the old television star's arm.

"Nothing like fresh young blood—gorging on a teenager and then partying. I sound terrible, don't I?"

Bile edged up in the back of Roy's throat. The edges of the room warped in his vision.

"And in return," Primrose giggled, "we give them nights of pleasure and fun they could never experience any other way."

Fedora had his arm around Roy's neck again. It seemed the man was made of garlic.

"Crazy stuff, huh?" He pulled Roy backward and spun him around. Fedora's face ballooned, his friend Rat's face floating beside it. "Come on, we gotta find Clooney."

A waitress with red horns and cloven-hoofed heels opened the doors down. A thudding onslaught of trance-dance music greeted them, and Roy felt himself in a kaleidoscopic maelstrom spiraling out of control.

Fedora yelled into his ear, "Welcome to Hell, my friend."

24

"Most people are worth more dead than alive. Did you know that?" Del asked.

She scrolled through an article on her phone.

Coleman kept his eyes on the road. His turn to drive today.

They had been called to a domestic disturbance at a house on the north side of Heckscher Park in the suburbs of Huntington, a nice area with nice middle-class families. But it was the end of the day, the time when husbands and wives got together to talk about things. The stress of the holidays was already in full swing. They got more domestic-disturbance calls during this time of year than any other.

Today was the first day of December. A light dusting of snow the night before had burned off by early morning, but it was chilly. A few yellow leaves still clung to the skeletal trees. Coleman slowed to check the GPS, then took a left turn.

"I'm serious," Del said. "You can buy a pair of eyeballs on the black market for fifteen hundred dollars. Scalp with hair for six hundred. A fresh skull with all the teeth for twelve hundred."

"You're trying to freak me out before this call?" Coleman replied. "And I know you'll be worth *nothing* dead, which is what you'll be if the chief finds out you're still talking about this Lowell guy."

"You can get a live heart for transplant for a hundred nineteen thousand in some places in Eastern Europe. A kidney delivered inside the US for two hundred sixty-two grand, or to China for sixty-two."

"Can't get none of that stuff at the bodega on my corner—at least, not last time I checked." Coleman looked at her for a second and shook his head.

"And look at this." Del held up another web article on her phone. "Transplant patients often take on the characteristics and even habits of their donors. This is just people who have heart transplants and liver transplants. Imagine what would happen with a *whole-body* transplant!"

"You gotta stop obsessing over this Royce guy," Coleman said. "You were nuts to go and stalk his family at that art event."

"I wanted to go anyway. It was just a coincidence."

"Hey, I'm your partner, right? Have a little respect."

"Okay, you're right. I *was* stalking them, but it's not just Roy. I get the feeling he's the victim." Del scrolled through more articles. "It's this Dr. Danesti. I mean, where'd he come from?"

She'd looked into Danesti, pulled up web pages and articles. He was adopted, had moved to America for postgraduate work in neurology when he was twenty-three, about twenty years ago. Became a citizen ten years ago. All the articles were vague about where he came from.

And then there was Eden Corporation, his company.

It had recently been reorganized as a nonprofit but had a lot of problems with financing, despite its glitzy locations. There was an article from Susan Collins at the *Tribune*. Del thought about giving her a call.

She said, "Eden Corporation is under investigation for ethics violations."

"Doesn't surprise me."

"There are stories linking them to the illegal organ trade."

"So you're saying this Dr. Danesti, in the middle of Manhattan, is buying and selling body parts for rich people. Seriously?" He grinned. "Careful you don't drop too far down that rabbit hole. Could be a long climb out."

She opened another web article on her phone. "The thing I don't understand is all the connections to surrogacy clinics."

"It's a big business, I guess." Coleman slowed the car. He squinted and looked out the window. "This is the address—Fifty-one Madison, right?"

Del put her phone away and checked the police display. "Some people are worth more dead than alive—being a cop, you see it all the time. But I wonder what someone like Roy is worth *alive*? And to whom? That's the question that's bugging me."

25

"Is this still Purgatory? Or are we back upstairs in Heaven? Or back in Hell?"

A white-uniformed woman with a gossamer blond bob hovered near the far white wall. "I'll get the doctor," she said to Roy before leaving.

She closed the door behind her, and Roy heard the lock click.

He was restrained, legs and arms, by thick padded leather straps. Bound to a gurney. Dressed in a blue hospital gown. A bag of clear liquid hung from an IV pole over his head. The walls were uniform white, but the space wasn't as big as he remembered Purgatory, and he was the only one here. No music. What just happened?

The door opened, and Dr. Danesti appeared, a parental grimace of concern creasing his cheeks and forehead. He had on beige khakis and a blue button-down shirt tucked in at the waist. It was the first time Roy had seen him in casual clothes. Also for the first time, he understood how people could think he and Danesti looked similar.

The doctor asked, "How are you doing?"

"Did you come to the party?" Roy was still disoriented.

Danesti shut the door behind him, walked to the bed, and began undoing the straps. "You're at Eden. The police picked you up last night and brought you here. We had to restrain you."

"The police? Why did they bring me here?"

"Because we asked them to pick you up."

"*You* asked *them*?"

"We had to. Your vital signs were ... We monitor you." Danesti tapped the side of his own temple.

The implants. He meant the sensors they had embedded under Roy's scalp and in his arms and legs. "And they track my location?"

"Their main job is to return data on your brain function, but we can triangulate your position to within a few dozen meters if you're near an open Wi-Fi connection. You need to be more careful, Roy. Your T-cell count was dangerously high."

"I've been taking my antirejection drugs."

"But your blood work last night—a whole cocktail of drugs. And alcohol. I told you to be careful with the drinking."

"I didn't drink last night." He had taken a handful of Oxy that he got from the kid in the park. Why hadn't he just asked Danesti for a prescription? *Because I don't want him to know.* But then, he didn't really know what was in the stuff he got from that kid.

Danesti said, "You must have had something on Saturday. I'm going to increase the dosage of your antirejection drugs. T cells don't generally penetrate the blood-brain barrier, but this procedure is still new. The cognitive effects are unpredictable. How are you feeling?"

"I'm fine ... Wait, what day is it?"

"Sunday."

Roy blinked. *Sunday?* He had gone out with Fedora on Thursday night. Another blackout?

He didn't remember anything from the past two days. Two whole days and nights, and then some.

The last image in his mind was the young woman whose blood Primrose took. The girl with blue eyes and red hair. The girl from his dreams?

What had he been doing for two days and nights? Did the doctor have a record of it?

Roy said, "I saw your rejuvenation party. One of them was just a child.

Sixteen, maybe younger." The thought of that girl pumping her lifeblood into the old hag Primrose overcame any fears concerning his blackout. An alien-feeling rage surged up in him.

"Mrs. Chegwidden did mention that you went to one of our outpatient facilities." Danesti finished undoing the last of the straps and removed the catheter from Roy's arm, taping an alcohol swab over the needle mark. "All our donors are eighteen at minimum, Roy. Maybe one of them looked—"

"Sixteen."

"That's not possible. I assure you."

"That's what Primrose said."

The guy didn't miss a beat. "Real progress in medicine does sometimes push the boundaries. Did you know that just a few miles from here, a Dr. Couney used to run a freak show on Coney Island, showing off tiny premature human babies in plastic bubbles? A young Cary Grant, a rising film star, worked as a barker, bringing in paying customers."

Roy rubbed his wrists. The chronic pins-and-needles sensation had numbed, and he felt the dull rasp of his fingernails on his skin. The knuckles on his left hand were still scraped, but fresh new bruises mottled his arms.

Danesti continued, "This Dr. Couney used the money to pay for the development of the first incubators—pioneered them in the early twentieth century. He saved tens of thousands of babies' lives. Perhaps even millions, by now—all by using a freak show."

"Using whataboutisms doesn't make something right."

"Sometimes, we need to push society. The media calls you Danestein's monster. I know the pressure must be terrible, and I am sorry for that. Do you want to return here? Stay in Eden?"

Roy was still disgusted, but now the fear … Should he tell Danesti he didn't remember anything at all from the past two days? Find out where he'd been? Those sensors in his head—what else could they read? What else could they do to him remotely? What he definitely *didn't* want was to get trapped here.

"Get dressed," Danesti said. "We have fresh clothes in the closet. I'm going to take you to our research facility."

* * *

Danesti pointed to an image of flattish-looking worms on a huge display taking up the wall of the room.

"These planarians can 'see' even after losing their heads. Sense light even without head or eyes. These decapitation-regeneration experiments copy sequences of events that occurred in evolution—a little like what you have experienced firsthand."

They had gone upstairs to Eden's developmental offices. Danesti said he wanted to make him understand why he, Roy, was so important. He'd given him a few minutes to get dressed, in khakis and a blue shirt that matched the doctor's. Almost like twins. Except for the blue handkerchief Roy had around his neck. He picked up the backpack and wallet that he'd had with him when they found him last night.

"Evolution was never really about survival of the fittest, but more about the symbiosis and connection of two separate organisms into one. Did you know that?"

Roy shook his head. He wasn't that interested in the research—not right now, anyway.

The doctor led Roy into a large room some fifty feet long with white counters to each side and high glass-fronted refrigeration units. Between them were rows of clear plastic tubs. He walked over to the nearest one.

A gelatinous semitranslucent mass glowed at the bottom of the container.

"This was originally a pig liver, but one now made with human cells infused onto the protein scaffold. We're also experimenting with 3-D printing of the scaffolding. It's a way to *create* organs for transplant.

"A hundred thousand people in the United States need organ transplants each year, yet only a third get them while the rest die. Mostly, this is because we can store a fresh organ for only four to six hours, so the donor must be relatively nearby. This is why we are leading a project to flash-freeze organs and then rewarm them, using nanotechnology to avoid water crystallization."

Danesti stepped over to the next plastic tub, which contained a small kidney that looked made of glass. "It's been cryogenically frozen for a month," he said. "But it's a real human kidney. Tomorrow, we'll rewarm it and implant into a pig. It means we can open the international market for organ procurement and exchange—if we can perfect the process."

"International? Where did you get that kidney?"

"America has only four percent of the world's population, but more than thirty percent of the waiting list for transplants. In many jurisdictions—Iran, for example—it is legal for living donors to sell their noncritical organs." The doctor fidgeted with a control on the side of the incubation machine. "This is all confidential, of course."

"You have offices in these places?"

"We have affiliations."

"Where?"

"Bangladesh. India. Even China. Of course, all with regulatory approval."

"You said an organ could only stay 'fresh' for four to six hours. What about my donor's body?"

"In your case, the entire body was used as a transplant."

"So you don't know when my donor died?"

"I understand your frustration. But even I don't get that information."

"But the Organ Procurement and Transplant Network has it?"

"If you're asking whether I'm on the board of the OPTN, then yes, I am," Danesti said. "But I don't have access to the individual donor data."

That wasn't Roy's question, but the admission stunned him. He was on the board of the OPTN. Wasn't that a conflict of some kind?

"Even without a brain, your donor body could have been kept functioning for days, even weeks. Some patients in vegetative states can live for decades."

"They're not dead, then? How can you use them as organ donors?"

"They're brain-dead. If the patient signed up for organ donation, and they're judged to be medically dead—"

"How do you determine that?"

"Determining when death occurs is a difficult problem, I agree, even with modern medicine. Come, I'd like to show you something."

The doctor led him to another set of plastic tubs. A tiny white mouse had fine tubes running into its mouth.

"This is a clone."

Roy wasn't as impressed as he felt the doctor wanted him to be. "There's a company in Texas that will clone your dog for fifty grand. I've seen it on TV. Mail order."

"But not one without a brain. We make a few tweaks to the genetic machinery to induce a kind of anencephaly. Create organisms that grow without brains but are genetically identical to the host. Once gestated, we nurture them in specialized incubators and grow them to maturity at accelerated rates. You and Mr. Sheffield were among the first to demonstrate that a body transplant is possible, but soon we won't need donor bodies. We can grow them."

He meant they wanted to clone humans, fast-grow them without brains. No worries of rejection.

"We don't show this to everyone, Roy, but I wanted you to understand the future. We can even improve—make modifications to the genetics of the clone. Make them disease-resistant, improve the new body. Imagine if we could have transplanted the mind of Stephen Hawking into a revitalized, healthy cloned body? What it could have meant for the world?"

It all looked so clean, so antiseptic. Something about it wasn't quite so clean.

"But you need to birth them."

"With surrogates. We implant fertilized eggs into surrogate mice."

"I meant with humans."

"The same process. We already have an active surrogacy program. Affiliates of Eden. It's very common these days."

Some of Roy's mother's friends had used them.

The doctor gave him a knowing grin.

Something about it said more than just the words he'd been saying. What was he hiding? Something buzzed in Roy's backpack, vibrated again, louder, and then started ringing.

His cell phone.

"Excuse me a second," he said to Danesti.

* * *

Angel had called, said he had dug up something important. That he'd been trying to get in touch the past two days.

Roy had said goodbye and thank you to Danesti, who at first told him he should stay in Eden, but then insisted that he at least go home and rest. Go back to the Hamptons. The doctor said that Penny had called him more than once and was worried. He said to call his wife.

Roy lied and said he would, then took the elevators down and walked across the street to the food court in the basement of the Bank of America building on Park Avenue. It was lunchtime, and the tables were packed with men and women in business suits, with fast-food wrappers scattered around them, all staring at their phone screens.

"Nice outfit," Angel said. He had a half-eaten burrito in one hand. "I like the ascot. Did your riding instructor dress you this morning?" He took a bite of his burrito and proceeded to talk through it. "Where the hell have you been the past two days?"

"I had to get inside Eden," Roy said.

He wasn't in the mood to talk about this latest blackout. He dropped his backpack on the table between them. "Anyway, weren't you supposed to have someone tailing me?"

"I did, right up till you went into that fancy party in Meatpacking. No way my guy could follow you in there. He waited outside all night, man. Said he couldn't see anybody following you."

"What did you find out? Did you get that list from Brixton yet?" Did they find out who his donor body belonged to? Could it have been that quick?

"No, man. Brixton won't give that up without some dirt on Danesti first."

Roy leaned closer to Angel. "He's got frozen human organs up there."

"Is that illegal?"

"Fresh ones that could be used for transplants? He said they had offices in India and Bangladesh." They had looked into Eden online, but being a private company, it could keep its structure and operations opaque. "Tell

Brixton that, and get that goddamn list. Tell him Danesti is on the board of the OPTN. That's got to be a conflict of some kind."

"How'd you find that out?"

"Because he told me."

"He controls the supply *and* the sales?" Angel said. "That's badass. So he's an organ dealer. That's what you're saying? What else?"

"He wants to build his own floating country on a platform out in the Pacific. He says religion used to be the only authority, but now science is the new religion. It's a cult in there."

Angel nodded thoughtfully and took another bite of burrito. "So basically, he's an aspiring Bond villain. Anything else?"

"He said my donor might have died months before my operation or have been brain-dead. I'm not sure."

"That doesn't help narrow things."

"Find a way to get that list from Brixton and put someone onto tailing me again."

The feeling was back. Roy felt eyes on him from somewhere in the food court. Was it Danesti? Someone from Eden? Nothing would surprise him.

He gave it up for now. "So, what did you have for me?"

"Ah, man, you're not going to like this." Angel scarfed down the last bite and swung his briefcase onto the table, opened it, and pulled out a sheaf of papers.

Watching him, Roy decided to open his own backpack. He'd felt something rattling around in there. Something glittered in the bottom of his bag. Jewelry? On top were two containers. He pulled them out.

Angel looked at the stickers on the two empty jars in Roy's hands. "Do those say 'Clooney' and 'Bieber'?"

"What do you have?" Roy stuffed them back into his pack.

Angel's eyebrows rose, but he didn't persist. "I found a lawsuit from a few years back. Your mother trying to get your money. Said I was your lawyer. Said I looked into it because you said Penny told you about it, or something like that. But this isn't that."

"It was from when I was in a coma?"

"No, man. Years ago, right after your dad died. It claimed that the terms of the trust were invalid, because you weren't their son."

"What? You can't be serious." Roy had seen pictures of his mother's brother, dead now, and he was a spitting image.

"You know the weird part? The court threw it out after they did a maternity test." He displayed a sheet of paper.

Roy stared without responding, trying to process what it all meant.

"I know, right? I heard of paternity tests, to see if someone is a kid's dad, because, you know, sometimes you don't know. But *maternity* test? How can you not know if a kid came out of you? I mean, did your mom not know? Why would she request a maternity test and then fail it?"

Dumbstruck silence. His mother had always been distant, but …

"You okay?" Angel asked.

"You go and get those files."

"And you?"

"I need to go home."

26

The overpass with its wire-and-steel cage swept by, quieting for a moment the drumming of rain on the windshield. Roy escaped Manhattan through the Midtown Tunnel, slid under the East River to emerge in the low-rise suburbia of Queens—mile upon mile of single-family dwellings and tarmac and concrete. The trees lining the expressway were half crowned, with more of their red and yellow leaves on the divider between the highway and the service road than on their branches.

Roy kept the window down and sucked in the cool fall air.

He had called his wife and his mother yesterday, even called Dr. Danesti, telling them he was going home. He didn't say he was going to stay, but they assumed it. Let them. He had other motives. They had volunteered to have one of the Chegwiddens' helicopter shuttles pick him up at the Thirty-Third Street heliport, but instead he bought a broken-down Chevy from a used-car lot on Avenue D. Paid cash. The fenders didn't match the body.

Emerging from the concrete canyons of Manhattan, the relief was palpable. It felt good to be out from under the oppressive weight of millions of people and all their problems and dramas. He imagined the crowds of people in all the houses and apartments as he swept past. Someone had just fallen in love. Someone was emotionally devastated having split with the person of their dreams. Another person somewhere out there had just died, and someone else was grieving. A roiling sea of human anguish and bliss that ebbed and flowed.

His own emotions were as flat as the gray sky.

Sleep had been short and fitful. He had dreamed again of the little girl with hair as red as her mother's, of the driving rain and the red-brown woman sitting in the grass. Always the same sense of impending doom.

After Hauppauge, the storm clouds cleared as sprawling suburbia gave way to rural Long Island. On a whim, he got off the expressway and wound his way up onto Middle Country Road, paralleling the highway but halfway to the water on the north side, near Long Island Sound. He wasn't in a hurry.

The countryside opened up—small farms and paddocks interspersed with broken-down homes and rusted cars on blocks. Dogs barked as he passed.

He mused over what had prompted him to get off the expressway. Maybe it was because he could have turned left into Hauppauge, dropped in at the medical examiner's office himself to see that report. But Angel was already on his way there.

Or maybe he liked the idea of driving past the Suffolk County PD headquarters in Yaphank and maybe seeing that policewoman again, Detective Devlin. Tell her what he had found out. Maybe turn himself in. *For what?* Roy couldn't shake the sense that he'd done something wrong, was being punished for some sin. The guilt followed him around.

Emotions in him sometimes felt like tsunamis, but not just because they were destructive. When someone close to him died, he withdrew, like the water emptying from the beach—a curious event that left fish stranded and gulping air while curious bystanders came down to see what was going on.

But anyone who knew Roy knew what was coming. A shift on the horizon, and then the onslaught that destroyed everything in its path. It had happened when he was a teenager, when a cousin he was close to died. At first, Roy didn't react. Then, a year later, he started doing drugs and almost dropped out of school. That was what happened when his father died. For a year or two he was okay, and then he started hitting the sauce. Maybe his dad knew that about him. Maybe that was why he created the trust fund.

Only this time, *Roy* was the one who had died.

* * *

Roy passed through the town of Coram, a one-light village with a single-story United Income Tax Center building at its crossroad. The parking lot was empty on a Monday, and a large red sign in the window said, "Karate Lessons."

In another ten minutes, he passed a sign for Brookhaven National Laboratories. This was the Department of Energy lab where, in the 1940s, they had conducted some of the world's very first nuclear chain reactions, which led to the creation of atomic weapons and other horrors. All he saw were leafy green forests and rolling pastures.

He drove past a sign for Tom's County Automotive, a ramshackle repair shop with dozens of rusting car hulks behind a razor-wire fence, next to a two-story Public Storage building in bright orange against the slate sky.

Something about the area calmed him, and he felt his stomach relaxing for the first time in weeks. He realized that this was the area where he had woken up after one of his blackouts. That night in the rain. He had driven up here without knowing it.

He kept driving.

The road hooked around south and connected with the end of the expressway in a Tanger Outlet Malls complex just outside Riverhead and Northampton. He drove south to the Montauk Highway, a two-lane road that was the only passage to the other end of Long Island. Crossing the canal at Shinnecock was like crossing the River Styx into the underworld.

His first stop was to see his old friend.

* * *

"Cheers." They clinked their beer bottles and drank.

Low clouds scudded over the Atlantic, but the rain had stopped. It was cold enough that Sam brought out two blankets so they could sit out on the deck by the sea grass. He loved sitting here surveying his private nature reserve, fifty acres of oceanfront sand dunes that were all his.

"Worried about you, my friend," Sam said. "Been, what, eleven days since we last spoke? I was getting separation anxiety. You changed your cell phone? That number you called from the new one?"

"Don't worry, they always know where I am." Roy pointed to his temple.

"Who's 'they'?"

"The ones tracking me."

Sam closed one eye and scrunched up his face. "You okay, buddy? Maybe you should go home for a bit. Or maybe stay here with me?"

"Dr. Danesti told me the implants track my location. That's how they found me the other night."

"Penny said they picked you up in Central Park. Another blackout?"

"Two whole days this time. I almost killed two kids the other night. In a bar fight."

His friend almost choked on his beer. "*What?* Never seen you throw a punch."

"Took down these two huge twentysomethings without breaking a sweat."

"Your knuckles do look beat up." Sam inspected Roy's hand and forearms.

"There was cocaine and ketamine in my bloodstream the night of the accident." Roy looked straight out over the ocean. "Any idea how that got there?"

A wave crashed in the silence, then another.

"Ah, damn it. You're the one that asked for it, but maybe that was my fault. You were drunker than a sailor on shore leave. I was the one that gave it to you."

"But *ketamine?*"

"It was New Year's. You're the one that likes that stuff. You hated going to the Chegwiddens'."

Roy didn't often take those rave drugs, but sometimes he did. At some parties. Usually with Sam.

"I'm really sorry, man," his friend added. "I've been feeling guilty about it. I mean, what if ... maybe the accident was my fault?"

For the first time in longer than Roy could remember, Sam looked sad.

"You should have told me before. And it was me driving, not Penny. Did you know that?"

"I did not know that." Still the look of sadness, but now also puzzlement. "Did Penny tell you?" His blue eyes narrowed. "Or that cop? Devlin? I met her on Friday, at your mother's art auction."

Roy was surprised for an instant. "At my mother's auction? Are they investigating me?"

"I got the feeling she's more just curious. More coincidence than anything else. Pretty girl. She's an artist. I gave her my number."

"There's no way that was coincidence. I hired a private eye. He's digging up the medical examiner's report from the Suffolk County Police Department records."

"And what does he think about all this?" Sam took another swig.

"He says to always follow the money."

A squall of wind whistled through the sea grass.

Sam said, "Heard you went to one of your mother's vampire parties the other night. Is that some creepy-ass stuff, or what? Think I'll stick to my beer and just let aging do its thing."

"My mother wasn't there."

"Now, that *would* have been weird. I mean, it's hard enough to imagine your own mother having sex, but seeing her drinking the blood of some young man? And not just metaphorically like she usually does?" Sam couldn't help trying to be funny, even at funerals. His grin had returned, but he sensed his humor had missed the mark. "You talk to Brixton more at the support groups?"

"He's helping me find out who my donor body is, but I need to dig up dirt on Dr. Danesti."

"You sure it's smart to bite the hand that sewed you together?"

"I'm feeling like I want to bite *all* the hands right now."

"I'm sorry if I haven't been a great friend. Maybe this was all my fault. Anything you need, I'm here for you."

Roy finished his beer. "I gotta go talk to my wife."

* * *

The old Chevy crunched across the gravel driveway, and Roy parked under the elms toward the end. No crush of beachgoers today. The sand at the end of Ocean Drive was empty, the boardwalk shops shuttered for the season, but the seagulls still squawked their lonely cries.

"You can't park that—" Penny was halfway out the front door before she recognized Roy in the driver's seat. "Sweetheart! I'm so glad you're back!" They always had problems with people parking in their driveway.

Somehow, she looked surprised to see him. It was a Monday afternoon, but she was done up as if on her way out for the evening: a lace silk shawl over her shoulders, a black dress, and two-inch heels. Maybe because she knew he was coming. But he'd said he was coming tonight. He had wanted to surprise her.

Roy got out of the car and inspected his house. Two stories of white-painted cedar siding, black windows. Small, for these parts—just four bedrooms, three thousand square feet. And yet, worth five million dollars in this corner of East Hampton next to the beach. It made no sense. What did Angel say? Follow the money? But the money here was everywhere.

"Come inside," Penny urged, still hanging in the doorway.

* * *

Roy sat on the same leather couch he remembered, saw the same white-themed walls and pictures and folding glass patio doors onto the pool deck. Why did it feel as if he hadn't lived here for years? Why did he get the sense that this wasn't *his* house? Instead of déjà vu, it was more like *jamais vu*.

Penny worked the coffee-pod machine in the kitchen and came back with two cups. "That car—I've never seen you drive something like that."

She put one cup on the mahogany coffee table—on a coaster—and cupped the other in her hands. She sat beside him, close enough that he smelled her perfume. Chanel. She was beautiful, perfect. The same woman he'd said yes to. Perfect teeth, perfect blond hair. Yet all he felt was a kind of revulsion.

She said, "I'm so glad you're home," again and took a sip.

"I'm not here for long."

"But I thought—"

"I know you weren't driving the car."

She'd never been a good liar. "But, I was, it was—"

"I read the medical examiner's report—from Suffolk County, not the East Hampton one."

Her hands trembled. "But Captain Harris … He said that—"

"The steering column went most of the way through my body. You couldn't have been driving."

Now the tears, her cup shaking so violently that Roy had to take it from her and put it down. No more revulsion. Just pity. He'd spent six years of his life with this woman, this fellow human, and seeing her cry made him want to cry. Her tears were honest. No artifice. The innocent—that had always been Penny, for all her other faults.

"I was trying to protect you," she said. "You already had two arrests for driving under the influence. A third one would have landed you in jail."

"But I was almost *killed*."

"It didn't matter. You would have lost your trust."

"If I was dead, it would be gone anyway." But not if he was in a coma, Roy suddenly realized. Could he be prosecuted when he was unconscious? She was right, though. He did have two convictions. Another would have sent him to jail.

"We did everything we could to bring you back, and now here you are!" His wife threw her arms around him.

And yet, it didn't feel real.

"Were you even *in* the car?" Roy asked.

"You drove off by yourself. You were drunk and stoned. And in a rage."

"About what?" So she wasn't even *in* the car.

The sobbing abated. He lifted her away from him and looked into her green eyes. "About what? What was I mad about?"

"I don't know." She looked away.

"Where did the scar come from?" The small nick on her forehead.

"I just … I hit my head. I don't know."

"Did you know about my mother's lawsuit?"

"I know she was trying to get at your money when you were in a coma."

"Not that. Fifteen years ago. She said I wasn't her son."

Penny's eyes widened. "*What?*"

"And what about Leila? What happened to my dog?"

At this, Penny pushed away and stood up. "What does that have to do with anything?"

"What did you do to her?"

"You're losing your mind, do you know that?" Penny backed away. "Nicky said this would happen, and it's happening. You need help."

* * *

The drive from his house to his mother's took fifteen minutes. *You were in a rage.* That was what Penny said.

At least that was honest.

One of the last things he remembered at the Chegwiddens' party before the accident was screaming. He hadn't been sure whether someone was screaming at him, or the other way around. But he'd been in a rage about something—what, Penny refused to say. But at least it verified his memory. Finally, a small piece of the puzzle.

But "*Nicky*"?

Nicky had told his wife that he would lose his mind?

He couldn't remember any of her friends named Nicky, and she refused to elaborate when he asked. He thought he knew most of her girlfriends. Maybe it was a new one.

He pulled into his mother's grand parking lot lined with replica statues from the gardens at Versailles. The sun was edging toward the horizon in the west, pulling behind the wall of storm clouds in the distance. The temperature seemed to drop by several degrees during the short walk from his car to the front door of his mother's house. He rapped with the large brass knocker.

"Come in," his mother said. Her face was pale, her lipstick crimson, her bob-cut hair streaked platinum and gold. She wore an asymmetric form-hugging dress with a strap over one shoulder, the other bare. Her smile showed off her perfect white teeth.

"We've been so worried!" she said. "But I understand you need time to yourself."

She already had a cocktail in hand. Soft music in the background, muffled voices downstairs. "I have friends over. Would you like to join us?"

"I'm only here for a minute. Is there somewhere we can talk?"

"We can talk here. Why don't you come in? Stay for a little while?"

Roy glanced at the row of pictures on the tables facing the entrance. Her with Diana Ross. With President Bush, the first one. And one of her with her brother. It was from thirty years ago, but it could have been a picture of Roy from yesterday.

"Why did you always laugh when people said I was the spitting image of your brother?"

"Because you remind me of him." Her brother was diagnosed with cancer the same year Roy's father died. He died the next year.

"And why did you file a lawsuit in 2004 to try and take the trust?"

"I haven't seen you in weeks, and you come in and start throwing accusations?"

"Why did you try to prove I wasn't your son? Not your *biological* son?"

She paused a beat. "That was just a mistake."

"Penny told me you tried to take the money again, when I was in a coma."

Virginia swallowed what remained of her cocktail.

"Why did you try to do a maternity test?" Roy asked again.

"Did your *wife* tell you how she got that scar?" His mother was half-slurring her *s*'s.

"I know she wasn't driving, and I know she wasn't even in the car."

"Trying to protect you—was that what she said?"

"That's what she said."

"You know why you left the party?" Virginia was clearly enjoying whatever she was about to share.

Roy remained silent. His mother dragged out the seconds.

"Because she was having an affair. Everyone at the party heard it. You were screaming. Your perfect wife was with some other man. That's why you drove off that cliff. *You're* the one who gave her that scar. You hit her. You think she wanted to save you?"

"I hit Penny?" A dim memory surfaced. Him screaming at her at the party.

"If you died, all the money would go to charity. Those are the terms of your asshole father's trust. Penny wouldn't get a nickel." She smiled at her cleverness. "Not unless she divorces you while you're alive—and have fully inherited all that money. That's the only reason she's being nice: to get you across that finish line so she can grab cash."

The venom of it was honest. He stared vacantly at the only picture of his father on his mother's mantel: standing with his arm around Steve Robinson.

"In a month, this house is mine, you know." He imagined putting his hands around her neck, squeezing the miserable life out of her. "Tell me the truth. Tell me why you tried to prove I'm not your son."

27

"I got a call today," Deputy Chief Alonzo said. "From Captain Harris, down at East Hampton."

Alonzo half sat on the edge of Del's desk.

He hadn't called her into his office, instead coming down into the pit. It meant that he wanted everyone else to hear what he had to say. "I thought I made it clear that we were cooperating with Harris, to make things smooth."

Del replied, "You did say that, Chief."

"What were you doing meeting with Royce Lowell-Vandeweghe a week ago?"

How did they find that out? Did Roy tell them? Did he complain to Captain Harris? That was possible. Whatever the source, there was no use denying it.

"Having a drink, sir."

"You do realize that New York City is not in our jurisdiction?"

"I was just having a drink. *He* called *me.*"

"And you called the Lowell-Vandeweghe house three times in the past month?"

"Trying to find out more information on that hiker. The one who was killed."

She cringed, waiting for the other shoe to drop—that she'd been at the

Lowell-Vandeweghe art auction, stalking Roy's family and friends—but it didn't come.

Instead, Alonzo said, "For a person who says they can see when someone is lying, you sure don't do it very well yourself. Explain to me how these are connected."

"Mr. Lowell-Vandeweghe was brought out on what he called 'field trips' before he was released from Eden. Into Long Island. And his family had a home not far from here—twenty years ago, before they moved into the Hamptons."

"You have something concrete on him?"

"I met him. Spent an hour talking. The guy is unstable."

"You know what he just went through, right?"

"Of course."

"Do you think you wouldn't have a few screws knocked loose after something like that? Of course there's something not right with him—he had his *head cut off*."

"Did you know his mother and wife don't even know where he is? He's run away from home."

Alonzo's eyebrows came together. "'Run away'? You do know he's a middle-aged man. And did you know there was a fight at the establishment where you had a drink with him, also involving him?"

That was news to Del. She shook her head.

"But you just happened to be there."

She asked, "What time was this? What happened? Did he get hurt?"

"I repeat again, Detective Devlin, this has nothing to do with us."

"Sir, with all due respect, we need to talk to Dr. Danesti at Eden Corporation. They have devices implanted in their patient that could give us time and location. I don't think Mr. Lowell-Vandeweghe is in full control of himself. And I've been looking into Eden—"

"Stick to your cases, Detective Devlin. The hiker? They've got multiple DNA fragments from the remains they found, right?"

"Yes, sir."

"We've still got an active killer in our jurisdiction. The feds have taken over the case, but maybe we can help out."

"The feds?"

"They think it's related to the Fire Island Killer."

"But it was only one."

Part of the MO matched, but not the pattern. The Fire Island Killer had worked in sprees. Seventeen bodies, cut up in pieces with some bits missing, had ended up in bags on Long Island's beaches ten years back. The hiker had been found in pieces, as well, but no more bodies turned up in the past two years. The Nissequogue murder was an isolated case.

Alonzo rubbed his crew cut with one hand. "No more chasing this Lowell-Vandeweghe around. Whatever you're doing, you've riled up some very important people who have suddenly decided to make my life difficult."

Del nodded but didn't say anything.

"Understood? I want to hear you say it. If you have something more to say on this, bring it to my office."

"Understood, sir."

* * *

"Hey, Del, there's some guy at the ME's office says he wants the Lowell file." Officer Coleman held up the black plastic phone receiver, cord dangling, as if the phone might explain the full picture. "You sure you want to do this?"

She'd kept the file on her desk. After meeting and telling Roy about the file, she assumed that he would come and ask to see it at the medical examiner's office, at which point she could return it and have a few words with him again.

She had been warned off contacting him, but she couldn't help it if they just happened to run into each other, could she? Better to ask forgiveness than permission.

"Tell him I'll be five minutes. I'll go alone."

She took the file and wound her way through the cubicles, past the slouched row of handcuffed waiting to be processed. She pushed open the exterior double door and bounded down the stairs into the autumn air.

It was a few minutes' drive down the road to the ME's office, so she took one of the unmarked cruisers. They'd be pissed, but she could handle a little of that. Minutes later, she pulled up to the uninspired beige brick building with the dark-blue-over-baby-blue logo of Suffolk County and jogged through the double doors, file in hand.

She scanned the lobby, looking for the bulky figure of Roy, but there was only a compact Latino-looking guy at the counter.

"Susanne, I have that file," Del announced.

The guy turned around. Yes, Latino. Behind the counter, her friend Susanne pointed at him and shrugged. This wasn't her problem.

Del started to say, "You're not—"

"I'm his lawyer. I'm Mr. Lowell-Vandeweghe's lawyer." The guy waved a piece of paper in the air.

"You're Atticus Cargill?"

Now, that would be two birds with one stone.

She had tried calling Atticus twice three weeks ago and got no answer, but already she could see it wasn't her luck today, either. Already the lines of *ishma*-red streaked down the man's face in front of her. It wasn't even close. He was lying.

The man looked left and right. "Ah, no, another lawyer."

Del walked up to him and took the paper. "Roy signed this? He wants the medical report?"

The *ishma*-red lines pulsed and faded. "Yeah, right on both counts."

"But you're not a lawyer."

His face fell. He was a good-looking man, high and tight crew cut as if he'd just gotten out of the Marines. Straight back. Squared away—trousers pressed, white shirt crisp. Maybe even a little *too* neat.

"Roy hired you, is that it?" she whispered. "You're a private detective?"

His eyes fell even further. Not used to being found out this easy. The guy looked tough in a military sort of way but wasn't trained in being purposely deceptive.

He said, "Unless there is evidence of a crime being committed, or about to be, I can't divulge any client confidentiality—"

"We already established you're not a lawyer. And we'll have to see about any crimes about to be committed." Del walked over to the photocopy machine and asked Susanne, "Could you authorize me for a dozen?" The machine's light turned green, and she began copying the medical report.

"My name's Angel," the man said. "And yeah, I'm helping Roy out. He needs help, that's for sure."

"Do you know where he is? I had a few more questions."

"I'll see what I can do," Angel replied. "I have one question myself: The car that was in the accident—it still in custody? I'd like to take a look."

"It was never taken into custody." Del picked up the file and the copied pages.

"Really? Is that standard operating procedure?"

"In East Hampton, they do everything differently. The Chegwiddens paid for the car to be removed, and the wife took custody afterward." Del paused a beat and then said, "So what are the leads you're following?" She handed over the file. "You got a card?"

"Can't be specific," Angel replied as he pulled a card from his pocket, "but always follow the money. That's my motto. So no forensics exam on the car?"

"Nobody died." She handed him her card and took his.

"Somebody *did* die," Angel said softly.

"Who?"

"Who is Roy attached to? Ever think about that?"

28

"Your own mother said you've always been a monster?" Angel said.

They were back in the private eye's loft on Third Street in Spanish Harlem, back in the jungle of hanging plants and potted eucalyptus trees. The windows were closed against the cold, the sky outside dark, with a faint reddish glow from the city lights below.

Charlie had just made a round of vanilla Earl Grey. He sat staring at two large computer monitors balanced on the dining room table. For the past two days, he had called in sick and stayed home sifting through the raw files from Brixton. Being a veterinarian made him the closest thing on their team to someone with a medical background.

"Those were her words," Roy replied to Angel. She refused to explain the lawsuits. She'd been drunk.

He had frightened himself at his mother's. He barely managed to contain his rage at her words, even knowing that they were designed to cut and inflict damage. Usually, he would just let her comments slide, but something was different this time.

"Did your mother hit you?" Angel asked. His expression was hard to read.

"At the house? When I was just there?" *No, but I wanted to hit her.*

"I mean when you were a kid."

"Never."

"And you're upset because she called you a monster? Dog, my *abuelita* would beat us with a stick if we just looked at her the wrong way. Being called a monster would be like her being *nice* to us. You *güeros* gotta thicken that skin some."

Roy and Angel also had computer monitors in front of them.

Three nights ago, Brixton had relented and given them the full list of past donors—a whole year's worth from before the accident. More than ten thousand people. They'd narrowed the list to those between eighteen and thirty-five years old, male, and Caucasian.

That brought it down to 1,820 names.

Beyond that, they had to search each record manually for cause of death—only some kind of head trauma, with minimal damage to the rest of the body.

"But … she meant it, like, literally," Roy tried to explain. "That I was *literally* a monster."

Angel said, "Have you looked in the mirror? I mean really looked … in … that … mirror?"

"Be nice," Charlie whispered from across the room.

"Because," Angel continued, "you got a whole huge red scar all the way around your neck. You're attached to someone else's body, and you got metal studs sticking out of your head. You are a bit of an oddity, my friend, and I say that with love. I know you been through a lot, but your mother has, too."

"Sometimes, you have all the tact of a scorpion on a wedding cake," Charlie said to his boyfriend.

Angel replied, "You can't always sugarcoat. You gotta face things head-on."

"Look who's talking," Charlie said. Then he said to Roy, "You're still letting her keep the house? Your mother?"

Roy's rage had dissipated as fast as it came on. "It's just money. Yes."

Angel snorted at that.

But it *was* just money. Maybe he had hoped he could win some love from her with the gesture. One thing was certain: he would earn her undying hatred if he took the house. She had lived in it for thirty years, helped rebuild it with his father. From his mother's point of view, he was an unlovable child who grew into an unlovable adult. But then, money overcame most obstacles—at least until his father died. And Roy hadn't been any help, had been just as destructive as she was, living up to her terrible expectations.

"I'm looking more into your mother," Angel said. "She's always on Page Six, yeah? Got forty years of celeb pictures on digital microfilm at New York Library on Fourth. I'm going down tomorrow."

"Hey, look at this one," Charlie said.

He and Angel were going through the raw files from Brixton. When they found possible matches, they sent over pictures and images they found on the web. Anything to get more images and information.

An email popped up on Roy's screen. He opened it. An image of a young guy's face, a news story about a train accident. Pictures of his family, of the site around the accident. The name and birth date. Five-foot-three. "Gotta be at least five-nine, and not scrawny," Roy replied after a few minutes of flipping through images. He took a sip of his vanilla Earl Grey.

"How did you ever get into the Navy SEALs?" Roy asked Angel. "I mean, why? It doesn't seem … I mean …"

"I'm Latino, man."

"What does that mean?"

"It means his mother," Charlie offered, his chubby pink face illuminated by the screens.

"It means that if my mother knew I was gay, it would have broken her Catholic heart."

Angel took a deep breath. "Maybe it would be different now. Things are different from twenty years ago. As soon as I came of age, I signed up for military service. From then on, I always took the hardest training, the hardest missions that sent me into the deepest, darkest holes this world has—"

"And that's not a figure of speech," Charlie chimed in. "Maybe not even a metaphor."

"Shut up," Angel said amiably. "I'm trying to tell my story. I saw some terrible stuff. Maybe I was hating on myself a little."

"Maybe?" Charlie said quietly. "But you won some of the highest military awards."

"The day my mother died, four years ago, I gave it all up in a heartbeat, but that don't mean it wasn't a powerful experience. I still have some of my closest brothers in there, and some others are having a hard time back in the world …" Angel's voice trailed off. "I'll never forget. So I'm happy. And the day I got out, the first man I met was Charlie. It was love at first sight. Haven't looked back."

Charlie said, "And did he tell you we're going to adopt? There's a boy in Colombia. He lost his family. We've done all the papers."

"That's really great, guys."

Roy had always wanted a family, but the possibility seemed further away than ever. When he'd married Penny, he thought that was what she wanted, too, but she refused—said she needed time.

The adoption idea sprouted a memory in Roy. "Hey, Dr. Danesti said he was adopted. Could you look into that? Find out from where? Who his parents were? And you're looking into his finances?"

"You think we don't have enough to do?" Angel said it smiling. "Sending over another one to you."

An email popped up on Roy's screen, and he flipped through the images, not seeing anything that rang a bell.

"I got that medical report, the one from Suffolk County," Angel said. "Said just what that cop said it said." He paused a beat. "And I met her. Your cop lady friend."

"Detective Devlin? You met her? Why?"

"She had the file. Seemed like she wanted to meet you, if you ask me. Crazy cop. Really pretty. But it was like she could see into my mind. Spooky."

"She knows you're working for me?"

"I didn't tell her anything. What I was trying to do was find the car from the accident, have a look at it. It's not in the Suffolk pound."

"You should have just asked me. The car is back at our house. All fixed up."

"Fixed up? But it went off a cliff."

"Sam fixed it—or at least, he paid for it. Penny helped him." Roy looked through another set of pictures. "Speaking of my wife, she's having an affair. That's what my mother told me."

"Right now? Your wife is having an affair *now*?"

"She was when I had the accident. It was why I was so upset at that party. I might have even driven off the cliff on purpose. My mother gave me that little tidbit. She said I screamed it out at the party, that my wife was sleeping with someone."

"Someone there was her boyfriend?"

"I didn't ask. Don't even care."

"We better find out who."

"Maybe her lover is the one that tried to kill you," Charlie mused. "And she tried to save you. That's kind of romantic." He grimaced after considering his own words. "Sorry. Actually, that's not romantic."

"She did say something odd," Roy said. "She said that Nicky said I would lose my mind. I never heard of a friend of hers called Nicky."

"Why not just ask her?"

"That's what I hired you for."

"And you talked to Sam? Your buddy?" Angel replied without rising to the bait.

"He admitted he was the one who gave me the cocaine and ketamine at the party."

"But if everyone heard you screaming about your wife having an affair, why didn't your friend Sam tell you about it? I looked into him a bit, through my friend in the financial world, and he says Samuel Phipps had remortgaged that house, like, three times. Also found out he's into the Matruzzi family for a few million in chits. Long Island mobsters are *still* mobsters, bro."

"He's always doing stuff like that. He likes gambling. A bit disorganized, but his family left him billions."

"Heard that, too. Speaking of that, you told me Atticus said the trust had eight million left in it. I saw the trust documents—there was ten-point-four million in there when it was registered. So if it still has eight now after all those withdrawals, he did you a good job."

That was good to know. At least all the pieces were falling into place. It occurred to Roy that maybe he was barking up the wrong tree.

His wife was cheating on him, his best friend was a degenerate gambler, and he had a stormy relationship with his mother. Maybe this was just part of the process: for him to find out everything going on around him, to start over, to find some peace of mind. But he still wanted to know who his donor was. The question ate away at him.

"Isn't Sam on your board of trustees?" Angel asked, still looking at his screen.

"Yeah, but he never goes in there, not while Atticus is in charge. I doubt Sam even knows how to turn on a computer."

"Your dad and Atticus started LCT Capital, right?" Angel said. "I looked up their press releases—your dad invested in all kinds of stuff. He was into medical technology, early genetics start-ups, even joint ventures with Russian and Eastern European companies. That's not nothing in the early nineties. He was a pioneer."

"I want you to find out about my dog," Roy said. His mind could never quite stop from circling back to that.

"Why didn't you just ask Penny again?"

"She never gives me a straight answer."

"I'm sending another one over to you," Charlie announced in a singsong voice.

Angel rubbed his eyes. "Did you ever consider one thing?"

"What's that?" Roy opened Charlie's email.

"That maybe you did this to yourself. Maybe *you* set this up somehow. Your memory has holes the size of Texas, and you had cirrhosis and who knows what else. You just said that maybe you drove that car off the cliff on—"

"Quiet one second." Roy held up one hand, palm out.

There, on the screen. The little girl with the red hair. The girl from his dreams. She was in the arms of a thickly muscled young man with a beautiful redheaded woman beside him. The man had died a week before Roy's surgery, about three months after the accident at the Chegwiddens'. He looked familiar, somehow. Roy had seen him before. He was sure of it. He read the news story. Suicide. Gunshot wound to the head.

"Jake Hawkins."

29

Rain drummed in waves of rising and falling sound off the hood of Roy's old Chevy. The temperature held just above freezing, but this place was two degrees away from an ice storm.

The house across the street looked tired, its white paint peeling from the wooden siding. The roof sagged. Lichens grew in expanding amoeba-like patches over the shingles near the chimney and at the edges of the single dormer window. A porch spanned the front of the house, the latticework beneath it broken into fragments, the mortar of the brick columns at each end cracked and crumbling.

The grounds of the house were halfway to being reclaimed by the sparse forest of birches and fir trees leaning in around it. No one had mowed the lawn in the past season. The knee-deep yellowed grass of the yard grew chest-high around the concrete blocks supporting an old Pontiac Firebird. Someone had been in the process of sanding down the frame maybe a year ago, maybe two, but now it was a rusted shell.

A stolen dream.

When someone died, they didn't lose just their lives; they also lost their family, their home, their kids, their everything.

The house had a single front door with a window to either side. Maybe four rooms in a square on the ground floor, two bedrooms upstairs in the attic. One entrance in the back. Roy had checked, walking around through the woods in the night. The nearest neighbor was three hundred feet up the road. Straight across was a boneyard of discarded implements from the small farm to the south.

A single streetlight stood near the front porch.

Roy had driven up here twice in two days, stopping last night in a light snowfall to watch the lights click off inside the house.

Tonight, he was parked in the junkyard across the street, staring for hours as the rain hammered down in a driving wind. He fumbled with a pack of cigarettes, took one out with his left hand and put it into his mouth, then clicked the lighter on and off before crumpling the unlit cigarette into the ashtray. He had never smoked in his life, but the urge pulled at him now—some part of the same irresistible force that brought him back to this hauntingly beautiful little house.

* * *

Two nights before, he, Angel, and Charlie had checked and rechecked the images. Jake Hawkins was twenty-six years old, had been an up-and-coming mixed martial arts fighter with a six-win, two-loss record and four straight wins. He was five-ten—about Roy's height. Excited stories described Jake as a contender for the middleweight MMA belt.

The fighter was a southpaw. There were pictures of him in the octagon, blood spattered across his face, arms raised high after a win.

Roy had taken his shirt off. Angel and Charlie had tried to match the pictures. Roy's new body was built like a tank, just like Jake's, although the muscles in the pictures were bigger and leaner. They had atrophied from the long time in bed, said Charlie.

There were two moles on Roy's back, in the same configuration they saw in the images of Jake. Jake's chest had a tattoo of two horizontal lines, whereas Roy did not—but they thought they could see the shadow of the tat. Maybe someone had bleached the tattoos away.

Roy's stomach had cramped, screaming at him.

Roy had read the stories of Jake's shocking suicide. A gun death.

The website connected it to other clips, suicides of boxers and football and hockey players whose deaths were linked to chronic traumatic encephalopathy. Was that what happened? Was Jake brain-damaged?

Roy had studied the images deep into the night, long after Charlie and Angel turned in. They told him to be careful, not to contact Jake's wife, to give it some time and think about it. That maybe Jake wasn't their guy.

Roy had obsessed over the pictures, stared deep into the fighter's eyes. *Is that you, Jake?* he had asked. *Is that you inside me? Are you talking to me?*

After midnight, he had fled Angel and Charlie's apartment and gotten into his car, succumbing to the irresistible pull that dragged him under the Midtown Tunnel and out along the expressway into the hinterlands of Long Island.

* * *

The front door of the house opened inward; then the screen door swung out. A little girl appeared.

Elsa.

Roy had learned this from his research. Five years old, with her red hair done up in pigtails, and a tiny yellow Minions backpack on. A woman came through the door behind her. Five-four, flowing red hair. She knelt and kissed her daughter.

Hope Hawkins.

Tears blurring Roy's vision. *Why did you do it, Jake? Why would you leave them?*

He had read the news story over and over.

A single gunshot through the head. Self-inflicted.

An orange school bus huffed to a stop, and Hope walked her little girl over to it. Both of them were hidden for a few seconds until the bus lurched forward. Roy waited for the woman to go back inside the house before starting his car.

He pulled forward through the mud and potholes and onto the pavement, following the bus at a distance. He put another cigarette into his mouth and champed at the filter. The bus angled into the driveway of a single-story building—Calverton Elementary. Roy waited to see the little yellow backpack appear, the girl's head down.

Not talking to any of her classmates.

He fought the urge to drive up and tell them he was her father.

But then what?

* * *

"Just coffee?" the woman asked.

Her red hair was pulled back. Pink lipstick matched her pale skin. Freckles were sprinkled over cheeks still ruddy from the chill outside. "No breakfast? We got a two-egg special."

"No, that's it," Roy said. "Thanks, Hope."

Her eyes narrowed, but her professional smile remained, her cheeks flushing a little. Maybe Roy stared a little too hard? It was difficult not to. He averted his eyes. Still, a gorgeous woman like that had to be used to men staring at her.

She glanced down at her name tag and relaxed. Of course he would know her name.

"A little early in the season for a scarf?" Hope asked as she poured Roy a cup.

"I got chills."

That was true.

Under the table, his knee bobbed up and down like a sewing machine.

Should he just tell her? Tell her that he had—what, exactly? Stolen? Grave-robbed? *Borrowed?*—her dead husband's body? But was he even right? The edges of the room seemed to warp, his vision blurring. *Not now. Please, please, please, not now.* If he blacked out, there was no telling what would happen, what disaster he would have to wake up to.

What was he capable of?

He had no idea.

Hope asked, "You from around here?"

"Just passing through."

"Oh, yeah, from where?" Still the cordial professional smile.

He hesitated. "New York. On my way out to Montauk."

"Not the greatest beach weather."

"No. No, it isn't."

He thanked her for the coffee.

She lingered an extra moment, as if she wanted to say something else, but then turned and left. A quick glance at Roy again before she went into the kitchen.

He had followed her yesterday morning to Tom's, a greasy spoon at the edge of the bluffs over the Peconic River on Highway 25, halfway between the Tanger Outlets and Riverhead. It was an old-style diner with chromed-metal-and-Formica counters, checked linoleum floors, and booths lining windows with views over the river and the scrub brush of Barrens Park.

Bacon hissed and popped on the griddle, overlaying the warm-comfort smell of freshly brewed coffee. At eight in the morning, just three cars were in the parking lot, including Roy's beat-up Chevy. Two more cars pulled in, and Hope brought coffee to the new patrons.

She slipped past Roy on her way back behind the counter, holding up the carafe—*more?*

He shook his head.

He left ten dollars for the coffee without waiting for the check.

* * *

"*Damn it.*"

Roy was soaked to the waist from wading through the wet grass, his hair sopping wet from the rain that streamed into his eyes.

Even through the pins-and-needles numbness, his hands and feet ached from the cold. He balanced on a mound of red bricks at the back of the house, straining to shove open the kitchen window. He had checked from a distance—no lights on. Nobody home. The girl would be at school till at least three, and Hope had picked her up from after school at five yesterday.

Groaning, he strained again.

Everything was locked.

What did he want?

He wasn't sure.

A hint of an explanation of why Jake had killed himself, for one. Something more than what Angel was able to scour from the internet. He couldn't send the man here. He didn't even want Angel to know he was here. He didn't want *anyone* else to know. This was his private mission. He needed to know more.

Break a window?

Not yet.

The house was locked down tight. Who locked houses like that out here? Wasn't this the countryside? Wasn't that the reason people moved out of the city? To leave doors open, keys in the car, trust your neighbor, and all that?

Roy circled the house again, shivering for real now.

He crouched in the grass when a car hissed by in the rain. He looked through the window of the double garage. A wall of tools gathering dust. A vehicle inside—could be an old Mustang. In the gloom he saw something else: stairs against the back wall.

He glanced up, blinking in the rain.

There was an upstairs to the garage. It would be warmer in there, at least. He tried the door to the side. Locked. Grabbing the handle, he put his shoulder into it.

The old wood frame cracked.

That can be fixed, a voice said in Roy's head. Nobody would know. *Nobody ever comes in here, anyway. The place is a wreck.*

He closed the door and paused for a few seconds to blow on his hands and stamp his feet. He circled the Mustang, ran his hand over it—*smooth*, the curves like echoes of a dream in the dim light. The smell of the engine grease, sawdust, dark patches of oil on the concrete slab—it all felt achingly familiar.

Roy took the stairs up to the attic and clicked on the light.

Two rows of fluorescent tubes popped and then clicked on. A heavy bag hung from the rafters at the end. A few pictures of Jake with Hope. One of him holding his little girl, Elsa. More pictures of other MMA fighters on the walls, many of them signed. A few pictures of Jake holding a tactical knife, dressed in camouflage in the woods. A weight bench and a heavy set of irons. Everything coated in a layer of fine dust.

A desk by the window looked out the back.

Roy opened the top drawer.

Two old plane tickets, some keys, stacks of receipts and business cards. He rifled through the side drawers. File folders stacked with bank records, what looked like contracts, old tax returns. He slung his backpack around, opened it, and pulled out the stacks of papers, emptied the contents of the top drawer into it.

"Put your hands up," said a voice. "Or I'll blow a hole clean through you."

Roy dropped the last handful of the contents of the drawer into his bag but kept his back to the voice.

"I'm not stupid. I saw your car across the road, two days in a row. Then when you pulled into Tom's today?" It was Hope, her voice quivering but angry. Solid. "You following my little girl? You goddamn sicko. Are you Lenny's people? I told them we got no money."

"It's not what you think."

How was he supposed to explain this? *Hey, I'm kinda your dead husband, so this stuff is sort of mine, in a way. Can we talk about this?*

He turned slowly, holding his left hand out, urging her to keep calm.

Hope still had her name tag on, the same clothes that she was wearing in the diner an hour ago. Her hands shook as she held a rifle, its barrel trained on Roy's chest at point-blank range.

Before Roy could say anything else, a strange keening noise, an animal wail, rose until it filled the attic room. It came from Hope. Her face creased up as the thin shriek rose into a scream.

30

Detective Devlin pulled up the collar of her wool peacoat against the wind howling up the cliff face. Ragged clouds dragged low and fast over the dull pewter surface of the Atlantic. It had snowed the night before, and patches of white remained in the northern lee of the gnarled pines leaning back from the prevailing wind.

She had to make this quick.

There were no cars in front of the house, and the lights were off, but the sprawling complex must have dozens of rooms, any of which might be occupied.

She had a prearranged excuse. Coleman had called in a fake report of a missing-person sighting, and that was enough to justify her encroaching on private property to do a check of the beach access. The excuse wouldn't do her much good if Harris got wind of it, though, and the Chegwiddens had to be some of the executive officer's favorite customers.

The puddles on the driveway had a thin plate of ice covering them, and she stepped carefully.

She had asked around about Captain Seamus Harris and learned that he took paid gigs to do private security for parties in the Hamptons. That explained why the East Hampton Police Department's second in command was at the Chegwiddens' that night, and why he was there to pull Roy from the car. But what wasn't he telling? What *really* happened that night?

"Security" was something of an overstatement for Harris's real function.

The Hampton crowd didn't want to be disturbed if a noise complaint came in, and they didn't want their guests getting searched for drugs. What better solution than to have the top cop from the local department sitting at the door? It wasn't exactly illegal, but she had a feeling Internal Affairs would look dimly on it.

Or maybe not.

She had been warned to leave Royce Lowell-Vandeweghe alone—friends and family, too. But then, why did the private investigator Roy had hired try to get back in touch with her? The car from the accident was never brought into the pound.

No forensic exam.

Even though Roy was as good as dead, the Chegwiddens' own contractor had dragged the wreck off first thing the next morning. Maybe the Chegwiddens were just obsessive about cleaning up their property. Maybe they were worried about a lawsuit. They were billionaires. Different rules applied, or people like that assumed they did.

Del wanted to get a look for herself.

She had parked her unmarked Crown Vic, a rust bucket ten years past its prime, two hundred yards up the gravel driveway, then walked in tentatively, pretending to check the bushes.

She checked the house again. No lights.

She had waited until the middle of the afternoon, but not for the temperature to warm up. She needed the sun's rays as direct as possible on the cliffs at the front of the house.

The new brickwork was obvious, the mortar clean and white, the stones pristine and lichen-free. She leaned over the edge. Thirty, maybe forty feet to the beach, but the new wall was built ten feet back from the drop-off. The rock had been scraped clean of auto paint, but she clearly saw the scratch marks where the car must have skidded past.

Straight off. No brakes, no turn skid marks.

"Hey, hey, hello?" called out a voice, the accent unmistakably British.

"*Damn*," Del muttered under her breath.

"Are you the police?" asked a man in a thick gray sweater and striped tie. He hung half in and half out the side door of the house.

"I should have rung the bell," she said. "I didn't think anyone was home."

"Well, well, so yes, you are the police?" the man asked again. He didn't look angry. If anything, he looked lost.

"I'm Suffolk County PD," Del said. "And you are …?"

"Charles Chegwidden. This is our property."

"As I said, I'm sorry for intruding, but—"

"I've already called you twice. Thank God you're here."

"Called *me* twice?"

"*Three* times—yes, three times, in fact, if I include last week."

"I think you've made a mistake."

"Mistake?" Charles asked. "But then, why are you here?"

"What's this about, sir?"

The man fidgeted with the door frame. "My wife, Primrose."

"Yes? What about her?"

"She's been missing for a week. Ever since a rejuvenation party thrown by Eden Corporation. In Hell."

31

Roy circled around Tompkins Park. Again.

The sun was still just below the horizon. Friday night had not quite given over to Saturday, but the eastern sky had faded from oil-slick black to gunmetal gray in anticipation.

In ones and twos, late-night stragglers appeared and disappeared between the cones of light cast under the streetlamps. Shapes materialized from the darkness. A huddled mass under a mound of blankets on a park bench. The jagged leafless branches of an oak tree overhead—the earth's nervous system reaching up from the cold dirt to feel its way into the shaded sky. Scrims of ice glazed the puddles in the tarmac path, trapping leaves beneath. The frigid air stung his nostrils on each deep breath.

He really had thought Hope was going to shoot him yesterday. He had almost wished she would, but as he held up one hand to her, she had crumpled, legs giving way, wailing like a trapped animal.

Had she been scared? Of course, but there was more to it than fear.

He had reached for her, but she shrank away, shaking, terrified of him.

So he ran, out the door and into his car.

And, as always, with the feeling that someone was watching.

He had driven for miles without thinking, just aware of the distance between himself and Hope. And Elsa.

The little house in Calverton had become the sun at the center of his universe, its gravity tugging at him. Even now, in Tompkins Park, he could feel its pull.

Before he realized it yesterday, he had driven clear out to Montauk, whereupon he turned around and circled back through East Hampton, resisting the urge to drive north. He drove past his house. Past his mother's house.

He had almost stopped in at Sam's house in Southampton. He had wanted to empty the contents of his backpack with his friend and sift through it, but his gut told him it wasn't safe.

He couldn't involve Sam. Couldn't put the people he cared about at risk.

He stuffed his hands deep into his jean pockets and took a side street away from the park, then another. He crossed back and forth, huffing clouds of white vapor with each breath. At the corner of Second Street and Avenue B, a red-orange neon star colored the gray morning. The Never Inn. Still no vacancy.

Was someone following him?

Maybe, but one thing was for sure: someone knew where he was.

The implants in his temples, against his skull, measuring his brainwaves. The implants in his legs and arms. Dr. Danesti knew where he was at all times. They were tracking him. Worse, were the implants affecting him in some way? Were they doing things to him?

* * *

"Come on, Jake," Roy said aloud. "What have we got?"

He had finally returned to his tiny basement apartment on Eleventh and Avenue C. He waited in the cold to make sure the landlady was still asleep upstairs before his stiff fingers fumbled with the keys. He pulled the drapes, then dragged a coffee table in front of the door and barricaded himself in before turning on the lights.

Then he emptied the backpack onto the bed. The stuff he'd stolen from Jake Hawkins's desk. Much of it was envelopes stuffed with crumpled paper. On closer inspection, they were just receipts. Phoenix, Arizona. Austin, Texas. Burgers. Taxis. A record of trips and travels.

"What else?"

A chain with a dozen keys, all different sizes—probably for the house and garage. Then a few separate keys. One looked as if it was for a safe-deposit box. Another had an orange plastic sleeve.

Three more keys, on another chain, looked similar to some of those on the first. He inspected each, tried to dredge up some feeling. What did his gut say? He smelled them, held them one by one against his cheek. Nothing registered.

A stack of bank records going back six years.

"Did you need money, Jake? Was that what made you do it?"

It's always *about the money,* a voice in Roy's head answered.

Was there some insurance claim? Did life insurance even cover suicide? He doubted it could. That wouldn't make sense.

And then another thought. Did Jake sell his body?

He had heard of people in India selling a kidney.

Angel had told him about it. One of the small towns where Eden had an office—"Kidneyville," they called it in one depressing documentary. Had Jake sold his body to Danesti? Was that possible? The doctor was on the board of the OPTN. Danesti had said how critical this operation was, to demonstrate further success on the heels of the Shelby Sheffield operation.

Roy leafed through the bank records. Jake Hawkins hadn't been rich by any stretch, but he had managed to save some money as well as pay down most of the mortgage on the small house.

I wasn't desperate, said a voice in Roy's head.

"Is that you talking to me, Jake? Show me. What else?"

He had read the stories of chronic traumatic encephalopathy. Had Jake suffered one too many left hooks to the head? But the regular stream of income, the carefully stored receipts right up until he died. He didn't look nuts.

In the pictures Roy saw, Jake still had a full head of hair. He didn't have the massive bulging muscles of a steroid junkie. He seemed organized, squared away. What could have made him want to blow a hole in his head?

There was a key for a safe-deposit box. But for which bank? Maybe he could get into that. He had Jake's passport, and it was still valid—at least, unless Hope had canceled it. He had looked it up. Dying didn't automatically terminate a passport. A relative had to cancel it. But had she? Would the bank teller even bother to check? He'd read about old voter rolls, how the government kept dead people on them for years. He leafed through the receipts. Boxing gloves, payments to Self Store. A computer from Best Buy.

Self Store. That wasn't a retail shop; it was a self-storage company. They had signs all over New York.

He glanced at the pile of keys. The orange one.

The receipt had an address.

* * *

"I just don't remember the number," Roy said to the kid behind the counter. "I have the key, though."

"Gimme the receipt again? Name's Jake Hawkins, right?"

The kid held out his hand.

He had blond hair combed straight back, and the eyes of a stoner in dire need of Visine. The kid seemed annoyed or impatient, or just high. Roy had interrupted whatever game he'd been intently playing on his phone.

The Self Store front office was twenty feet square, with a huge orange logo taking up one wall, stacks of packing boxes and tape for sale on another, and two plastic chairs in front of the counter. The entrance door was set in a wall of safety glass crisscrossed with embedded wire. The place was ringed by a twenty-foot chain link fence topped with razor wire—not exactly Fort Knox, but you'd need a good reason to want in.

The location was right on Middle Country Road, just past Brookhaven and not far from Calverton. On one of his first blackouts, Roy had woken up in his Range Rover not a hundred yards from this place. It couldn't be coincidence.

The kid studied the receipt, tapped a few strokes on the keyboard. "Yeah, I got you here." He sucked air in through his teeth. "I'll need some ID, too."

"Passport okay?"

"Sure," he replied, eyes still on the screen in front of him.

Roy bet he was from the rural end of Long Island. He might not even have *seen* a passport before.

Roy had his wool hat pulled low. He adjusted his sunglasses, the scarf still wrapped tight around his neck. Not unusual attire for the middle of December, but still, this kid could be a problem. Roy held out the passport, his thumb half over the photo. He and Jake might look similar from a distance, but there was no way Roy looked in his midtwenties.

The kid didn't even look up. "You're locker sixty-four," he said. "One of our biggest."

Roy put the passport away. "Thanks." He turned to open the door out.

"Hey, man, you owe six months' rent on that unit," the kid called out as Roy walked away. "It was scheduled to go up for auction."

* * *

It wasn't one of the outdoor lockers. Roy took the cargo elevator to the second floor of the main building. Indoor. Climate controlled. Polished concrete floors, exposed steel joists and corrugated metal ceiling. The air was stale, smelling faintly of mothballs.

The main corridor was lit, but the access corridors off it were dark. The place was deserted, creepy, even at 9 a.m. He found the sign for his locker grouping, clicked on the light timer at the start of the corridor, and walked down to number sixty-four.

After unlocking the unit, he put the lock and key in his pocket and rolled up the metal door. He felt around for the light cord and pulled it, and a single incandescent bulb lit up. Exposed aluminum studs held up exterior drywall along the left side, the wall unfinished on this side. Cheap. The enclosed space smelled of fresh rubber, like new tires. At the back, cardboard boxes were stacked almost to the ceiling. A pile of tents and camping gear and fishing rods lay near the front. It was a big unit—twenty feet square.

Roy got to work.

Boxes full of Christmas lights. Others filled with books on nutrition, running, and weightlifting. A box of obsolete electronics, old cordless phones, wires. A washer and dryer covered with a tarp, an old dog crate. Going through the camping equipment, he found a switchblade knife and three years' worth of *Penthouse* and *Playboy* magazines.

This was a waste of time, he realized.

His stomach was knotted, but maybe he was just hungry. It occurred to him that he hadn't eaten an actual meal in two days.

There was nothing of interest in here.

He rolled the door back down and locked it, then walked down the hallway to the elevator, keeping his eyes on his feet the whole way. Maybe he should find the safe-deposit box. There had to be something in there, though he doubted the passport trick would pass muster at a bank.

He had to call Angel.

Roy strode down the hallway to the elevator, counting the linoleum tiles underfoot—an old habit. Still looking down, he stopped at the elevator, just at the entrance to the next corridor.

He turned and took twelve measured strides back up the hallway, back to Jake's storage locker. He opened it and took measured strides toward the back. He made only five, but it was twelve strides corridor-to-corridor outside. Maybe the other side had deeper lockers. But no, the kid said Jake had one of their biggest ones.

He inspected the back wall.

The same unfinished drywall, but no exposed aluminum studs this side. Was it just better finished in the back? He tapped the wall in several places. It sounded hollow, but then, it should. Each four-by-eight sheet had screws along its edges. One didn't.

He pushed the boxes away from the wall, then grabbed the knife from the camping gear. Fitting the blade into the joint between the unfastened drywall sheet and the adjoining sheet, he worked up and down the joint until he had opened a half-inch gap—enough to get his fingers around the end of the sheet.

The drywall board shuddered against the floor but slid open another three feet. There was no lighting behind the wall—only the illumination from the single bulb at the front of the unit. Metal shelving ran from just behind the drywall, to the next unit, three feet behind the false wall.

The shelves were stacked with jars. Preserves or home-canned vegetables? On the shelf below the jars were piles of clothing. Everything had a light covering of dust.

Except for one corner.

One of the jars seemed to be a more recent arrival, the dust just disturbed, the glass still clean.

Roy got his phone out and clicked on the flashlight.

The jars were filled with a translucent tea-colored liquid, and each had something in the bottom. Roy leaned closer to get a better look at the one in front of him. He turned the jar, and the blob inside spun lazily around. It was an eye.

The cornea was opaque, but there was no mistaking it. Bits of gray flesh stuck around the edges, and the ragged end of an optic nerve trailed from the back.

The hair at the back of Roy's neck prickled.

He looked at the next jar. In the bottom lay a human finger, right up to the third knuckle. And below this was the clean new jar. The liquid was clear. At the bottom lay an ear, still red and ragged where it had been cut off.

Roy staggered backward and fell on his backside in the pile of camping gear.

32

With a shaking finger, Roy punched in the number. One ... six ... four ...

Damn it. He pushed the off button. He had already tried twice, but his hand shook too much to key the numbers. *Deep breaths.*

He sat on the edge of bed in his basement apartment on Avenue C, surrounded by the bank statements and receipts from Jake's house. He barely remembered leaving the Self Store, though he did remember going back upstairs twice to make sure the unit was locked.

He paid the kid at the desk whatever was owed, plus a year in advance. At two hundred bucks a month, that was almost four grand from his dwindling supply of cash. The kid had watched, wide-eyed, as Roy peeled off the bills. He told him to keep the change from the last hundred.

The drive back into the city was a blur of constantly looking up through the windshield for helicopters and waiting for police lights behind him. And always the feeling that someone was close, just out of sight.

What was Jake doing with a locker full of human body parts? *Only thing possible,* said a voice inside. *You know what it is.*

"But that's *not* possible," Roy muttered, answering the voice.

He had ditched his cell phone on the drive in—threw it onto the shoulder of the highway and picked up a new one at a CVS. The first thing he did was call Sam to ask for the Chegwiddens' number. Sam protested, saying they needed to talk, but coughed up the number anyway.

Roy asked whether Sam had heard any news of their neighbor, the one who hated cats, who Penny had said went missing a few months back.

Sam hesitated but said that no, it was still a missing-persons case. The whole neighborhood was talking about it. Roy hung up halfway through Sam imploring him to come over because there was something else they needed to talk about.

Should he have emptied the storage locker? But, how would he? Just cart out a dozen jars of human remains on a trolley, past all the security cameras?

Anyway, *why* would he? It was Jake's locker, not his.

Whatever it all meant, it wasn't Roy's fault. He should just call the police. Call that Detective Devlin at Suffolk County PD.

Except …

That jar with the ear. A segmented golden fish earring lay in front of him on the bed. Roy had pulled it out of his backpack. Was it Primrose's? Was it possible? He had blacked out for more than two days after the vampiric rejuvenation party at Hell. He remembered being disgusted by Primrose. He had never really liked her—despised her, if he was being honest.

It would answer the mystery of why Jake killed himself. The man was trying to protect Hope and Elsa from himself.

Roy squeezed his hands together to stop the shaking. He tried the number again.

Six … three … three …

The line began ringing. "Hello?" said a British voice.

"Charles, it's me, Roy."

"Ah, my god, Roy, it's good to hear from you." Charles paused. "The news isn't good, I'm afraid."

Roy had been about to ask to speak to Primrose. "About what?"

"Yes, yes, she's gone, just gone."

"Primrose? Since when?" Roy felt the bottom falling out of his perception, as if the ground were opening up to swallow him.

"One of those blasted rejuvenation parties that Eden holds. The police haven't been able to find anything."

Roy paused a beat and then asked, "What police?"

"Ms. Devlin, that wonderful detective woman. She was here just yesterday, and Captain Harris was over as well. Nobody can find my dear Prim. I'm just beside myself with worry."

* * *

Music blared out through the half-open entrance. Roy had knocked twice and got no answer, so he pushed the massive black wooden door in. The leaves of the spider plants hanging from the rafters ruffled in the breeze over his head. He had phoned earlier, said he needed to speak with Angel in person. It was late, past midnight.

"*These are a few of my fa … vo … rite things,*" sang a hulk of a man in an olive-drab T-shirt and ripped jeans. His sloping shoulders came almost up to his ears, the muscles bulging as he raised his arms wide. His jaw was wider than his temples, and thick cauliflower ears stuck out from a close-shaved head.

Behind him, Julie Andrews sat in bed with two children to each side of her, a thick blanket pulled up to their chins. Lightning flashed on the TV screen.

The big man saw Roy and smiled but just kept singing. "*Girls in white dresses with blue satin sashes …*"

"*And Blackhawks and M-Sixty fragging grenaders,*" Angel sang, joining in the next verse. He stood to put his arm around the hulk's waist. The man was at least a foot taller than his Puerto Rican chum. Angel gave Roy a sheepish grin and waved him over. He waggled his beer bottle in the air, did Roy want one?

The Sound of Music played on the big wall screen to one side of the apartment. Charlie was on one of the couches, waving his arms to conduct the sing-along. Another man, almost as big as the massive one and with the same battle-tested look, sat man-spread on the other couch. Empty bottles littered the table between them.

"Come in," Angel called out as Roy held back. "We're celebrating."

"Maybe I should come back."

Angel let go of his big friend and covered half the distance to Roy. The other men kept singing along with Julie Andrews, giggling at their improvised lyrics as they danced and mimed the characters on the screen.

"What was so important?" Angel asked.

"What are you celebrating?"

"Our adoption papers are finalized."

"Oh, right. Congratulations again."

"Tomorrow we're picking up little Rodrigo. He just turned five." Angel was wobbly. He put an arm around Roy's shoulders. "Guys, guys, this is Roy, my friend I'm doing some work for." He pointed at the hulk. "This is Alpha"—he moved his finger to the other man—"and this is Dog."

"Fellow SEALs?" Roy asked.

"You know it. They just rotated back into the world. Came by for a few drinks."

Roy mumbled hello, and the men nodded back in greeting. "And are they, uh …," he said to Angel under his breath.

Angel frowned but then laughed big, throwing his head back. "Gay? Now you think *all* SEALs are gay? No, man, these are just my brothers from other mothers. Both straight as a gun barrel, sad as that is."

Alpha and Dog wore amiable grins. Dog had the remote in his hand and fast-forwarded the movie.

"Do you have somewhere we can talk privately?" Roy whispered.

Angel leaned back and sized him up. "Come into my bedroom."

He walked past the couches and into the back room, stopping to grab some papers from the kitchen table. The bedroom was spacious, with white walls and a king-size bed covered in a cream comforter. A gray couch stood against the left wall. Candles burned on the bedside tables, filling the air with the scent of lavender. A single painting hung on the wall—a stylized image of the phoenix with flaming yellow wings, rising from the ashes.

"I think I'm attached to the body of a killer," Roy blurted out as soon as Angel closed the door.

Angel wagged his head to one side. "No kidding. That Jake Hawkins was an animal. Saw some videos of him taking people apart in the octagon. That fight in Hartford, man—"

"No. I mean, he *really killed* people. Not just in the ring."

"Come again?"

"He was a murderer."

"And you know this how?"

Roy was about to tell him about the storage locker, but he felt a weight in the pit of his stomach. His gut, telling him no.

Angel's face brightened. "Ah, I get it. You went and talked to his lady. Hope Hawkins. She's beautiful, from what I saw in the pictures. She said he killed people? I don't know, man. Talking to her wasn't a good idea. No telling what she might say."

"You know I talked to her?"

"I got that tail on you. You asked for it, remember? My boy Romero. He's been following you, but he hasn't seen any other tails. You're clean, man. He's good at this."

"And he followed me all the way out to the Hawkins place?"

"He stopped following you in the Midtown Tunnel. I told him to stop. The way you were heading out there? In a hurry, in the middle of the night? I figured where you were going and thought it better that Romero *not* follow you."

"Don't tell Charlie, okay? I'm dangerous, Angel. This thing—"

"Being a dangerous man can be a good thing. I know whereof I speak." Angel was really drunk. His eyes skittered from one side to the other.

"Let's cancel your investigation," Roy said. "Can we do that?"

From behind the door, the muted singing of Julie Andrews bidding so long and farewell and auf Wiedersehen.

Angel said, "But we're not done yet. I'm talking to this doctor, at the hospital where you were born—"

"You don't need to do that."

"I don't like to leave jobs half finished."

"This is for your own safety."

"*My* own safety?" Angel's eyes leered comically. "From who?"

"From me."

He snickered. "I'd like to see you try." He put his arm around Roy again.

"I'm being serious."

"Me, too," Angel said. "I'm the one worried about *you*." He jabbed Roy in the chest.

Roy had been trying to be nice. He had come here to end things, to protect Angel, to call this off, but the guy was drunk, hanging off him, his face right in Roy's. That new-but-now-familiar cresting wave of anger boiled up. *Get this guy off me.*

"I told you nice. I'm canceling the investigation." He shrugged Angel's arm off. "And get that tail off me permanently. Your Romero guy—get him to stop following me."

"I took your money, my friend, and I'm going to help you. No matter what. I leave nobody behind."

This guy just didn't know when to quit. Roy remained silent.

The idiotic tunes of *The Sound of Music* blared beyond the bedroom door. They stared at each other. Roy glaring, Angel puzzled-drunk.

"I'm worried about you," the detective repeated.

"Worry about someone else."

"That dog, your girl Leila?"

"What about her?" Roy's frustration vanished. "Did you find out something?"

Angel took the papers from his hip pocket—the ones he had grabbed from the kitchen table. "She died five years ago." He gave the papers to Roy. "From the East Hampton vet. Charlie got them."

"Five years ...?" Roy took the papers. They were for the cremation of an animal. "Leila," it said at the top. The signature at the bottom. Roy's. Unmistakable. "I don't understand. I remember she was alive before the accident."

"Yeah, three *years* before. Did you have another dog?"

The painting of the phoenix on the wall seemed to flutter, the flames warping. The room tilted on its axis. *No. No. Not now.*

Roy clutched the papers. "I need to go."

He pushed past Angel, past the SEALs still singing along with Julie Andrews, his mind flowing out ahead of him, down the stairs and out into the frigid air.

33

"Yeah, that's it," Del said. She pointed at the second and third video feeds. "Try that."

They flipped through archived footage from cameras positioned at Ninth and Fourteenth, and Tenth and Hudson. In the fast-forward view, the late-night crowds of the Meatpacking District scurried about like ants. These weren't like the old security cameras with grainy black-and-white images. These were high-definition, in vivid color. The NYPD applied all kinds of algorithms to them to find people—facial recognition, gait recognition, and more.

"Gotta get this done before the other guys get back from lunch," Officer Esposito said. "You got that thing for me?"

Officer Coleman, Del's partner, slipped an envelope from his sport jacket to Esposito, who slipped it into his desk drawer without taking his eyes off the video feeds. Coleman said, "Good to see you."

"Yeah, man. Been a while," Esposito said. "And good to see you, too, Del. Say hi to your dad for me."

"And good thing *your* dad has fifty-yard-line season tickets to the Giants," Del whispered to Coleman. To Esposito, she said, "Go back to the feed on Ninth. I think that has the best view. And rewind to eight p.m."

The images on the three monitors in front of them switched up and scrambled into reverse.

"I'm still not sure this is a good idea," Coleman whispered to his partner.

Del's eyes remained on the screens. She said, "You want to make an omelet …"

"We're not breaking *eggs*. These are laws."

"'Bending' would be a better description."

"Alonzo's going to 'bend' our legs if we get found out."

"So don't get found out," Del replied. "You want to be a detective? You gotta *detect*."

From the sixth floor of One Police Plaza, the *new* New York Police Department headquarters, there was a view of the trees of City Hall Park, just at the foot of the Brooklyn Bridge. Beyond the park stood the neo-Gothic magnificence of the Woolworth Tower, its green copper crown framed by the glass-walled Freedom Tower behind it.

LCT Capital was in the Woolworth Tower, Del remembered. Maybe she would pay a visit over there and talk to Atticus Cargill. Find out about Roy's trust fund from the administrator himself.

Or maybe she wouldn't. That would set off Captain Harris's alarm bells and land her in hot water with her boss, Alonzo.

Coleman had gotten them into the NYPD's SOC—the Security and Operations Center. They had to go through two sets of double doors and be photographed twice to get in, but Del and Coleman had credentials. And Coleman's buddy Francis Esposito was the tech nerd who, in addition to loving the Giants, managed the physical infrastructure side of the SOC.

It didn't hurt that Esposito knew Del's father, too.

It was here that the NYPD integrated all the incoming cyber threats, alarms, and physical threats—the new real-time crime-fighting center, where they merged all the credible threats into a single stream of information to disseminate back to the cops on the street. New York's Finest in the twenty-first century.

The SOC wasn't quite as exciting as it had sounded on the drive over.

Del had imagined an evil-genius-style control center with wall screens tracking orbital assets. After passing security, Del had been ushered into a city-block-size open room of gray cubicles. It smelled of new carpet, old pizza, and body odor.

"Stop there," she said to Esposito. "Put the cameras from Ninth and Tenth on these two monitors and roll forward at triple speed."

Esposito checked his watch. "That'll only get you to ten at night. I gotta turf you out at one."

"You want to keep those tickets?"

"One-fifteen, and I'll roll at five times speed. I'm telling you, it'll pick up."

They had fed several of Primrose's pictures into the facial recognition system. Del wanted to see the woman entering the bar.

"Okay, do it," Del said.

Two days ago, when she met Charles Chegwidden at the house in Montauk, she was forced to call in to the East Hampton Police Department to check on the missing-persons report. This had ignited a firestorm. Captain Harris had shown up within half an hour, his face redder than his hair. Del had feigned surprise, saying she was just chasing down a missing-person sighting that was called in.

Harris didn't believe her, of course.

He said they knew that Primrose had been called in as missing but that she often went off-grid for a few days when her show was in the off-season.

Del found out later that Charles had a bit of a sad reputation as the cuckolded husband. He called in several times a year to report her missing, when his wife was just out enjoying herself—with other men—in the city. They started to ignore his calls after a while.

This was different. Ten days missing already. Despite all the attempts to track her down, no one could find her.

A missing billionaire TV celebrity wasn't going to escape the media for much longer. Her last known stop was at the bar Heaven, in Meatpacking, or, more accurately, at Hell, in the basement of Heaven.

Eden ran an out-patient rejuvenation center there, Del had discovered, but there was no way any video footage of inside the bar or from Eden's own systems was going to get into the public eye. Harris had petitioned the commissioner to make sure it stayed under tight security, and Del and Coleman weren't invited to the party.

The public system of outdoor cameras the NYPD maintained was another matter, however—as long as they didn't get found out.

Why was she risking it?

It was something the private eye, Angel Rodriguez, had said. *Someone was killed.* Whoever Roy was attached to was dead.

There was a body.

The links to Eden and Primrose were too much of a coincidence. The missing hiker reported on Roy's street—that was another dead body. And now his neighbor was also missing. She wasn't ready to bring it to her boss yet. She needed more.

She had tried the cell phone that Roy called her from before, but it was disconnected. She tried his friend Sam, whose private number she had, but he didn't answer. It was too risky to Del's career to try calling Roy's wife or his mother, the socialite-queen of the Hamptons. She tried calling back Angel, Roy's private eye, but got only an answering machine.

Roy's case had become an itch that Del couldn't quite scratch, and that drove her nuts.

"And the download of all Royce Lowell-Vandeweghe's facial-recognition hits?" Del asked Esposito. "How long?"

That was the real reason they had come. She knew that Roy was in Manhattan. If she couldn't go to Eden Corporation to find out his location, she still wanted to know where he was and what he was doing. This may be another way to find out.

"It'll be a raw dump of all the hits," Esposito said. "I put the filter wide, just like you asked, but you'll be getting thousands of false positives you'll have to sift through manually. It'll be done in a few minutes."

The time stamp on the video feed scrolled through 10:00 p.m., then 11:00. It froze and then began stepping forward a few frames at a time.

"There she is." Esposito pointed at a red square highlighting a woman's face.

It was Primrose Chegwidden, no doubt about it, walking down Ninth Avenue to Heaven.

"Do you think you can find out who those people are?" Del pointed at the half-dozen oldsters following in Primrose's wake.

"You want me to ID citizens?" Esposito said. "Tracking down a perp or two from photos, that's one thing. Doing a database search—that's a whole—"

"Set of playoff tickets?" Del said suggestively.

Coleman groaned.

"I'll see what I can do," Esposito said.

The image on the screen froze again. This time, not just one red square highlighting a face, but a green one, too, on a different face.

"Jesus Christ," Del muttered under her breath. "Zoom that in."

The two faces ballooned in size.

It was Roy, talking to Primrose. Her golden-fish earrings waggled and sparkled even in the dim light. Roy followed her into the bar.

"Can you add that video stream to my download?" Del asked Esposito.

"Sure thing."

"And double-check that we get all the facial recognition hits on that guy." She pointed at Roy. "I want to know *everywhere* he went."

"That guy?" Esposito squinted at the image. He zoomed in so Roy's face took up the whole screen. "That's your head-transplant guy? I read all about him in my technical journals."

Del said, "One more thing."

In the picture on-screen, she pointed at a Latino-looking guy with a mullet and a mustache, his shirt unbuttoned almost to his navel despite the freezing weather.

"Find out who that joker is."

34

"Hello? Sam? That you?" Roy said into the phone.

He was alone in the dark in his dingy apartment, with the heating off.

The cold brought with it pain, so he at least had some sensation from this bastard body. He sat naked and cross-legged on the stained mattress of the bed. Two fingers held the pull cord of the lamp on the nightstand.

Every few minutes, he would click the light on and stare at his pale reflection in the mirror of the vanity he had ripped from the bathroom wall and propped up on a chair in front of him. He would stare back into his own eyes, wondering what was lurking in the depths.

Who was in there?

What was in there?

He would stare at the red scar ringing his neck and fantasize about digging his fingers into the edges of it, ripping the skin apart in a gush of blood. Separating himself to become one again, not two.

Then he would click the light off, and the room would go dark again.

And the sensation returned. That he wasn't alone.

The body had two brains; that was what Dr. Brixton had told him.

Is that you in here with me, Jake?

Stop talking to yourself, a voice answered. *Focus. Get a grip.*

His dog had died a full three years before the accident, but hadn't he spoken to Penny about it? Or Sam? Even his mother? Was that why she was so upset when he brought it up? Because it made no sense? What else didn't make sense?

It didn't matter.

He could just sit here and wait for it to end. Stop taking his antirejection drugs, and his head would explode. Or rot. That was what he'd heard would happen. His brain would decay from the inside out while his eyes and tongue bloated.

That was all he had to do to end this pain.

"Hello?" a tiny voice said in the darkness.

He'd forgotten he had just answered the phone. He clicked the light on and lifted the phone to his left ear.

"Sam?" he replied.

Only Sam had this number, unless it was a telemarketer. Now, *that* would be icing on the cake. Maybe he could invite them over. Show them just what he thought of telemarketers. Add another prize to his collection.

Roy asked, "Who is this?"

"Hope."

* * *

It took Roy's mind a few seconds to process. It felt like days. Weeks.

He became aware that he was sitting completely naked and staring at himself. He clicked the light off to hide in the darkness.

"Who?" he said into the phone.

"Hope Hawkins," said the all-too-familiar voice.

Even now he felt the pull—even in the darkness, that tug toward the center of a universe he could never be a part of. Was he hallucinating? Was this real? How could it be possible? He hadn't left anything at the house. She didn't know who he was. She didn't even know who her husband had donated his organs to, if she even knew that he'd been a donor. And she certainly didn't have Roy's phone number.

He remained silent.

"Roy, are you there?" Hope said.

"You've got the wrong number."

"Please, don't hang up," her voice pleaded, on the edge of tears.

In the silence, a battle of Titans raged inside Roy. His thumb hovered over the button to end the call, but instead he said: "How did you get this number?"

"I called your house. Your wife gave me your friend Samuel Phipps's number, said if anyone could reach you, it would be him."

"But how ... how did you know?"

"Those hands ..." She started weeping but managed to contain it. "I would recognize Jake's hands anywhere."

He remembered her staring at his hand as he held it up to her in the garage to try to keep her back.

"He was the sweetest man." Hope's voice trembled as the words tumbled out. "When we got married, he said that if anything ever happened to him, to donate his organs. He was firm about that, about helping someone else. That's who he was. When I saw you—saw Jake's *hands*—I thought I was seeing things. But I went online, saw that they did hand transplants, and then I read the stories about whole bodies. I saw your picture. I saw your *face*."

After a pause, Roy said quietly, "I shouldn't have ..."

But what could he say? That he was sorry? He was sorrier than the world had words to express.

"You wanted to know about Jake," Hope said. "I can understand that."

"That's right."

"Then I'll tell you everything. Where are you?"

* * *

Roy ran around the apartment like a teenager who had just asked his prom date over. He put sheets back on the bed, tried to arrange the comforter on top with some pillows that weren't stained. Tried to stick the vanity that he'd ripped out of the wall back in place, but had to settle for pinning a towel over the gaping hole.

At least clean the toilet. That he could do.

And take a shower.

No clean clothes, but he put on deodorant and turned the boxers he had on inside out. Gross, but at least they felt clean. Swept what dirt and dead flies he could under the couch.

She was leaving Elsa with a babysitter, she said. She'd be there in less than an hour. The whole time, thoughts raced through his head.

Did she know that her husband was a killer? Not just in the ring, but a *serial* killer? A murderer with a collection of body parts just a few streets down from their house?

How could she know?

Serial killers were secretive, Roy had read online. Sociopaths. They often hid in the open with a wife and family, just like Jake. Blended in by appearing normal. They were often extremely intelligent and charming.

But what if she did know?

Had he just uncovered their stash? Was she on her way here to silence him? The thought of Hope killing him felt comforting, somehow. He looked into the mirror and combed back his hair, stared into his own eyes.

His thoughts turned even darker.

What if she was coming over here to reunite with her dead husband? To conjure Jake up from his body to take over Roy's mind? For the two of them to embark on another killing rampage?

Roy shook his head.

That's insane, said a voice in his head. *She doesn't know. Don't get stupid.* And then …

What if it wasn't safe for her to come here? What if Jake had killed himself to protect her from himself? Was Roy now leading her back into the lion's den? What if he blacked out again?

A rap at the door.

Roy stopped combing his hair. He'd been raking it for half an hour, trying to cover the protrusions of the sensors embedded in his scalp. He pulled his scarf tight around his neck and went to unlock the door.

All his questions collapsed in on themselves.

There stood Hope, trembling under the streetlight, her mascara and eyeliner smudged and streaked down her cheeks from the tears. She still had on the name tag from the diner. Her red hair was matted. But she was the most beautiful thing Roy had ever seen.

"Come in," he said simply. There was no way any of this would be easy.

She hesitated, so he stepped back to give her space. After reaching the bottom of the stairs, she stopped. With his eyes, he indicated the couch and that he would sit on a chair beside it. He filled an old kettle and turned on a burner on the stove before sitting down.

"Did you get my letters?" he asked. "From the Organ Procurement Network?"

Her head quivered up and down, her lips tight together. "And you didn't want to answer them?" He knew they were anonymous and that she couldn't have known it was a full-body transplant.

"I couldn't. It was too painful."

And now Roy had just shoved himself into the open wound. "I'm sorry."

"It's okay." Hope's voice gained some volume. "Jake would have wanted me to know you."

He would bet that wasn't true. "Did you and Jake ever come to New York?"

"You mean around here? He loved the East Village. I wasn't surprised when you said that's where you were."

A creeping tingle in Roy's scalp. "And the Never Inn? Did you go there together?"

The forced smile on her face faltered. She shook her head. "I don't know it."

"The *Never* Inn?"

Her shoulders scrunched. *Sorry*, they seemed to say, *never heard of it.* Clutching her purse tight, she said, "He was the sweetest man."

Should he tell her that her husband was a psychopath? His stomach clenched at the thought. *Is that you, Jake? What do you want me to tell her? Tell her you kept eyeballs and fingers in glass jars so you could take them out at night and—*

"Can I touch your hand?" Hope asked.

"What …?" She was still like a wraith to him—a vision that could be seen but had no real substance.

She reached out and put her hand on Roy's. Her fingers were warm. Soft.

Without warning, she leaned forward and buried her face against Roy's forearm. He flinched but didn't resist. Didn't pull back. She got halfway to her feet and pushed her whole face into his chest, breathing deep.

The sobs began, her body convulsing with little weeping gasps.

She slumped back down into the couch and held one hand over her face. "Oh, God, you smell like him."

Roy didn't know what to say, so he said, "Would you like some tea? I put the kettle on." He got up, got out of there. *Too close, too close.* Waited with his back to her until she stopped weeping.

"He's gone, Hope," he said quietly.

"But you're here. Most of you *is* him."

"I think I know why he killed himself." His stomach flared again. Could he tell her? Should he?

"No, you don't," she said. She wasn't crying anymore.

Roy didn't say anything.

"You don't know," Hope said, "because Jake was murdered."

* * *

A shrieking whistle pierced the air.

"Roy?"

Steam shot out into roiling clouds of vapor that dissipated as fast as they formed.

"Roy, are you okay?" Hope said.

He blinked twice and, in slow motion, took the kettle off the stove. Time stutter-stepped forward and skipped a beat or two.

"How do you know Jake was murdered?" A dull throb blossomed between his temples.

"I just know. He loved"—her voice hitched—"he loved our daughter, Elsa. So, so, much. He would never leave us like that. He was the kindest, gentlest person I ever knew."

"But he was a fighter."

Roy had seen the same videos as Angel, of Jake Hawkins spattered with blood, beating the crap out of his opponents. There were things Jake's wife didn't know or couldn't understand. Not the way Roy knew him. *Felt* him.

"He had to make a living."

"There are other ways."

"What would you know?"

"Excuse me?"

"I read about your family. How would you know what it means to struggle?"

Roy's eyes were still focused on the steaming kettle. He turned to face Hope. She was on the couch, still clutching her purse, but the plaintive fear in her face was replaced with something more defiant.

"You're right. I have no right to judge," he said. "But my family came from pretty humble roots—and does this seem like a happy place I'm in? You think I'm not struggling?"

Her gaze dropped, but the edge of defiance remained. She was a fighter, too. "I … this is …," she stuttered.

"You need to go." A searing pain behind Roy's eyes. "You don't want to be part of this."

"I can stay. I want to help."

"You *need* to go."

* * *

Roy sprinted the ten blocks to the corner of Second Street and Avenue B, where the Never Inn stood. He went up and down the street but couldn't find it. It had disappeared.

He checked his phone, did a search for the Never Inn, but came up empty.

The place had never existed except in his mind.

35

"There are reported cases of transplant patients assuming characteristics of their donors," Dr. Brixton said. "It's common, in fact, though disputable. I'm afraid you are in somewhat rarefied territory. You are your own guinea pig."

In the dark corners of the room, the hot-water radiators grumbled as if struggling to shed some heat into the damp chill of the church basement. The Englishman's gray wool sweater had a hole at the neckline, and Roy became obsessed with the idea of grabbing the errant thread and unraveling the whole thing.

"Hallucinations, certainly. I'm not surprised," Dr. Brixton continued. "Your mind has undergone considerable stress. Dementia. Psychosis. These are to be expected and even predicted in your case."

When Roy didn't respond, Brixton added, "You should admit yourself to a facility. I'm being serious. Paranoia is another projected effect of your condition—a gradual blurring of reality. You are on a slippery slope, Mr. Roy."

Brixton had a habit of calling him this ever since Fatmata had written it on his name tag sticker in the first meeting. Roy hated it. He sat hunched on a folding metal chair in front of the doctor, one knee bouncing up and down.

Roy asked, "How do I know if something is real or not?"

The doctor bared his teeth as if he had bitten into something unpleasant.

"Just give me something I can use," Roy said. "Something practical."

"Well, a shared experience. Does someone else see it? Does something make sense in the wider context?"

Roy hesitated, then reached into his backpack and pulled out Primrose's earring. "Do you see this?"

"A golden fish."

"So it's real."

"Assuming *I* am real."

"Jesus Christ," Roy muttered under his breath.

"You see the problem," Brixton said, "but I assure you, I *am* real." He smiled. "What does that object in your hand signify to you?"

Roy put the earring away. "What about the dreams? I dreamed of that little girl, and then I found her. Doesn't that signify something? You said my body has two brains now. Is Jake talking to me?"

"Let me ask you this. Did you want a family? Before the accident?"

There was no use ducking it. "Sure, but my wife wasn't ready."

"And your wife, Penny—did you feel close to her?"

She cheated on us, said a voice in Roy's head. "Not as much as I wanted to."

"And now," Brixton said, "you have a woman who seems ready to give you unconditional love, beyond even any expectation. With a ready-made family."

"So you're saying she might be a figment of my imagination?" He pulled from his pack the scrap of paper that Hope had written her cell phone number on. He had tried calling it already, twice, to be sure—and she had answered both times.

"More a product of wishful thinking, perhaps, on your part and on hers. I'm not saying it isn't true. I'm just saying to be careful."

"She said Jake was murdered."

"Of course she wouldn't want to believe that her husband committed suicide. What are the odds that you really found your donor so quickly? And one almost next door? One with a beautiful woman as a wife, with the little girl of your dreams?"

"I have no idea."

"How many people were on that list I gave you?"

"Twenty thousand, maybe more."

The doctor remained silent, but that sour look returned to his face.

"The moles look the same," Roy said. "On my body, from what I saw in the pictures."

"Did the wife inspect any birthmarks? Anything *very* specific?"

"She said I smelled the same. Said she recognized his hands." Roy held them up for the doctor to inspect.

"What does Dr. Danesti say about all this?"

"I'm staying away from him."

"And why is that?"

The doctor's face now had the obsequious expression Roy had seen on Primrose's face when she was trying to psychoanalyze him. *I thought you hated Danesti. Now you want me to bare my soul to him?* But he remained silent.

"I can see I'm not going to convince you," Brixton said after a few seconds of silence. "Why don't you go and talk to the only other person on this planet who shares your experience?"

* * *

The rest of the transplant support group sat in their chairs, back to their droning conversation. This was what they did on Friday nights?

He paced in front of the coffee machine.

Fedora stood next to him, inspecting the two jars marked "Clooney" and "Pitt" that Roy had just pulled from his backpack.

Hope hadn't asked for any of Jake's possessions back when she left his apartment. Why was that? He stole them from her house, and yet, she left them all with him. It felt as if she was marking her territory, like leaving a toothbrush after a date.

What did meeting her prove?

That she didn't know that her husband was a psychopath?

"You know how much this would have been worth?" Fedora said. He held up the empty Clooney jar.

"Just give me a second." Roy pulled out his phone and called Angel.

The detective answered right away. "Are you okay? I've been trying to call you all day."

"Angel, listen. I'm sorry about the other night."

"Sorry about what?"

"Telling you to cancel the investigation. I still really need your help."

"I never leave anyone behind, bro. Don't worry about it. But I'm going to send you something. You might want to sit down."

Roy didn't bother looking for a chair.

He paced past the coffee machine and turned and walked back again. His phone pinged with a text message. An image: two people, locked in an embrace. Kissing. He zoomed in on the image. It was his mother, much younger. The image looked scanned from a newspaper. Who was the man she was kissing? He zoomed in further.

"That's your friend, Samuel Phipps," Angel said, his voice small and tinny through the microphone.

Roy put the phone back to his ear. "That's *Sam?*"

"From the Saturday, July eighteenth, 1987, edition of Page Six, the gossip and celebrity column. Looks like your mother and your friend had some benefits."

Roy was just nine years old when the picture was taken. His mother and father had been married for … fifteen years by then. He looked at the image again. "Is that what you wanted to tell me?"

Angel had called six times already.

"Are you sitting down?"

"Sure." Roy stopped pacing to refill his coffee cup. He hadn't slept in two days.

"I went and talked to that doctor, the one I mentioned? He's in an old-age home in Queens, in his late eighties. Not quite all there, but he says he signed your birth certificate. Southampton General wasn't built until two years *after* you were born. So I asked him how it was possible, if it was a mistake. I didn't expect him to even remember, but he remembered *you.*"

"Can we hurry this up?" Roy downed the cup of barely warm coffee in one gulp.

"You sure you're sitting down?"

"Hey, man, you want some water?" Fedora asked. "You don't look so good."

Roy thanked him and took the bottle but didn't open it. "Angel, just spit it out."

"The old doctor said he didn't care anymore. Said he was too old. He says your dad paid him to fake the birth certificate. I think maybe your mother didn't give birth to you."

"What?"

"Maybe a surrogate, in India. At least, that's what this guy said."

Roy remembered his mother's friends talking about using surrogates. Eden had subsidiary offices over there. "Are you serious?"

"The old doc was a real hoarder. I got a picture and a name. Grainy and black-and-white. Adhira Achari, an Indian girl in Chennai. Except she must be in her sixties now. I don't know, maybe this is nuts. This doctor has Alzheimer's. He doesn't even remember his own daughter when she—"

"I need to see it."

Another ping on his phone. Another image. The Indian girl.

Angel said, "Let's meet. I'll show you more and we can talk it out."

"I need to go somewhere first. Maybe tomorrow?"

"I'm going to look into LCT Capital," Angel said. "That okay with you? Your friend Atticus? I'm going to look in his safe."

"Sure." Roy felt the room wobbling. "I'll call you later." He hung up.

His friend Fedora watched him. His lips pursed.

"I can't go out to Meatpacking," Roy said.

Fedora shrugged—no big deal. "Can I keep the jars?" When Roy nodded, Fedora added: "You should drink some water, my friend. You don't look good."

* * *

The taxi dropped Roy outside a multispired mansion on West Eighty-Seventh Street. The house was stately but decrepit looking. Its cornice gargoyles crouched between two of the four-story brownstones that were the signature architecture of the Upper West Side near Columbia University.

He'd heard of these country homes built in the 1700s that had survived the Gilded Age housing boom in Manhattan, but he'd never seen one with his own eyes. A holdover from the *old* old money of New York, and now it was Shelby Sheffield's home—the only other person on the planet who had undergone a body transplant and lived.

None of the lights were on.

The house looked dead.

Even the streetlight out front was dark.

Roy paid the taxi driver and walked up the stairs to the front door. Rang the doorbell. Waited.

Sheffield hadn't answered Roy's first phone call an hour ago, but he rang back right away after Roy left a message explaining who he was. He said he'd been waiting for Roy to call him. That *they* were listening, that he couldn't talk over the phone. He said to come over to his house right away.

The taxi ride up from midtown, straight along Broadway, had taken on a cinematic feel, as if he were watching a movie with the colors too bright. Sitting in the back seat, he started to fall asleep, felt his eyes drooping, right up until the taxi driver was yelling at him. Telling him they had arrived.

Was he sure he had the right address? The house was dark. Roy opened the bottle of water Fedora had given him, and took another sip, tried to wake himself up a bit.

A creaking sound.

Roy squinted into the darkness. Below the staircase, in the shadows, a hand beckoned.

"Come on, hurry!" Shelby Sheffield said.

* * *

"Can I turn the lights on?" Roy asked.

"I've disconnected the power," Shelby answered.

The man hung back in the gloom, hunched over. Two candles, burning on a wooden table covered in a thick layer of dust, illuminated a small patch of the damp basement. It smelled of earth, of worms, the sweetish whiff of rotting garbage.

"Only one telephone, an old landline," Shelby added. "But I keep it in the back. Under a lead box. I knew you were going to call. I've been waiting for you. For months. Years."

He didn't look anything like the man Roy had seen in the pictures.

Shelby Sheffield had been the head of the International Monetary Fund, a celebrated banker and manager of a billion-dollar hedge fund in the nineties. In his pictures, he had been square-jawed, with a full head of natural black hair.

Even in the videos of Sheffield leaving Eden almost a year and a half before, the banker had looked impressive. Seventy-four years old, but the media said he looked more like fifty. The creature before Roy now looked about the same age as this eighteenth-century house. Thin, greasy hair dangling from his pallid scalp. Folds of skin drooping from his cheeks. Open, festering sores.

Roy had forgotten why he came. He took another sip of the bottle of water in his hand. "I wanted to ask you some questions."

"And I have the answers," Shelby hissed.

The candle flames seemed to sparkle in purples and golds, the colors bending the dim outlines of the walls. Shelby moved toward Roy, his face fully illuminated for the first time. Roy recognized the staple scars ringing the neck, the same as his. He put a hat on. It looked like tinfoil. At his temples were jagged marks in the skin, the wounds barely healed. He had dug out the implants.

Shelby's eyes were wide.

"The vibrations—they're tuning into my mind." Shelby adjusted the crinkled aluminum foil covering his head. "You must feel them, too. That's why I stay underground."

"What do you know about Dr. Danesti?" Roy asked. "Where does he get his money?"

He felt his eyes drooping despite a growing fear of the person in front of him. Who left him like this? The man was stick thin. *Someone should put this thing out of its misery,* said a voice in Roy's head. *It would be a service.*

"Ah, yes, yes, the good doctor Nicolae Danesti. Saved my life, to turn it into *this*? Not one, but two." Shelby took a step back into the shadows. "Have you talked to your body? To the person whose body you stole?"

"Did you give Danesti money?" Roy said, ignoring Shelby's question. "How much? Did he speak about me?"

About me? The voice in Roy's head became louder. *Did he speak about who? You mean Jake? You mean me?*

"Don't trust the doctor." Shelby's voice echoed in the darkness. "There is a connection between you and him. A hidden connection. I would kill him, if I were you. Before it's too late. But don't say I said that. Not me. Not me." ·

Time oozed to a crawl. The candle flames seemed to freeze in space. A face emerged from the darkness, but it wasn't Shelby.

It was Jake Hawkins, his face lit from below.

"Have you talked to me, Roy?" Jake asked. "Because we have a lot to talk about."

36

Shouts and hooting laughter from the streets below penetrated through the closed windows of Del's loft. It was Friday night in Greenwich Village, but she and Coleman weren't quite finished with their week. They had finally gotten the download of all the facial recognition hits from Esposito. She had to go back down to One Police Plaza and get the memory key physically.

Esposito didn't want to send this stuff over the wires. Those were his words exactly.

She dropped her backpack by the entrance and fished in her pants pocket for the device Esposito had given her. She clicked on the lights. Coleman followed her up the stairs and into the loft, then began his regular inspection of her paintings. He went to the newest first, just by the front windows.

He said, "You said your family is Creole but not Cajun? What's the difference?"

"'Cajun' is a contraction of 'Acadian.' They were French people kicked out of coastal areas up around Canada in a war in the 1750s. The Acadians came to Louisiana. That's who Cajuns are."

Del sat down at a beaten-up wooden desk halfway down the loft. She opened her laptop. "'Creole' just means 'pidgin,' for lack of a better word. A blend. Original French settlers mixed with Africans, Cubans, Germans, and anybody else who got their asses over here back then. Basically a melting pot."

"I think I can see what you painted. It's kinda greenish?" Coleman had his face a few inches from the painting at the front of the loft. He squinted.

"Oh, shoot, I almost forgot." Del got up from the desk. The laptop was still starting up. She walked over and switched off the main light.

Coleman said, "What are you doing?"

She clicked another switch, and a black light buzzed and then popped to life over their heads, dousing them in a faint blue glow. Speckles of white lint glowed bright on Coleman's navy shirt in the darkness.

"Wow," her partner whispered.

On the painting in front of them, a four-foot blood-red image glowed bright—an image of what looked like a scarecrow, but with crimson fire seeping down into the ground below it.

"I grind up spinach in alcohol to extract the chlorophyll, then mix that with titanium oxide," Del explained. "In normal light, to you, it still looks mostly white—but this black lamp emits long-wavelength ultraviolet, and the chlorophyll phosphoresces and glows red. So now you can sort of see what I see."

Coleman was mute for a few seconds. "Is that ... what I think it is?"

"Yeah. Pegnini. Sorry, maybe I shouldn't have chosen that one to show you." She clicked the main lights back on.

"That really got in your head, huh?"

"Hard to get out."

The computer had finally booted up, so Del returned to her desk.

"I looked up that thing you do," Coleman said. "Being able to *see* if people are lying? I read a science article saying they can use thermal imaging to detect deception with ninety percent accuracy. Increased blood flow around the eyes and forehead."

"So you're saying you don't think I'm lying to you?"

Coleman laughed. "I didn't think that. I'm *saying* it's interesting."

Del inserted the memory key from Esposito. A directory appeared with a massive list of thirty-three thousand files.

She clicked on one.

A grainy black-and-white image appeared with a red box around the suspect's face. Not all the cameras in the network were as clear as the ones in the Meatpacking District. From this angle, it was hard to tell whether it was Roy. She had done her undergraduate degree in fine arts, but with a minor in computer science, mostly with an interest in digital image processing. She had told Esposito to widen the recognition filter. Maybe too much.

She squinted at the picture, shrugged, and clicked to the next one. It was just as inconclusive. The guy in this one had on a baseball cap.

Thirty-three *thousand* of these?

"Hey, are you going to help?" she said. Coleman was looking at another of her paintings.

Del opened up more images and tried to understand what she was seeing, but the time stamps added an extra level of complexity. Another dimension. She still had no idea whether any of them were really Roy. She opened another window on her desktop and began clicking multiple images. She picked a few and opened a digital map of Manhattan in another window and tried to correlate the image locations and times, to make sense of them.

"This is your mom?" Coleman had switched walls. He pointed at a picture.

It was Del's mother, back in the seventies, at her first vernissage. Del loved the picture. "Yeah, that's her." She smiled. Her mother dressed up in an African kaftan, showing off hermaphroditic sculptures in bronze. She was such a firebrand back then, but then, she was still active in the community now, just in different ways.

"Holy cow!" Coleman murmured.

Del turned to look at him. "What?"

"Your dad is *Sergeant* Devlin of the Seventh Precinct?" He pointed at another picture, of Del's mother and father together.

She returned to looking at the images on her screen, shaking her head. "And you want to be a detective?"

"I just figured—"

"My last name is Devlin. You *did* notice that, right?"

"Yeah, but I didn't make the connection. He's *Irish*. I mean, really Irish. Like more Irish than Jameson's."

"And your point is?"

"No wonder Esposito let us into One PP," Coleman mused. "And I thought it was just because we were friends."

"It was," Del replied. "Plus who my dad is. Plus Giants tickets. The parts add up—we're *part*ners, right? Now, come on, help me."

Coleman took one last look before coming to sit down beside her. "What do you want me to do?"

Del opened another set of pictures. This was going to be impossible.

Thirty-three thousand images.

They needed another way to look at these. She needed to visualize the images together, find a way to see them clearly in time and space.

Human vision was foveated, which meant that the eye's cone-shaped light detectors became exponentially denser near the center. In effect, this meant that humans really didn't see everything clearly—in fact, barely seeing anything more than movement and shadows in the peripheral vision. It was a trick the brain played. The eye really saw clearly, in detail, only an area about the size of a quarter held at arm's length. The brain painted in the rest of the image to give us the *impression* we saw everything around us, but we didn't, not really.

She needed a way to get past this limitation.

"Call your buddy Esposito. I have a little programming job for him."

37

Angel Rodriguez squatted on top of the fancy toilet, his door still locked. He doubted the octogenarian night security guard would bother checking each stall. At best, the guy might just come in and take a pee. He bet the old guy had to do that at least a half-dozen times each night, so Angel wouldn't have long to wait.

That would give him enough time between the rounds.

He was used to waiting. He had gotten adept at squatting on his tours of duty in Afghanistan and Iraq, and in the Kashmir Valley during training with the Indian troops. An easy way to suspend your ass over the ground without sitting, and get to your feet fast if you needed to. He could squat like this for hours.

For most Westerners, it was hell on the knee and hip joints, but Angel was supple and strong. He could fall asleep in this position for hours but be wide awake at the snap of a twig. Was he afraid now, sitting on a toilet? Locked in an office after hours? About to break into the safe of a senior hedge fund manager? He laughed to himself. The only danger here was maybe a night in jail.

On more sorties than he cared to remember, he'd been left alone in the dark where any small mistake would have gotten him killed. Where he had to kill to survive, thousands of miles from home in a hostile country. This was a cakewalk.

In the worst case, he was sure he could explain it away by saying he had a job here, or get Roy to intervene. Roy had a seat on the board of directors of LCT Capital after all, and he had said he was okay with Angel getting the papers from Atticus's safe.

He was doing it for his new buddy, Roy.

Nobody left behind.

That said, he was worried about Roy. The poor guy was clearly starting to skip a groove. The money Angel was getting from Roy would make it possible for him and Charlie to buy their own little house in Brooklyn, to put down the deposit. He appreciated it.

They needed to finish this investigation as fast as possible and get Roy back on track. Clear the air. Get everything in the open. Roy deserved that much.

Angel looked at his watch. Nine p.m. He hardly even needed to look. His brain had a hardwired counter in it. He could squat here, eyes closed, and know almost to the minute what time it was. A skill he had needed to hone. He focused on his breathing.

He had spent this afternoon taking his new son—*his new son!*—Rodrigo, out for a walk in Central Park. He and Charlie had flown to Colombia months before to meet the five-year-old but had brought him back here only this past week.

They were now a family of four, counting the mutt, Columbo, that they had just rescued from the pound. What kid didn't need a dog as a best buddy? He rocked back and forth on his haunches, a grin on his face.

After all the crazy stuff he'd been through, he couldn't believe he had made it to this point in his life. His own family! He was going to give this kid such a great life; he was going to be the best dad *ever.*

Rodrigo Rodriguez. His son's name. It just rolled off the tongue, didn't it? Didn't that sound like a Latino pop singer's name?

The main door to the bathroom creaked open. Soft-soled shoes ambled over the ceramic floor, and then the tinkling sound. Angel checked his watch again. Nine twenty. He waited for the outside door to creak shut again before stepping panther-like off his perch. He opened the stall door and crept out, opened the outside door a crack. The guard was probably already back at his station, halfway back to sleep in front of the security monitors. Angel had disabled the one for Atticus's office by rewiring the feed from the office next door. Simple enough, but still risky.

Keeping low, Angel made his way between the cubicles to Cargill's office and slipped a card into the locked doorjamb to open it. In the dark, he felt his way back to the credenza and pulled open the painting covering the safe.

Roy had said that Atticus was old-school. Said he didn't keep important files electronically, didn't even keep them in a bank safe-deposit box.

Angel clicked on an ultraviolet flashlight and lit up the keys on the safe. This model of safe had a five-digit code. He had slipped some UV-sensitive ink, invisible to the eye, onto a document he gave Atticus today. That was the easy part—the longer part had been getting hired as a file clerk using one of Roy's unwitting friends as a reference.

Angel had waited to see him open his safe from outside the room, through the glass wall of Atticus's office. He'd been careful not to watch directly, but just from the corner of his eye, enough to catch the elbow motions. Watched him open the safe three times in the past week. To the top left, then down, and to the side and back. Now, under the UV light, the keys Atticus had pressed glowed bright.

Angel just had to guess the sequence.

Only four of the keys glowed. One. Three. Six. Nine. He remembered the motion of the elbow. Up. Then down. And back. A number popped into Angel's mind: 19-3-66—Atticus's granddaughter's birthday.

Not too smart, old man, but a sweet sentiment.

Angel keyed the sequence into the safe's keypad. The door clicked open. This was the risky part. Atticus might have a silent alarm on the door—an email or text message alert that was sent out each time the door opened. He'd looked up this model of safe, and it was an option, but if Atticus's lax security protocols were anything to go by, maybe he had never enabled it.

This had to be quick. In and out.

Angel pulled out a sheaf of files and leafed through them, a plastic flashlight in his mouth. Still no noise from the front office. It took only a minute to find a file marked "Lowell-Vandeweghe."

The rest of the files were for other clients, and the rest of the safe was filled with what looked like bonds and checks. He closed the safe and locked it.

He read through the file using his flashlight. He stopped on a page. Frowned. Switched to the calculator on his phone and punched a few numbers, then looked at a web page. He looked at the next page in the paper document, and his eyes went wide.

He whistled quietly, then dialed a number.

Roy picked up on the first ring.

"Hey, where are you?" he whispered.

"Uptown," Roy answered. "Downtown."

"You okay?" Angel took the pages of the file and opened the safe again to put them back. Better to get done as quick as possible.

"I'm fine," Roy replied.

"Man, I got something I gotta tell you."

Angel heard a shuffling noise in the office toward the front.

"Yeah? What?"

"Can we meet? I gotta get out of here."

The detective scribbled on a scrap of paper and stuffed it into his pocket.

* * *

Angel stamped his feet in the cold and pulled his wool hat lower around his ears. Just over a week till Christmas. Man, they had to get a big Christmas tree up in the loft! Decorate it. Get some presents under it.

Focus, he said to himself. *Get your mind back on the job.* Still, it felt as though everything was coming together and the mystery had been solved.

Snowflakes began to drift in the orange glow of the sodium streetlamps. He had spoken to Roy, who said to meet him in ten minutes, two blocks from the Woolworth Tower on Madison Street, right beside the NYPD headquarters.

That was fine.

Maybe Roy wanted to speak to the cops. With the information Angel was about to give him, he might want to. Maybe he already knew. That was possible. Was it illegal? Angel didn't know. Probably not illegal, but certainly surprising.

A shape appeared on the corner, just beyond the huge concrete blocks on Madison that blocked the street so nobody could drive up it. Terrorist-proofing.

He waved, and Roy waved back.

Angel recognized the green-and-red parka that Roy had worn the last time they met. Roy had the hood of his coat pulled up against the snow.

Angel walked toward Pearl Street, the falling snow lit up by the fluorescent lights of a Rite Aid pharmacy glowing bright on the next block. "Check this out, bro. You're not going to believe this."

Without thinking, automatically, Angel suddenly reacted—twisted his body sideways and slammed one hand down. The wind was knocked out of him, as if he'd been punched in the gut, but he felt nothing. He gasped for air and looked down. A wicked blade stuck halfway out of the side of his chest.

He clawed at it, but Roy gripped the handle tight and ripped it out. He tried to make another stab, but Angel managed to dodge, and the knife went through only his coat. But the damage was done.

Angel dropped to his knees, his fingernails gripping Roy's coat. Still no pain, but a sudden fear. *Not now. Please. I'm so close.* How hadn't he seen it?

His last thought was of Charlie, and then of Rodrigo's little face smiling in the park, before the blackness took him.

38

Roy tightened his grip around Primrose Chegwidden's throat and squeezed. Her face turned mottled purple, and then as red as that stupid colored hairdo. Her head separated from her body and floated away.

Just like Roy's.

He let go and put his arms out to get some lift, to hover over the ground. Angel looked up at him, gave him a thumbs-up, but Roy couldn't stop himself. He dived down, straight into Angel, straight into his heart.

His eyes opened to blackness. He gasped for air.

The darkness felt as if it were constructed of invisible Styrofoam cubes. Soundlessly, the cubes of darkness squeezed into each other, pressed, and then came the awful teeth-gritting squeak of the foam collapsing into itself. New cubes formed from the old, and the process repeated, the empty black space reforming and reshaping, gathering speed.

He blinked. He was lying on his back. The dim light of the streetlamp outside bled in past the tatty, washed-out curtains of his apartment. It was still dark out, and freezing cold in here. His lips were parched, his mouth filled with sludge. He needed water. He struggled to roll to his right, and then left, and then just to get up onto his elbows.

Nothing.

He sucked in another lungful of air and smelled the stale sweat, the metal tang of blood in his mouth. He felt the cold and the prickle of the cheap mattress against his skin. He could breathe, but he couldn't move, couldn't budge so much as a finger.

What had he done? What happened? The last he remembered, he was in the basement with the crazed Shelby Sheffield. Was that what lay in store for him, too? He would kill himself first. He remembered thinking someone should put Shelby out of his misery.

And then what? How had he gotten here? Had he injured himself? Severed his spinal cord somehow? Gotten into a fight again? He took another breath and tried to calm a rising panic. Again he tried to move an arm, even a finger. Nothing. God, he was so thirsty. His head throbbed.

What have I done?

How long could someone survive without water? *A day? Two?*

When did he last take the antirejection drugs?

He remembered an article he'd read in the *Times*. The Japanese had a word for this: *kodokushi*. The lonely death. People dying alone in their apartments, remaining undiscovered for weeks while their bodies decomposed.

How much time had he paid the landlady for? Two weeks? Or was it a month in advance? Would he die of thirst, his desiccated body rotting for a month before anyone came in? He doubted it would be the first time someone had died in this dump.

And then another thought.

Had Danesti done this to him? The implants still in his temples, under the skin near his skull, in his legs and arms. What were they capable of? Had Danesti disconnected the implants? The bastard. Would he leave Roy to rot here? Had he pissed him off too much? Become too much of a liability? What else could those implants do? He didn't feel as if he had his exo-suit on—he usually took it off and put it in his backpack at night.

Roy closed his eyes and tried to calm down. *Breathe deep. Just breathe.*

* * *

Bam, bam, bam.

Roy's eyes shot open.

Bam, bam. "This is the police," called out a voice. A man's voice.

Without thinking, Roy rolled over and fell out of the bed. He stopped for a second, crouched, realizing he could move again. Had he only been dreaming his paralysis?

"Open up!" yelled the policeman.

What did they want? Did they find Primrose's body? He paused a beat before thinking. Did they find the storage locker?

There had to be cameras. He shouldn't have been so stupid. He should have gotten rid of the evidence. But why? He should just turn himself in. He scrambled in the dark to find his jeans and put them on, grab his phone and wallet. He put on his sneakers and grabbed his backpack with the exo-suit. He felt in the pack to check—it was rolled up inside.

Don't let them catch you, said a voice in his head. *You don't want to be caught like this. Like an animal.*

"Roy, we know you're in there," said another voice from outside the front door.

A woman's voice.

He knew that voice.

39

"*Damn it*," Del muttered.

White puffs of vapor billowed out with each exhalation. It had to be five degrees below freezing. It had been snowing on and off for two days, and a few flakes were drifting down.

A clear set of footprints led into the apartment. They had to be from this morning. One set of prints.

She and Coleman had sat in their cruiser across the street and waited. It was a long shot. She had asked Esposito to reformat the data he'd sent her, but to put it into a three-dimensional visualization color-coded with a frequency map of the facial recognition hits. With this new tool, she'd had him expand the filter even wider to gather more hits. Once it was done, she could cycle back and forth through time and see the hot spots.

In just a few minutes, it had zeroed her in on a set of cameras over a bodega on Eleventh and Avenue C. She had distilled the images. That was definitely Roy in a few of those frames. Down the street, too, from some cameras over a traffic light, more images of Roy.

She and Coleman had spent yesterday canvassing the street, until the lady upstairs from this place said the picture of Roy looked sort of familiar. That maybe it was the guy she had rented the apartment downstairs to.

Maybe. The guy paid cash. No ID. It wasn't illegal, the old lady had reminded them.

The events of two nights ago had added urgency to their search.

"War Hero Gutted like a Fish in Front of Commissioner," was one sensational headline in the local papers yesterday.

Angel Rodriguez, a decorated former Navy SEAL team member, had been stabbed in front of One Police Plaza. Right at NYPD's headquarters, with a dozen cameras watching it happen. Angel had been gravely wounded and had lost a lot of blood, but he was tough and had managed to fight off his attacker long enough to save his life—maybe. Angel was hanging on by a thread in a hospital uptown, in a coma.

The suspect had just strolled away into the City Hall subway station as if he were on a Sunday walk. The cops streamed out, but in the ten minutes it took to react, the suspect was gone, melted into the Saturday-night crowds on the station platform. He could have gone out to Brooklyn, uptown, or downtown. Become one of millions.

His face was covered by a parka and scarf and didn't show in the video.

Del and her partner were the only ones who knew that Angel was working for Roy—at least, the only police who knew.

Forty thousand other officers of the NYPD might like to know what she knew. The largest police force in America was on the case. In effect, it was the fourth-largest army on the planet, and someone had just kicked the beehive, but if she brought up anything else about Royce Lowell-Vandeweghe to her boss, it would not go well for her.

So she and Coleman had waited in their car.

Maybe she could have checked Angel's apartment, but he was listed as single. Also, the NYPD would be all over his place. She was a long way from her jurisdiction of Suffolk County. So she decided just to wait and hope they could catch Roy coming back to his apartment—or the apartment they thought he was renting.

But Coleman had nodded off on his watch.

When Del woke up, right away she spotted the fresh tracks in the snow, leading into the apartment.

She banged on the door again.

They waited a few seconds for a couple to walk by. When the street was empty once again, she yelled, "Roy, come on out. We just want to talk." If Roy complained to his billionaire friends, she might be out of a job—unless she was right.

Silence. No lights inside the apartment.

"Is there a back way out?" she asked Coleman.

"No way. I checked. Just one way in and out. What do you want to do?"

Snowflakes drifted.

"Kick it in," Del said.

"We got no warrant. You sure?"

"I'll take responsibility. You kick it, and I'll go in first."

She unholstered her Glock.

"You sure you need that?" Coleman asked.

"You sure you don't?"

He thought about it for a good second before unholstering his own weapon. "We're coming in," he announced.

"You shouldn't have said that," Del whispered just as Coleman lunged forward to piston-kick the door. It was cheap and splintered right away, swinging straight in.

"Whoever's in here, just stay cool," she said.

She swung her pistol out. The door had thudded against the wall and swung slowly back.

Inside, it was pitch black. Still not a sound.

Del edged forward, then back, but had to move in before the door swung closed again. She took a step over the threshold, down a step and then another.

Coleman came in behind her.

Her eyes adjusted to the darkness and then to the subdarkness. Even in what other people perceived as utter blackness, she could discern shapes, especially if they were warm.

There was a faint glow in the middle of the room. A bed?

She took another step forward. Coleman came beside her, and she heard him groping around on the wall for a light switch. Something was in here with them. Some presence. She sensed it too late—the glowing outline of a hulking figure hurtling toward her.

"Coleman!" she yelled as she ducked sideways.

An elbow glanced off the side of her face. Then the figure grabbed Coleman and literally threw him into space. Del sprawled sideways and crashed over a table. By the time she got back to her feet, the attacker, whoever it was, had gone. Her partner said he was okay, so she dashed out to the sidewalk.

Her hands shook. She saw nothing out there, not left or right.

A man came out of the bodega and froze, staring at the woman with a gun in her hand. Del looked at the footprints in the snow. People were already out, going to work. Too many footprints to pick out one set.

"Damn it."

* * *

"You okay?" Del asked Coleman.

Her partner was shaken but didn't look hurt—at least, he wasn't cut anywhere. "I'm fine." He sat on the edge of the bed, nursing his elbow. "What on earth was that? That thing threw me ten feet in the air like I was a bag of laundry. Did you get a look?"

"I just saw an outline," Del said. "A man."

"All I knew, I was suddenly airborne. Do you want to call it in? Get some backup?"

"We just broke in illegally. Who, exactly, would we call?"

They had just turned the lights on. The place was a mess. Which was probably to be expected, given the state of the rest of the building and the chain-smoking landlady upstairs. Papers were scattered all over the floor. They looked like receipts.

Coleman picked one up. "Who the hell is Jake Hawkins?"

40

God, it was cold. Roy stumbled forward and slipped on a patch of ice, putting one hand against a lamppost to keep from crashing onto the sidewalk. A woman in a heavy coat and matching scarf, latte in one hand, recoiled, crinkling her nose. She gave Roy a wide berth on her way into the Astor Place subway station.

The morning commuters streamed around him, parting like water around a rock, giving a wide berth to the undesirable in their path.

What were all these people doing out on a Saturday morning? Buying Christmas gifts?

He wrapped his arms around his body in a vain attempt to stay warm.

He had on only a thin cotton T-shirt and jeans and his backpack, while everyone around him wore parkas and scarves and heavy boots. He had run blindly through Tompkins Square Park, where some of the kids paused from their sledding to gawk at him, and before he knew it, he was on the Bowery. The street used to be the most notorious junkie jungle in America, but now it was all glass storefronts and Starbucks. Not a place someone like Roy could hide.

He scampered north to St. Mark's Square, hobbling a little without the exo-suit. There would be more street people around St. Mark's. There always were.

Had he hurt that cop? He hadn't wanted to. He just needed to get away.

They didn't seem to have followed him, but he saw a city cop at the base of the subway stairs. Roy reversed course back onto the street, where he spotted a McDonald's. The snow was falling faster now, whipped into flurries by the wind. He ran across the street, huddled over against the storm, and banged through the door of McDonald's.

The line of people inside glanced his way, then went back to whatever they were doing. This was New York City, after all—there wasn't much they hadn't seen.

Roy went into the bathroom and closed the stall door. He checked his bulging pockets: four thousand, three hundred eighty dollars in cash. He still had Jake's passport and his own, and he still had his wallet, though he didn't dare use the cards.

He had a pocketful of antirejection pills, but no idea when he last took them. Maybe that was the reason for the ripping headache.

"Sir, you can't stay in there," said a young voice outside the stall. "The bathrooms are for paying customers only."

Apparently, the kid had drawn the short stick to have to come in and talk to him.

"One second."

He flushed the toilet to maintain the fiction that he had come in to relieve himself. He tried to slick his hair down and straighten his T-shirt before opening the door.

"I had a really bad night. Drinking, you know? Too much partying."

The pimple-faced kid shrank back but dutifully held his ground. "But like I said—"

"How about this?" Roy held out a hundred-dollar bill. "Go get me a few bottles of water, a coffee, and an Egg McMuffin. And keep the rest for yourself. I just need to clean myself up. Can I do that?"

The kid paused a beat, but again, this was New York. He took the hundred and said, "How about I put the cleaning sign out front? Give you some privacy? For another hundred?"

Roy attempted a grateful smile, but the kid's eyes went wide. He realized he didn't have anything around his neck. In the mirror behind the kid, he saw the neck scar, purple and red against his pallid skin. He tucked his chin.

"And do you think I could buy a coat from one of your friends? A hat and scarf?" Roy waved a few more hundreds.

Working at McDonald's had made the kid a pragmatist. "I'll see what I can do."

"One more question. Why are there so many people here on a Saturday morning?"

The kid gave a knowing grin. "Because it's Monday, dude."

* * *

"Three days," Roy muttered aloud. He looked into the bathroom mirror. "What have you been doing for three days?" He was looking into his own eyes but speaking to Jake somewhere back in there.

For two hours, he'd had the kid block off the bathroom and shuttle in coffee and eggs. He had cleaned the blood from his hands—his own blood? His hands and forearms looked like a junkie's, complete with the tremors and full of cuts and scratches. He shaved with a razor the kid provided, and he had a new shirt and even a sturdy winter coat that he had to pay five crisp C-notes for, but then, he wasn't in a good position to negotiate. He thought about plugging in the exo-suit, but he didn't really need it anymore. It had become more of an encumbrance than anything else. Not sure how many antirejection pills he should take, he downed five.

He stared into the depths of his own eyes.

He remembered being tired at Shelby Sheffield's house. Was that how Jake got out? When he went to sleep or when his mind grew fatigued?

And how had they found him? How did Detective Devlin know where he was? Did Hope tell them? That was possible, but it didn't make sense.

The sensors in his head.

He looked at the small bubbles of skin where the devices were inserted. Two on his temples, two high on his forehead, two over the ears. One each at the big joints. What were they doing? Were they even now broadcasting his location to the police? No. If they were, the cops would already be here. But he would bet Danesti was tracking him.

The doctor had his own agenda, Roy was sure of it.

Even here, he had the feeling he was being watched—as if someone were in here with him.

Which they were.

He tried calling Angel but got no response. He didn't leave a message, and on second thought, he dumped the cell phone into the garbage.

* * *

"How much for the big one?" Roy pointed at a knife in the display case. Its point looked sharp.

The pawn-shop manager replied, "That's, ah, fifty bucks."

"Forty?"

The man leaned back and stroked his gray goatee. A wall of guitars hung behind him. Glass cases lined both walls, with steel cages above them.

The guy said, "Sure. Forty."

Roy paid, pocketed the blade, and left the shop. It was afternoon already. He had spent the day hiding out in McDonald's, his back to the wall, sipping coffee. Trying to think. What was real? What wasn't? Maybe his mind was playing tricks again. He needed to go back out to that storage locker, see if he had really seen what he thought he saw. Bring one of the jars back. Take it to the police?

First, he needed to do something.

He walked down St. Mark's Place and crossed a few alleys to get back to Tompkins Square Park. He had a wool scarf tight around his neck again, sunglasses on, his thick new winter jacket pulled tight around him. He was warm, at least. He spied some of the kids he had talked to before, when he got the painkillers. Two of them scattered, but one remained on the park bench.

"Don't got no more Oxy, man," the young crustypunk said.

"Where's Rudy?" He meant the Afro-haired kid Roy had met first in the park. The one who got him his OxyContin.

"We don't know. People been disappearing, you know?" The kid looked scared.

"I need something to keep me awake. You got some amphetamines?"

The crustypunk frowned. "You mean like Adderall? Vynase?"

"Will it keep me awake?"

"Like Scarface and his little friends, bro. How much you want?"

"Everything you got." Roy pulled out his knife. "I need help with one more thing, and you're not going to like this."

41

"Hey, guy, you need a doctor?"

"Just drive," Roy said. "I'm fine."

"You don't look fine. There's a hospital—"

"I fell down some stairs. I need to get home. Please, just drive."

The Indian driver didn't look convinced. Roy could see his brown eyes glancing back at him in the rearview mirror. He had a red turban on. Didn't that mean he was Sikh?

They don't cut their hair, right? Roy had an internal monologue going again. No, a *dialogue,* actually. Questioning and answering himself.

I'm not sure. Maybe it's just a big hat.

Roy's knowledge of India was embarrassingly weak considering his new knowledge that he may well have been born there. He'd better start learning.

He had made two more calls from pay phones, but Angel hadn't picked up.

The taxi rumbled along the Cross Bronx Expressway, a concrete-canyon-walled racetrack for semis that mere cars entered at their own peril. Even with the windows rolled up, the roar and echo of the thousands of vehicles screaming through made it difficult to talk to the driver.

This was his third taxi.

It was too risky to go back to his Chevy, and anyway, the keys were in the apartment, now a no-go zone.

So he had taken a taxi, first out to Union City in New Jersey, through the Lincoln Tunnel, and jumped out to run through alleyways before grabbing another cab north to the George Washington, and then a third to double back. He had dumped the exo-suit and backpack in Jersey. It was the first time since coming out of the coma that he felt free.

He touched the wound at his left temple and winced. Blood oozed down the line of his scalp. The driver's concerned brown eyes flashed again in the rearview. Roy tried to get a look at himself in the scratched plastic mirror against the divider behind the front seat.

The Tompkins Park kid had done his best digging out the sensors, but the holes were deep, and the skin had flayed around the edges of the wounds. Six of them in his head. He pulled his wool cap back down and wiped away the blood. His jeans had dark patches of blood on them as well. Eight more wounds in his arms and legs. Good thing he had a big supply of Oxy.

The taxi wound its way through Throg's Neck, over the bridge, and then down onto the Long Island Expressway. If it wasn't there, if he couldn't find it, he would just turn himself in.

* * *

"Mother of God," Deputy Chief Russ Alonzo said to Detective Devlin.

With a latex-gloved hand, he held a mason jar aloft. A slightly decomposed finger floated in a transparent but slightly greenish liquid.

"How many more of these are there?"

They were on the second floor of a self-storage facility outside Calverton. Two junior officers were setting up floodlights.

"At least thirty containers," Coleman replied. "Ears. Eyes. Worse. And a bunch of bags of clothes—all sorts of stuff."

The junior officer couldn't hide his excitement. "Gotta be the Fire Island Killer, right? This is his treasure trove?"

Ten years before, seventeen women's bodies had appeared, one by one, on beaches on Fire Island, and others on Long Island. Wrapped in sacks and dumped into shallow graves between the sand dunes, cut up in pieces, with some parts missing. It was one of the biggest unsolved and still-active serial-killer cases in America.

"Totally different MO," Del said. She turned to the junior officers setting up the lights. "Hey, keep back. Don't disturb anything. This whole area is a crime scene."

"Put this back, then." The deputy chief handed Del the jar, grimacing as he did. His black mustache twitched in disgust.

"I'm going to take this one into Forensics right now." She held a larger glass jar in her hand. The liquid was clearer than in the others. A fresh ear, the edges ragged and pink. "This one looks more recent. Might be tied to the hiker we found."

From the pungent and slightly irritating smell of the jars, she could tell they were stored in formaldehyde. Or rather, formalin, which was a mixture of formaldehyde—a gas at room temperature—with water and methyl alcohol. This by itself was interesting, since modern labs mostly used a formaldehyde-free alternative for storing biological samples, so this had an old-school feel to it. Some of the samples were different colors, which meant that not all the formalin concoctions were of exactly the same proportions. And that was about the extent of Del's knowledge on the topic. Surely the forensic teams would have a lot to go on here.

"Let's get some fresh air," Chief Alonzo said as he left the room.

Del waited for Coleman to place the mason jar back and explained again to the junior officers that they were not to disturb anything or let anyone in. She caught up with the chief at the elevator.

"Tell me again how you found this," he said.

The elevator door slid open. Del kept both hands on the jar with the ear in it. An image flashed in her mind, of her dropping it, splashing bits of flesh on Alonzo's perfectly shined black shoes. Coleman entered the elevator behind her and shot her a conspiratorial look.

"Just by luck, sir," Del replied, concentrating her focus on her boss's slick black hair. Anything but his eyes.

The elevator dropped.

"Luck?"

"The locker is registered to Jake Hawkins, sir," Coleman said. "He lives just around the corner—or did before he blew his brains out two years ago."

"So our main suspect is dead?"

"Seems that way," Del said.

Almost two years ago. The coincidence wasn't lost on her. Just before Roy's operation. Gunshot wound to the head.

She didn't have access to the confidential files of the organ transplant network. She had called the OPTN right after she looked up Jake Hawkins on her phone. The network was protected by a web of impenetrable data security and privacy laws set up by Congress, but she was sure somebody would have a way in.

So was the main suspect dead? Maybe.

Del said, "Somebody still alive had to know about it."

"How so?"

"Someone came here a few days ago and paid up the rent in full. It was about to go to auction."

"Family member, maybe?"

"Maybe, but the cameras aren't working. They're all just fakes for show. The kid said some weirdo did come in, but the kid's so stoned, I'm not sure he'd be a very reliable witness."

"Do we have prints?"

The elevator shuddered to a stop. Why was it these places always smelled like mothballs? Or was it rat poison?

When the door remained shut, Del pushed the "open" button, being extra careful with her gruesome prize.

"No fingerprints for Jake Hawkins, nothing on file. He had no record, not even a parking ticket."

"Sounds just like a psychopath, right?" Coleman said. "Hiding under the radar? No arrests? No record?"

Del ignored him. "The lab team is on the way here to dust for prints and collect all the bio samples."

Finding this place really had been luck. Of a sort.

They had looked through all the papers and receipts in that apartment this morning, but Del could see that one set of papers was different from the rest. They had the oily smudges of having been handled over and over again. They were storage-locker receipts.

On a hunch, she had driven back up here with Coleman, and anyway, she was feeling uncomfortable being in the NYPD's jurisdiction. Better to chase leads in Suffolk County. They had just asked the kid at the front—stoned and playing video games on his phone—and showed him their badges. They said they had reason to believe that someone was hiding drugs in Hawkins's locker.

He used bolt cutters to open it, and it took only a second for Del to see the smudges from fingers that had pried open the back sheet of drywall.

They exited from the building into the razor-wire-encircled parking lot. The frigid air smelled of the evergreens bordering the lot. Already, a dozen Suffolk County police cruisers were jammed into the gravel parking lot, their flashing strobes lighting up the bushes and the building as twilight descended.

"Do we have a body? I mean, Jake Hawkins?"

Now, *that* was an interesting question. "Officially, he was cremated, sir," Del replied.

"Officially?" Deputy Chief Alonzo's brows furrowed together. He stopped to pull the lapels of his long wool coat.

"That's what's listed on the death certificate. We have someone going over to talk to the widow, Hope Hawkins."

"So we have no DNA, either? Can we get some from his house?"

"No need. The guy was an up-and-coming star in the mixed-martial-arts rankings. His day job was landscaping—cutting grass and blowing leaves—but by night he fought on the circuit."

"An MMA fighter?"

"That's right. They require that all fighters get regular blood tests. The labs have to keep them."

"Thank God for that."

Del held up the jar with the ear in it. Whoever cut it off had been in a hurry.

She caught some motion from the corner of her eye. Two dark cars pulled off from the road to stop behind the Suffolk County cruisers. Behind the cars was a New York City Yellow Cab. What was it doing all the way out here?

* * *

"You want me to stop, sir? You get out now?"

The red-turbaned cabbie turned in his seat but kept the security latch closed. It was clear he didn't care for Roy as a passenger and wanted him out of his car as soon as possible.

"No, uh, just … uh …" Roy was transfixed by the scene.

There was Detective Delta Devlin, holding up the jar with Primrose's ear in it. He had almost cracked her and her partner's skulls a few hours ago. Judging by all the police cars, they'd been here a while.

So they weren't scouring New York for him. There wasn't an all-points bulletin up for a mass murderer on the streets on Manhattan. Otherwise, he would never have made it out so easily.

He doubted they had even seen his face at the apartment, but somehow they'd found him. It had to be Danesti's sensors. But more important and to the point, the jars with the body parts were real, not a figment of his imagination.

Del had one of the grisly mementos in her hand, inspecting it. Then she looked straight at Roy. Or maybe just at the taxi. He shrank away from the window. The cops' lights gave the scene a kaleidoscopic air. Should he just stop and get out?

Roy fished another amphetamine tab out of his shirt pocket and swallowed it dry.

No.

He banged on the plastic divider. "Just keep moving. Keep driving."

"To where?" The driver slowed almost to a stop.

"Past Calverton a few miles. Just keep going."

* * *

Del watched the yellow taxi accelerate and pull away. She was about to give the glass jar to Coleman, jump in one of the cruisers, and follow the cab, when someone called out her name.

"Detective Delta Devlin?" said a woman who had just stepped out from one of the dark cars.

Del nodded.

"I'm Special Agent Conroy, and this is my partner, Special Agent Fitzgerald. We're with the FBI."

"Of course," Deputy Alonzo said, striding over with his hand out.

"We're going to be taking over the crime scene," Conroy said.

Del said, "I was just going to take this to get analyzed." She held up her glass jar.

"We'll take that," Conroy said. "And, Detective Devlin, we do have one question."

"Yes?"

"Exactly how did you come upon this?"

42

"You want a cookie, mister?"

The boy, who looked to be about six years old, held out a white-chocolate-macadamia-nut cookie. He had lips like a rose, and milk-white skin that was almost translucent. His face radiated the benevolent innocence of a cherub.

"Don't bother the nice man," his mother said. She wore yoga pants and a tight-lipped smile.

What she really means, my little friend, is don't talk to strangers. Especially strangers like me. Roy smiled and shook his head, thanking the boy, but no. *She does have a point. You never know what monsters are lurking, what hungry beasts are roaring silently, fangs out, hidden right in front of you.*

"But it's Christmas," the kid protested, resisting his mother's tug. "You said to give to those less for-shoo-nate than us."

Take your mom's advice, kid, because if she turns around, you might disappear. Roy closed his eyes and tried to stop the voices.

Stop it. Stop talking.

When he opened his eyes, the kid and his mom were gone.

Was the boy even real? It was hard to tell. It wasn't even that important.

It was a quiet Tuesday morning at the Starbucks on Main Street in East Hampton. The pumpkin-spice latte displays had been replaced with glittering toffee nut, the aroma of coffee fighting with cloying peppermint for dominance. Two students were studying, their books spread out on a wooden table. A man in a rope-patterned wool sweater sat in a copper-rivet-studded green leather chair beside the cheery gas fireplace.

Roy hunched in a corner, a cold coffee in his hands, his heavy coat pulled high, hat pulled low, bloodstained scarf tight around his neck despite the heat inside the shop.

Just two days before Christmas, and the weekenders were back. The rich and aimless making their pilgrimage out of Manhattan to their palaces in the countryside. He had been one of these people just weeks ago, but he couldn't risk anyone recognizing him now.

He was so ripe, he could smell himself.

The joggers and the mothers with nannies in tow lined up to get their lattes, averting their eyes from him. Maybe they didn't even see this vagrant in their midst. That was how well trained they had become.

But the little boy had seen him. The cherub.

He thought of Elsa, his little girl. His baby. *Jake's* little girl, he reminded himself. What was she doing? What had happened? Last night, he had the taxi take him past the Hawkinses' place. He had wanted to see Hope and … what? Warn her? Tell her how he felt, that he wished she had stayed with him that day? But it was too late. Dark sedans had been parked in front of the house. Lights on inside. People inside. Police people.

He told the cabbie to keep going, but the guy had started insisting that he needed to get out. Driving him around aimlessly, the guy had finally cracked, said he would call the police. Lucky for him there was that plastic divider. Bulletproof. Knifeproof.

Roy had paid him the full fare plus a generous tip—better to leave the man happy. Then he got out in the dark and cold, somewhere between East Hampton and Sag Harbor, and just started walking. He looked up at the stars and the skeletons of the trees and popped another amphetamine.

When dawn colored the eastern horizon, a police cruiser had eased to a stop beside him, crunching on the gravel shoulder. The officer had wound down his window, hand resting on the butt of his service revolver, and asked what he was doing.

Roy said he was just going for a walk, Officer. He had no fear, no worries.

The guy had said he needed to see some ID. The voices inside Roy debated whether to just kill the kid, but it seemed too messy, so he produced his wallet. Said he lived just down the street on Ocean Drive.

The officer had looked at the ID and then back at Roy, shined a light on his face, and said to have a good night, Mr. Lowell-Vandeweghe. He said that he shouldn't be out here all by himself so late at night. It could be dangerous.

Dangerous? Roy had almost laughed. *Do you know who you're talking to?* There was no danger if you were the apex predator.

* * *

Roy finished his cold cup of coffee. The servers behind the counter kept looking at him. They would call the police eventually, or at least a security guard. He was free now. Nobody knew where he was. So why was he back in the Hamptons? Roy tossed his paper coffee cup into the garbage. Because he was home.

Time to see the family.

* * *

Roy knocked on Sam's door, then just opened it. His friend never locked things.

A wide staircase off the expansive entryway wound up to the second floor, but the place seemed empty. Were some of the pictures gone from the walls? Was that the same couch in front of the attending table? It seemed different. An open metal pot was in the middle of the floor, which seemed curious until a drop of water plopped into it, and then another. A leak in the ceiling thirty feet overhead had made a dark spot on the white-painted woodwork.

For a seventy-five-million-dollar home featured in *County Living* magazine, it seemed to have gone a step below shabby-chic. Then again, Sam was a bachelor. He really lived in only two rooms of the forty-room complex, and he didn't care a hoot what anyone thought, as he always reminded Roy.

"Sam, hey, you home?" Roy called out.

The dining room's twenty-place cherrywood table was set as if for dinner tonight, but everything was covered in a fine layer of dust.

He heard banging—someone outside?—then a thudding and the squeak of metal. Through the latticed windows toward the ocean, Sam's bushy-bearded face and wild gray hair appeared.

Roy grinned.

Sam had a shovel over one shoulder. He'd been out doing yard work.

He motioned for Roy to join him on the deck. Outside, the slate-gray Atlantic rolled on, impervious to the concerns of man. The grass-topped dunes were still frosted on the shady side as the sun fought its way through the low clouds. The inshore salt breeze, clean and strong, blew frothy white tops over the sea.

"Jesus, Mary, and bloody Joseph!" his friend exclaimed. "What happened to you? Are you hurt? You've got blood down the side of your face."

"Did you know?" Roy said quietly.

"We've been worried absolutely sick about you, my friend."

"Did you know about my mother?" Roy didn't have the picture Angel had sent him. He'd thrown that phone away. He had nothing, no papers, just a memory he didn't trust.

"Know what?"

"That she didn't give birth to me."

The edges of Sam's mustache quivered in the wind, his wild-man bush of gray hair blowing with his beard. Despite the cold, he was dressed in an open-necked linen shirt. He had on heavy boots, though, and gloves. His shoulders sagged inward. "Ah, jeez, come on inside and we'll get some coffee."

* * *

"Yeah, I had an affair with your mother," Sam admitted. "I wouldn't even call it that, though."

They sat on stools at the pink granite island in the kitchen. Their voices echoed. His friend looked worn down, exhausted. For the first time, Roy considered the effect all this was having on everyone else in his life.

"Why didn't you tell me?" Roy said. Not angry, just curious.

Two mugs of coffee steamed on the counter between them. Roy was so wired, just the thought of drinking another cup made him jittery.

"Tell you what? That I had sex with your mother?" Sam put his face in his palms. "I was twenty-two; she was forty-seven. She was this glamorous socialite, the wife of a friend. She knew everyone. I didn't know what I was doing."

The problem was easy enough to solve: Just dig a hole in the dunes and roll Sam into it. Roy smiled, wondering what his friend would think if he knew his thoughts.

"And yet, you and my father remained friends?"

"He knew how she was. I apologized. It was a mistake."

"So you told my dad?"

"He saw that picture."

And then another thought. "Wait, are *you* my father?" Roy asked without warning.

Sam's mouth literally fell open. "Are you insane?"

Roy replied, "Have you taken a look at me? You're really asking that?" Somehow, being with Sam pulled a veneer of normality over the weirdness, allowing him to joke about it.

"I heard your mother and father had trouble getting pregnant. I wasn't around then. I mean, how can she be a Hampton matriarch without a family to domineer?"

Sam tried to laugh, but it sounded forced.

He added, "Your dad was into all kinds of stuff back then—real pioneering. So maybe he found a doctor in India. I bet half your mother's friends have done it."

"So why all the secrecy?"

"You think your mother wants all her friends to know her kid was born to a poor brown woman?"

"They do it all the time now."

"Now is not back then."

He was about to ask whether that was the reason his father hadn't written his mother into the will, when the front door opened. *Speak of the devil.*

Roy's mother appeared, followed by his wife and two very large men in white. Two more men appeared through the patio doors from the ocean side of the house.

"Sorry," Sam mumbled.

"Baby, just stay calm," Penny said. She lifted her hand. It shook.

The four men tightened their circle around Roy.

"We knew about the apartment," his wife said. "The one on Eleventh and Avenue C? Nicolae was just letting you have some space. To work things out for yourself."

"Please," his mother said. "Don't make this worse."

"*Worse?* I know what you did."

"I'm sorry you found out like this."

Found out they had used a surrogate? Or about her affair with Sam?

Roy eyed the big man to his left. The men had approached from all sides. Big mistake. He just had to dart out, disable one, and he'd be outside their circle. Back up a step, and they would have to come to him. He could take them out one by one. The plan evolved in his mind.

Penny said, "Shelby Sheffield was found dead in the basement of his house."

Roy's fists relaxed. "When?"

"Two nights ago. He cut his throat. He went insane. We won't let it happen to you."

Shelby cut his own throat? Won't let what happen? Let me be killed? "I can't stay here. You don't understand."

"Then make us understand."

He raised up an inch.

"The police aren't looking for you," his wife continued. "We've taken care of all that. You don't need to worry. You're safe."

43

"Tell me you are not goddamn serious," Deputy Chief Alonzo said.

His boss's boss, the Suffolk County police commissioner, remained seated behind his vast mahogany desk. It was an appointed civilian post, not filled by someone who came up through the ranks; thus, it came with all the attendant concerns about *re*appointment. Commissioner Basilone didn't like to get involved in the nitty-gritty details of police work, but he liked it even less when those details threatened his chances at climbing the political ladder.

Basilone growled, "We bust open the biggest unsolved serial-killer case in thirty years. We got maybe twenty bodies, and it was discovered through an *illegal search*?"

In front of the commissioner, also seated, was the borough president of Manhattan. He was a shoo-in for mayor when the billionaire businessman currently in office retired next year. Borough president was three steps down from the mayor's office, but senior enough for his presence to be a little unusual. Two men in expensive-looking suits—obviously lawyers—flanked him. Behind them, almost hidden, was Dr. Danesti, and Captain Harris of the East Hampton Police stood to one side of the pack.

Del and Coleman had just been called into the commissioner's office. No one was ever called in there except when something was about to hit the fan.

It just had.

Alonzo glowered at his subordinates and said, "If this ever goes to court somehow—"

"Technically, it wasn't illegal." Del had been anticipating this. She was studying law, after all. "We were doing a facial recognition—"

"Breaking into a home without a warrant isn't illegal?"

Ah, that. "We had reason to believe—"

"That Mr. Royce Lowell-Vandeweghe was there?" Alonzo finished her sentence for her. "Is that what you were going to say?"

Del shook her head. "I believed that a crime was in progress. I'd like to add that Mr. Lowell-Vandeweghe is *not* a suspect in what we found at the storage locker. It's just—"

"What? Just what?"

When pressed earlier, Del had to explain that they had found the papers that led to the storage locker, by tracking down Roy against express orders not to. But Del hadn't actually seen Roy in that basement. She didn't have an explanation, so she kept quiet.

One of the lawyers stepped forward and laid a paper on the commissioner's desk.

"The FBI has interviewed the owner of the building, Mrs. Rivera, who says that Detective Devlin and Officer Coleman were showing around a picture of Mr. Lowell-Vandeweghe. She said she told them it looked familiar, but now she's saying it definitely wasn't him."

Not what she told us, Del thought. "As I said, we had positive facial recognition—"

"Of our client going into the convenience store on the corner of that street." The lawyer produced another sheaf of papers: photographs from surveillance cameras.

They were the same pictures Del had used to narrow down Roy's location. The only way they could have gotten those was through Esposito. These guys moved fast.

"Is that true?" Commissioner Basilone asked.

"He assaulted two police officers," Del said. "My partner and me."

"Who is 'he'?" the lawyer asked. "Did you get a positive ID? Because the owner of the building has no record of our client. The FBI is doing a thorough forensic examination of the apartment, but there are prints and DNA from a dozen different people, none of which match our client. *Someone* may have assaulted you, but I can assure you it wasn't Mr. Lowell-Vandeweghe. Your only way of coming to this conclusion was some illegally obtained images of him buying milk at the convenience store nearby."

"Is that true?" Commissioner Basilone asked again, his voice getting higher and louder.

Del gritted her teeth. Bending the truth was one thing, but outright lying was another. "That is true, sir."

"I might add," the borough president of Manhattan said, "that this is outside the jurisdiction of Suffolk County and that a dozen different statutes of our citizens' rights to privacy have been—"

"With all due respect, sir," the lawyer cut in, "we don't need to go there."

He looked directly at Del, made sure they held eye contact. "Today is a day to applaud the diligence and intelligence of our fine men and women in blue. And Detective Devlin, despite"—he pursed his lips—"bending some rules, has, whether unwittingly or by pure instinct, led to the uncovering of the Fire Island Killer. She should be commended. All we're saying is that any media or files involving our client, Mr. Royce Lowell-Vandeweghe, or any ongoing investigation into him, must immediately be stopped and expunged."

"You're trying to tell us who we can and can't investigate?" Deputy Chief Alonzo said.

Del's scalp tingled. Alonzo was defending her right when she thought she was about to be thrown to the wolves.

The lawyer gave an ingratiating smile. "I'm saying that this has been a breach of my client's rights, but that we won't pursue the matter if it is rectified immediately."

"I think Roy was involved in the Plaza attack," Del blurted out. "Angel Rodriguez was working for him."

"Mr. Rodriguez was working for a lot of people, and we anticipated this conclusion from Detective Devlin, given her intense focus on our client." The lawyer produced yet another paper from his folder and dropped it on the commissioner's desk. "We released DNA samples, videos, and images of our client to the FBI, and a gait analysis of the video of the Plaza killer is not remotely a match to Mr. Lowell-Vandeweghe."

Gait analysis. Del hadn't even thought of trying that.

She said, "But the clerk at the self-storage facility said that someone paid for that locker just a few days ago." Why was nobody even talking about the gorilla in the room? "Roy just underwent surgery with Dr. Danesti, attached to someone else's body. Primrose Chegwidden is missing, and one of his neighbors is missing. Angel Rodriguez was working for him. He's still out there. I think he thinks he's attached to—"

"Our client is at home; he is not 'still out there.' I honestly do not understand how Detective Devlin is making this connection."

Captain Harris said, "One of my officers met Mr. Lowell-Vandeweghe on his morning walk, just a few hours ago, in East Hampton. Getting some exercise, no doubt, to help heal from his surgery. We have a video log and time stamp."

Del's face must have dropped, because the lawyer's smile became that much more vicious. "And our client is currently having lunch at his close friend Samuel Phipps's house, together with his mother and wife. Right now. Would you like to call them? Talk to him?"

He produced his cell phone for theatric effect.

"That won't be necessary," Commissioner Basilone said.

The lawyer said, "I didn't want to be forced into this, but Detective Devlin's apparent overenthusiasm has forced our hand." He held his phone up.

Del wondered what he was about to do, when Coleman's voice began playing from a recording: *"Yeah, I'd like to report seeing a missing person I saw on your website. Up by the sixteen-mile marker of Ditch Plains Beach."*

Her partner's face went bright red.

"This is Officer Coleman calling in a fake report so that Detective Devlin could illegally enter onto the private property of the Chegwidden estate," Captain Harris said. "And this was after her senior officer had given her a direct order to stand down, according to what Deputy Chief Alonzo told us."

* * *

They left the top floor quietly after Commissioner Basilone assured the lawyers that Mr. Lowell-Vandeweghe's rights and civil liberties would not be infringed on in any way, and that his name would be removed from any association to the investigation. Deputy Alonzo shepherded Del and Coleman downstairs and into his office, where he all but grabbed them by the ears.

Del stood at attention in front of her boss's desk. "Chief, something is going on here."

"You're right about that." Alonzo hadn't even bothered to sit down yet; he just stood there scowling at his charges. "You just got that detective badge, and you were supposed to be helping Coleman get his. Now you're about to lose your badge, and Coleman maybe his job."

"It was my fault," she replied. "I asked him to do it. I'll take the blame."

"I did it," Coleman interjected. "It's my responsibility."

"I've got a lot of respect for your father," Alonzo said to Del. "Why didn't you just hand whatever you had over to him? What were you thinking?"

"It was just a hunch, sir. Instinct."

"You're both on suspension." Alonzo's head sagged. He looked at the floor and said, "Just take it as a vacation for the holidays. You're off tomorrow anyway. Two weeks. Full pay. I'll handle Basilone."

Del didn't protest. It could have gone much worse.

She said, "I'm sure Royce was involved in the Plaza attack. He might have changed the way he walks. How can they even know *how* he walks? The guy has a new body."

She suspected that Roy was losing his mind. Transplant recipients sometimes took on the characteristics of their donors or, at least, thought they did. In Roy's case—*a whole-body transplant*—that sensation had to be amped up a million times.

Alonzo still stared at the floor. "Mr. Angel Rodriguez is a real war hero, and we all thank him for his service, but from what I read, that kid did a lot of bad things to a lot of bad people in a lot of bad places in the world. Who knows why someone tried to gut him in front of

NYPD headquarters? Someone was sending a message, that's for sure."

"But you *know* something is going on," Del repeated.

"I'm not stupid, whatever your opinion of me might be."

"I met him," Del said. "This Royce guy is not right in the head. We have to keep some kind of watch out for him."

"Now *I'm* thinking *you're* stupid," Alonzo said. "Do you know who those people are? The people those lawyers represent?"

"Rich people?"

"'Rich' is when you can buy a nice house in the country. These people are the kind that get presidents of the United States elected. Multibillionaires. They might look like normal people, but they're not, and Dr. Danesti is their golden goose."

Del said, "I'm sure Danesti is involved in whatever is happening. He's at the center—"

"Do you know," Alonzo said, "that the prime minister of Russia is coming to Eden's Manhattan office for a treatment next month? Meeting personally with Danesti? The prime minister of goddamn *Russia*. It's a diplomatic field day, and Basilone is trying to get in on that action. There's stuff going on here that's way above our pay grades."

"Murder is murder," Del said. "Royce is dangerous, and he's on the loose."

"He's not on the loose. Didn't you hear them? You've got that special skill of yours, right? You tell me. Do you doubt what that lawyer just said?"

Del didn't. She had watched the lawyer's face. It hadn't changed color, not the way a liar's would, even a really good one. Everything the lawyer had said in there was true—or at least, he thought it was—and it knocked down her theory that Roy was on the run. "I think he thinks he's attached to the body of Jake Hawkins."

Alonzo didn't even know how to respond to this. "Look, this is all someone else's problem now. The FBI has taken control." He pointed at a file on his desk. "Remember the DNA match of that hiker you were looking for? It matches Jake Hawkins. They say the woman had an aunt near there who used a lawn service. Hawkins did landscaping. That's how they're saying he cased his victims."

"But most of the Fire Island victims were prostitutes," Del said.

Alonzo closed his eyes and took a deep breath. "You applied to the FBI, right? That's where you want your career to go?"

"Yeah, I did," Del admitted. It wasn't a secret.

"Then let me help you by convincing you to let them do their job."

* * *

The sky was a brilliant, almost royal blue. It was always colder on cloudless days in December. New snow squeaked underfoot as Coleman and Del left the building.

"You okay?" Del asked her partner.

"Yeah, I'll just tell the wife I got some extra time for the holidays."

"Let the chief cool off. Basilone will be onto bigger and better things in the New Year. It'll blow over. Trust me."

"Sure."

"Did you notice one thing?" Del asked. "At that bigwig meeting upstairs?"

"I noticed a cool breeze blowing in my asshole."

"Atticus Cargill—where was he?"

"The old guy? Did you ever talk to him?"

Del shook her head. "Cargill is Roy's attorney. Was one of his dad's best friends. He's been the Lowell-Vandeweghe family lawyer since Roy was in diapers. Why wasn't he in that meeting? How did Roy suddenly become the 'client' of those slick bastards without Atticus making an appearance?"

"I don't know, but I'm not sure it's a good thing for you to find out."

"We need to find a way to put out watch alerts for Hawkins."

"Why?" Coleman stopped at his car, his hand on the latch. "Jake Hawkins is dead."

Del shielded her eyes from the bright sun. "I'm not so sure."

44

"Whatever you did or *think* you did, we're going to protect you," Penny said to Roy.

Her face seemed younger than the last time he saw her. Her hair was done up in a new style. She wore a cream silk top and the string of fat pearls that he'd given her for their first anniversary. This close, she smelled of sandalwood and musk. That distinctive perfume from India that she so loved. A thousand dollars a bottle, he remembered.

Always follow the money.

They all had moved into the dining room, with Roy in the middle, one of the big men across the table, two behind blocking the patio doors, and one blocking the exit to the entryway.

Roy's wife sat facing him on one of the dining room chairs, holding his hand.

Except that it wasn't *his* hand. It was Jake Hawkins's.

The big men had taken his scarf and hat. Now his neck scar was in the open, exposed for all to see. He hated the feeling. Penny had applied some antiseptic and gotten some Band-Aids to cover the wounds on his forehead and temples and over his ears.

They had taken his coat, too, and found Jake's passport, his stash of drugs, and the knife.

"Did you do the incisions yourself?" Roy's mother asked. Virginia didn't sit but wandered the perimeter of the room. She already had a gin and tonic in hand. "That is some nasty work." With one finger, she touched the left Band-Aid on his forehead. "But nothing that can't be fixed with a little plastic surgery."

Roy didn't reply.

"Who was that woman who called?" Penny asked. She squeezed his hand. "Hope? She said her name was Hope? Was that some kind of payback? You're having an affair?"

She had obviously talked to Roy's mother. The truth was in the open about her own indiscretions. "I gave her Sam's number. I was trying to help, even if I didn't understand what was going on."

"And who is Jake Hawkins?" Sam asked. He sat at the head of the table.

A large oil painting of a sea battle hung over the side table. Sam hadn't changed the decor since he took the place over from his parents ten years before. He thumbed through Jake's passport. "What have you been doing, buddy?" he asked as he put the passport back into the coat pocket.

"I hope you haven't been visiting Shelby Sheffield," Virginia said. She took a sip of her drink. "Now, that would be awkward, if that knife of yours made it into the hands of the police."

Roy squeezed Penny's hand, but not because he appreciated her patience—even though she had just accused him of having an affair, without seeming to care much about it. He squeezed her hand at the thought of Shelby Sheffield; it made him tense up.

What happened that night?

He remembered being in the apartment, remembered speaking to Angel. Angel said he had something that Roy had to see. More flashes of half memories. It wasn't just the papers about his mother; there was something darker.

He remembered blood.

Angel hadn't called him back. Hadn't answered any of Roy's calls.

Thinking about Rodriguez triggered a shooting pain in the bottom of his stomach.

Penny's cell phone rang, and she let go of his hand to stand up. She said hello and walked away a few paces. The big man near the door let her pass, keeping his eyes firmly on Roy.

"Nicolae will be here soon," Penny said to Virginia. She meant Dr. Danesti. To Roy, she added, "They're going to take care of you, dear. Don't worry. We'll get past this. He's bringing his people."

His people. The words seemed to echo.

Two heads are better than one, said a voice in Roy's mind. Two brains in the human body. An ancient brain in the gut. *What should we do? Stay here?*

If Danesti's people get their hands on us, we're never getting out again, the voice answered. Or worse. Shelby Sheffield. The image of his leering eyes came out of the darkness at the back of Roy's mind. He closed his eyes and tried to quiet himself.

What did his gut tell him? He glanced at Sam. His stomach twisted again, even more painfully.

"I need to go to the bathroom," he said.

"Can't it wait?" Penny said. "Nicolae is almost here."

"I can go in my pants if you prefer. I need to talk to Dr. Danesti, too. I didn't try to run when you came. I know I'm not right in the head, but I do know when I gotta go to the bathroom." He paused and added, "I'm sorry, sweetheart, I know I've been difficult."

Penny kept her eyes on him for a second, then looked at the big man by the door, who nodded at the two men behind him.

The big man indicated for Roy to come forward.

Roy stood and reached for his coat.

When the men reacted, he said, "My antirejection drugs are in the pocket. I need to take them."

The knife was on the table but far out of reach. They had searched him already.

"That's fine," Penny said.

Roy stayed relaxed and slouched until he was just past the door frame. Part of him just wanted to take a whiz, but another part of him …

He turned as if he'd forgotten something. The two men behind him were still on the other side of Penny, the fourth at the far side of the table.

He felt the guy following him stop, and the guy in front took a quick step toward him.

Unhurried, Roy let his weight carry him around. He ducked and brought his left leg out in a sweeping motion. It clipped the first man's left calf just as Roy's palm hit the hollow of his left shoulder. The man yelped as he fell backward, banging the back of his head on the table edge.

The men still in the dining room lunged forward, but they had to navigate past Penny and a few chairs to get through the narrow door. Roy needed only a second's head start.

He slammed the dining room door shut behind him and heard a body bounce off it. The man at the far side of the table had dashed around from the kitchen, only to trip over the ottoman that Roy shoved in front of him with his foot. He rolled, and just as he came up on his feet, Roy caught him under the chin with an uppercut, and he was out.

Roy dashed out the front door and down the porch steps, to Penny's Range Rover. She never took the keys out of the ignition—a habit that annoyed Roy, but not today.

As he grabbed the door handle, he had a fleeting realization that he'd made a mistake. Shadows darted forward in his left and right peripheral vision at the same time.

He had miscalculated. It was his last thought before a hammering blow knocked him back.

45

Searing white lights blinded Roy. His mouth had the coppery taste of blood, and his throbbing head wouldn't stay upright.

"You think we damaged him?" said a familiar-sounding voice.

"I don't think so," another voice replied.

"I mean his neck or something. You hit him pretty hard, and I think maybe we gave him too much sodium."

"He's at least two hundred pounds. I don't think ... Hey, he's awake."

"What?" Roy tried to bring a hand up to rub his eyes but couldn't.

Was he paralyzed again?

But no, he was sitting up.

He struggled some more.

"Mr. Lowell-Vandeweghe, can you hear me?"

Ropes held his hands behind him. He looked down and tried to focus his bleary eyes. His feet were tied to the legs of a wooden chair. The spotlights were so bright, he could feel their heat on his face.

Roy stuttered, "Who ... what is this?"

The voice asked, "Why did you hire Angel Rodriguez? Are you working for Hizb-i-Gulbuddin?"

"How would this guy be connected to *them*?" murmured the other voice.

"Eden Corporation has tentacles everywhere. Maybe they're making some kind of supersoldier."

"Let's start simpler. Not go crazy."

Roy blinked hard a few times, trying to clear his eyes. He struggled briefly against the ropes binding his hands. Those voices.

"Dog? Alpha? Is that you guys?"

Silence for a few beats, then hushed whispers. Two loud clicks, and the spotlights dimmed. The room came into focus. Rough concrete walls. Stacks of twisted sheet metal beside a green dumpster. Little white clouds puffed into the cold air with each labored breath. Two men were silhouetted against a job light hung from an extension cord behind them.

Roy said, "Where's Angel? Is he with you?"

Was this some kind of rescue operation? He was still groggy. The last thing he remembered was trying to escape from Sam's house. He'd gotten outside and was about to jump into the Range Rover, then noticed that someone else was outside. Something had hit him in the head.

"Can you guys untie me?"

One of the men approached. "When did you last see Angel?" It was Dog, the one with the gorilla jaw.

"Angel's not with you?" Roy strained against the ropes. The wooden chair flexed under him. "I saw him. After Dr. Brixton. Last time I saw him was with you guys."

"When were you with Dr. Brixton?"

"A day ... maybe two days ago? I'm not sure."

"I'll tell you what we're sure of." Dog walked back toward the other man, between the two floodlights on tripods. He picked up a cell phone from a pile of objects on a table between them. "You were the last person to talk to Angel. The cops tracked the phone number, but it was to a burner phone, paid for with cash at a CVS in midtown. They don't know who bought it, not yet, but we do."

"What do you mean, *last* person to talk to Angel? Where is he?"

"Charlie said that number was your number. He hasn't told the police yet. He wanted to wait till we talked to you."

"I still don't understand. Can you guys untie me?"

Dog put down the phone and picked up some sheets of paper. He walked back to Roy and clicked on a flashlight. Held the papers out. Images of Angel splayed out on a sidewalk, half-covered in snow and congealed blood.

Roy felt nauseated.

He turned his head away, but Dog pushed the pictures closer in front of his face. "That's where Angel is. You talked to him five minutes before that. Did you meet him?"

"I don't … I don't remember."

"You better start remembering, or we're telling the police who the owner of that phone number was."

"I black out sometimes. Ask Charlie."

"We have asked Charlie. That's the only reason your body isn't at the bottom of the East River … yet." The man's face creased up. "You know what Angel went through, man? They'd just got their boy, started a family." His face resumed its expression of hostile blankness.

Roy asked, "Is he dead?"

"He's hanging on by a thread, in the ICU at New York Presbyterian."

"Did he say I did that to him?"

"He hasn't woken up yet. Maybe won't ever."

Dog went back to the table and put down the pictures. He picked up Roy's coat.

"We've been through your stuff. A few thousand in cash, some passports. Looks like you were ready to run." He held up a clear plastic bag with a black-and-white picture in it. "Who is Adhira Achari?"

Roy leaned forward in the chair and felt its joints squeak. "A woman in India. Angel got her name from an old doctor."

"And who is she to you?"

"I'm not sure. Maybe my mother."

"Your …?"

"Surrogate mother. Angel found out I was maybe born to her."

Dog took a second to process this, then held up another paper, encased in clear plastic. "And what does 'Heaven all benefits, trust to all highoz' mean?"

"I have no idea."

Dog brought the paper closer. "What does it mean?" he asked again.

Roy looked at the scribbled piece of white paper.

"It was in Angel's wallet. The only thing we couldn't make sense of, apart from that picture of the Indian woman."

"I don't know. It means nothing to me, either."

Alpha shook his head and said to Dog, "I think we need to give him some time to wake up. Let's go get some coffee." He turned to Roy. "You go anywhere, and we kill you—you understand?"

* * *

Roy listened to the two men's voices recede into the distance.

Angel was attacked?

He remembered a fuzzy memory, talking to Angel.

These guys are going to kill us.

Roy listened hard to the sounds around him.

He heard the distant white noise of cars sweeping by on a freeway. With a grunting effort, using the balls of his feet, he pushed the chair back. It went up onto its back legs, then rocked forward. Leaning with it, he put all his weight onto his toes, then jumped back with everything he had.

The chair and Roy together shot up into the air a foot, tilted at an angle, and crashed onto the concrete floor. The chair's back legs broke off, and the back separated from the seat. He gasped for air, strained, and pulled his hands under himself, then under his feet. He leaned to his side and got onto his knees, then stood. The ropes were loose now, and he pulled his hands out of them and untied himself.

And listened.

Still nothing.

He hobbled forward and grabbed his coat. He was freezing cold and shivering. He checked the pockets. The cash was still there. He grabbed the two plastic envelopes with the picture and scribbled note and limped in the opposite direction from where Dog and Alpha had gone.

There was a set of stairs to the rear.

* * *

"There he goes," Dog said.

He lay on a mat on the fourth floor of the half-finished apartment complex.

"Let me see." Alpha took the night-vision binoculars from his partner and adjusted the focus. A grainy green image of Roy scrambling through bushes came into view. "He's making for the freeway."

"You think he did it?"

"I don't think he even knows what he did."

"But you think he attacked Angel?"

Alpha gave the binoculars back. "Charlie said that Angel got hurt trying to get whatever was on that paper to Roy."

"I seen some weird stuff out in the world, but this ..." Dog kept the night-vision gear on Roy as he scampered away.

"We track him. We see where he goes. Who he meets. Follow him everywhere."

"Yeah."

"But if he ever comes back near Charlie or looks like he'll hurt someone else ..."

"We put him out of everybody's misery."

* * *

"Can you call me a taxi?" Roy released a pile of chocolate bars onto the counter.

He had already opened a bottle of water and was halfway through guzzling it down. He put on his coat and zipped it up tight around his neck.

"There's a pay phone out beside the propane tank," the Quickie Mart cashier replied.

The teenager didn't register the least surprise at the vagrant dirtbag who had emerged from the bushes in the darkness. Not much was unusual for a New Jersey Turnpike gas station.

Roy produced a crumpled hundred-dollar bill. "Can I get a few dollars in change? Keep twenty for your trouble."

The cashier held the bill up to the light, then punched up the total and handed back three twenties and a pile of quarters. "Have a good day."

A car pulled into the gas station, and a woman got out to come inside.

Roy stuffed the chocolate bars into his pockets and hunched, keeping his face concealed. He pushed open the doors to the outside and watched the cars hissing past on the turnpike. Angel's friends were going to kill him, and who knew what else those maniacs might do.

He looked down the road, felt that familiar tug. Toward the small house on the north side of Long Island. Toward Hope and Elsa. He couldn't let himself give in to the urge, didn't know what he might do—what Jake might do—if he let himself go back there. He dropped a quarter into the phone and dialed a number.

It rang twice.

"Hello?" his wife answered.

"Baby, it's me."

"What happened? Who were those men?"

"Just some friends."

"Where are you?"

"Don't worry. Just give me a little time. I'm coming home. For Christmas."

46

"So you got into a bit of a pickle with Basilone, I hear," Del's father said.

They had settled on the sitting room couch in the three-story red-brick house on Brooklyn's Eighth Avenue, just a block from Prospect Park.

"Always follow yer instincts, and find a way to do t'ings, but the key is don't get caught doing it. Remember, 'Devlin' means 'fierce' in Gaelic. Live up to your name."

"I thought you said it meant 'unlucky.'"

Her father smiled sideways. "Depends which Paddy you're speaking to." He paused. "What I'm meaning is, always find a way to do the right t'ings."

"Of course."

Del paused before asking, "Why is it you've never gone back to Ireland? You've never taken me, never gone back yourself in thirty years."

"That's just the past, is all."

"But you had a brother. And your dad is still there."

"Brother died a long time ago." Her father took a sip of his drink. "And I just don't get on with my dad." He changed the topic. "Always try to do the right thing, Del, but don't get caught doing it." He winked and smiled.

He hadn't really answered her question, but she let it go. She always let it go, sensing some old wound, but one day she needed to know what had happened.

Her dad said, "When it seems there's nothing more to be done, there's always something more to be done. You think about that."

She nodded.

"Don't believe anything he says." Her mother sang the words from the kitchen. "*Est-ce que tu va rester la nuit?*" Was Del going to spend the night?

"*Oui.*" Her mother always tried to slip in a little Creole French when they spoke. Del rolled her eyes and smiled at her dad before adding, "Hey, Mom, I was meaning to ask you, did you work with the Phipps family a lot back when you were starting out?"

"*Qui?*"

"The Phipps family. Out in Southampton."

"Never heard of them."

"You never heard of the Phippses? They have that massive estate out there."

"My ears are working perfectly," her mom replied. "Are yours? I told you, I never heard of them."

That was odd. Del filed the information into the back of her mind, behind the other thoughts that kept circling through her head.

The NYPD had searched Angel Rodriguez.

With her dad's help, she had managed to get a look at the evidence. One thing he'd written on a scrap of paper and put in his wallet: "*Heaven all benefits, Trust all highoz.*" The NYPD detective in charge of the case had attributed it to a religious quote of some sort, hadn't paid it much attention, but it stuck in Del's mind.

"Are you feeling better, Dad?" she said. "No chest pain?"

Her father had learned a long time ago not to try to lie to her. "Just a little, here and there. I keep the stress down."

"Maybe you shouldn't be drinking that."

He frowned at the glass of whisky in his hand—and that was "whisky" with a "y" and not "ey" as he was fond of pointing out to the less enlightened. "It's Christmas, and a wee dram isn't going to hurt. And"—he nodded at the vodka soda in her hand—"I'll not let a lady drink alone."

She asked, "Have you thought about retiring?"

Thirty-four years in the NYPD had taken its toll. He had remained a beat cop as long as they would let him—almost twenty-five years—before forcing him up the ranks. He loved the electricity of being in the streets, but it had made him older than his years. Turning sixty this year, and he'd already had two heart attacks. With his pension and the value of the house that they bought thirty years ago—just before Giuliani began the cleanup of New York—he didn't have to work anymore. But then, what would he do with himself?

He picked up the painting Del had brought for her mother. "When are you going to start painting with colors?"

The doorbell rang, and Del's mother, her beautiful black hair now streaked proudly with gray, swept past them to open the door. "And when you are you finding a nice boy?" she said as she passed. "That Officer Coleman seems very sweet."

Del rolled her eyes. "He's married, Mom."

She got up to greet her sister and her husband. Their two kids, three and four years old, ran in screaming and yelling to greet the new puppy, who made just as much noise.

Del's phone pinged.

Her mother's face scrunched up while she was still hugging her son-in-law. "I thought we said all cell phones were to be off."

"I'll turn it off now," Del promised, but she pulled it out just to check.

It was a text from Esposito.

"Mom, Dad, just give me a second, okay?"

* * *

Del locked herself in the bathroom and opened her text messages.

"Sorry about giving you up to Basilone," Esposito's message read. "Had no choice. But I did track down that Latino-looking guy Roy was with. In front of that bar? Goes by the name of Fedora. He's a small-time hood that works with the Matruzzi family out of Queens."

She had never heard of Fedora before, but the Matruzzis—why did they always seem to turn up in this?

The next text read, "Here's the high-res video of the Rodriguez attack you asked for. Forty-eight-bit color, unencrypted. You'd better look at it on a big screen."

She had already seen the footage, and although she had no way to see the full face, there were flashes of the side of the attacker's face, and some of his arm that became exposed. She wanted to look at it in more detail.

She forwarded the link to her regular email.

"One more thing," said the next text message, "and make sure you delete this as soon as you get it." Esposito was obviously worried about getting in trouble for helping her again. The message bubble was an image, not text. She clicked on it. It was a picture of Royce, standing in line.

"That was from a day ago. Philadelphia International."

Del stared. The lawyers had said Roy was with his family. Had they gone on a trip? That wasn't impossible, maybe even likely. Eden had offices all over the world. She didn't see anyone else she recognized in the picture.

She whispered, "What are you doing?"

And was it Roy or Jake Hawkins she saw in that image, looking back up at the camera?

47

A red and gold terminator carved the stratosphere in half. The horizon, seen from forty thousand feet up, was bent into the slightest of curves. The middle pane of the airplane's window was frosted over in a fine spiderweb of crystallized water. Roy leaned his forehead against it, trying to soak in the minus-sixty-degree air rushing by at hundreds of miles an hour just inches away from him.

His eyes drooped.

"Sir, your water."

He blinked and turned from the window.

The flight attendant smiled, a plastic cup balanced in her slim fingers. She had to lean over from the aisle, over the guy beside him, who was trying to pretend he was sleeping. Roy threw two pills into his mouth, took the cup from the flight attendant, and downed its contents in a gulp.

He handed the cup back to her. His hand trembled. "Thank you."

"You're welcome." She hesitated. "Are you feeling okay, sir?"

Were the airline staff trained to watch out for infections? People who looked unwell? He had read online about reports of another bird flu outbreak in the Philippines. Would she report him? He'd felt stinging in the back and side of his neck earlier and, taking a closer look, had found small lesions.

"I'm fine. Flying just makes me a little nervous. I'm taking my anxiety pills. I'll be fine."

"Do you need a pen to fill out the customs form?"

He nodded, so she handed him one. "Just tell me if you need anything else."

She smiled again and adjusted the red and blue kerchief tied around her neck before walking back up the aisle. The deep-blue mood lighting of the Boeing 777's cabin shifted to a brighter shade to harmonize with the rising sun.

Roy watched the flight attendant go.

Ten hours stuck in this coffin, sweating in this tiny seat. How did she expect him to feel? Then again, it could be worse. He felt sorry for the guy beside him, who couldn't escape Roy's stink.

His seat thumped forward, and Roy gritted his teeth.

Two assholes behind him had been drinking the whole flight. Ten hours, and they'd never stopped jabbering and ordering more drinks. When the flight attendant refused to serve them anymore, he heard them giggling as they filled their cups from a bottle of whiskey they'd gotten from the duty-free shop. College buddies, on their way somewhere.

Ten hours out of Amsterdam, each minute an hour, and Roy's brain hadn't stopped circling around and around. Unable to sit still, he squirmed and fidgeted in his seat, his knees bobbing up and down. He bit his fingernails raw.

Images flashed through his mind: of Angel, his body covered in congealed blood; of Shelby Sheffield's insane eyes and the flash of spurting blood as a blade pierced his carotid artery; of Primrose Chegwidden—strangling her, cutting the ears from her head to get rid of those damned earrings.

Roy's eyelids drooped, but he balled his fists. He had to stay awake. Had to keep the monster away.

The intercom crackled. "This is your captain. We're beginning our descent. We'll be on the ground in half an hour, so the cabin crew will be coming around to clean up."

A slight forward pressure as the airplane decelerated, the nose edging down. The sky outside the window gained color. The horizon brightened. Roy pressed his head against the window, closed his eyes, and tried to force the gory images from his mind.

His seat bumped again.

"You going to take that?" Jake Hawkins asked.

Roy opened his eyes. The dead man sat in the seat beside him, clear as day. He stared straight at Roy, his face bright, every detail sharp, even the two-day-old stubble. Jake looked rested, healthy, his short blond hair combed back, his blue eyes clear.

"We're almost there," Roy replied.

Jake said, "I wouldn't take that. I would tell them to shut up."

Again the back of his seat thumped forward.

This time, Roy turned in his seat. "Hey, can you guys quit it?" He still had the pen in his hand.

His chair jerked forward yet again. The two guys behind him were wrestling or something, horsing around. Roy unclipped his seat belt and turned to look over the back.

"Can you stop that?"

The guy behind him had a full, thick beard and a red plaid shirt, a drink in one hand. He said aggressively, "What did you say?"

"I said, can you stop hitting the back of my seat?"

"Just relax, man. Chill out."

"If you don't stop hitting my seat …"

"You'll what?" The kid took off his seat belt, too, and stood up, their faces just inches apart.

"Sit the hell down." Roy shoved the kid back into his seat, but instead of just sitting, he bounced back up and swung a fist at him.

With his left hand, Roy grabbed the kid by the shirt collar and twisted it so that it half-choked him. He gritted his teeth as a wave of rage boiled up inside.

A crunching to the left side of Roy's face sent his head swiveling around. He tasted blood.

The kid's friend had punched Roy and was winding up to hit him again. Roy reacted without thinking, the pen still in his right hand. He jammed the point of the pen right into the kid's friend's neck. Hot blood spurted into Roy's face.

The guy gurgled and clawed at the pen stuck in his throat. Screams. Someone jumped on Roy from his right side.

He still had the first kid by the shirt collar, and literally swung him around, lifted him out of his seat, and used him as both shield and bludgeon. The fury surged. He let go of the kid and stabbed at another person trying to restrain him. More blood spattered the aircraft's interior.

Someone yelled for everyone to get back.

More screaming filled the cabin as people clambered over each other to get out of the way. Everyone terrified. Everyone staring at Roy. He stood up straight and turned to find the voice telling everyone to get back.

Ten feet away, a man stood up straight, a gun in his hand. Horns sprouted from the man's head. He identified himself as an air marshal, told Roy to freeze or he'd shoot. Roy charged, letting loose a guttural scream. The gun went off once, twice, the bullets hitting him but hardly slowing him down.

Roy grabbed the air marshal by the throat and jammed the pen into the side of his head.

* * *

The ground crew peered in through the window. They had just brought around the jet bridge to connect to the 777's front exit. The flight crew had locked themselves inside the cockpit, refusing to come out.

Paramilitary airport guards in flak jackets urged the airline staff back. The lead officer lowered his visor and unclipped his semiautomatic weapon from its single-point harness, raising his other arm. His fist straightened into two fingers pointing forward. He pulled on the latch to open the door.

It slid open, and he stood back, weapon out.

Blood spattered the cabin from floor to ceiling. Two bodies lay slumped on the deck. Cries and whimpers came from inside the cabin. The man hesitated, then inched forward. From inside came a grunting noise like a hog feeding, and then a roar.

* * *

"Mr. Lowell?"

Roy jumped in his seat, his fist tightening around the pen.

"Mr. Lowell, we've arrived." The flight attendant smiled nervously. She kept her distance while waking him.

He blinked and rubbed his eyes. The cabin was empty, the lights on full. Bits of paper were scattered on the floor.

"I think you fell asleep, sir. Welcome to India."

48

"I'm very sorry, but there is nothing that can be done." The little man in a suit two sizes too big for him gave a dishonest smile, his head wagging back and forth. "Now, go. Go."

Mrs. Achari was Tamil, and the man spoke Urdu. In Chennai, these two languages were the most common, but they were speaking in English at his request, to lend a sense of legitimacy to a process that was anything but. The man's eyebrows twitched as he waited for her to get up from her chair, and he glanced at the man behind her.

What lawyer needed a bodyguard? Only one who had something to fear.

Honking cars and cries of street vendors in the alleyways two floors below echoed through the open windows, with the smell of fried food accompanying the noise. The veneer-wood-paneled office had no air-conditioning.

She waited.

Waiting and staying in place were about the only weapons she had. A small Tamil woman of the Harijan caste didn't have many options. That she had been admitted into his office at all was a sign of the times, a generosity that untouchables of her generation could not have imagined fifty years ago when she was growing up here—but that was not to say they would listen. Times were changing, though, and she was determined to help them along.

"There are elections coming, Mr. Deepak," she said, not moving.

"Mrs. Achari, you are squatters, nothing more. It is an illegal slum."

"Half the village was made legal during the navy construction."

"Which permits have now expired. This is prime oceanfront property which for too long has been unlawfully occupied. There will be relocation." Mr. Deepak dabbed his bald head with a handkerchief he pulled from his breast pocket. "Kidneyvakka is a dark stain on Chennai's history and will be cleansed away with the construction of the new World Trade Center Towers."

"I have seen your relocation," she said. Even after the government outlawed the term "untouchable," new insults were found to make her people less than human. "You are tearing these families apart."

"Which are not real families on real property."

"Have you no heart?"

He nodded at the man by the door and waved his hand. "Go now. I said to go."

Mrs. Achari's knuckles lightened as she gripped her small purse. Inside it was the demand of the villagers. "We have a lot of fight left in us, Mr. Deepak. I assure you that."

The man laughed and said, "All the best parts of your people have already been taken."

49

"Welcome to Nissequogue State Park," announced a weathered green sign half obscured by a patch of bayberry bushes. Del scanned left and right at the crosswalk, paused to check for oncoming traffic, and then picked up her jogging pace.

To her right, the imposing brick facade of the Kings Park Psychiatric Center towered high over the bare branches of oak trees around it. "Insane asylum" was a more apt description. The massive complex of dozens of buildings was so ruined by time and asbestos that no one could redevelop it, despite its location right next to the river.

The asylum had peaked at ten thousand patients in the 1950s, she had read, and was originally a farming colony complete with a piggery. It was also one of the first institutions in the world to use shock therapy and lobotomies. By the late 1980s, it had housed a ragtag collection of the criminally insane. Thirty years ago, it closed after one of them escaped—into the very woods she was running into now.

The place gave her the creeps.

Feeling the asylum looming behind her, she ran harder up the gravel path, between the orange-and-white-striped metal posts marking the trail entrance, slackening her pace only after she had gone a few hundred feet into the leaf-carpeted forest of naked maple, white birch, and poplar. Just a few days before New Year's, and the temperature hovered above freezing, the air crisp, the faint smell of wood smoke from a chimney somewhere.

Maybe it was her mother's Creole background, but a part of Del didn't altogether disbelieve in spirits and ghosts and such, no matter how much the analytic side of her brain tried to dismiss it as childishness. Places like Kings Park had a dark energy that was hard to dismiss, a feeling of *dépaysement,* as her mother would say—the French word for an emotion that had no English equivalent: a feeling of disorientation from being out of your home country, or in a place you simply couldn't understand.

She had that sensation all the time now.

They had gotten a call from the medical examiner's office yesterday.

They had analyzed the body parts found in the storage locker. One of them matched the hiker who was last seen in these woods. The ear matched tissue samples from Primrose Chegwidden, but they hadn't released this to the media yet. Jake Hawkins's DNA was found all over the storage locker, along with DNA from at least half a dozen other people the FBI was trying to match.

All this made sense, but there was a new mystery. All the rest of the body parts were from cadavers stolen from the research wing of Stony Brook Hospital the year before.

Why?

It didn't make sense.

And where had Roy gone?

Why had no one sounded an alarm?

And why had Roy been hanging out with a hood connected to the Matruzzi mob? She had gone over the images from when Roy went to Hell. That Fedora character had gone in with them. Shouldn't the FBI be looking into the Matruzzis? But nobody would listen to her. She had gone and talked with Dr. Brixton's support group, and they said Fedora was there legitimately. He had body dysmorphia issues, but no one had seen him lately.

Maybe.

Even small-time gangsters had mental problems—maybe more than most.

And then there was the scribbled note that private detective Angel

Rodriguez had on him when he was attacked: "Heaven all benefits, Trust all highoz." Rodriguez was still in the ICU at Presbyterian and hadn't woken up yet. Maybe never would. They were worried about brain damage now. She hoped he would make it. He seemed like a nice guy.

At the center of it all was Eden Corporation and Dr. Danesti.

How did it all tie together?

She crested a ridge, and the trees thinned. She stopped at a sandy bluff overlooking the mouth of the Nissequogue River, emptying into Long Island Sound. Gray ocean stretched across the horizon. She bent over, hands on her knees, and took a few deep breaths, then straightened up to look again at the view.

The sun was just near the horizon.

This was the spot and almost the exact time of day that the hiker who disappeared here was last seen, almost two years ago. This was what the woman, the same age as Del, had seen just before she died. She closed her eyes and tried to feel the woman's spirit.

Speak to me, she whispered to herself. *Tell me what happened.*

She opened her eyes.

A family walked by her. A woman with three children, all of them dressed in fleece and proper hiking pants and boots. Del smiled at the woman but didn't get a smile back. She waited a few seconds and then began to follow them along the trail at the edge of the beach. The woman glanced over her shoulder at Del from time to time.

It wasn't hard to understand why. A dark-skinned person walking behind them.

Del shrugged it off. She tried to ignore little details like this, but when your job was being a detective, it was hard not to notice. Having an Irish father, straight from the old country, had drilled a stubborn practicality into her, not to bother with such trivialities—and even, perhaps, a touch of melancholy about the plight of simply being human.

The job required some of that. Maybe that was why the Irish made such good cops.

She glanced again at the family walking away. Perhaps she was wrong. Maybe the mother was just protective of her kids, no matter who was following. Human beings were tribal by nature. Skin color wasn't always the core issue. It could be religion, sports, or any other way people identified. Her father had told her stories of horrible bigotry between the Irish Catholics and Protestants—two visually indistinguishable groups of Caucasians.

How did she identify?

She was still working on that.

For whatever mixed-up thing Del was, most people couldn't see the beauty she saw in the world. For a few minutes, she stood in awe and watched the sun go down, her private palette of millions of hues stretching from infrared to ultraviolet, lighting the clouds in frenetic psychedelic glory.

Roy was a monster sewn together from parts, but in an increasingly schizophrenic world, maybe everyone was a little bit like him now—except that he was a murderer and still on the loose. She had to find him. Or someone had to, and soon.

* * *

"Yes, hello?" said a woman's voice.

Del took a deep breath. There was always something more you could do, even when you thought there wasn't. She replied, "Is this Interpol?"

"This is the Washington Bureau Office of the Department of Justice. We interface with the Interpol organization regarding international warrants. Are you a law enforcement officer?"

"Yes, well, no."

She had come back to her parents' place in Brooklyn. It was late, and everyone else was asleep. She had the couch in her mother's studio to sleep on, while the grandkids and her sister and her sister's husband fit into the small spare bedroom. Her family liked to stay together over Christmas, and more than a few drinks had no doubt been imbibed tonight.

No one else was up, but Del had just plugged in the Christmas tree lights again. She loved Christmas trees. Loved the smell of the sap, and the warm feeling of peace the corny little lights seemed to emanate.

"How did you get this number?" said the woman's voice on the phone. "This is restricted to law enforcement personnel only."

"I'm a detective with the Suffolk County Police Department."

"And do you have an arrest warrant for a suspected flight risk?"

"Not exactly, and look, I'm not calling in my official capacity."

"Can I get your name?"

Del rubbed her eyes.

She couldn't call the FBI, or rather, there wasn't anything more to say. They had already made it clear that they were handling the investigation and thanked her for all her help, but said they would take it from here. Some of the biological samples from the apartment in Alphabet City matched Jake Hawkins, but the age of the samples was in question.

The idea that Royce had been surgically attached to Jake's body had been entered into the possible theories regarding the case, she had been assured, but there was pressure from above to keep that on the sidelines. Right now they had their man, Jake Hawkins, and he was dead.

This phone call could get her fired, and she wasn't even really a police officer at the moment, but she hadn't tried to call from an anonymous number. She wanted them to be able to confirm who was calling.

"Delta Devlin," Del said after a pause. She heard keyboard clacking on the other end.

"And your organization?"

"This isn't officially from my organization. I'm acting as a private individual." She knew that this didn't matter, or shouldn't matter. She was still in law enforcement.

"Ma'am, as I said—"

"There is a very dangerous man who got onto a flight from Philadelphia International two days ago." She wasn't even really sure whether he had gotten on a flight, or with whom, or to where—but her instincts were lighting up.

She had barely slept last night.

"The man's name is Royce Lowell-Vandeweghe, but he may be going under an alias: Jake Hawkins, who is deceased and is the object of a current investigation by the FBI."

"Could we speak to the FBI case officer?" the woman asked.

"I'm warning you that this man is very dangerous and should be watched."

Silence on the other end. "And there is no arrest warrant?"

"None."

"We appreciate the call. Thank you very much, Ms. Devlin. We've taken down the information." The line went dead.

Del held her phone and looked at it. Had she just thrown her career away?

Or done nothing?

Or both?

50

After two days of wandering the slums in the north of Chennai, Roy was beginning to comprehend the futility of his quest to find the woman in the picture that Angel had sent him. Chennai was a city of five million people, and Achari was the second-most common surname of the poor Tamils who made up most of the population living in these huts and tin-roofed hovels.

Piles of garbage clogged the intersections, and a pervasive and overpowering stench of rot clung in the humid air. Nothing in this place seemed fixed, everything shifting and moving in much the same way that Roy's vision swam in a slow-motion, sleepless hallucination of this impoverished shantytown.

What were the chances, armed with nothing but an old black-and-white, of finding a woman from forty-four years ago in a place where the life expectancy wasn't even forty?

For two long days, he had been slogging through the mazes of unpaved alleyways and open cesspits with his guide, showing around the picture with his new friend Ramya. The night he arrived, he had gone straight to a hotel in the city's tourist core. He asked the concierge to recommend someone to show him around the slums to the north.

After protesting long and loud that it wasn't a place to visit, finally the concierge had relented. Half an hour later, a lanky young man in a polo shirt and baggy pants arrived. His name was Ramya, and he would be very happy to serve the American gentleman. The man had gleaming black hair combed in a high pompadour, and eyebrows that connected one temple to the other in a continuous dark band.

Roy had checked into the hotel downtown using Jake Hawkins's passport. He figured it was safer to use Jake's, in case Roy's name had been flagged from a flight manifest. He'd had to act fast. They hadn't expected him to run, but the noose was tightening. It wouldn't be long now.

He was out of antirejection drugs.

But not out of amphetamines. He was now popping another one every few hours. His feet and calves were swollen, probably from the flight but perhaps also from the stress on his heart. Maybe he would have a heart attack before his body rejected his head.

Either way.

He had checked out of the hotel on the first night after realizing he really didn't need it. He would just stay in the slums until it was over.

* * *

"You see, Mr. Jak-baba?" Ramya said to Roy.

He called him "Jak-baba" because Roy was using Jake's name. Ramya was Punjabi, and the honorific "baba" meant "wise old man" in most of the languages from Turkey to Singapore. It was mostly a way to make Roy feel important, he decided, and it must be having the desired effect. He liked Ramya.

They stood on a dusty mud road at the outskirts of a slum to the west.

Three young Indian boys lifted up their shirts to expose the smooth crescent-shaped incision scar from a kidney removal operation. The boys stood on a mound of plastic bottles they had separated for recycling—a booming racket they had cornered on this side of the slum. Open sewer pits ran on both sides of their business operation.

Roy struggled to focus. His vision swayed in the dust and swelter. He said, "That's okay, thank you," and motioned for them to put their shirts back down.

He wore the scarf despite the sultry heat, and not just to obscure his neck. He also used it to keep the flies and gnats out of his nose and mouth. The constant nausea from the smell made him feel always on the verge of gagging. His neck scar itched. He wanted to scratch it, just dig his nails into it and tear it open.

Three barefoot young men wearing baggy trousers walked past. One, in a Dallas Cowboys jersey, turned to look at him. Roy blinked. It was the face of Jake Hawkins again, looking right at him. He saw Jake everywhere.

He remembered the parties at the Chegwiddens', the flashing silverware and diamond necklaces and jokes about the cost of a new liver. This was the underside of the miracle, the part that no one saw, here in the dirt of a wretched slum where teenage kids would sell a kidney and their future for sixty bucks. Most of the donors suffered medical complications and didn't live long or well.

It was illegal, of course, but that didn't mean a great deal here in Kidneyville—"Kidneyvakka" in local speech—and this was far from the only place. Every big city on this side of the planet had places like this, in India, Bangladesh, China, the Philippines—wherever grinding poverty and anonymity made it something less than a crime.

On every intersection here were men and woman and children missing a leg, an arm or hand, an eye. Were they so desperate that they would mutilate themselves for sympathy, just to earn a rupee on a street corner? Or sell a piece of themselves? Or did someone else mutilate them?

The boys still stood in front of Roy and Ramya. They kept smiling but stayed put.

It took Roy a second to understand why they still stared at him, but then he pulled out a handful of rupees. Worth about a cent and a half each. He rummaged in his pocket for some hundred-rupee notes. He felt cheap, but he had to conserve his cash. "Show them the picture first. Ask them for help."

"Yes, Mr. Jak-baba, that is what they are waiting for."

Ramya pulled out the dog-eared picture of Adhira Achari and showed it to the boys. They squinted at the image, but all shook their heads.

"Sorry, Mr. Jak-baba. But we press on, yes? Back to the car?"

"Internet," Roy said. "I need to check the web."

"Yes, of course. We have the most wonderful internet here in Chennai."

* * *

At the edge of the slum was a bustling market, and Ramya led Roy to a little stall with walls of plastic sheeting. Ramya negotiated with the woman at the entrance, pointing his finger at Roy, and a minute later came to collect him. He ushered Roy to the back of the stall, to an old box-type computer with a curved CRT screen.

It was slow, but it worked.

"Fire Island Killer Found!" announced a website headline.

The media now knew that the police and FBI had found the collection of body parts in the storage locker. Jake Hawkins's DNA was all over it. There were pictures of Hope Hawkins, trying to hide her face from the cameras. Roy went online a few times a day, whenever he could, to read any developing stories. Old habits died hard. So far, the name Royce Lowell-Vandeweghe wasn't attached to anything he read, but that didn't fool him.

The authorities had to have made the connection by now, despite what Penny had said. Despite her assurances that they could protect him. There was no way Dr. Danesti could hide this. They had to have issued an arrest warrant for him by now, but none of that mattered.

He could have turned himself in, but he could also just die, stop Hawkins on his own. He would kill Jake, once and for all.

"Kill" was too aggressive a word. He would die anonymously out here in this sea of anonymous people. Curl up in a corner of a sprawling slum and let nature take its course, let the antirejection drugs clean themselves out of his system, and Jake's body could begin to attack Roy's head, ending both.

He wasn't sure of the mechanics of it. He had heard that the white blood cells, the T lymphocytes, couldn't pass the blood-brain barrier. So Jake's immune system couldn't attack his brain, but it would destroy everything *around* it: eyes, skin, connective tissue.

What would it be like to die that way? To have his face and head rejected by the body? Tumors growing out of control? He imagined his face ballooning as if a fungus were sprouting from under his skin. He had read that rejected body parts, like transplanted hands, literally began to rot like dead meat. His mind kept wandering, imagining it.

Apart from the last hour of the flight to Chennai, Roy hadn't slept in four days. The dream of him butchering people on the airplane seemed more real than the kaleidoscope of colors and smells around him now. Amphetamines were easy to find in India, he had discovered. He had a pocketful, and kept eating one every few hours, trying his best to keep track of whether they were the white-blue or double-strength red-blue ones he'd recently found. He had taken his last antirejection pill in the morning. A headache pounded behind his eyes, or maybe it was his eyeballs throbbing in their sockets.

Roy rubbed his temples and looked away from the computer screen.

Beyond the seesaw jumble of corrugated metal, a glistening wall of concrete rose a hundred feet in the air—a new shopping mall. Yesterday, they had gone in, or rather, Roy had gone in while Ramya waited outside. Marble floors and cool recycled air. The contrast with the squalor outside was dizzying.

Roy had learned on the web that the Ramaputra clinics inside the mall were affiliated with Eden. He had walked to one and loitered, fantasizing about going in and telling them he was Dr. Danesti's patient and that he needed more drugs.

You seriously want to do this? asked a voice in his head.

Jake Hawkins's face leered at him from the next stall, a sheet-plastic wall held together with string. *You kill me, you kill you. Why don't we go back to the clinic?*

"Shut up," Roy said aloud. "We're not going back to the clinic."

He got up from the computer, found some bills to give to the woman.

Ramya didn't say anything—just smiled and led the way back. He had come to understand that Jak-baba would speak to the invisible one who followed him around.

* * *

The rickshaw taxi stopped in a haze of blue-gray exhaust at the light.

A bullock clomped up beside them, pulling a cart. On the other side of the oxcart, an electric Tesla whirred quietly to a halt. In the grass at the middle of the intersection a man squatted behind a satellite dish to defecate, while a robotic forklift unloaded a pallet of ceramic cooking pots on the far side of the road.

Roy glanced at himself in the rearview mirror. He had dyed his hair blond yesterday, to look more like Jake in the passport photos.

"We don't need to do this," Jake Hawkins said.

The dead man sat next to Roy in the back of the rickshaw, as real and as solid as the ox standing beside them.

"We're not going back," Roy said to Jake.

If he feared anything, it was that Jake would finally take control. Roy fished in his pocket for another upper. The ocean of anonymous people in the slums would provide an endless hunting ground for a serial killer. He couldn't let that happen. He kept a knife in his pocket—if he felt another blackout coming, he would have time to slit his own throat first.

The last blackout had lasted three days. Maybe the next time, he would never come back. Would Jake head for the clinic? Get antirejection drugs? Explain some clever scenario to Dr. Danesti about how he liked it here? All the doctor wanted was to parade Roy-Jake around like a prized steer to show the success of his operation—the key to everlasting life.

What a joke.

Maybe not a joke. Jake Hawkins had clawed his way back into the land of the living.

The dead man leered and said, "We should just stay. We're safe here. Or we could go back. I'm sure Danesti would protect us."

Roy felt the pull, as strong as ever, toward Hope and Elsa. In his mind's eye, he could still see the little red-haired girl.

"We're not going back," Roy repeated.

51

"I'm not coming home with you," Roy said.

But Ramya persisted. "Not my home. But I have very good place for you."

Roy had just explained that he would meet him tomorrow to continue the search. They had exchanged email addresses, and Roy had a new phone they had just picked up. When Ramya asked where he could drop him off, Roy said anywhere. He was just going to walk the streets alone. Just him and Jake.

Ramya would have none of this. "I have a hut. You can sleep."

"I don't want to sleep."

The Punjabi man clearly thought Roy was crazy—and probably dangerous, from the jumpy way he kept his eyes on him. But he seemed more afraid of not bringing home money to his wife at the end of the day. "Then at least a place you can be most wonderfully safe while you stay awake."

* * *

The drive five miles east along the traffic-choked roadways to the coastal slum of Nagar Navy took most of an hour in the rush-hour traffic. Roy agreed to go there, mostly because it was a place they hadn't been yet.

Ramya was excited to show him his home, and Roy couldn't help but feel a tingling appreciation for the simple hospitality that this man he barely knew seemed determined to extend to him.

Jake Hawkins rode along in merciful silence the whole way.

The day was winding down, the sun dropping toward the horizon behind them as they parked the rickshaw beside a crumbling brick wall. The last of the wet season's gray haze blurred the lines of a haphazard wasteland sloping down to the Bay of Bengal a mile away. Goats browsed in the heaped debris, and a pack of dogs trotted purposefully by on their way somewhere. Groups of men and children sat along the ruined concrete fence outlining the edge of the slum. They watched the rickshaw arrive and nodded at Ramya.

"Come, come with me," Ramya said.

Roy and Jake followed him through a gap in the concrete fence, into a maze of colorful laneways and hanging fabrics. Places of business bustled. People saw Ramya leading this Westerner around and waved cheerfully at Roy from their small abodes along the sheltered passageways. A growing throng of children tagged along behind. The air smelled clean—delicious, in fact, with the scent of roasting cardamom and cumin drifting in the air.

Roy glanced behind at the children following them. The kids smiled and giggled. Barefoot, but they looked well-scrubbed, healthy, and happy. Roy asked, "Should I give them money?"

"Most certainly not. There is no begging in the slum."

"You mean, sharing a few rupees is viewed as wrong?"

Ramya's face creased up as if he were trying to solve a math puzzle. "Not wrong. I mean there is no begging, but anything from your heart is your choice, Mr. Jak-baba."

Men dug black soil from under large paving stones along a narrow pathway running into an empty allotment, hoping to clear drainage areas of the last monsoon downpours. Roy felt as if he were walking through a dream, with Jake Hawkins's dead face peering out between the cheerful dyed fabrics hung from second-floor terraces. A large German shepherd came up the lane with a small boy in tow. The dog was old, and its hips had almost given up on it. A father called out, and the boy smiled shyly at Roy and ran sideways into an alleyway, the dog in tow.

Halfway to the oceanfront, Ramya took a left into an alleyway and stopped.

"Here you can stay and do your meditations," he said. "I called ahead and arranged for you. This is all for you by yourself, Mr. Jak-baba."

A six-by-six patch of hard-packed earth was covered by a lattice of wood poles and a blue plastic sheet. The ground was swept clean. A fresh-looking square of cardboard with a thin red blanket folded in the middle.

"This is great," Roy said. "Perfect."

The Punjabi's smile widened, and his head wagged from one side to the other. "And you come with me for some chai? See my family?"

"I'm sorry, not tonight." Roy didn't want to see Ramya's wife, didn't want her to see the claws in his eyes. "Will I be bothered here?"

Roy was worried less about his own safety than about some poor local trying to steal from him or getting in his way. He wasn't sure how he might react—how Jake might react. The dead man stood beside Roy and looked at the hut with some disgust.

"You don't need to worry, Mr. Jak-baba," Ramya said. "The people here are already ruined. There is no need for them to cause you any harm."

"One thing," Roy said. "Do you think you could get me some steel wire?"

The little Punjabi's forehead creased up. "Some wire?"

"To fix the top." The wooden lattice of the roof looked loose. "In case it rains."

* * *

Roy waited for Ramya to return with a spool of wire before taking a walk down to the water. He passed a mother wrapped in a gold-and-red sari squatting on a concrete ledge and washing her two gorgeous children in a metal basin under a water spigot. She smiled proudly to Roy.

The sun had set over the city behind him, and a bluish-purple fog filled the eastern sky ahead. He found his way onto a crumbling stone shipway foundation nestled between Indian navy docks to the north and south. A rooster strutted past him, annoyed at having his territory disturbed. Roy sat cross-legged at the end of the pier and watched the luminous haze over the Bay of Bengal slip into darkness.

Was this the land where he had come into this world?

In the semidarkness, he surveyed the water's edge. Garbage-strewn sand dunes between the ocean and the crumbling seawalls. No one went down there. A good place to bury things, he mused as he fiddled with a length of the wire Ramya had given him.

* * *

Children in matching yellow-and-brown uniforms streamed through the alleys in smiling packs of three and four. It was early morning, and they were on their way out of the slum and off to school.

Roy had spent the night prowling the streets, always moving. In the darkness, he had imagined himself a shark. He read that they could never cease moving forward through the water. If they stopped, oxygen wouldn't flow over their gills and they would suffocate. If he stopped, he might fall asleep and never wake up—at least, not as himself. The throbbing pain behind in his eyes now radiated into every cubic inch of his skull.

He needed water.

Young women filled clay jugs at the communal water tap. One by one, they balanced their pot or bucket on their heads and walked off. Roy waited. One of the girls had on a red sari. She noticed him looking at her and pulled the covering over her lower face as she knelt to place her jug under the spigot. Roy pushed closer, focused on the red dot on her forehead, and squeezed the spool of wire in his pocket.

She flinched and shied away. Her clay pot rolled onto its side.

"Mr. Jak-baba, Mr. Jak-baba!" Ramya said excitedly. He pulled on Roy's arm.

Roy blinked and rubbed his eyes. By the time he looked back, the young woman was already hurrying away, water slopping from the clay pot on her head. The other women had moved away from him.

"I have the most wonderful news!" Ramya said, pulling again on Roy's arm. "Last night I was asking people about the person we are finding."

He nodded encouragingly at a small figure in front of him. It was a little girl, her dark eyes reflecting light like the water at the bottom of a well. She held a yellow paper in her hand, a photocopy of an elderly woman's face. There were words in Tamil that Roy didn't understand, but at the bottom, in English, very clearly: "Mrs. Achari."

The little girl pointed to an alley and scampered away.

"Today I have just heard of this Mrs. Achari who is trying to save the village," Ramya explained. "Today posters appeared all over the streets. The girl says she knows the woman."

Roy was already following the girl.

The edges of the lanes warped and blurred in his vision. Plants in ceramic hanging baskets swayed from second-floor balconies. Brightly dyed clothes fluttered like banners overhead, beckoning him forward. The stink of an open sewer wafted up as they jumped over. Roy lurched ahead, the girl stopping every now and then to smile and urge him forward. The huts and structures gave way to a dusty field at the top of the slum. Before them, a green forest stretched over the hard-packed earth.

"This is the Great Adyar Banyan tree," Ramya explained. "A very good and holy place."

"That's *one* tree?" The grove extended hundreds of feet to each side.

"Just one tree, but many trunks."

They reached the edge of canopy. Thick gray-brown trunks rose up, and dozens—hundreds—of branches dug their fingers into the hard-packed earth. The rising sun cast speckled shadows through the green leaves. The roots glowed.

Ramya said, "The Great Banyan is just one tree, but thirty thousand root-trunks go into the ground and back up—over five acres. Four hundred years our great banyan has been here."

The little girl stopped. Waved again.

Roy wiped stinging dust from his eyes. The roots and branches around him seemed to be conducting signals. Pulsing lights streamed along them. Neurons in a brain, the canopy above them a green skull against the sky. Three men squatted in a circle, deep in conversation. Everything interconnected, and all to the tree.

Straight in front of Roy, the little girl stood beside a woman. She sat at a manual sewing machine, her foot moving the treadle up and down, over and over. The girl tapped her shoulder. The woman stopped and looked up at Roy.

He stared, dumbfounded.

She had on gold-rimmed spectacles, her gray-black hair pulled back under a red lace shawl that covered her body. A streak of white paint ran down her forehead to the bridge of her nose, and a red dot hovered over the middle of her forehead. He took the photo from his pocket and held it out in front of him.

"Ms. Achari?" he said softly.

"Yes?" she replied.

"Adhira Achari?"

"Yes, Adhira Achari is my name."

"Is this you?"

She lifted gnarled fingers and took the picture from him. Studied it.

Seconds drifted by. Roy leaned forward, and a sweat droplet fell from the tip of his nose and soaked into the earth. He still had a scarf wrapped around his neck. The heat was suffocating.

The woman glanced behind Roy. She handed the picture back with one shaking hand. "This is me. This *was* me." She hesitated, then seemed to shrink into her sari. "I've been waiting for you."

"You have?"

"You must be my son."

Roy slumped to the ground.

The branches of the tree shimmered around him as the air left his lungs. Jake Hawkins circled through the pulsing banyan roots at the periphery of his vision. "Can we go now?" the dead man asked. "Are we done here?"

The Achari woman looked scared more than anything else. What was Roy expecting? She had been used and discarded by his family, like an empty milk jug. His fingers dug into an earth that seemed to crater upward around him. The woman looked at Roy and then at Ramya and the little girl, then back at Roy, her eyes darting back and forth.

"What's wrong?" Roy asked.

She gripped the saffron fabric she was sewing and squeezed until her fist shook.

"Twins," Jake Hawkins said. "She had twins, didn't she?"

Why would he say that? "Did you have twins?" Roy whispered to the woman.

She looked terrified, but then, as if seeing there was no escape, she relaxed and nodded.

52

Heaven all benefits. Trust all highoz.

The words floated in space in front of Delta Devlin, came apart into their individual letters, and spun into the maelstrom, sucked into endless white. Royce's face merged with Jake Hawkins's, their combined being resisting the pull of a white tornado that consumed everything around them. The white bled into red. Angel Rodriguez, Shelby Sheffield, Roy's mother, Atticus Cargill, Samuel Phipps—they all were pulled up into the churning abyss.

The image of Roy's father persisted.

He was the first to die, so long ago. The picture of him with his arm around Steve Robinson, the famous tech entrepreneur, now also dead. All circling, all connected in an accelerating orbit.

* * *

Del woke up in a sweat.

Snowflakes whipped past the window of her loft. She swung her legs out of bed and found her fluffy slippers before padding off to the kitchen area to make some coffee. Coffee before anything else. She pulled on a warm cardigan and sat down at her laptop to scan the morning's news.

The top story was about a Chinese tech company becoming the first to join the five-hundred-billion-dollar club in value, joining the select club of just a few other companies. She poured her coffee and took a sip, her eyes moving on to the next story, about unrest in the Middle East.

She stopped, the coffee cup halfway to her lips. *Five-hundred-billion-dollar club.* That picture of Roy's father with his arm around Steve Robinson.

Robinson had taken back the helm of his company, HighSoft, back in 2001, just when the huge tech meltdown began. Steve Robinson and Roy's father had been good friends. She keyed in some search words. HighSoft was now one of the world's most valuable companies, producing everything from cell phones to search engines and artificial intelligence.

She searched for and looked at the stock price: $28.25 as of this morning. When Roy's father died back in 2002, it was just under three dollars. So it had grown almost tenfold in value over twenty years.

Not bad.

Heaven all benefits.

Angel Rodriguez had done enough cloak-and-dagger work to start coding his messages, but he hadn't thought he was going to get caught with anything. He probably didn't even think he was in any danger. The man had fought his way out of some of the most dangerous places on the planet. He hadn't thought there was any risk—but still there would be a reflex.

Heaven all benefits.

This could mean that Eden Corporation was the beneficiary of the trust. She'd had the thought before. Eden. Heaven. It made sense. She had no way to verify it, but it was possible.

Trust all highoz.

Why the "oz" on the end of "high"? It didn't make any sense. When she met Angel, he had said his motto was "Always follow the money."

Unless ...

Follow the money.

Maybe the "z" was a "2." Did Angel mean "Trust all HIGH 02"?

Del did a quick calculation. So the ten million dollars of the original trust in 2002, if it was all HighSoft stock, could be worth a hundred million now. That was a huge amount of money to anyone. Atticus Cargill was the manager of the trust. He had to know, despite the confidentiality clauses. But then, how much of that would have made it to today? After all the withdrawals and conversions? A lot would still be left, right?

If this was even true.

So where was Atticus? This was another question. The man had disappeared right after Angel Rodriguez was assaulted right next to Atticus's office. The old lawyer was a Vietnam War vet. Had he attacked Angel and then disappeared with the money?

Del did another search online, into Eden Corporation. It was registered as a charity organization. You could make donations. Get tax write-offs. Had the lawyer, Atticus Cargill, changed the trust? How could she find out? It was supposed to go to a charity if Roy died—or if he went to jail, and either scenario seemed increasingly likely.

When she spoke to Roy, he had wondered aloud how Eden could afford to pay for his surgery. The cost had to be astronomical. He said the trust had paid for part of it. Or maybe the trust had paid for *all* of it. Was Eden Corporation profiting from the estates of its patients?

She did another search and found an article crying foul from the estate of Shelby Sheffield. His children, all middle-aged men and women, said that their father had made a massive donation to Eden Corporation in his will, robbing them of tens of millions of dollars and leaving them with nothing. They were going to contest the suicide ruling. The story had been dismissed as sour grapes. His kids were already wealthy.

Was this how Dr. Danesti was funding his company?

How did one check to see who held the stock of a public company? She did another search and found that the major shareholders, any holding more than a few tenths of a percent of the stock, were publicly listed. She scrolled down through the names for HighSoft. The list ended after only about two dozen names. They didn't list everyone. A dead end. Maybe she could …

A name popped out near the bottom of the list of top institutional holders: RLV Trust Corporation, with 0.54 percent.

She got up so fast, she knocked her coffee over, spilling it all over her kitchen table.

She didn't stop to mop it up, but ran straight for her stack of file folders, under the new bag of painting supplies she'd bought yesterday. She pulled the files out and spread them on the floor, then pulled one up, ran back to the table, and put it down on the section not covered in coffee. RLV Trust Corporation was Royce Lowell-Vandeweghe Trust Corporation, and 0.54 percent meant it was worth—she almost dropped her calculator—1.64 billion dollars.

Was that possible?

She went back and checked and rechecked the stock price, until it popped out: HighSoft's stock had split four times since 2002, with one of those a four-to-one split. So it hadn't grown by ten times. The stock had grown to more than *three hundred times* its original value when it was placed in the trust. It was right there, out in the open, at the bottom of a public ledger.

Royce's trust was worth close to two billion dollars.

Had Roy's family made a deal with Dr. Danesti, for him to save Roy's life in exchange for becoming the beneficiary of the trust? Two billion dollars was enough to make people do a lot of things. Was it possible Roy's mother agreed to this, or his wife, Penny—or Atticus? Where had the old lawyer disappeared to?

And where was Roy?

In three days, the trust would liquidate. Nearly two billion dollars of HighSoft stock would convert to cash. The money would go either to Roy or, if he should be dead or in jail, to the charity named in the trust. But where was he? What if none of those outcomes became possible to determine? All that cash would be stuck in legal limbo for years. Two billion dollars …

Her fingers hovered over the keyboard.

53

"Twins—now, *there's* a twist," Jake Hawkins said.

The dead man's face floated over the computer screen.

Roy sat in a small internet café at the edge of the slum, a single fan blowing a merciful stream of cooling air at his face and sweat-drenched body. After talking to the Achari woman—his birth mother, was it possible?—he had wandered back to check the latest news, promising to return to see her. His last-ditch effort to close the final loop before he killed himself, to know the truth. But the truth had opened a whole new Pandora's box.

He had a twin.

Roy was born in a test tube, his head later cut off and attached to someone else's body. He felt ill but couldn't throw up, was suffocating but wouldn't die. The needling headache had transformed into rhythmic tremors throughout his whole head. He could barely focus enough to read the letters on the computer screen before him.

The practice was common, he had learned. Ramya had explained it on their walk back. It wasn't unusual for surrogate mothers to have twins—a result of the combination of fertility drugs and hormones, and the process of egg harvesting and implantation into the uterus. All designed to maximize the odds of a successful pregnancy, but also upping the odds for twins.

The problem was that the rich families subsidizing the process might not want twins, and this risked an unhappy customer, so sometimes the managers would hide the twin birth. They would proudly deliver a son or daughter to the family and keep the unwanted child for another customer, another adoption.

Roy clicked through web pages detailing the practice. It was an easy though illegal way to make extra money, and who needed it more than these people?

And here I was, thinking I *was your twin.* Jake's face wobbled in the air.

"Shut up," Roy said. "Just *shut up!*"

With one shaking hand, he got out two amphetamine pills and dry-swallowed them.

He did a web search for Hope Hawkins. A new article appeared, in which she was telling reporters that her husband was murdered, that he wasn't the Fire Island Killer. He had trouble clicking the buttons, could barely focus on the images and words on the screen. Everything seemed to vibrate: the walls, the floors. Everything shook and trembled.

Roy sat upright. Had his father known about his twin?

He had asked the Achari woman, and she said she had met his father. She said they were about to tear down the slum, that she'd begged him for help. Roy asked questions about the doctor who had delivered him. Who was it? She said it was a Russian man, that it was an experimental program back then. He felt as if his brain were stuck in tar, hot and slow and frying in the heat.

"Let's just go to the clinic," Jake said. The dead man took an empty seat beside Roy. "We have something else to investigate. We can't stop now. Do you think your mother knew about this?"

"She couldn't have known."

"Maybe Virginia was the one who told him to throw your twin away with the rest of the garbage. Sound like her? Ever think about that? Maybe that's why your father cut her out of the will."

"Quiet, please." Roy rubbed his eyes and tried to clear them.

Everything was blurry, the room floating in and out of focus. He felt to make sure the switchblade was still in his pocket. If he felt that particular feeling of blacking out, he knew what to do.

Roy opened another search box, typed in the keywords to see if the story back home included his name yet. He clicked on the top story and had to read the headline twice: "Eden Corporation Set to Receive Two-Billion-Dollar Bequest from Estate of Lowell-Vandeweghe."

The story ran on for a page.

It wasn't the *New York Times*, but a smaller news outlet. It talked about how Royce hadn't been seen in more than a week. Rumors were that he was dead. The story had gone viral and was linked to reports of Shelby Sheffield's family claiming they were going to sue Eden Corporation.

The reporter had tried to get in touch with Atticus Cargill, the director of the trust, and then Gary Thomas and Samuel Phipps—the people listed as secondary contacts. No one offered a comment. No one could get in touch with any of them.

Toward the end, the stories veered into conspiracy, and for the first time, he saw his name linked to Jake Hawkins. Another reporter said she had a source who said that Roy had been surgically attached to the body of Jake Hawkins, now known to be the Fire Island Killer. The story appeared only in a fringe gossip column, but still, it was out there.

"So they finally found out," Jake Hawkins said. He read the story over Roy's shoulder. "Took them long enough."

"Let me think." Roy slumped forward and pressed his hands into his face over the keyboard.

Two billion dollars. Could it be true?

He willed himself to focus and did another web search. The story about the value of his trust was even in the *Wall Street Journal*. It was enough money to make people do crazy things. Atticus had to have known. He had lied to Roy's face and told him the trust was worth eight million when it was really closer to *two billion*. Now the old bastard was missing. He had to have conspired with Dr. Danesti to change the terms of the trust and make Eden the beneficiary. Had Roy's mother known? Was she part of this? How did Dr. Danesti think he could …?

Dr. Danesti.

Roy's thoughts became clear for the first time in many days.

Dr. Danesti was adopted from outside America. He had an Eastern

European accent. The man who delivered the twins—Mrs. Achari said that she thought he was Russian. That was close enough to Romania, wasn't it? The languages sounded nothing alike, but both were behind the Iron Curtain back then. The Russian could have delivered twins and spirited one of them away, eventually to be raised in Romania. He remembered the party at the Chegwiddens' house, how everyone said he looked just like Dr. Danesti. They were the same age. Everything fell into place. This was no accident, no random chance.

This was revenge, pure and simple.

Dr. Danesti was the twin.

Jake Hawkins smirked. "I told you it was a twist."

Danesti must have lived a life on the outside, gone to medical school. Had Roy's father discarded the twin? Left him here to rot? That would make a person crazy for revenge, wouldn't it? He remembered how Dr. Danesti had a fascination with his mother.

And his wife?

She'd said "Nicky." That Nicky said Roy was going to go crazy. Nicolae. Nicky. His wife had to be having her affair with Danesti. The man was trying to steal his life.

Not just steal it, but create a monster, make Roy suffer a fate worse even than death. Seek revenge and attach his twin's head to the body of a serial killer, and in the process inherit all of Roy's family's money—take his wife and his life. Danesti was behind all this.

And he must have murdered Jake or had him killed.

So Hope was right. Her husband was executed in some conspiracy, just not the one she imagined. If Hope was determined to uncover the truth—and expose a billion-dollar theft and murder and cover-up of a serial killer—there was no telling what Danesti and his people might do to her and Elsa to protect his secret.

54

"Give me half an hour," Del said into her phone, knowing that it would be more like three times that.

Getting a cab at this time on New Year's Eve in Greenwich Village? She'd be better off walking.

"Want me to come get you?" Coleman asked.

The only date she could get for New Year's was her partner, who was coming with his wife. She needed to get online and start dating, or something. This was embarrassing.

Del said, "I'll be there soon. Don't worry."

"Keep us posted. You have the address?"

"I got it. Don't worry." She hung up and went back to scrubbing paint from her fingernails.

Del had on a simple black dress and her Manolo heels, ones she took out only for special occasions. Her law books were spread across the paint-spattered table in the middle of the loft. Her fourth year of night school, but she wasn't sure what she would use the degree for. She enjoyed learning about the law and structure of government, but more to the point lately, she'd been focused on libel.

Could she be sued for what she had done?

Certainly, she could lose her job, but that would depend on whether anyone found out it was her. She had opened up a new online email account and used an anonymizer to try to hide her IP address. She had used the same process when she was a teenager, to access illegal peer-to-peer file-sharing sites and download free music and movies.

Except that they weren't free, as her father had explained when he found out. Grounded her for a whole month. Still, she had learned how to create an anonymous path onto the internet, but who knew how much scrutiny that could withstand from a determined investigator?

She still couldn't see the full picture, but she could sense its outlines.

Her blank canvases hung up and down the walls of her loft, but they weren't blank to her. To everyone else, they were bland strokes of different shades of white, but to her, the paintings sparkled in vibrant colors. Images and shapes that nobody else could see. She had always imagined she could apply the same talent to being a detective, seeing lines and shapes invisible to others.

Was she right?

Her leaked story had gone viral almost instantly. Two billion dollars in limbo for a man who'd had his head cut off and was missing? Possible links to a serial killer and one of the world's most valuable tech companies? The internet went crazy.

Within a day, the investigative minds of the fourth estate were digging into the crack she had pried open. Bright lights peering into the dark corners of the finances and practices of Eden Corporation. Into the details of RLV Trust Corporation.

Where was Atticus Cargill? Had he escaped from the country, with a few hundred million in hand? Sordid details of LCT Capital and Gary Tarlington, Atticus's partner, had emerged.

She had even let slip a rumor that Roy was attached to the body of Jake Hawkins, the Fire Island Killer, but that story seemed so far-fetched, it had gotten traction only on the conspiracy websites' outermost fringes. The story had gained momentum, but it was also drawing a lot of criticism and anger from the very people who had warned her off.

Very powerful people.

She used a nail file to scrape off another fleck of white paint from her fingernail, and her phone rang again. She tapped the answer button without looking. "Coleman, I told you, I'll be there soon."

"Detective Devlin?" asked a female voice.

Del stopped cleaning her nail. "Who is this?"

"Are you alone?"

"Is this a joke?" A prickling sensation crept up the nape of Del's neck.

"Answer the question."

"I'm going to hang up."

"Jake Hawkins's passport was just used to clear passport control at JFK."

"Who is this?" Del asked again, much more calmly now.

"You called us, remember? We've alerted the FBI and local law enforcement. We sent the images from the cameras at JFK to them. It's Royce Lowell-Vandeweghe."

"Did you stop him?"

"Jake Hawkins was not on any watch lists. He is deceased, at least officially. Roy will be arrested, at minimum for passport fraud—when he's found. *If* he's found. Our office has issued an arrest warrant, but tonight half the NYPD is out on crowd control."

"When? When did he go through customs?"

"An hour ago."

"Why are you calling me?" *An hour?* That meant Roy was already in the city. Twenty minutes in a cab from JFK, maybe less.

"Because, Ms. Devlin, you're the one who set this train in motion. We know about your leaks to the press. I believe your intent was to get Mr. Lowell-Vandeweghe's attention?"

Del felt the blood drain from her face, felt as if it pooled in the bottom of her stomach.

"Seems that you've succeeded, Ms. Devlin. The FBI will take a few hours to respond. I suggest you use that time wisely."

The phone cut off. Del pressed her hands together and wobbled on her heels.

What had she done?

55

"Can I look at the big one?" Roy pointed at a large knife in the display case. "What's that called?"

He'd been asking the pawnbroker, but dead-man Jake answered first: "I believe that is called a bowie."

"A bowie," the clerk said. He took the knife out and handed it to Roy.

"See? I told you I knew my knives." Jake Hawkins pressed his hands against the glass display top, then clapped them together. "That's American pioneer Jim Bowie's own design. A beautiful tool for gutting an animal. Always better to do a job right, with a sharp blade, than wimp out and use a gun. That's what I say."

Buying firearms wasn't an option. Too risky in New York. Too much attention. On the glass in front of Roy was a machete, its blade a foot and a half long. He had asked the clerk to sharpen it for him. Three more weapons, all switchblades, were on the counter.

"I told you, don't call them switchblades," Jake said. "Those are assisted-opening knives. Only gangbangers call them switchblades."

"Yeah, yeah, I get it," Roy replied.

"You sure you're okay, sir?" the clerk asked. He leaned over the counter with the bowie knife. The man's left eye drooped downward and his front teeth stuck out.

"I'm fine." Roy took the knife. This guy wasn't going to win any beauty contests, either. "It's an allergic reaction. Sunflower seeds I ate on the plane. I already took an antihistamine."

The same thing he had told the passport officer at the airport.

Open sores had broken out on his neck and cheeks—his skin beginning to rot and slough away. The left side of his face was swollen and hurting. His eyes felt as if they might burst from their sockets, and his vision was blurry. The vibrations from the walls and floor grew more and more intense. He had gotten a dozen blister packs of OxyContin before leaving India. It helped, but it wasn't masking the pain anymore, only keeping enough of a lid on it that Roy wouldn't scream.

The deformity had probably helped him get into the country, by making it impossible to tell that he wasn't the man in the passport picture. And on the inside, too, there was no difference between them anymore. Two had become one.

The dead man leered at two young women who banged through the front door of the pawn shop. They were drunk, dressed in short skirts despite the cold. One had on black tights and a fur-lined bomber jacket. They held on to each other for balance, took one look at Roy, then made mock horror faces at each other and giggled. They walked down an aisle, giving Roy a wide berth. Customers were coming in and out of the shop to buy New Year's paraphernalia. It had taken Jake three tries to find a pawn shop open this late, this close to Times Square. Right next to Ray & Frank's liquor store, conveniently enough. The girls reappeared with a box of sparklers and paid the clerk.

Roy tested the edge of the bowie knife. Carefully. He held the blade up to the face of the girl in the bomber jacket. "What do you think? Like it?"

She staggered back a few steps. Her friend grabbed her to make sure she didn't fall over and gave Roy the finger. "What the hell is wrong with you?" she said.

"I bet you could give yourself a clean shave with that," Jake said. He watched the girls leave the shop. "Don't worry about them."

"I'm not worried." Roy tested the edge of the blade with his thumbnail.

"Did you say something, sir?" The clerk leaned over the counter again, fixing Roy with his good eye while the other wandered off to look at the floor. The guy smelled of sweat and sausage and yesterday's booze.

"I'll take them all."

The clerk paused a few beats to calculate in his head. "How about a hundred and forty?"

"How about three hundred?" Roy pressed his last three bills onto the counter.

For what he was about to do, he didn't need money.

"But one more thing."

"I got no more knives."

"Do you have a menswear section?"

56

"Do you need me for anything else, sir?" Nicolae Danesti's administrative manager hung halfway in the door to his office, her business suit already exchanged for a modest yet modern evening gown. "Everyone's arrived."

"I'll be down in half an hour," Nicolae replied. He checked his watch. Ten forty-five.

"Do you need any help with your bow tie?"

"I'm fine." He adjusted it himself, admiring his tuxedo in the reflection from the floor-to-ceiling windows. "Dim the lights," he said.

His manager left him alone. Tonight was a big night. Half the fifty-eighth floor—the entire rehabilitation wing—had been redecorated to host Eden's New Year's Eve celebration. Many of the world's elite were here, having traveled from all over the planet.

How could they not?

The richest people in the world were the oldest, and they needed him. You couldn't take money with you into the afterlife, but Dr. Danesti sold the dream of hanging on to this one. To those who hungered for more time, this promise was worth any price. They all wanted to be here for the special announcement he would make at the stroke of midnight.

As the lights dimmed, Nicolae's reflection in the window faded, replaced with a view of the blazing lights of Manhattan's skyscrapers.

From a thousand feet up, he gazed out at the world laid out below him. The media attention on Royce Lowell-Vandeweghe in the past few days had been troubling, but sometimes, to change the world one had to endure criticism.

His financing had been secured, and his backers didn't seem to care about the negative publicity. In any case, wasn't the maxim "no publicity is bad publicity"? Everyone understood that this was a process. Shelby Sheffield had lived two years longer than he would have naturally, and Royce … well, that was still to be determined. Nicolae had learned from the experiences, had become stronger from them.

"Sir?"

His bodyguard now leaned in from the doorway to his office.

"There's a call from downstairs. A Detective Devlin just entered the building."

"What does she want?"

"She was invited by one of the guests. Just thought you might want to know."

"Keep an eye on her, but that's all."

It didn't matter. His sources suspected the detective in the leaks to the media, but better to keep the devil close, where you could keep an eye on him—or her. Keep the *Devlin* close. He laughed at his little joke. She was just doing her job, or trying to, and he understood that. It wasn't personal, and it wouldn't make any difference, or even be her job for much longer. He couldn't imagine anything that would derail his plans now.

The dream of his lifetime was coming true.

"They can all wait a little," Nicolae said to his bodyguard without taking his eyes from the skyscrapers before him. Clouds, illuminated from below by the city lights, skimmed the tops of the buildings, threatening something between snow and rain. Dots of water flecked the outside of the window.

"Antoine," he said to the bodyguard, "we're going upstairs, and I don't want to be disturbed for the next half hour."

He needed to gather himself for his big speech.

Nicolae didn't enjoy these parties. All the dinners with the glitterati, the rubbing elbows—it was all a means to an end, something to be endured. His real passion was always the work, his revenge on a world that had treated him so shabbily.

* * *

The lab was dark, the ceiling and the stainless steel refrigeration units along the walls lit only by the cold blue glow from the vats lining the center aisle. Nicolae Danesti walked the length of the room, hands clasped behind his back, admiring his babies in the glowing tanks of liquid.

And he did think of them as *his* babies.

Bonobo chimpanzees at varying stages of embryonic development in the first row of containers. Artificial wombs in which he had implanted fertilized bonobo eggs—but eggs genetically modified and bathed in fetal growth factors. Bonobos were the closest living relatives to humans, sharing over 99 percent of their DNA, yet were just two feet tall and sixty pounds at maturity. The perfect tool for the next step in his research. Normally, they gestated in eight months, just a month less than humans, but in these artificial wombs, he'd sped up the process to just three—albeit with some deformities, but he was getting closer.

The next row of vats held bonobos in more advanced stages of growth—complete fetuses, and then complete animals in incubators. Bonobos reached sexual maturity in twelve years in the wild, but he had accelerated the development of a fully formed fifty-pound male to just under a year. They looked perfect, their small arms and legs wrapped around them, their eyes closed—but then, their eyes would never open, not by themselves.

He had genetically engineered these primates as anencephalic—grown without a brain.

Next month, he would perform the first brain transplant into a manufactured body, from a thirty-year-old bonobo into the year-old body of its brainless clone. For humans, this was equivalent to putting the brain of a seventy-year-old into its own eighteen-year-old body. Not the body of someone else, but its *own* body, just a much younger version.

He checked his watch again. Eleven twenty-three. Almost time.

The regulatory hoops he'd had to jump through to get to this point were the hardest part of it. Experimentation on great apes had been banned in much of the world, but he had managed to get a special permit that sidestepped the Endangered Species Act in America by proposing a research plan that would enhance the survival of the species. He had certainly achieved this goal.

He could clone bonobos, grow them in these artificial wombs. The transplant experiment wasn't a part of the protocol, and he would face sanction, but this was the price of pushing society forward. And after tonight, he would be free of regulatory rules forever.

He inspected the face of the most mature bonobo in the incubator at the far end of the lab. So peaceful and dreamless. Just an organic husk waiting for the root graft of its dreaming tree. This bonobo was the one he would use in the experiment. He imagined what the chimp would think when it opened its eyes for the first time. How much stronger it would feel! How long would it live? This was the real question.

A juddering thud pulled Nicolae out of his reverie. He straightened up. "Antoine?"

No reply.

He turned and repeated, "Antoine?"

A figure emerged from the dark at the back of the lab, but it wasn't his bodyguard.

"Hello, brother," Roy said.

His face looked contorted, grotesquely deformed yet grinning.

The intruder held a machete in the air. Its blade glinted dully in the blue light.

57

"You really thought you could get away with it?"

Roy had watched the doctor inspecting one of his horror-show curiosities for a few seconds before entering the room. He drank down the cool tonic of the moment after so many hours of fantasizing. The pain in his face, in his head, was beyond agonizing.

"Just kill him."

Jake Hawkins danced around the vats of fetuses. The dead man was excited, too.

Dr. Danesti's mouth dropped open and his eyes went wide in the dim light. He retreated a pace, his back almost against the window wall of glass and the thousand-foot drop beyond. His teeth flashed in something resembling a snarl, but then the blank inspecting-an-insect-in-a-jar look that Roy so despised dropped over his face.

"It's good to see you, Roy," the doctor said after a beat of silence. "I was worried."

"Worried you wouldn't get all my money?" Roy advanced three steps down his aisle, making sure he could cut right, to the next aisle, to block any avenue of escape.

"I had nothing to do with that." Danesti held his hands up, palms out.

Jake hung back to Roy's side and leered at the doctor. "He's lying."

"I know he's lying."

"Who are you talking to?" Danesti asked.

"None of your business." Roy took another two steps toward the doctor.

The blue vats and pygmy chimps rolled in waves in his vision. The walls and the ground under his feet vibrated in a disjointed but building rhythm. The shrill whine of the electromagnetic dishes in the communication tower above the skyscraper drilled deep into the inner folds of his brain. He had seen the antennas and heard their shrieking before he entered the building, but he had no choice.

It had been easy enough to get in.

He still had in his wallet the plastic entry card that gave him near-unlimited access to Eden's inner sanctums. He was one of the corporation's most valued customers, after all. He had used one of the side entrances, keeping his face down, but a security guard stopped him at the second-level elevators. He told the guard he was Royce Lowell-Vandeweghe, and showed him his access card, confiding that he was the big surprise of the evening—that he was to be the big announcement.

Of course they had heard of him, he said. Of course it was a surprise—didn't they know there was a big shocker planned for tonight? He had on a black tie and jacket, after all.

Dr. Danesti asked, "What are you doing with the knife?"

"You like experimenting, don't you?" Roy took another two steps toward the doctor. His hand shook a little.

"What did you have in mind?"

"You cut my head off. It seems only fair that I return the favor."

Jake Hawkins hovered eagerly in the fringes of his vision.

"Think I'll go downstairs," Roy continued. "Meet the world's media that you've so kindly congregated. Hold your severed head up and explain to them how you'll live forever—that image should stick around in their minds for a while."

"You're having a psychotic break, Roy," Danesti said, and Roy could hear the confidence returning to his voice. "Your face is swollen. Your body is rejecting the tissue. You need to take some antirejection drugs."

"I think he's right," Jake said to Roy. "Maybe we get some more? Fix

us up? We could still escape, you know. Just cut his head off and leave it."
The dead man brightened. "Or take it with us."

"Roy," the doctor said, "you need to stop."

"Stop what? I know where you come from. What you're doing. You
want my mother. My wife."

"We can talk about that."

"About you stealing a billion dollars?" Roy bounded forward. Just one
last vat holding one blue chimp clone separated them.

"I'm refusing the donation. I had nothing to do with Eden being
named as your beneficiary."

The good doctor did his best to maintain the expression of concerned
reason, but it didn't last. The edges of his mouth curled up in a terrified
grimace. The fear bled out into eyes that widened, darting back and forth
between Roy's eyes and the blade in his hand.

"So you admit it."

Roy lunged forward and grabbed the doctor's tuxedo lapels with his
right hand, wrapped his big fingers around the fabric, and twisted, lifting
Danesti off the floor. Energy flowed into his limbs. The man felt weightless
in his grasp.

"You should have just told me the truth. That we're twins. It didn't
have to come to this."

He hefted the machete in his left hand. He could sever the spinal
column with a single blow. In his mind's eye, he watched the doctor's head
tumble from his body.

"Do it," Jake urged.

Roy's arm twitched as a searing new pain eclipsed the banging in his
head. He almost doubled over in agony. Danesti trembled in his grip, his
feet still dangling above the floor.

58

"Roy!" Del shouted.

She was soaking wet, her hair stuck to her head. She had ditched the heels for her Nikes and run the three miles from her loft in Greenwich Village to the Eden skyscraper in Midtown. She didn't even try to get a taxi. Her father always said to keep in good shape because you never knew when it would come in handy.

Her body shivered uncontrollably as it tried to warm up. She still had on the little black dress, and it hadn't been much protection from the sleeting rain. She held up one shaking hand with her Suffolk County detective badge, the other down low where she would normally carry her gun.

She had left her personal sidearm in her father's lockbox. They had gone to the range yesterday and were going again tomorrow, and the chief had taken her service revolver when he put her on suspension. She had no weapon, but he didn't have to know that.

In the semidarkness at the far end of the lab, Roy held Dr. Danesti aloft like a child's toy. He had a long blade in his hand. It didn't take a lot of imagination to see what came next.

"Roy. Listen to me for a second. Just stop." Clicking the light on, Del put down her badge and pulled her phone from her purse. "Tell him what I told you to tell him," she whispered to the man beside her.

"What was that again?" he murmured.

"I'll repeat it for you," she whispered. Then she yelled, "Roy, I've got Sam with me. Your best friend. Listen to him."

On the run over, she had called Phipps, leaving audio and text messages. She figured he would be in Manhattan for New Year's. She had done her research. A few days ago, she'd gotten a copy of the invitation list to Eden's New Year's gala. It was one of *the* parties for the who's who in town. Roy's mother was here, too, but Del didn't see her as especially useful.

Also on the run over, she had phoned the NYPD to confirm the arrest warrant for Roy, but she couldn't find anyone above a desk clerk she could speak to in her desperate scramble—so she'd called her father.

Roy looked back over his shoulder at her. Danesti swayed in the air, scraped his fingers ineffectually against his attacker's muscular forearm.

"S—Sam?"

"Yeah, buddy, it's me," Samuel replied, his bushy gray beard and wild hair haloed by the blue glow of the vat beside him. He stood straight, hands up in an attitude of surrender.

"Tell him Danesti didn't know about the money," Del whispered. She held her phone's light out so that it illuminated Sam's face.

"Danesti didn't know about the money," Sam repeated.

Del watched him, then glanced down to the end of the room to see the effect on Roy. He looked confused.

"How do you know?" Roy said to Sam.

"Just tell him Atticus was the one who changed the trust," Del whispered urgently.

Sam nodded and said in a loud voice, "Atticus was the one who changed the trust."

Two security guards behind Del edged forward, but she put out one hand to hold them back. She had brought security, of course. Had them try to contact the doctor's bodyguard, and when they couldn't, they came up here.

She'd said it might be a hostage situation, that she was a negotiator with the police, and flashed them her badge. Dr. Danesti was promising a big announcement at the stroke of midnight, just fifteen minutes from now. This was likely not what he had in mind.

"What now?" Sam whispered to Del. "What do I say now?"

Roy's face contorted, and he said through gritted teeth, "Sam, you have no idea what I know." He turned to Danesti and drew back the machete. "This stops tonight."

Del looked at Sam's face one last time and shoved him back. She ran forward four paces and stood up straight.

"Listen to me, Roy!" she yelled. "We don't want to have to shoot you."

Roy swung Danesti's body around to put him between them. "You want to shoot me? I can't be killed, because I'm already dead."

He charged at Del, the machete held high.

59

Hope Hawkins pulled the last plate from the kitchen cupboard, wrapped it in newspaper, and placed it gently on the others. The small kitchen was stacked with boxes of all sizes. Discarded ones she'd taken from the grocery store, the liquor store—anything that she could use to pack in.

The start of a new year. Anything had to be better than the last.

She sat on the edge of a wooden chair with wobbly legs and held the knuckles of one trembling hand her to mouth. She had grown to love this house. She knew all its imperfections, every creaky floorboard. The house was tiny, but that didn't matter, because it had been filled with a dream, its sagging beams held up with love. It had been theirs—hers and Jake's—and now they had to leave it.

Two nights ago, someone had spray-painted the front of the house with something so vile and horrible that she forced it out of her mind. Yesterday, she went straight to the store to find as many boxes as she could.

Today, just getting out of bed was all she could manage.

The doctor gave her sleeping pills, but that didn't stop the nightmares. She hadn't slept in two weeks, ever since the police showed up on her doorstep. Since the FBI came in their unmarked cars. Asking questions and more questions. Names and dates. They had dug up the entire yard and uprooted half the surrounding woods. They hadn't told her what they found there, but they did tell her what they found next door.

The storage locker. Filled with body parts.

And the headlines in the newspapers: "Jake Hawkins, Fire Island Killer."

The thought screamed through Hope's mind. She had cried for days and nights. Her mother had taken Elsa to begin with, but she went and got her back. She tried to protect her, tried to shield her, but the kids at school were cruel. So were the adults. She had lost her job at the diner. The boss said it wasn't his fault, but he needed to run a business. A *family* business. He couldn't handle the crowds of curiosity seekers and the rumors. She understood.

She had no money and no idea what she would do, but she had to be strong.

Little feet padded down the stairs. "Mama, are you crying?"

Hope hadn't even noticed that she was sobbing quietly. Tears dripped onto the scratched parquet floor. She wiped her eyes with the back of one hand and swept back her long red hair with the other. "I'm just packing up, honey. We'll get going soon."

Elsa came around the corner and into the kitchen. The same red hair as Hope, the same freckles. Just five years old, but her pretty eyes now had the look of someone older, their pale blue washed with a sorrow as deep as time. She had on her pink My Little Pony pajamas. "I'll help, Mama," she said. "You wanna empty the bottom ones, too?"

The little girl had been through so much in the past two years. First the shock of losing her father, and now this? It made Hope feel as if she were screaming with lungs full of water at the bottom of a dark ocean, yet, somehow, they had to carry on.

She said to her daughter, "Yeah, let's empty the bottom ones."

She opened the baseboard cupboards and arranged a new box, and Elsa began a determined campaign to get everything out. Hope watched. Each item her child placed in the box reminded her of Jake. Of where they had bought that slow cooker. Of her telling Jake they didn't need that food processor.

"We're going to go somewhere far away," she said to Elsa. "Somewhere nobody knows us, okay? Somewhere warm. It's going to be nice. You'll see."

"Okay, Mama." Her daughter continued working on the bottom shelf.

How could Jake have done what they said he did?

The psychologists had come over with the FBI that first week. They told her it wasn't her fault, that she bore none of the blame. They said that psychopaths were often charming, that it was impossible to tell, that they lived normal lives right out in the open. Told her that she and Elsa were just cover, just a smoke screen for Jake to hide his true nature.

So her whole life was a lie? Worse, she had loved a murderer? Given birth to his child? Revulsion and fear warred with her love and dedication. She gritted her teeth and willed back the tears. All those tender moments with Jake—all lies, fabrications. Jake had promised that he would always take care of them, never leave them, that he would never let go.

A loud rap came at the front door. Hope flinched. Not again. *Leave us alone, please.* Another knock, and another.

"Just a second," Hope called out, her voice wavering.

She scooped Elsa into her arms, held her snug, and walked to the front door. She took a deep breath and opened it. A huge man stood in the rain on their front steps.

Royce.

His face was misshapen, and red sores encircled his neck. His clouded eyes seemed to look straight through her.

"What are you ... What do want?" Hope stammered.

She took a step back and clutched Elsa in her arms. She looked left and right for anything she could use as a weapon.

The huge scarred man lumbered through the open door, his massive frame blocking out the light. He reached for Hope and growled, "We need to bury the past, once and for all."

60

Officer Coleman pulled his wool cap lower to cover his ears, turned his collar up, and rested for a second. He leaned on his shovel and looked out over the snow-crusted sand dunes and a gray Atlantic dotted with whitecaps.

When he signed up to be a police officer, he never imagined that he would end up here, doing this. He took a deep breath, then stood up straight and thrust the shovel into the sand.

It thudded against something.

"I got another one," someone behind him yelled.

That made eight so far today. He pressed his shovel down. Maybe nine.

The officers twenty feet to his left and right put down their shovels and walked back to the voice, but Coleman stayed there, dread tingling through him and raising the hairs on his arms and neck. More gently this time, he pushed his shovel into the soft sand and scraped it back. Something gray. And blue. He dropped to his knees, letting the shovel fall to one side. With his hands he scooped away the sand, brushing it away with his fingers. A swatch of red hair emerged.

His head sagged. He was going to be sick.

After two deep breaths, he got unsteadily to his feet. The sleeting rain was finally letting up. "I got one," he said. Then louder: "I think I found her."

He looked back down at the red hair. Yeah, definitely her. The bodies weren't even really dug into graves—just dumped between the dunes and covered in sand, as if the person who left them didn't care anymore. Coleman tried to calm his stomach and lifted his nose into the sea breeze to take a deep breath.

* * *

Delta Devlin struggled up the side of a steep dune, the sand spilling down with each step. BB-size pellets of ice fell from the sky. She topped the ridge to find Officer Coleman gazing at his feet.

"You okay?" She trudged over to him and looked down. "Yeah, that's Primrose Chegwidden."

The press was going to have a field day over this one—in what was already a sensational case. She wished there were some way to protect them, but Primrose was beyond all that.

"Want to sit down?" she said to her partner. "You don't look so good."

They backed up twenty feet, to a respectful distance from Primrose's body, while forensic technicians scrambled over with plastic sheets and cameras in hand. Coleman and Del sat in the sand and stared at the ocean.

"How did you know?" Coleman asked.

"I didn't, not really, not until the very end." Del glanced over her shoulder at Samuel Phipps's house.

61

Roy woke from sleep and bolted upright.

The memory of four nights ago was still etched into his mind. Every time he closed his eyes, his brain seemed to want to relive it, to go back over every detail of the glowing monkeys in the blue vats. He turned onto his side, the new exo-suit whirring to help him, and pulled down the blankets covering him. The couch he lay on was surrounded by packing boxes.

The two Suffolk County police officers guarding him roused in their chairs opposite the couch. One rubbed the back of his neck and said, "You sleep okay, Mr. Lowell-Vandeweghe?"

"Roy—just call me Roy."

The young man smiled. "You want some coffee, sir?"

"That would be great."

Outside the window of the Hawkinses' place, Roy saw two more Suffolk County officers standing guard. They were guarding this place as if it were the White House, but still protecting Hope and Elsa from him as much as from anything outside. They didn't quite trust him yet, but then, this would be a process for everyone to adjust to.

Himself most of all.

Detective Devlin had stopped him that night.

She had screamed at him that it was Sam who killed all those people.

That he was hallucinating. She'd said that it wasn't Atticus who changed the trust documents, but Sam. Explained that it was Sam who had originally tried to kill him by sabotaging his car that night two years ago. She had told him to think of Hope and Elsa. His friend Sam's expression had changed from leering glee to empty disappointment and then to anger as he turned to run. It was then that Roy had dropped the doctor and the machete.

By that point, a dozen NYPD officers from the Seventh Precinct had flooded into the lab, grabbed Roy, and handcuffed him.

Detective Devlin had insisted that the real perpetrator was Samuel Phipps. When they refused to arrest him, she had arrested him herself. It was her own father who had come up with his officers. If it had been anyone else, Roy doubted they would have let her arrest Sam.

Danesti and Devlin had defended Roy, told the police that he needed medical attention, so instead of taking him down to the station for booking, they had taken him into Eden's emergency center. There, with officers guarding him, they pumped him full of sedatives and antirejection drugs.

He'd slept for two full days. When he woke up, the visions of Jake Hawkins were gone, the voices in his head quiet—or at least, quieter.

While he was asleep, Fedora, the man who had befriended him at the Brixton support group, had come out of the woodwork. Fedora'd heard that Samuel Phipps was arrested, and he'd come forward and admitted to the police that Sam had hired him to follow Roy, to drug him with water and coffee laced with ketamine and flunitrazepam.

That was what had induced Roy's blackouts.

He hadn't been losing his mind, wasn't slipping his grip and ceding his volition to Jake Hawkins. He'd been drugged. Each time he blacked out, either Sam or Fedora had given him a bottle of water or beer. They kept him strung out for days sometimes, with almost complete memory loss.

It was Fedora's confession that day—and an admission that he'd also helped Sam steal the cadavers from Stony Brook Hospital and fill the storage locker with pieces of them—that had secured the search warrants for Sam's house. Roy picked up the newspaper from the coffee table. "Long Island Gambler Is the Real Fire Island Killer," read the headline. It had a picture of Sam beneath it.

Penny had always thought Sam was a creep. Roy should have listened to his wife. All those times he'd gone to visit his friend in the past months, he had a feeling of impending doom, of something wrong. It wasn't something out there, though—it was Jake trying to tell him about Sam.

Sam must have killed Jake Hawkins. The police found records of him calling the labs where Jake had done his blood tests for the MMA fighting circuit. When he heard they were waiting for a body donor, he did his research and found a close enough physical match to Roy. He must have found out Jake had signed his organ donor cards.

Had Sam tried to kill Roy to begin with? Fed him drugs at the party and sabotaged his car? The man wasn't speaking—was denying everything—so the details were emerging slowly. Who else knew about the trust? Atticus? Roy's mother? His wife? For how long? He didn't know yet. Didn't want to know.

Roy glanced through the rest of the article.

The story detailed how Sam had changed the terms of the trust, tried to make it look as though Dr. Danesti and Eden Corporation were trying to steal the two billion dollars. Sam knew that it would never happen, that the conflict of interest would never pass in the courts. And with Atticus gone, the money would spend years in legal limbo.

Sam would have been left as the sole administrator, able to siphon off money from it, drag it out forever while Roy and Jake were implicated as the Fire Island Killer. Sam even had some kind of rationale. The paper quoted him as saying that what Eden Corporation was doing was against God and that he had to stop it.

Sam still didn't admit to the other killings, even though they had already dug up twenty more bodies in the dunes in front of his house. He still seemed to think he could get away with it.

62

Danesti was not Roy's twin.

It was a delusion, part of Roy's fever dreams. Roy had been born to a surrogate, according to testimony from his mother, but no record of it remained. Was the woman he found in Chennai really his birth mother? It was possible, but Adhira and Achari were two of the most common Tamil names. Even so, to ease Roy's mania, the FBI did a DNA test on Danesti and Roy. It came back negative. They weren't even remotely related. And because a surrogate was not genetically related to the child she bore, there was no way to determine whether the woman he found in India had birthed him.

Dr. Danesti hadn't been having an affair with Roy's wife, either. Someone else was. They questioned her and found out she'd been seeing someone from the charity where she worked. This was another merging of reality and fantasy that Roy's mind had invented—but even so, he had helped uncover the truth behind Jake Hawkins's murder.

Del explained all this to Coleman as they made their way across the dunes toward Samuel Phipps's house. Four more bodies had been found in just the past hour.

"So you used your trick—that thing?" Coleman said. "To figure it out? How'd you know it was Sam?"

Del replied, "For one thing, when I met Sam, he lied about supporting my mother's work in the seventies. It was an obvious lie, easily found out—yet he did it anyway. It's a habit of psychopaths. They just don't think they'll get caught."

"And he invited you here, didn't he? Tried to get you to come to his house?"

Del literally shivered at her partner's words. She hadn't made the connection. She had found Sam charming, had even considered coming out here to his home—for police work, she'd told herself—and she couldn't help feeling some attraction to him at the time. She might easily have ended up in one of these bags, buried in the cold sand.

She said, "When Sam showed up at Eden, I told him to tell Roy it was Atticus who changed the trust documents, that Danesti didn't know about it."

Samuel Phipps had repeated those exact statements to Roy.

She had watched his face in the blue glow from the tank beside him and saw the flicker, the telltale narrow lines of color that only she could see. Was she positive? She would have bet that he was lying, but it was still a gamble. She had seen the same flickers when he said he'd supported her mother.

She also knew that Samuel was second in line, after Atticus, to administer the trust. They had just dug up the old lawyer's body, fifty feet from the house. No DNA test yet, but Del had looked at that hulk of a body. It was definitely Atticus Cargill.

When the NYPD refused to arrest Sam that night, she had taken the risk, arresting him herself and dragging him off into a cell in Suffolk County. From a strictly legal point of view, it was valid—a police officer could make an arrest in a neighboring jurisdiction if she was invited, and she had made sure, on her run over, to ask her father to invite her into Manhattan. Even so, she'd had to endure an avalanche of legal and career threats from the commissioner and a parade of lawyers, but she stood her ground.

She hadn't really been 100 percent sure about Sam until they got the warrant to come and dig on his property. Angel Rodriguez had finally woken up, and in his weak state, he had been able to tell the police that it wasn't Roy who attacked him. At first, he'd thought it was, but when they showed him pictures of Sam, he changed his mind.

It all made sense once she saw the angles and lines. Ten years ago, before he inherited this place, Sam had lived out in Long Beach—where they thought the Fire Island Killer might have lived. He'd even been interviewed by the original case detectives. He'd been under financial stress back then—from gambling, of course—before his parents died and he inherited the lavish beach home worth eighty million. His business had failed years ago. He had mortgaged the house to the hilt, and ten years later he was broke again.

Sam had a way of hiding out in the open as only the very rich could, but psychopaths had a hard time evaluating risk. He always thought he would win. At the end, Delta had realized that if that was who he was, he wouldn't be able to resist watching his final victory. So she called him, gambling that he would come with her to face Roy.

"So you're the hero," Coleman said.

"Nobody's a hero in this."

Del surveyed the scene. Orange flags dotted the dunes, detailing the locations of all the bodies.

She said, "The real hero is Roy. He's the one who uncovered the clues, knocked all the apples off the tree for me to find."

"That guy's nuts."

"Roy is the victim. He could have killed Danesti at the end, but he stopped himself despite the delusions. If he'd killed the doctor, we might never have been able to put the finger on Sam."

That was true. If Roy had killed Danesti, there would have been no way she could maintain any semblance of control and arrest Sam. He would have gone free that night and probably would have tracked down and killed Fedora, maybe even finished off Angel.

Coleman muttered, "This is definitely one for the weird books."

The roar of the tumbling ocean waves felt soothing. The sun came out. Seagulls squawked overhead.

"Danesti didn't press charges," Del said. "Roy is still Eden's golden ticket for new customers, so the doctor downplayed the incident. Said it was simply a misunderstanding. He even asked me to officially make Sam's arrest in Suffolk County. The doctor didn't cancel his press conference. He still made his big announcement at midnight."

Coleman pulled a clump of grass out of the sand. "Somebody needs to stop what he's doing. It's not right. He's guilty in this somehow."

Del didn't disagree, but then, what could she do about it? She'd heard Dr. Danesti had secured billions in funding to build a platform in the Pacific, create his own city in international waters that would be free from regulations. That was his big announcement. It was beyond creepy. Frightening. The future was arriving faster than she felt prepared for.

"So Roy's okay?" Coleman asked.

"I guess."

Once they had calmed Roy down that night at Eden, they gave him sedatives, and Danesti administered massive doses of antirejection and anti-inflammatory drugs. The poor guy had slept for almost forty hours straight, and she had learned that when he woke up, he was calm and lucid. By then, the FBI agents were on-site and explained what they could to Roy. They didn't have anything more serious than passport fraud to hold him on, and Danesti insisted he didn't want to press charges, so Roy had been free to go—with an escort, of course.

And there had been only one place he wanted to go.

Her phone rang. She didn't recognize the number but answered anyway. "Hello?"

"Detective Devlin?" said a voice. "I'm calling from the Washington Central National Bureau. My name is Agent Dartmouth."

"I'm sorry, who?"

"We're with the Department of Justice and interface with Interpol. We're the ones who called to warn you about Mr. Jake Hawkins's passport being used at JFK."

"What can I do for you?"

Was she still in trouble? Were they going to tell her boss? Even after all this?

"It's what *we* can do for *you*."

"I still don't understand?"

"Detective Devlin, we'd like to offer you a job."

63

Hope unwrapped the last of the plates and put it in the cupboard.

The house was still full of packed boxes, but she had decided to unpack just this one. Outside the kitchen window, footprints crossed the new snow. Elsa was on the swing out back, and Roy stood behind her, leaning down to push the swing, sending her higher. One of the two Suffolk County police officers standing on either side of the swing set nodded at Hope.

She had scarcely seen her little girl smile in more than a year and a half. On a backswing, Elsa looked over her shoulder and waved. Hope waved back, then held the hand to her mouth and fought back yet more tears.

What a difference a day and half made. The story had broken that morning, right after the first of the bodies turned up on Samuel Phipps's fifty private acres of beachfront sand dunes. Roy had wanted to come here, to tell them first before they heard it on the news, but he was still in poor shape. Shaking. His face was still swollen, with bandages over his sores, and his eyes were bloodshot. He looked as if he had woken from the dead, but he insisted on dragging himself out here to talk to Hope and Elsa, to make sure they heard it from him.

He hadn't known what to do with himself afterward, so Hope had demanded that he stay. She laid him down on the couch, surrounded by boxes, and covered him with a blanket. She told him to sleep. A doctor had come by to check on him.

More police had arrived in the middle of the day, and more after that, but not to deal with Roy. A flood of media and television trucks had jammed the small highway and roads leading in and out of Calverton. The story had gone global. Out of respect, the Suffolk PD had sent a small army of officers over to cordon off the Hawkins house. They even had cops posted in the woods.

The diner had called this morning to offer Hope her job back.

* * *

Elsa got off the swing and took hold of Roy's hand. She led him back to the house. Hope went to the back door and opened it, shooed her daughter inside, and told her to get cleaned up. "I have to speak to our guest," she said, and pulled on a coat to step outside.

"I can't stay," Roy said as soon as the door closed.

The two police officers in the backyard kept a respectful distance.

"Come sit with me," Hope said. She sat down on the wicker back-porch swing and patted the place beside her.

Roy said, "I'm not right. In the head."

With a shaking hand, he lifted his baseball cap to reveal the scars in his forehead and temples. "I did that to myself. And I almost killed someone."

She remained silent, unsure what to say.

This man was a stranger to her, and yet … *most* of him was her husband. Her Jake. A juddering collision of strangeness and familiarity splintered in her mind. Her emotions shattered and recombined, revulsion and attraction struggling for dominance. *Till death do us part*—that was what she promised Jake, but was he really dead? Was a part of him still alive? She didn't know how to rationalize it, but she could not deny what she felt.

Roy said, "I'm not safe to be around Elsa."

"You'd never hurt her."

"How do you know?"

She hesitated, then put a hand on the forearm of his parka. "I just know."

"I talked to him." Roy's jaw muscles flexed. "At least, I thought I talked to Jake. I was hallucinating, but Jake *did* stop me from killing Danesti. I felt him."

She couldn't imagine what this man had been through—was scared of him even now, if she was being honest. But he had risked his life to come back here and protect her and her daughter. Moreover, he had put his sanity on the line, risking something perhaps even worse than death.

"I can tell you that Jake loves you and Elsa more than anything. I felt him pulling me back here, no matter where I went. I can still feel him." Roy put his hand on his chest.

"What are you going to do?"

"I asked Penny for a divorce. This morning. Even back before the accident, she had met someone else. Our marriage has been over for a long time." Roy looked away. "What happened to your husband was my fault—"

"It wasn't your fault."

"I'm still to blame."

She didn't try to argue with him. One thing did bother her, though. Of the stories she had read online, some talked about the prodigious body count, but just as many were more interested in the cash, the trust fund. "The Two Billion Dollar Man," they had started to call Roy. They seemed more interested in the money than the lives lost.

"What about the trust?" Hope asked. After all, it was the reason her husband was murdered.

"Those were the other calls I made this morning. I gave it all away. Gave it to charity."

"Excuse me?"

She didn't let go of Roy's arm. If anything, she held it tighter. It wasn't what she had expected to hear.

"Not quite all. I put five million in an account for you and Elsa. Left the same amount for myself—what I thought I was owed. Probably need it for medical expenses—I've cut all ties with Dr. Danesti." He looked away, as if feeling guilty. "I can cancel all that if you want. I'd understand. I also gave some money to a friend of mine, for his kid, Rodrigo, but that's it."

"You gave all the rest away? *Two billion dollars?*"

"Do you want more? I could get some back, maybe, if you—"

"No. I don't want any of it."

Roy looked into the forest, his eyes focused on a spot a million miles beyond.

He said, "Just think about it. I'm sure Jake would have wanted you and Elsa to have it."

One heartbeat, then two.

"I better go," Roy said.

He leaned forward to get up.

"We have a spare bedroom," Hope said. "Why don't you stay today? Go to the hospital tomorrow? If the doctors think it's okay?"

Elsa had opened the porch door and looked at her mother, who nodded. The little girl walked over, and Hope pulled her into her lap.

"I'm not right in the head," Roy said. "I told you."

"Then we'll help you *get* right."

Snowflakes drifted over the forest. Roy's body sagged. He sat back down.

Hope said, "We'll find a way."

She pulled him toward her, and he let his massive body collapse onto hers. It wasn't only men who could promise never to let go, no matter what. She held him and Elsa tight in her arms.

She whispered, "Come rest that weary head."

EPILOGUE

"Mrs. Achari, come and sit," said the lawyer, the little man in the oversize suit.

"Little-Man-Big-Suit" was what Mrs. Achari had started calling him in the slum while she distributed leaflets. The name had stuck, and she laughed about it, but this morning she was summoned into the city by two police officers. They'd been very insistent. Could she be arrested for making up nicknames? More likely, she might be arrested for disturbing the peace.

Or was it the incident with that man?

The crazy one she had met under the Great Adyar Banyan tree. Ramya had insisted that she meet him. Her name *was* Adhira Achari, that was true, and years ago she had been a surrogate for a Western couple, when she was still almost a child herself.

The experience had ripped her soul.

She had always wondered what happened to the boy, and when this clearly delusional American came along, her heart had leaped. But she couldn't be *sure* that it was her in the photo. She couldn't see very clearly, even with her glasses. Ramya had insisted that it was her. He said that she could ease the man's pain, that he was in great emotional and spiritual suffering—and the man had frightened her. He'd been babbling like a lunatic. In the end, she had told him whatever he wanted to hear, and after that, he just disappeared.

Was that why the police had come for her? What had she done?

Little-Man-Big-Suit gave his trademark dishonest smile. His head wagged back and forth. "Please. Please. You *must* sit down."

The honking cars and cries of the street vendors echoed through the open windows. The man's bodyguard was still here, but now there were two more men. Different men. Huge men, directing evil grins at her. Even sitting down, the men towered over Mrs. Achari. She sensed their menacing presence behind her.

"You can't force me to do anything," she blurted out straightaway.

The lawyer extended one shaking hand. "Can you please verify this list of residents?"

"I will do nothing."

"You misunderstand me." He glanced nervously at one of the burly men behind her. Mrs. Achari looked back as well, over her shoulder. The men were both Caucasian. They smiled back, revealing straight white teeth.

"These men ..." The lawyer stopped to clear his throat. "These two men are here to ensure a fair and proper distribution of a ... a gift." He held up a piece of paper, leaned over his desk, and handed it to her. "You are to refer to these men—"

"As Angel's Guardians, ma'am," said one of the men. "We will be here with you through the transition. This is a two-year operation to serve and protect."

Mrs. Achari was completely lost. "Serve? Protect?"

"Your village," said the man. He stood up. He looked as tall as a tree. "My name is Dog, and this is Alpha."

"You're not here to throw us out?"

Dog laughed and shook his head. "You *own* that land now. Over two thousand acres—the whole stretch of land between the navy docks, all the way to the water. Look at that piece of paper in your hand."

Mrs. Achari did as he said. "There are too many numbers."

"That's how much money was just deposited into a charity in your name. It's to be distributed among everyone in your village."

She looked again at the piece of paper and held it out at arm's length. She still couldn't see it properly. "This is in rupees?"

"Dollars, ma'am. Almost two billion dollars."

"Is this some joke?"

"No, ma'am."

Mrs. Achari's hand shook as she tried to count all the digits in the number on the paper. "I am very sorry, but English is my third language. Do you mean you are my guardian angels?"

"We'd prefer 'Angel's Guardians.'" Dog gave her the sweetest grin she had ever seen on a man so huge. "Or just your Angels."

AUTHOR'S NOTE

Dear Reader,

I hope you enjoyed this journey with me. In the next section is a discussion of *The Dreaming Tree* in real life, some background material, and parts of my process in creating it.

Also …

The adventure continues for Detective Delta Devlin in my next book, *Meet Your Maker*, in which Devlin begins to work for Interpol and investigates the mysterious murder of an American art dealer.

THE DREAMING TREE IN REAL LIFE

First off, thanks so much for reading. I really appreciate your support and your interest in my work. Feel free to email me if you want to chat about anything in the book. My contact info is at the end of this section and also on my website.

There is a lot to unpack in this book.

If you've read any of my other work, you'll know how much I love to mix reality with fiction until the line between them gets gray and blurry. Much of this book is based on real-world events and technologies—from the impending event (planned for this year) of the first human head transplant operation, to tetrachromats (real people who do indeed see a hundred million more colors than the rest of us), artificial wombs, the freezing of whole organs for transplant, and even the Gilgo Beach Killer (whom I renamed the Fire Island Killer in this book)—which is an active and ongoing investigation and still one of the biggest unsolved serial-killer cases in America, even though someone was recently convicted in two of the killings.

The saddest truth, however, is the brutal and highly lucrative international trade in human organs for transplant, which we will discuss a bit later in more detail.

To kick off the discussion, *The Dreaming Tree* is an homage, of course, to Mary Shelley's *Frankenstein*. I purposely finished it around the two-hundredth anniversary of *Frankenstein*'s original release, as a celebration, but also to coincide with the eve of the very first human head transplant about to be performed in the real world.

In the world of Mary Shelley, the book was pure fantasy, a way to reflect on the realities of the world of that time. But now this topic takes on a whole new dimension as humanity contemplates crossing this threshold.

"Who was I? What was I? Whence did I come?"

These words are from the creation of Dr. Frankenstein in the throes of its existential dilemma, and I wanted to touch on some of these same ideas in *The Dreaming Tree*. There are strong thematic elements related to Milton's *Paradise Lost*, of Satan as the fallen angel, so for fun I included a strong secondary character named Angel, who is sacrificed defending our fallen hero and, ultimately, is the one who brings redemption. I invite you to tell me what you think of the parallels.

On the topic of human head transplants, if you search the web, you'll see that Dr. Sergio Canavero announced recently that he will be attempting the first human head transplant. The very audacity of Canavero's project shocks us, but the technical hurdles to performing such an operation have already been overcome. *Technically*, it should be feasible, but morally and ethically? This is another question entirely. However, history shows us that once something becomes possible, it isn't long before someone crosses the threshold, come what may.

When in vitro fertilizations and heart transplants were first proposed, the ethics and morality were vigorously debated, with many at the time saying that such daring experiments were against God. But now such procedures have become commonplace.

And during the writing of this book, the world was stunned when a Chinese scientist announced the birth of the first gene-edited babies—even if technically feasible, this was an ethical boundary most had considered taboo. It is banned in most countries around the world, and yet, in an instant, that boundary was crossed. Genetically edited humans have become a real thing.

Only time will tell whether the same becomes true for head/body transplants, something else that is now technically feasible.

How does consciousness form? This is still an open question. Another open question concerns how big a part the rest of our nervous system, outside the brain, plays in our identity. The ancient brain around the gut isn't something I made up—this is a real thing. If you research the early evolution of chordates—in basic terms, the phylum of organisms with a spinal cord—the original nervous system and "brain" before this evolutionary step was centered in the gut. It is the most ancient of our sensing and "thinking" systems.

This is a topic I would love to discuss more with readers, so feel free to message or email me to start a thread online on my Facebook page.

I did take some liberties in *The Dreaming Tree*—for instance, I doubt that human "head transplants"—technically better termed whole-body transplants—will be allowed in the United States anytime in the near future. Too many bioethics questions are still unresolved. Whole-body transplants may well not happen for many years, despite predictions to the contrary.

For now this is the domain of fiction, and one of the reasons I decided to undertake this book now was to explore the idea with readers and continue the conversation about this and many other topics touched on in *The Dreaming Tree*.

Sadly, one of the things that made the biggest impression on me while researching this book is the brutal and highly lucrative trade in transplant organs, which is largely controlled by international criminal networks. Even more shocking are the reports, in recent years, of prisoners in China being executed and their body parts harvested for transplant.

Right now on the dark web, you can buy a pair of human eyeballs for fifteen hundred dollars, a skull with teeth for twelve hundred, and so on. The most surprising thing was learning that it is possible—though illegal, of course—to get a human kidney delivered into a private clinic in the Western world for something like three hundred thousand dollars, or a pair of lungs for about a million.

The question, of course, is where these human body parts come from. And unsurprisingly, the source is often the desperately poor who can be preyed on.

Roy's visit to northern Chennai's "Kidneyville" was designed as the other end to his arc that reaches from the opulent homes and dinner tables of the Hamptons to the poorest of slums, where teenagers sell their own living organs for a handful of dollars. "Kidneyville" isn't really one place. There are slums with similar names dotted all over the globe, in almost any place with large populations living in grinding poverty.

Almost unbelievably, during the process of writing and discussing this book, I came upon the story from a friend of mine who was abducted in Central America, with the express intent of murdering him to sell his organs. He managed to negotiate his way out of it by promising a large reward, but I found this story, so close to home, shocking, to say the least.

I invite you to investigate for yourself on the web. It's easy to be horrified, but at the same time, people in desperate straits make desperate decisions—and for good or for ill, these choices are largely shaped by how much money one has—and, obviously, one's own moral compass.

Finally, while the trade in human organs is growing, so are the technologies for artificially growing organs using 3-D printing and scaffolding. So perhaps, the future isn't quite so dark. Perhaps, technology can save us all in the end.

I'm interested to know your thoughts. If you'd like to get on my mailing list for new releases, or just want to talk, please email me at Matthew@MatthewMather.com.

Best regards,
Matthew Mather
January 1, 2018

The 200th anniversary, to the day, of the publication of *Frankenstein*.